Forest Brothers

by

Geraint Roberts

Circaidy Gregory Press

Copyright information

'Forest Brothers' text copyright © 2013 Geraint Roberts. Cover Art copyright © Rita Roberts, inspired by a photograph by Kalli Piht. All rights reserved. No part of this publication may be reproduced, stored in a retrieval system, rebound or transmitted in any form or for any purpose without the prior written permission of the author and publisher. This book is sold subject to the condition that it shall not be lent, resold, hired out or otherwise circulated without the publisher's prior consent in any form or binding other than that in which it is published.

ebook ISBN 978-1-906451-77-6
First published February 2013
paperback ISBN 978-1-906451-69-1
First published February 2013

Printed in the UK by
Berforts Group Ltd

Published by Circaidy Gregory Press
Creative Media Centre,
45 Robertson St, Hastings,
Sussex TN34 1HL

www.circaidygregory.co.uk

Acknowledgements

It was my first date in Tallinn with my future wife. Sub-zero temperatures and a wind to freeze the extremities. I was admiring the snow-covered Old Town as we navigated from warm café to warm café. At the back of the medieval tower known as Fat Margaret, I spied a plaque sporting a white ensign. Closer inspection revealed a declaration of the gratitude of the Estonian Nation to the Royal Navy for their assistance during the Estonian War of Independence of 1918-1920.

This surprised me, for I felt I had a good knowledge of 20th century UK history but this campaign hadn't appeared in my school books. In fact, the part of the world including the Baltic nations went all but unmentioned. As I stood pondering this, a Welshman in a far off land that felt somehow like home, Huw Williams was born.

My literary journey has been overwhelming at times. I came through because I was blessed by acts of kindness, generosity and encouragement by friends along the way.

Steven Loveless taught me the building blocks of creative writing. I have found my voice with the help of Sally Spedding, Rod Duncan, Dave Martin, Marianne Whiting, Liz Ringrose, Margaret Penfold, Kay Green, Catherine Edmonds and Sarah Evans. I have got inspiration from the Earlyworks Press writers, from Leicester Writers' Club and my Northampton circle, with their meetings described as 'Lit Luvvy days'.

This book would not have come into being without the hard work of Kay Green and Alex Bell. Steve Hughes and Helena Castro offered invaluable proof-reading help on the "warts and all" version, whilst Kalli Piht provided beautiful images of the Estonian landscape.

My family have shown remarkable patience and tolerance on this journey, so this is dedicated to them. My children, Evelin and Gareth. My in-laws, Maie and Jaan. My late father, Roger, my mother, Rita, Deb and Rob Lea, and importantly to my wife Aile in particular. Love you all.

Foreword
Historical Background

To give a brief background to Estonian history of the 20th century is a Herculean task, but some events are worth explaining to assist those who have no knowledge of the country. I will do my best to explain.

Estonia's proclamation of independence from Russia occurred in February 1918 following a smuggled declaration being posted in Tartu. The day after, it was quashed by the advancing German Army, taking advantage of the gap created by the disarray following the Bolshevik revolution of 1917. When Germany finally retreated upon armistice, they handed power to the first Estonian government.

Very quickly, the fledgling nation and its neighbour Latvia were fighting for their political lives on many fronts. A regrouped Russian Army invaded from the east and a 'Baltic German' Army from the south. The force included units of Latvian and Estonian communists.

Estonia urgently needed to train and deploy an army. They were supported by troops from Finland and the 'White' Russian royalist army while the Royal Navy secured the coast. Other units came from Latvia, whilst small Danish, Swedish and Ingrian[1] units renewed their ancient ties with the Estonian people.

The Estonian army proved to be the dominant force and they won their independence by driving back their enemies east to Russia and south to the gates of Riga. Much use was made of armoured trains, sending mobile units into attack. Finally a peace treaty was signed by the Bolsheviks renouncing claims to the land in perpetuity.

The first republic lasted 22 years. Only twelve of these were as a democracy. The depression and the rise of political extremes led to an autocratic government, lasting until Estonia was broken up and distributed under the terms of the Molotov/von Ribbentrop non-aggression pact. The Soviet Union took control of the country in 1940 and independence was quashed. Destroyer battalions were let loose to cause chaos and keep the populace in fear. 10,000 people were deported to Siberia in an episode known as the 'Red Terror'.

---

[1] Ethnic Finns from the Russian side of the Baltic

As the then ascending German Army drove the Soviet army back, many hoped that Estonia would be given back its independence as had happened in 1918. It was not to be. Estonia moved from being a Soviet republic to become part of the republic of Ostland.

Many who had fled the Red Terror took to the forests. Many more joined them as the German Army took control. Another wave fled for fear of deportation or killing when the Soviet Army regained control in 1944. These people were known collectively as Forest Brothers – the Metsavennad. Some were partisans, looking to strike a blow for insurgency, others were refugees. Most only wanted to be allowed to be Estonian.

When the opportunity arose with Glasnost, Estonia and its neighbours took it with open arms. The singing revolution and the human chain across the Baltic states – the "Baltic Way", were iconic events that helped Estonia rediscover itself with a return to independence in 1991.

My novel is a work of fiction but the background events, such as the atrocities at Kadrina (Ch 7) and the commissar's encounter in the forest (Ch 8) are documented. See, for example, Mart Laar's *War in the Woods*.

All characters are fictitious and any resemblance to anyone living or dead is purely coincidental. Although certain roles are clearly defined in history, like that of ship captains for example, all the characters in this novel are fictional. I do not know the people who played those parts in the real world. I do not know, and therefore do not aim to judge, any specific individuals.

Note on Estonian pronunciation

The Estonian language is phonetic and also contains four vowel sounds that English does not have:

õ – unique Estonian vowel described as 'halfway between the e in get and the u in *hung*
ä – makes the a sound closer to an e, as in hat pronounced as *het*
ö – like German, makes the o more of an ur
ü – like German, makes the u more of an oo sound, as in 'view'

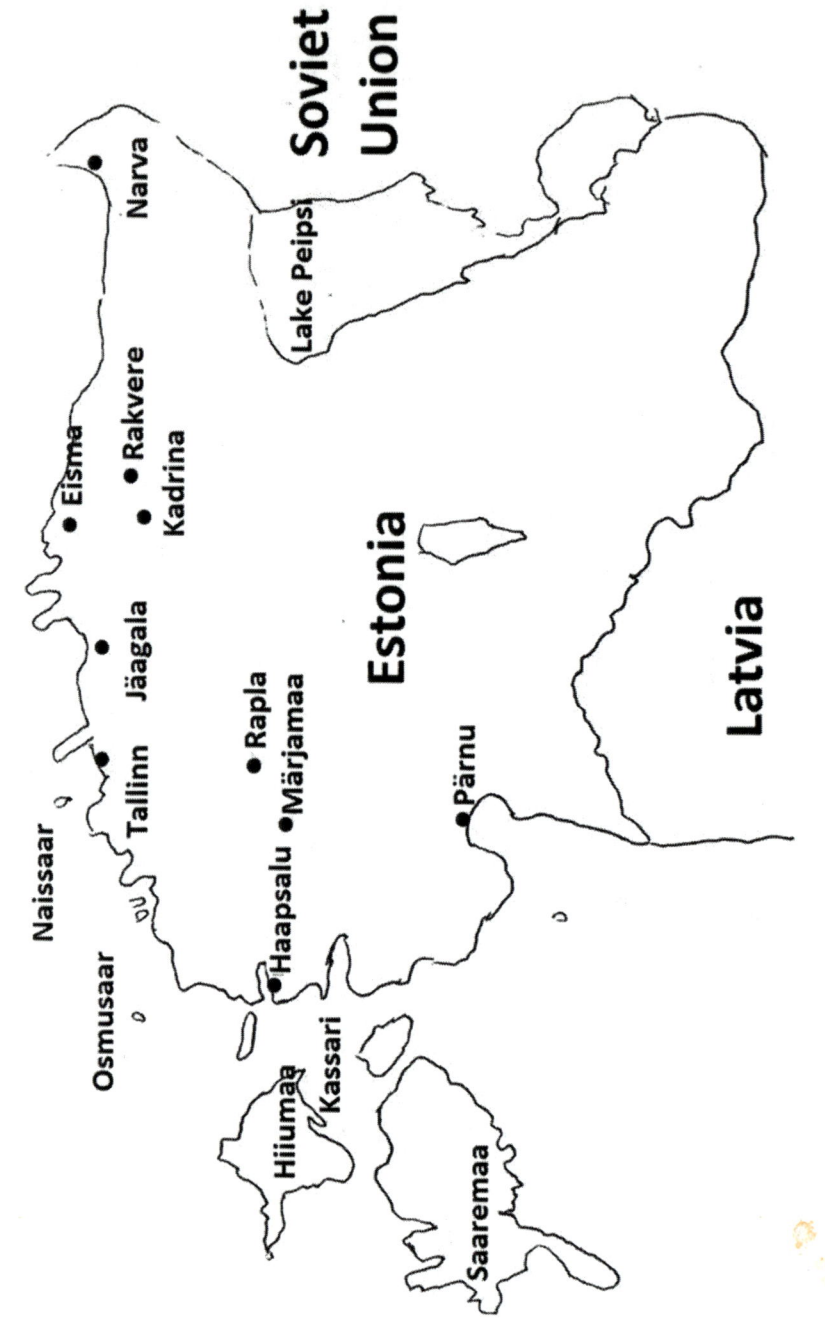

Chapters

1	The suit	1
2	Metsavennad	7
3	The baker	15
4	The hammer and the anvil	21
5	Brothers and sons	29
6	A matter of trust	39
7	Kadrina	47
8	Rabbit stew	59
9	Forest ambush	69
10	Redemption or revenge?	79
11	A curtain of water	87
12	To catch a baker	97
13	He swears in different language	107
14	The promise	119
15	Dirty linen	135
16	Märt and Maarja	147
17	Captured	155
18	The island of women	167
19	One of the Finnish boys	171
20	The hill of crosses	187
21	Our time is done	197
22	In the light of a star-shell	209
23	Cymru am byth	201
24	The smell of fish	223
25	Everyone but the Germans	233
26	Scalloway	241
27	The spy unmasked	247
28	The gentlemen of Whitehall	258
~	Epilogue	

Chapter One

The suit

'Why me?'

Huw cursed as he looked out of the window of his shabby room. A group of men had rounded the street corner and were heading for his front door. One wore a suit. In this part of Swansea, that was too smartly dressed to be a local.

'A bastard spook,' Huw growled to himself.

The suit was accompanied by a naval officer and a rating. The sound of a knock on the front door confirmed Huw's suspicions. Keep them away from me, he prayed. Keep them all away.

It was a futile wish. Moments later, his landlady was showing the men through to Huw's room, wringing her hands in her apron, gazing at the suit-wearer as awestruck as if she were being visited by royalty. 'Mr Godfrey has come from the government, Huw,' she whispered.

'And he can go right back there. I've been on nights down the docks and we had a heavy raid last night. I'm done in.'

'Huw Williams!' The tone was disapproving, reminding Huw so much of Sunday school in chapel. Something in her expression stayed his anger though. He had no argument with Mrs Edwards. She did her best to look after him, despite his sour moods. God alone knew why.

'I'll go and make a nice cup of tea,' she said.

'Don't bother, they are not staying,' Huw replied. Then he took a deep breath. 'I don't want you to be put to any trouble, Mrs Edwards. I think these men are here only fleetingly.'

'Come on Huw,' the officer spoke softly. 'Don't worry, Mrs Edwards, we are old friends.'

'Taylor?' Huw said, looking at the navy man for the first time. 'A commander now, John?'

'Good to see you, my friend.' Taylor replied with a warm smile.

Huw nodded slowly. 'It has been a while. It's alright Mrs Edwards, I promise I will behave.'

Mrs Edwards departed in despair.

1

You know me too well, Huw thought, as he turned round to reach for his waistcoat, still muttering.

'Why me?'

'We're looking for a volunteer,' Godfrey said, without bothering with formalities.

'Nobody ever volunteers,' snorted Huw.

'Well, perhaps you've been volunteered. It's an opportunity to change your life.'

'Or end it.'

There was a pause as Godfrey smoothed a crease out of the crown of his trilby hat. 'They said you'd be difficult,' he said.

Huw laughed. 'The last time one of you lot came to visit me, you certainly did change my life.'

'What did you expect? You'd jumped ship. That's desertion. In the last war you would have been shot at dawn.'

'I was gone, in the middle of a foreign land, miles from the effing sea. I wasn't hurting anyone and I had my life.' Huw slammed his fist on the wall. 'You bastards went and took it from me.'

Godfrey sat down and lit a cigarette. He didn't bother offering one. 'We reclaim our own, Williams. Let's face it, if we didn't, nobody would hang around on those stinking tin cans out at sea.'

Huw hated the oily smirk on the man's face. He was being laughed at and cajoled at the same time.

'I don't care what you think, balls to the lot of you! I was doing alright there and when the bloody navy had finished with me, I was unemployable. I've been scraping farthings where I can since then, because as soon as people know about the dishonourable discharge they can't wait to get shot of me. I'm lucky the Nazis have killed so many dock-hands that I'm actually tolerated here.'

'Easy, Huw,' Taylor soothed. 'No-one's saying you haven't had a rough time.'

Godfrey shrugged. 'I'm not really the sympathy type. You shacked up with some foreign bint in a backward land and expect me to feel sorry for you when it all went wrong?'

The man slumped to the ground at the end of Huw's punch, born of 23 years of frustration. The rating jumped towards Huw, but was stopped in his tracks by a sharp command from Taylor.

'You're an idiot, Godfrey,' he told the blindly stumbling man. 'Seaman, get him out of here before I finish off the job. Take him back to the car.'

The sailor dragged the man out. Godfrey, holding a now blood-soaked handkerchief over his face, was still groaning.

'Make sure he doesn't get blood on the carpet,' Huw snapped. 'Else Mrs Edwards will kill me.'

Taylor sighed, closed the door and moved to sit down.

'Christ, Huw you just broke his nose; I could have you thrown in the nick for the rest of the war.'

Huw knew, but his fist was still throbbing with the memory of the punch. In the circumstances, it was not an unpleasant feeling. 'You know damn well he started it,' he replied, 'and besides, it seems you need me.'

'Yes my old friend, I admit there are better ways to approach a man like you and I wish we could have a bit of time to catch up, but you are right, this operation does need you. We need a man in the Baltics, someone who knows the territory, its culture and speaks the language.'

'Why not ask the Russians?'

'Ah yes, our allies in the East, good old Joe! They would only tell us what they want us to hear. Also, Russians have a limited shelf-life in occupied Estonia. They aren't fondly remembered for their behaviour in 1940; blotted their copybook there with a few atrocities. Russian agents tend to turn up at the door of the German army. Sometimes they are still alive.'

Huw snorted. 'The Estonians are not so anti-Russian; it's just that the Germans offer the better of two evils. A puppet state is better than none.'

'Precisely, but what's going to happen when the Germans are driven out?'

'The country dies again.'

There was a brief pause, as Taylor rubbed his thumb and forefinger from the edges of his mouth down to meet on the lower lip. 'What if we intervene?'

Huw choked back a curse. 'Come on John, this isn't 1918. The Russians are already at the doorstep and the German army is still inconveniently in the way of them.'

'Wasn't it then?'

'We're not going in though, are we? Where were we when the Communists tried an uprising in '24? If we didn't go then, why now?'

Taylor raised his hand.

'Look, we can debate history all day and you obviously know more than I. Just take it from me, we are very keen to keep an eye on the Russians and need people we can trust to report back. Someone who can blend into the local population and not be seen as a threat.'

'How would I get there?'

'The Russians will take you.'

Huw roared with laughter. 'Pull the other one!'

Taylor smiled and held up his hands. 'To them, you will be helping the invasion. Reporting back where the Germans are weakest, rooting out local sympathisers and so on. Only we will be telling them what they want to hear, whilst you go to ground. You will be supported by the local partisans. They are called Metsavend. Doesn't that mean Forest Brothers?'

'No, that's only one of them. The word is Metsavennad.'

'There you are Huw, you're already prepared.'

Huw shook his head. 'What do I get out of it?'

Taylor smiled sympathetically.

'I at least know you better than most. I thought you were a lucky blighter when you jumped ship for that girl. Always had a tinge of jealousy there, you know. She was a lovely thing. I have read your file and I know you were betrayed after many years and sent back here in chains. I know since you were released, you've been struggling to find a way to get back. The Depression never helped and nobody's given you a chance since to earn enough. I suppose I'm offering you the chance now to go back and find her.'

'Too late,' Huw whispered. 'She's gone,'

'The land is still the same, Huw. Perhaps you can discover a new path there. You've certainly not been given a chance here, have you? We'll train you up in what you need to survive, you'll be fine.'

'I can watch my own back. The docks have taught me that already.'

Taylor chuckled. 'Perhaps, but there are a few things we know that the docks won't have prepared you for. Look, my friend I'm sorry it comes down to this, but I think you are the man for the job. Will you take it?'

Huw closed his eyes. 'You don't know me any more. I'm a shell of the man you bunked with on *Caradoc*.'

He walked over to the window and stared out at the street. The miserable weather matched the depressing scene of decaying and bomb-blasted terraced houses. It was not much of a place to regret leaving.

'How do I get out afterwards?'

'Perhaps you won't want to leave, if we forget about you when it's all over?'

'What's going to stop me being betrayed again?'

Taylor shrugged. 'Your education in the docks? You'll be in the forest with all the others hiding from the invaders. After that, it's up to you.'

'And the part about the Allies intervening, John?'

'As you say, this isn't 1918. We can't do much until the Germans oblige and get the hell out of the way.'

Huw was eating in the canteen of an army barracks, not caring about all that went on around him. The six weeks training had given him something to focus on, a meaning to his life beyond the hurt and anger. He had decided to give it a try, if only to allow him to die in the one land that had ever shown him respect.

He heard footsteps and out of the corner of his eye saw a man in navy uniform approaching. Huw didn't bother looking up; some things were not going to change and his hate for the navy was one of them.

'I just wanted to see how you are getting on,' Taylor said with a smile of greeting.

'Well you know, or you wouldn't be here,' Huw replied without humour.

'What do you mean?'

Huw indicated with his knife to the food on his plate. 'Two eggs. You only get two eggs when you're about to go off on an op.'

Taylor grinned. 'That's the spirit. Training go alright?'

Huw shrugged, he still could not meet Taylor's eyes. 'Well I thought the docks had left me savvy with the art of street fighting and distrusting everybody, but there is so much more than I had ever given thought to.'

Taylor laughed and pulled out a pack of cigarettes. He took one and lit it. Huw refused the offer to join him.

'Don't want to get into the habit. It might give away my position, having a quick fag in the forest.'

'We never did get time to catch up properly,' Taylor said.

Huw managed a weak smile. 'You've done well for yourself and I am a walking disaster. There, we're up to date.'

'You might find her, Huw. Estonia is a small place.'

'I've been training for the north coast and we lived in the middle of the country. She was ex-government, so was probably shipped out on the first cattle truck east.'

'So why are you bothering?'

For a brief moment Huw looked into his teacup, trying to block out the inevitable image of her face from his mind. For once the mask dropped.

'It gives me the chance to do something, put something right. I don't know what or why, but I have to go. Besides, you asked me.'

'You'll be alright, Huw. You're a survivor. It's like you were born for a purpose.'

'John, you're a good man, but you don't half talk bollocks sometimes. At least I don't have to worry about wanting to kill myself. There'll be plenty over there to do that for me.'

It was a harrowing flight from Torshavn, which had attracted the full attention of the Nazi army defences in Norway and the winds from hell. By the time they landed, Huw felt lucky to be alive. He fell out of the plane at Murmansk to a waiting escort. He was manhandled into the back of a covered lorry and driven to a railway goods yard at speed. Then he was bundled into a cattle truck with a guard posted either end. It felt like a trap. 'This is it,' he thought. 'One way ticket to Siberia, or worse. What the hell was I thinking?'

It was a long and tortuous journey of darkness, with only the smell of the previous occupants of the truck for company. Huw settled down to sleep, there was little left to do.

The train stopped after many hours and the door was thrown open revealing a grey cold morning. Huw had little time to appreciate it before he was bundled into yet another covered lorry and driven to a dockside. It wasn't amusing, but then the Soviet Army was not known for its entertainments. It was late when he was finally invited on board a submarine at the point of a gun.

Chapter Two

Metsavennad

'Good luck, old chap.'

Huw stared back from the bunk he hadn't been allowed to leave since they cast off. The irony of the words rang in his ears. They were not meant to be that way, or were they? It was so difficult to tell. The sailor didn't smile, his eyes were as flat as stone – but then weren't they all like that in this damn country?

The English words spoken with a foreign tongue, yet said as if it was a natural expression for this occasion. *Good luck old chap* – Even the RAF didn't say it; nobody did outside of movies, for Christ's sake. And these had been the first words spoken to him for the whole journey in a language he could understand. No promise of borscht for his rumbling stomach. 'I'm Welsh, you ignorant bastard,' Huw eventually replied.

The sailor stood and waited. The normal ignorance exhibited by an outsider to the passionate nationalistic pride of the United Kingdom of four nations. Huw contemplated singing *God save the King*. Now that would be ironic. Not half as much as the maker's plates on the submarine, that proudly declared this dung heap of a sub to be a daughter of Vickers, the shipyard in Barrow-in-Furness. Or the fact that this once proud defender of free Estonia was taking Huw back to her home base of long ago: a return to where his dreams had been shattered and his career in the navy had foundered all those years back.

Huw stretched as waterproofs were thrust into his face. He dressed quickly and was ushered forward through the cramped chambers to the base of the conning tower, where a few men had gathered like a mock guard-of-honour. The prospect of fresh air from the open hatch proved too much of a draw for them.

'Do not hurry,' said one of the men in Estonian. Huw shrugged off the surprise.

Judging by the movement of the vessel, the sea outside was not flat calm, but Huw had had enough of Soviet hospitality. Even a hardened submariner could feel sick in this iron coffin, as it wagged like a pendulum. A quick retch and he left a colourful calling card.

They wouldn't forget him, he thought with satisfaction, as he was bundled up and out of the hatch.

The cold Baltic air greeted him with an icy hug. He was dismayed at the sight of a perfect silver moon, perched high in a cloudless sky. Searchlights could not have done a better job of picking out the coastline in that autumn night. He groaned at the scene. 'Shall I fire some flares to make me more obvious?'

There was no reply. 'Useless,' he muttered, as he clambered down to where a sailor held a kayak near the prow of the submarine. Huw wondered briefly how they had managed to get the kayak there, but dismissed the thought. Just as long as it was there, ready for him to get away. With his pack shoved inside, Huw got in, fixed the skirts around his waist and grabbed the paddle. Without warning, the sailor kicked the kayak and it slid off the side at a crazy angle. Huw hit the water sideways and only some quick paddling and wriggling stopped him capsizing. His parting wave was more like homage to Agincourt. He heard no reply.

The Baltic that night was not as bad as he had feared. Certainly his training in the North Sea had been rougher. The coastline ahead seemed only to offer a line of silver silhouetted trees. To find one poxy little island in this darkness – Damned Island! It was bloody well named, he thought, and a bloody foolish place to aim for.

He moved towards the shore, hoping for a light to guide him, and most of all hoping it would be a friendly one. His rhythmic paddling made his mind drift to other days in the Baltic many years before…

Armistice had come and gone, but the navy was still hard at work. A squadron had been dispatched to protect the fledgling nations of the Baltic from the Bolshevik revolution. Huw had been a conscript in the war, but had missed what little action there had been on the sea. Jutland, a bloody stalemate lauded only by the media, had passed him by. The most danger he had experienced was running aground on Caradoc, *off Fair Isle.*

Now the country got over the celebrations for the end of the war, licked its wounds and looked forward to a new dawn. Meanwhile the squadron's flotilla sailed on to a lesser-known part of Europe, to meddle in someone else's conflict.

Huw's war had been a sham, spent refitting in the Shetland Isles whilst others made their mark on the fields of Flanders. One old friend had even sent him a white feather. It was the last spiteful act of a young fool, soon to be cut down in the mud near Fromelles. The boy was just sixteen, one of many boys full of bullshit jingoisms and dreams of glory on the battlefield...

Perhaps they'd all deserved to die for being so stupid, Huw thought as he paddled.

...The flotilla had moved slowly up the coast from Latvia to the Estonian capital. Huw had the night watch and he was wondering when it would end. Midnight in December on the Baltic Sea was not a place to be without being swathed in scarves, goggles and a fur hat and Huw was thankful for them. The wind would bite into any exposed part of the flesh. It was difficult to look ahead without his brow feeling encased in ice.

Huw watched the wash of the boat and dreamed of his bunk. He tried not to imagine the sea as having ice, but his mind picked out small phantom bergs at every opportunity. He wished he was home. He imagined Ernest Shackleton, eating his dogs on his ill-fated polar trek. He wondered if the ship's cook on Caradoc *could ruin that meal also.*

The explosion came from nowhere and, for a brief moment, Huw saw the outline of the nearest ship in an orange and white glow. For a fleeting second, he could have sworn he saw it jump out of the water. Slowly, Huw realised that someone was shouting, 'Report Williams! Give me status!'

'One of the frigates is hit sir, looks like Cassandra*.' Huw replied, snapping to attention, despite his mind being in free-fall. The communication lamp on the other vessel was winking urgently to him.*

'How?'

'Unknown sir, submarine attack?'

The officer cursed. 'In this weather and light? Probably hit a mine.'

'Where on earth had that come from, sir?'

'One the sodding Germans forgot to tell us about, no doubt.'

It was soon obvious that Cassandra *was dying. Westminster rushed to her side, to rescue the crew. A swell lifted* Cassandra *up to nearly smash onto her rescuer. Westminster withdrew and the Aussie* boat **Vendetta** *came aside. Huw watched the men stream across from the stricken ship, scrambling up the rope nets as quick as they could. Huw was transfixed by the sight, especially as he watched one man slip and disappear into the icy waves below. All the while, the signal lamp winked furiously, telling the world of the danger. Then with a metallic groan, the* **Cassandra** *sank down beneath a mass of bubbles and swirling water.*

'Did we get them all off? What about the stokers?'

Like losing children on a Sunday school trip, Huw thought. Naïve children who'd thought this would be a breeze against a weak opponent. He could see the world for what it was; little reward and plenty of danger. One of the men started crying.

'My brother's on there!'

The cold, and the sight of a seemingly invincible craft sinking in less than an hour, was too much. Huw stopped functioning, was relieved of duty and sent to quarters.

A sharp explosion woke Huw from his reflection. The kayak rocked wildly as he started, and fear gripped his body. Mines! Another blast came from the shore and Huw turned to see the outline of the submarine lit by the explosion. All signs of humanity had disappeared from the deck.

'What the…?'

Huw's mind was racing. The light of the explosions made him feel painfully exposed and he searched desperately for cover. What the hell were they doing dropping him off next to a gun battery? Incompetent arseholes!

Paddle flashing, Huw struck out for shore, steering towards the shadows made by the half-submerged boulders that were ubiquitous on this coast. A high rectangular lump offered protection. His fingers found the surface and started scrabbling for handholds. He clung on, and caught his breath as he tried to limit the kayak's movement in the rolling sea. His fingers warned him that this could not go on for long, but he had to find a way to shore without alerting the defenders or he'd be dead before he had even started.

Why would the Soviets go to so much trouble to ferry him down there, only to get him shot? There had been plenty of opportunity to do away with him along the way, dump his body and then shrug nonchalantly to the SOE.

There was a movement on the beach, on the submerged causeway to the island. A group of men made for the forest. Huw had no great knowledge of the German language, but he recognised the tones and inflections. This was a welcome party, but not a local one. It appeared however that their attention was diverted to the submarine and by great fortune, he would be missed. That was as long as he stayed out of the way.

Huw closed his eyes and focused on the sounds of movement above the noise of the waves raking up the shingle beach. He had no idea where to go now, but no desire to be killed for that ignorance.

His fingers begged to let go of the rock, but he had to hold on until he was sure there was nobody left on the beach. His contact was either dead or chased off. He would have to scramble ashore when it was safe and work his way down the coast. Perhaps he could find the Forest Brothers? He tried to make his mind drift into the past, to shut out the pain and fear, but a voice broke through the dark. No nasal Russian or aggressive German tones: this was a metronomic staccato, musical in its lilt to him. A language Huw had once embraced as his own.

'Perhaps you should think of coming ashore?'

'Can I trust you?' Huw gasped back. Even in the dark, he could sense the man shrugging.

'It is your choice, stay until morning and be caught, if you wish.'

'I will need help.'

'For sure.'

Huw's fingers were curled up in cramp. He could barely grip the paddle and certainly not much else. The stranger waded in and helped him up to the beach, where Huw collapsed.

'There is no time, you must come.'

'Who are you?' Huw said through gritted teeth.

'Metsavend.'

'Forest Brother? What is your code?'

'There is no time, you trust me or not, I don't care. If I am to betray you, you are already dead. We need to hide this boat. Further down there are marshes where we can sink it with rocks. Come.'

'Where then?' Huw gasped

'Towards Eisma for now. There is time for talk, now is not. Come.'

They were keeping to shadow as much as possible, yet moving fast. Huw struggled to keep up and talking was out of the question. Despite removing his oilskins, he was starting to sweat and prayed for gusts of wind to cool him down. In time, they moved onto a gravel road and made steadier progress.

Suddenly, the stranger turned and grabbed Huw, throwing him into the ditch. Huw tried to roll away, but was caught and pinned down.

'Listen!' The man hissed.

Far off, Huw could hear a lorry, its engine moaning in complaint at the uneven road. A white light grew as the vehicles approached. Then they were past; a motorcycle and sidecar with a lorry full of helmeted silhouettes. The German patrol moved on but the man's hand kept Huw down until the engine noises had died in the night.

'We go.'

'Where?' Huw whispered.

'Away from this place, there are too many soldiers about. We must move to a safer place.'

'In the forest?'

The man sighed. 'You are in forest.'

They moved on in the dark shadows. Huw tried to follow, navigating by the faint breathing noises being made by his guide. Their journey appeared to be taking forever and Huw felt it taking its toll on him. Finally he knew he had lost the man in the dark.

All he could see was the faint fuzzy outline of tall, thin trees and a busy starry sky above. Huw sat against a tree trunk and tried to relax. What the hell had he been he thinking, coming here?

Deep down he knew he had nowhere else to go. Nothing to look forward to and no prospects back home. Fate had dealt him a duff hand for most of his life, what was there left?

Huw thought about what to do next. He would sleep now and then make for the village in the morning – if he could find it. Then south to see if his old homestead was still there.

He was woken by a hand on his shoulder, shaking him roughly.

'Come, we must not rest. There is little time and we must make camp.'

'Don't you have a shelter we can stop at,' Huw complained. 'I'm dead on my feet.'

'No more.'

'Why's that?'

'When you see a friend get blown up visiting it, you stop building them. Come.'

Her hair was the colour of gold in a morning sky. When her mouth curved into a smile, her cheeks dimpled and her face lit up. His breath was taken away by her beauty...

Huw's dreams dissolved and he found himself alone again. Only the faint light from the starry sky above bore him company. A shooting star blazed a bright silver trail across in a blink of an eye. Huw wished for all the madness in the world to stop.

The man was by Huw's side again, tying a cord to his arm.

'This will keep you with me; I cannot waste time finding you again.'

'Charmed, I'm sure.' Huw muttered. 'I still don't even know if I trust you.'

'This is your choice.'

Huw mouthed a curse and questioned his own judgement. 'I can't go any further.'

'Then you will die.'

'Is that a threat?'

'No. It is fact.'

The sing-song lilt of Estonian vowels made Huw think of better times, as again his mind tried to dull the pain.

Her eyes were clear blue and time stopped when he looked in them. The perfume of her body was his clover. He just couldn't stop thinking of her...

It was a village dance, the girls wore traditional costume. She had flowers in her hair and her smile was loving, inviting. He knew there could be no other for him.

'You must dance,' she said. Her voice was music to his soul.

'I don't know how!'

'Hah! Then I will teach, it is not hard.'

She took his hand and led him forward into the throng. Her eyes...

'We are here.'

The vague shapes that Huw could make out looked no different from the rest of his journey.

'You make enough noise to bring soldiers with you,' a voice muttered out of the gloom. Huw was surprised at how quickly he was remembering the language. He was so tired he hadn't realised his mystery companion had been speaking Estonian to him all the way from the beach. The accent was familiar and as he was taken somewhere to sleep, Huw wondered why the voice echoed in his mind.

'Here we stay.'
  'Here we stay.'

Chapter Three

The baker

Huw awoke to the sound of subdued voices, the clank of metal and the smell of cooking. He looked around and saw he was in a shelter of sorts, with branches leaning against a tree and a small covering of sacking. If he was in a shelter, he thought, he must be at the base. He heard footsteps, the sacking was hitched and the silhouette of a tall young man appeared. Huw screwed his eyes shut against the sudden burst of light.

'Food,' the young man said. 'And this,' he added, passing a bottle. Huw opened it and took a swig. The vodka burned down his throat, making him gasp.

'Don't kill him, Juhan!' A cheerful voice rang out and the young man smiled.

'You use it for insect bites, Englishman.'

'I've been here before, I don't have this problem.'

'This is good.'

Juhan left and Huw began to itch. He peered out of the hide, at the small hollow in the woodland. A few men stood around the fire, cooking mushrooms. Some rifles were left against a nearby tree. Further off, Huw made out a figure keeping lookout, and he guessed there were others at various points doing the same. He hoped to God this was only a temporary camp, but he knew he would be disappointed.

His guide's voice came over from the fire. 'Come and eat and then we talk. You must tell us everything before we can go any further. It is important that I know.'

Huw looked at the man, his silver-grey hair rubbed with dirt to make it less obvious. His lined face spoke of many years of toil. The cool, blue eyes held hidden thoughts. But there was something else…

'What's happening, kallis?' She whispered with fear.

'They've come for me.' Huw whispered. 'I've got to get away. I'll come back soon, darling. I promise, I'll be back soon.'

A man rushed through the door. 'Huw, you have to go. They will catch you. Leave from back, head south and stay hidden at river. I'll reach you when it is safe.'

'Thank you, Märt,' Huw said. 'I will remember this.'

He looked into the cool, blue eyes. He looked...

Huw blinked. 'I know you.'

The grey had taken the place of the sandy hair of many years ago, the lines were heavier and the mouth perhaps sadder, but Huw remembered him.

Märt nodded without a smile. 'Yes, I know this. First you eat and then we talk.'

'Yes,' replied Huw. 'Yes we will.'

'Juhan, keep watch. Tell men to go and we will follow,' Märt said curtly. Juhan gave an easy smile, nodded and disappeared. Huw's mind was numb with shock. Märt had been the baker in Märjamaa, a hundred miles away south of here, not Metsavennad material for sure. He was the quiet one, who kept to himself. Huw had been on edge as it was. Now he felt his world had been turned upside down. Märt shouldn't be here. Huw began to wonder how much of all this was someone else's plan.

Could he trust Märt? The Märt he used to know had never been interested in politics, had never embraced the fascism of the League of Veterans, the collectivisation of the Reds, even the nationalists of the fledgling Estonian nation. Just as long as his bread was baked and sold, Märt had not appeared to care. Now he was in the forest, demanding answers like an intelligence officer.

'First you tell me why you are here,' Huw replied. 'Trust goes both ways.'

'I went to forest when Reds came. They looked to take some of our village folk away. Trucks arrived and they started rounding up those they found. Some of us began to fight, but we were beaten off or killed. Then they rounded up those who did not escape and took them to Siberia. I found forest more to my liking.'

Huw's heart leapt in alarm. *Maarja!* He wanted to ask about her, but was equally desperate not to face the answers he might get. He found it hard to contain his feelings, suppressed for so many years, for the only woman that had loved him...

Huw shivered as he was taken below deck before being wrapped up in a blanket on his bunk. The doctor would be down to see him later, if he had the time. The voyage had suddenly got dangerous and the unknown threats of mines in the water had everyone on high alert. Huw lay on his bunk listening to the throb of the engines as Caradoc *moved on.*

He knew the shock of the blast had unnerved him, but he couldn't understand why. He'd shown himself to be brave enough in the past – climbing to the crow's nest in heavy seas... but he had just watched a ship jump out of the water. He knew he should sleep, but there was a nagging doubt in his head. Caradoc *could hit another mine. He had to be ready to get up on deck. He had to be there to help the wounded get off the ship. He had to stay awake, he just had to...*

Huw woke up to the sound of seagulls. The ship's great engines were silent. A quick scan through the porthole told him they were in dock. This must be Reval. The castle walls of the hill-town embraced a number of church steeples. It looked so different from other places he had visited.

He heard footsteps approaching and on a whim jumped back on his bunk and feigned sleep. The door opened and after a pause, closed again. He could hear the conversation outside.

'What's going on, Doc?'

'He's still sleeping off the effects of shock; a combination of action, cold, exhaustion and perhaps a lack of experience. A bit of rest and he will recover.'

'Will he? What would stop him losing his nerve again?'

'Give him time and he'll pull through. He's a good lad, that one. Smart.'

'I hope you're right. I can't afford to carry anyone on this patrol.'

'We'll have to see then, won't we?'

Huw sat down, pondering the old memories. Was he a good soldier? What makes a good soldier? Could he trust Märt? Would he have, when times were different? Probably. Märt had no quarrel with anyone. He just got on with his job – or that's how he used to be, before the bitter suffering that Estonia had faced, as bad as many others in Europe.

17

There was no choice. If the man was a plant, they already knew Huw was coming and why. Better to take the leap of faith, however bizarrely fate had dealt it, but still keep an eye out for a quick exit.

'Märt, I'm here for the Allies, to try find out what is happening at the Eastern front. Find places of weakness and report back.'

'To British or Reds?'

'What do you think?'

'That you report to British and they choose what they say to Reds,' Märt's face showed a sudden flicker of emotion.

'I thought so too,' Huw replied.

'Where is contact?'

'No idea, Finland or Sweden. Neutral countries don't always know what happens inside their borders.'

'And what do you do when Reds come?'

'Hide.'

Märt shook his head angrily. 'There is nowhere to hide, you have no idea. Those of us left, those who have not been killed or shipped to Siberia, they have opinion about these Allies of yours. So be careful about who you talk to, most will not welcome you trying to help the Reds back here.'

Huw grimaced. 'So the country fights for Hitler?'

Märt shook his head. 'The country fights for Estonia. In this world of two evils, Germans offer better future of bondage.' He rose and shouldered his rifle. 'We wait for Americans and British to give us our land back. For that, you must stay alive and keep reporting to your people. But be warned. If I find you reporting to Moscow, I will kill you.'

'Who are you?'

'White Fox.'

'Thank God.'

'Yes, because you would have been dead after torture if I was not. You talk too much.'

'What the hell do you mean?'

Märt picked up his pack and turned to leave. 'You are spy. For British on Germany. For British on Russia. Trust no-one.'

'Except you,' Huw muttered with sarcasm.

'You are fool.'

'What happened to you, Märt? I never did you wrong.'

Märt began to walk off and Huw hurried to follow. After a while, he got a reply.

'My world has ended. You will not recognise this Estonia. There is much to fear, little to trust. Germans, Reds; they both kill us, but in this land, we kill ourselves also.'

The Red Army was static, stuck across a deep river valley. The city of Narva, shattered but proud, stood taunting its foes on the other bank. The bridges between were long destroyed.

A pair of officers scanned the city through binoculars, watching the occasional spout of masonry from explosions. One cursed and spat.

'You would have thought they would get fed up of this punishment.'

The other grunted, his steel-grey eyes showed no emotion, as he looked at his comrade. 'These are people fighting for their land. The Germans are leaving them behind to fight us and they know what awaits them with defeat.'

'What of the British spy?'

'He has landed.'

'And soon he will be sending us information.'

'Yes,' the response came with a mirthless grin. 'Soon he will sing to us.'

Chapter Four

The hammer and the anvil

'Why then would people want to help the Allies,' Huw said. 'If the Russians are so unloved here?'

Märt was silent for a long time as they walked, his gaze always focussed on something in the forest. Huw knew he was in tune with the land, looking for any sight, smell or sound that warned of danger. Eventually, he replied, low and quick.

'The country is not all united. Many see Germans as our old landlords, many see Reds as same; both coming to kick us into mud once more. Some people here are Russians. Some think communism is our answer. Some even hope Swedes will come back and reclaim their ancient land.' He stopped and looked at his colleague. 'But you know this already or you have forgotten your life here.'

Huw had not forgotten. He would not forget.

'What do you want me to say to the people?' He asked.

'You say nothing.' The tone was final, yet it left Huw unsatisfied.

'What do *you* believe, Märt?'

His companion spat. 'That you may have wasted your time or come too late. Nothing changes here. We have not learnt to live together or trust one another. There is enough hatred within this land that people will steal, betray, even kill. We don't need foreign armies to do it for us. Before Germany stops fighting we will all be in forest – or dead.'

'So why are you helping?'

The baker shook his head. 'You would not understand. You have not lived in a land where others are at war. When Reds came three years ago, they sent in their Destroyer battalions. Those animals killed, raped and maimed in farms and villages, to keep our land in fear. For days they killed anyone they saw, this they were ordered to do.'

He was angry now, his hands had curled into balls of tension and his voice had dropped to a low threatening tone. 'They drafted lists of people to send to Siberia. They made Estonians do it and those wretches were grateful. Grateful! Because they thought they would save their own skin at expense of others. Reds were chased away by Germans and they burnt everything before them. I want to stop that happening again.'

'So you do not think I should have come?'

A figure appeared in the shadows ahead, giving a cheery wave; Juhan. Märt cursed his free spirit, then sighed.

'No, I think you can help us in this fight, though I wonder if you can truly save us from ourselves, Huw.'

'Then what is there to do?'

Märt held his arm to stop him before they reached Juhan.

'Survive. I am telling you our only hope is to keep safe in forest. If you really want to trust people, trust me, trust Juhan. Say nothing to any others. If you want to help, stay alive. Talk to British, tell them that my fears are wrong and there is still hope.' He started walking again. 'If it gets too bad, we will send you back and you can tell them what bloody mess this all is.'

How? The question stuck in Huw's throat. He did not feel it would be answered. Silence fell...

Some of the fleet had been down the coast to Narva, where the Red Army had been pressing the White. The fledgling Estonian army, led by Laidoner, had fallen back to protect Reval from the expected attack. The ships went to cause the Red Army some problems and give Laidoner time to regroup and build defences.

It was not what the admiral had been told to do, but he knew what was needed and his hard-pressed crews were getting restless. At least he knew it would stop the mutinous mutterings of his wartime conscripts for a while, giving them less time to nurse their grievances.

The men of the squadron came back with a spring in their step. They had caused havoc and enjoyed relating how they had watched the enemy running for shelter. Vendetta *was in the thick of it again and Huw wished he were Australian, as he made his way to the ward room to meet the captain. He had visions of demotion for his actions at the sinking. What he got felt worse.*

'We need to set up an office, a liaison in the city between us and the Estonians. Whilst you are still recovering, Sub-Lieutenant, I want you to be part of it.

22

'I'd rather stay, sir,' Huw had pleaded. *'I need to prove to you I am no coward.'*

'I never said you were, young man. I need someone organised, diplomatic and able to communicate quickly. I saw that in you when we shoaled on Fair Isle, you didn't panic.'

'Yes sir.'

'You're the best man for the job, Huw.'

'Yes sir.'

I'm the only one you can spare, thought Huw sadly.

'Good, that's settled. You can move in a few days, so you'll be in before Christmas. Start getting things ready now and report to the consulate.'

Huw sat outside the consul's office, cap in hand. As he waited, all he could see was his naval career falling down a big plughole. He already missed the salt air and the waves, even if the wind made it too cold to face the Baltic without goggles. He watched the clock, and brooded.

A door opened and a woman came in to sit opposite. She made no effort to acknowledge him and sat as if trying to take in the warmth of the room, whilst brushing the snow from her blonde hair. Her eyes looked tired and her cheeks slightly pinched, but Huw could only marvel at her beauty. She sighed to herself and her face showed dimples. Huw could not stop looking at her; he hadn't seen an Estonian woman before and if they were all like this...

'In my country, it is rude to stare.'

Huw saw her lips move, but the words seemed distant, the voice musical. He blinked and she sighed in annoyance and looked away, which woke him from his dreaming.

'I'm sorry,' he blurted. *'My mind was somewhere else.'*

She looked away and her lips twitched in distaste, making Huw flush.

'No ma'am, I was thinking of the journey here. I meant no harm. I am... I mean I did not expect to meet an Estonian today.'

'So, you did not expect to meet an Estonian in Estonia?'

'I...no, I mean here – in the consulate. You speak English.'

'Yes, I know this.'

Huw could feel his ears begin to glow. *'I mean... I will start again. My name is Huw.'*

'*Who?*'

'*No, Huw. Say the vowel like the e in eggs. English people say Hyoo, which is not right...*' Christ, I'm babbling, he thought. '*I'm here to provide liaison to the Estonians. Um...you.*'

She nodded. '*You are liaison with English navy, yet you are not English?*'

'*Welsh. Wales? The world keeps on calling us English, but Britain is made up of England, Scotland, Ireland and Wales,*' Huw took a deep breath. '*I'm sorry, I'm rambling on.*'

'*Perhaps if you let people tell you how to say your name, you allow them to call you what you are not, Huw.*'

She said his name correctly and it sent a tingle down his spine.

'*What is your name?*'

'*Maarja. MAH-R-YAH,*' she replied deliberately and then giggled. '*And have you enjoyed your journey here?*'

The tone was mocking, and amusement played in her eyes, but the words were sobering for him.

'*I watched a man die, if that's what you mean.*'

She sighed. '*It is hard the world over. I should perhaps ask how you have liked Tallinn?*'

'*Tallinn?*' Huw looked blankly back.

She smiled. '*Reval is a German name and today, we are saying things as they should be said.*'

'*I think it is nice, the little that I have seen.*'

'*Perhaps you should walk around and see how beautiful it is.*'

'*I would need someone to show me.*'

There was a pause and she smiled and narrowed her eyes. Huw noticed the long dark eyelashes.

'*I work for the ministry. I have come to say there is a party to be held in honour of the English. I mean of course,* British *navy. A dance also.*'

'*This is nice,*' Huw replied, not knowing his right foot from his left where dances were concerned.

'*You may also hire ladies for occasion.*'

Huw coughed violently at her words. He had swallowed and it appeared to have missed his stomach. '*What?*' He croaked.

'*For dance? You may hire partners.*'

'*Oh!*'

'Well what did you think I mean?' She suddenly flushed and her hand leapt to her mouth.

'I am so sorry,' Huw had to splutter. 'It was just the words sounded... not right. I am not used to this idea for dancing.'

'The Reds have our land and we have nothing. People are starving and food costs more money. They need to do this.'

'Yes, I am sorry,' Huw said quickly. 'We are here to help end that, too.'

This caused a flicker of anger. 'Yes,' she said, 'you fire your guns from afar. It is Laidoner that we must hope for.'

Huw was annoyed too. 'We do our bit, Maarja. We just destroyed the Reds at Narva.'

'Narva? Do you know where that is?'

'Yes, on the border to the East. The road is now cut. The Red Army needs to regroup and while they do this, your Laidoner can grow stronger and prepare.'

She pursed her lips. 'Perhaps, Wales man.'

'Perhaps we are allies?'

'Perhaps,' the smile was back in her eyes and Huw felt light-headed.

'Then perhaps I may hire you for the dance?'

Maarja looked away in embarrassment. 'I did not ask for this.'

'You are taken for another?'

'There are others you could choose.'

Huw nodded. 'But I would like to go with someone that I know.'

She shook her head. 'You do not know me.'

He smiled. 'You are the Estonian I know the most. For me, that is enough.'

The camp was basic; just a few shelters camouflaged by brushwood. Not many people appeared to be there, as they approached. Huw spied Juhan, who smiled in greeting and threw a bottle over.

'This one is for drinking!'

Huw nodded thanks and took a swig, leaving some drops on his fingers which he dabbed on his body.

'Some friends have made me more welcome.'

The young man laughed and moved away. Huw looked around the clearing, noting how Spartan the set up was. There were signs of a fire, but no permanent hearth. There was a sudden rustle beside him and a man appeared as if out of the ground to walk past him.

'You have a tunnel?' Huw asked Juhan.

'No, a bunker,' he replied. 'We always knew Reds would be back, so we made ready.'

'How long do you expect to stay here?'

'Until Estonia is restored,' Märt said, returning. 'Until Atlantic Accord is fulfilled. As your Mr Churchill and President Roosevelt have said, all countries will be restored at end of this war, like last time. Perhaps you should rest again, before you report.'

Huw was shown inside the bunker, following a scramble down to an oblong room dug out below. It was empty but for a few crude beds, and a small store of ammunition in the corner. Huw could clearly hear the men talking outside, but was dog-tired and lay down on one of the beds. Soon, their voices blended in with his slumber.

'Why did you bring him?'

'He is our link to the West, Peetr.'

The man curled his lip in a sneer, the long scar on his face making him even less attractive.

'What good is that? They watch and will do nothing.'

'Peetr,' a silver-haired man soothed. 'Germany is in the way for now.'

'Raio is right,' Märt replied. 'And don't forget promises of their leaders. We will be free after this, just like last war.'

'And Stalin?' Peetr spat. 'Did anyone tell those Reds?'

'Stalin will listen.' Raio said calmly.

'Well, he didn't listen in 1940. What will make him listen now? Reds hate West as much as West hates Reds.'

'So,' countered Märt, 'Americans will not stop until they dump Stalin on his fat arse? This is not true, for Russia keeps Germany busy for now and that is good enough for Yankees.'

He took out his knife and started to shave a tree branch. 'This man will help; he lived in my village for a long time. He will know what Reds would do. He'll give us chance to tell our tale, it was reason us Finnish boys went to fight for our cousins.'

'That's it, bring up Finland again,' Peetr muttered. 'I know I wasn't there.'

'No, but you were there when we were Erna, you joined us. Let's encourage him. Let's face it, he's feeding back information to West, let's tell him what to say and think.'

'So you say,' Peetr said darkly. 'I for one will not turn my back to him.'

'Watch is relieved,' said Juhan as he approached the glade. 'Where is fire?'

'Where it always is, idiot,' Peetr muttered.

'Why are you talking of English man?' Juhan asked nonchalantly.

'How do you know, Smiler?' Raio asked and Juhan shrugged.

'They could hear you in Rakvere. Isn't he here?'

'He is in bunker.'

'Oh. Can't he hear you then?'

There was a silence, as the men gathered their thoughts. Raio leant forward to kill a horsefly that had landed on Peetr's back. There was no response from the morose man.

'There is another thing,' Märt said, throwing the stick away. 'Huw can remember how we were when Estonia was free. Can we?'

Chapter Five

Brothers and sons

The steel-grey eyes gazed through a pair of binoculars over the ruined landscape, to the hills beyond Narva. It was becoming more and more silent as the defenders grew fewer. His colleague brought a flask of vodka, which was half emptied in a gulp.

The eyes didn't waver from looking across the shattered city. The man was not tall, like his comrade, his face showing a tinge of former youth in complexion, incongruous to the piercing gaze that hinted of struggle and pain. He didn't smile, but nodded his thanks.

'They are nearly done, Oleg,' his lean, athletic companion said hopefully. 'It is days now, hours even.'

'Good, then we will get busy.'

'Why not go over now? The line is broken in the south. The army is across Lake Peipsi.'

'No I can wait; I have business in the north.'

'We'll find the agent soon enough. Nobody in Estonia can keep a secret from us.'

Oleg nodded grimly.

'Why do you want him so bad?' His colleague said. 'He is nothing.'

'It is personal, comrade Yuri, nothing more.'

Märt had taken Huw down an endless maze of forest paths. He had not explained why, which no longer surprised the Welshman. Juhan went with them and walked next to Huw. He was eager to talk and Huw wanted to learn more.

'Märt seems to not trust anyone.' Huw muttered, getting an inevitable grin back.

'It is his way; he shows caution from seeing too many friends die. When we came here from Märjamaa, it was because our local Reds had begun to shoot who they did not like. Those who escaped, they went into forest. A few went back and killed Reds. So we are all as bad as one another, perhaps?'

They were interrupted by the harsh, low sound of Märt's words.

'You are a fool, Juhan. As you talk, we slow down. Anyone listening is driven to us like biting insects.'

Juhan just smiled and shook his head. They continued for a while in silence, but not for long.

'They say you lived in my village, Englishman. I always wanted to see what you were like.'

'And now you see me?'

Juhan shrugged. 'I dunno.'

Huw welcomed the small conversation; it was a breath of warmth in the icy air that surrounded Märt.

Soon, they reached a crossroads. The sunlight came through the canopy in streams and Huw was conscious of birdsong in the air. His training had been in the woodland of Leicestershire, where bright yellow fields of rape had been visible through the trees. The feeling of being close to humanity was always present – an old quarry, the sounds of a nearby railway. Now, he felt he was walking through an immense wilderness. All around him, the woodland disappeared into gloom. It was as if the light had been sucked into the limp tangles of dead wood strewn at the foot of trees. In front of him, Märt was crouched on the floor, head to the ground, looking at a bush. Slowly, he approached and reached in to lift out an electrical wire. He found another and gently moved it also. Huw stopped breathing.

Märt moved the bush to expose a hollow. Reaching in, he lifted out a sack that clunked metallically. He set it on the ground and exposed a radio set.

'Who did this?' Huw asked.

'Raio.' Juhan replied.

'The grey hair?'

Märt nodded. 'To stop those who would look too hard. I will speak with him, for today it was obvious. Here,' – he handed Huw a headphone – 'it has not much battery.' His face spoke the words of exasperation as Huw fumbled. It was not that Huw did not know how to use the radio, but he felt uncomfortable with Märt standing over him. The Estonian rolled his eyes and moved away.

'It's not as if you have to piss. Tell them Arctic Fox is with you.'

Huw found his frequency and started tapping out a standard greeting. 'Gracie, respond. Gracie.'

The crackling of the radio noise washed over him and the forest faded into black, as Huw focussed on the crackling. In time, a sound was heard and Huw felt the world had become one with the faint morse beeps, as he strained to hear.

'State code?'

'Glyndwr,' he tapped. Then quickly added 'Arctic Fox is here.'

'Understood.'

'Can I trust him?'

There was a delay. Perhaps, Huw thought, the contact had gone to get his codebook. Then a flurry of signals came back. Huw took the headphones off and looked strangely at Märt.

'What are your best bowling figures?'

Märt cursed and looked even more fed up. '3 for 6 off 1. Don't you English think of anything but cricket?'

Juhan looked confused as Huw asked for orders.

'Bear close to Narva hills, keep vigilant,' came the response followed by a call-off.

Märt stashed the radio back in its den and without a word, moved out on the path they had come from. Juhan and Huw were left scrambling behind.

'How do you know cricket, Märt?' Huw asked as soon as he caught up.

'I was taught, in Finland, by an Englishman,' was his curt reply.

Huw gave up. Presently, Juhan picked up the conversation. 'Do you belong to a unit?' he asked.

'Not as such,' Huw replied and Juhan broke into a sly grin.

'Ah! Commando.'

Huw shook his head. 'Sorry, not even close.'

Huw still wanted to sit and talk alone with Märt to find out what had happened to his former wife. He yearned to find out about Maarja, but Märt's icy responses were getting him nowhere.

'Pretty strange we should meet again here, Märt,' he tried.

'Not so, there are only a few of us left in Estonia,' came a reply that ended any hope of a dialogue.

Huw shrugged. 'It's best I don't talk about those things, son,' he said to Juhan. 'Some things are best kept private.'

'Son?' Juhan looked surprised by the word and Huw stopped. He glanced at Märt who had carried on oblivious to the exchange. It still made Huw flush.

'Only a saying, Juhan. In my country we say it to men younger than ourselves. Sometimes we do, anyway.'

'So,' Juhan nodded slowly. 'You must teach me these sayings.'

'But not now,' Märt said returning. 'Now we stop talking and start listening for enemy.'

'You lucky bugger, what's she like then?' Taylor's enthusiasm grated on Huw. The man was revelling at the prospect of the dance. *'We got invited by the skin of our teeth,'* he continued, *'and I bet the Top Brass will get all the top picks. What she like then? Ugly as sin, I bet.'*

'That's right, Taylor.'

'And that's why you're meeting her early? She up for it, you think?'

'You don't know what "up for it" means! What's up with you? You're like a puppy in his first season. You're acting as if you've never met a woman before.'

'Oh come on,' came the reply. *'They are all supposed to be gorgeous here.'*

'Compared to your mother, she's an angel.'

'I knew it; she's a honey, isn't she?'

'That's right, Taylor, whatever you say.'

Others came into the room and, bored of the conversation, Huw left. He could still hear Taylor in the background.

'Yes, he's got a bird already, lucky beggar! Oh, I don't know, something about Fat Margaret. Sounds like he has his hands full already – and more besides!'

How did it all come to this? Huw had not been prepared for the shock of returning to this land. The past was stuck in his mind, at times as if taped over the present. Memories were flowing, vibrant and full of life. The present was grey and senseless by comparison.

'How do you communicate with other groups?' Huw asked Märt, as they sat around a fire with the others. Toomas had managed to kill an elk and they were all eating well for once. Huw appreciated the warm meat, although he still pulled his coat over his back to keep his exposed side warm.

'What are you talking about?' Märt replied. 'We have no contact. This is not an army, we are just groups of people trying to survive.'

'And we will,' said Raio, 'some people make sure we do not starve. We know a few other Forest Brothers and where they are.'

'Perhaps in south they were better at forming resistance,' said Märt. 'Germans were good at stopping it here; they made everyone join SS.'

'What do you mean?'

'It is simple. German army is stretched. It needs men, some people in this country and other lands go willingly. Others are forced. There are many people here who made money from German squires in older times. They miss old ways. Germans make units of them all in SS.'

'So what do you hope to achieve in the end?' Huw asked. 'Political change?'

'We just hope to live,' said Peetr. 'And if we survive, future will write itself.'

'We have help,' said Juhan.

'He has been told that and he does not need to know,' Peetr snapped. 'All this talk! I will not cause any problems for our friends.'

'It is alright, Juhan,' Huw said quietly. 'I don't need to know, in fact it is better if I do not know names.'

He was stung by the venom in Peetr's voice and yet understood it. Huw's mind was living the Estonia as it had been: farming communities and chic city dwellers, proud of their independence and the chance of a future. All he saw now were people like Peetr, hounded into the forest and forced to live hand to mouth.

'Huw, go help Juhan, we need wood,' said Märt.

'We're surrounded by bloody wood,' Peetr muttered behind them, as they left.

'You've made a friend,' Juhan said with a grin. 'Be warned, he thinks you are spy.'

Huw bit his tongue and started gathering kindling. They returned with armfuls of dry wood and Huw found Peetr still glaring at him with open resentment. It was beginning to be mutual and Huw felt close to snapping.

'Peetr, we need food. Get Toomas and go searching.' said Märt.

33

Peetr cursed. 'What? Are we the women now? Go send our idiots.'

He nodded towards Huw and Juhan. Wounded, Huw began to approach him, but Märt pushed in front.

'Juhan, take Huw to learn where we find food. Peetr, we talk, now.'

'Come,' said Juhan. 'I teach you how to find mushrooms and berries. We must eat!'

They journeyed for a long time in silence, for Huw had no desire for conversation. Inwardly, he raged at the putdown until he managed to close himself away, hoping his temper would cool. Juhan was at his side talking about berries and mushrooms; when and where to find them, what not to take and so on. Huw patiently listened, even though he knew a lot of the woodman's skill from long ago. Juhan was at least good company.

He heard a faint rustle and touched Juhan's elbow, circling the bush the noise had come from. They carefully edged forward, waiting for any sign of movement. Huw was worried that it may be a soldier stalking them. Only Juhan had a rifle. Did he know how to use it? They would surely be dead by now if it was a soldier. Besides, there was not enough room for a fully-grown human in that bush. A small animal?

Huw grasped a sturdy branch, the size of a club. He wondered if he could deal with anything larger than a rabbit. Many years back, he had hunted boar in the Estonian forests. It had proved to be a dangerous struggle against an angry beast. He crept on, hearing short, panting breaths. Light on his feet, waiting to spring, Huw indicated to Juhan to make ready and raised his stick.

There was a sudden rustle from the bush and a small yellow-haired girl shrieked as she ran out straight into the waiting arms of Juhan. He laughed as she struggled in his arms.

'Piret, be calm, my beauty. Juhan wants musi.'

The girl still tried to break away, but more from the threat of a kiss. Juhan put her down and she immediately punched him in the stomach, making him whoosh with expended air. She was no more than eight and her fair hair was tangled and wild. Red scratches on her hands and face showed she had run through the bushes without a care for safety.

'Soldiers, Juhan, they hurt Papa.'

Juhan's grin disappeared.

'How did they hurt? How many?'

'Three, I think. They hit him with gun,' she looked at Huw suspiciously.

Juhan frowned. 'There is no time.'

'We must get help,' Huw said.

Juhan shook his head. 'There is no time,' he repeated and crouched down next to Piret.

'Kallis, go and see your aunt, we will come for you,' he kissed her head, for once looking serious.

'Have you ever fought soldiers?' Huw hissed.

Juhan shook his head. 'I have not, but these people are good to us, they share their food. We have to help.'

'Alright, we'll go and look and then decide what we can do.'

They reached the outer barns without any sign of trouble or noise. The farm appeared deserted. The air missed the sounds of work.

Juhan gritted his teeth. 'I cannot walk away. These people keep us alive in winter.'

'That's fine, Juhan, but we cannot just run in without knowing where the soldiers are and how they are armed. There's no vehicle, so perhaps they've left. We'll go slowly. You follow my signals.'

Huw kept low and crept to the end of the barn. He had practised combat for many months, but had never faced a situation that could leave him wounded, captured or worse. His bladder felt full to bursting, even though he knew he would not panic, could not panic. A vision of the stricken *Cassandra* came into his head; *the shouted orders, the cries amid groans of metal twisting under pressure, the rush of water...* Huw shook his head, clearing out the dream. He felt his body trembling and forced himself to focus. Another memory: *Caradoc* shoaled off Fair Isle. *He was shouting orders, directing people down to repair the ship...* The image faded. He looked back and Juhan gave a less than convincing smile. Huw knew Juhan wouldn't walk away and he felt a wave of protectiveness and responsibility for him. He spied a narrow gap between the barns and worked his way towards it. There was a rustling noise behind him and Juhan came to his side.

'I told you to stay!' Huw hissed.

'Yes, but you have no weapon,' Juhan said, passing him a hunting knife. The edge was keen, but it made Huw feel less prepared; it signified the start of close-up conflict.

'I am going to those bushes and then to the door.'

'You are old and slow,' Juhan whispered. 'I will go.'

Without warning, he had sped past Huw and was at the edge of the doorway. He flashed a quick grin to Huw and then disappeared. Huw cursed him for a fool. He cursed himself for freezing. He cursed himself as he started to go after Juhan, albeit cautiously, waiting, listening and looking for signs of trouble. Yet still there was no sign of life at the house. Huw licked his dry lips as he reached the threshold, his teeth gritted as he tried to remember his training.

Relaxing his jaw before his teeth cracked, he moved inside. A shadow appeared from the first room and Huw tensed, relaxing when Juhan came into view.

'I thought you would not come,' he said.

'What the hell?' Huw spluttered. 'The soldiers?'

Juhan shrugged. 'They have gone. They ran when we came. Come, woman is fine, but man is hurt.'

Huw went inside to find an elderly couple; the man sat on the floor against a chair, the woman by his side. She was tending a cut near his left temple, now swelling with bruising.

'They did this?' Huw asked.

The woman looked up. 'They were boys, nothing more. They were scared, just boys wanting to go home. Siim spotted them and tried to chase them away, but they were tired and hungry and scared. They were very sorry after. Those poor boys…'

'I am alright,' Siim said, waving off her ministrations. 'They surprised me in barn.'

'They robbed you?' Huw asked.

Siim shook his head, touching his temple in pain.

'No, they brought me back, they were very sorry,' he finished with a bitter laugh. 'They were so frightened, just needed some food. They had not eaten for days.'

'They were runners?' Juhan asked, and the wife nodded.

'Frightened boys, a long way from home and nowhere to go.'

'Germans?'

'No, others, Flemish perhaps.'

Huw helped the farmer onto a chair while his wife went away to empty the bowl of water.

'Anna gave them food and they ran when they heard you,' the farmer said to Huw. 'You are no woodsman, too clumsy. They won't last long, for they have no idea where to run.'

'Why did she do this?' Huw asked.

'We have two sons – they fight, yet we do not know where. Narva perhaps or Võrumaa. We don't know if they live, even. Anna thinks that if she shows kindness, then it will be repaid. Somewhere, she thinks, there will be farm that will repay this kindness for our sons.'

He tried to get up, waving away help. 'I will be all right, if I sleep headache away.'

'Piret is with your brother,' Juhan said, and Siim nodded and waved his hand as he left the room. 'She is better there today.'

Chapter Six

A matter of trust

'You did what?' Peetr grabbed Juhan by the throat. 'Are you mad? Are you really that stupid?'

Huw sprung up in an instant and grabbed Peetr to drag him away. Peetr lashed out, sending Huw sprawling, but he quickly rolled to his feet and crouched ready to spring.

'If you want a fight, Peetr, you choose me.'

Peetr nodded and moved forward, wiping his mouth in anticipation.

The camp became alive with people trying to separate the two. Raio dragged Huw away and a few took Peetr.

'Gently, friend,' Raio said. 'This is not time to start war.'

'He needs to stop picking on Juhan,' Huw snarled.

'It's his way.'

'Not good enough,' Huw wrestled himself free and moved to Juhan's side.

'What is this?' Märt shouted, racing in from the woodland. 'Do you want to bring Germans here?'

'He has all but done so already,' Peetr snapped, glaring at Juhan.

Märt held a hand up for calm. 'I will hear it from them first.'

Juhan recounted what had happened at the farm and Märt nodded.

'Peetr, what is your problem with this?'

Peetr quivered with anger. 'You know what that idiot has done? He has exposed us. Those soldiers are deserters, they will get captured and they will tell everything about who and where they got help. Then old man will be forced to tell them everything, including about foreigner and they will start hunting us down like dogs, to find spy!'

'Peetr has point, Märt,' Raio said quietly. 'But I was thinking perhaps these soldier boys will be killed first and will not know where they have been. However, what if they had been there and Huw was shot? Where is our future then? Huw can tell English what we are facing. We need to protect him.'

'I can look after myself,' Huw said and moved to warm himself by the fire. He was cold and fed up. 'Do none of you respect what Juhan has done here? These people help you and you are saying that when they needed him, Juhan should have turned away?'

'They were not in danger,' said Raio.

'And had they been?' Huw raged. He grabbed a log and threw it in the fire, sending up red sparks to match his anger.

'I have heard you all,' Märt said, 'and I think there are some other things to say. He called the camp in, but sent Juhan and Huw away to guard.

'Keep watch, whilst we talk.'

Juhan nodded and picked up his rifle, moving off. Huw followed, cursing the fact that he could only hear the rise and fall of their voices. He desperately concentrated on what words he could catch:

'Flemish SS are helping to hold Narva hills.' Märt said 'That deserters have come this far tells me one thing. There is not much time, if it is not already too late. We must get ready for this. We need more ammunition, rifles and so on. I aim to go to Kadrina, to old friend, perhaps to steal from Germans.'

There was a gasp from the others.

'Kadrina is far,' said Peetr. 'Rakvere is nearer. Why Kadrina?'

'Rakvere is too big, too well guarded. Kadrina will be easy to get in unseen. We will find out what is happening there also.'

Märt drew a map in the earth as he spoke, marking out the roads. He underlined Kadrina.

'Who will go with you?' Peetr asked.

'Juhan and Huw,' Märt held up his hands again. 'Yes, don't worry Peetr, I will make sure Juhan does nothing stupid. Raio, I will keep safe our spy also. He must see our world beyond forest. We leave at dawn.'

Everywhere Huw went in the town involved the feel of snow compacting under his boots. He was so glad of those boots, but knew he would need to change for the dance in the afternoon. Maybe he should carry his dress shoes rather than wear them to the hall and risk dampening and freezing his feet?

Maarja stood by the side of a great round tower in the castle walls that marked the entrance point to the medieval part of town.

Huw looked at the thick walls of the tower; they would definitely withstand a pounding. Then his focus was drawn away to Maarja. She wore a fur coat and hat, and Huw briefly wondered whether Estonians greeted their friends by hugging. That would certainly make him so much warmer in more ways than one. The snow fell silently and yet it was as if it did not land on her. She smiled a greeting and gave a small wave.

'Today we walk old town.'

Her soft voice echoed in his mind, casting shivers down his spine. The streets looked deserted, making Huw struggle for something to focus on – to cling onto in the engulfing sea of doubt that gripped him as he saw her. He gritted his teeth, trying to keep a semblance of order, if only to keep her by his side.

'So, why do they call this Fat Margaret?'

Her smile was quite patient. 'These walls are thick – fat, no?'

Huw decided he daren't ask who Margaret was and they stood in awkward silence before she took his arm.

'Come, I will show you old town.'

'People always walk arm in arm here?' *His teeth grated at his stupid question, he could not believe how he was floundering. Maarja squeezed his arm.*

'In winter, it is good to have help,' *she replied.* 'For when I slip, you will stop me falling.'

Her face looked serious, but the eyes mocked him and he loved the experience.

They made their way past tall buildings that flanked the narrow streets. Huw wondered if they were the only people in the city, such was the lack of activity in the freezing wind. His last port before this tour had been Copenhagen, a city that glowed with humanity and commerce – a buzz of activity. Even the Lettish capital of Libau had been positively animated in comparison to Tallinn, but by now he welcomed the space. In the hilly cobbled streets, there could have been a thousand people around, but he only had time for the warmth of Maarja's touch.

The cobbled road proved awkward to cross in the slush. He slipped once and had to use Maarja to support him as they entered a spacious town square. On one side was an extensive medieval building, with a narrow bell-tower.

'This is Raekoja Plats.' She said softly. 'We have our um... Rathaus here.'

For once her English faltered, so she pointed at the building and Huw thought about it for a while, before settling on it being the town hall. It could have been Portsmouth for all he cared, as long as he was with her.

'Perhaps we should walk to top of Toompea?'

He shrugged, although the cold made him shiver a bit. 'I have no problem.'

She stopped, looked at him and snorted. 'Yes you do. You are not dressed for this. You look more blue than your uniform. Come.'

She headed into a dimly lit corridor, which opened up into a shop that sold woollen clothes. Huw was grateful to get indoors, away from the freezing air. As his jaw ached back into warmth, he realised how cold his face had become. Maarja started fingering some scarves and Huw noted her desire for him to spend money. He felt she was trying to help the shopkeeper make ends meet. Still, he could do with a scarf...

He chose a dark woollen scarf and quickly donned it, only for Maarja to reposition it with a slight frown, as if moving a piece of art. With a small nod and a grunt of approval, she was ready for them to continue up the street. There was little conversation. Huw listened to the crunch of their feet in the snow and the faint sounds of their breathing. He desperately searched for something to say, but was only left with his thoughts. They soon reached the base of a flight of steps leading up the hill outside the town walls. A medieval tower stood separate – close to, but not quite touching, the wall.

'What is it?' asked Huw.

'Kiek in de Koek,' she looked at his face and paused, frowning in incomprehension. 'What is problem?'

Huw kept his mouth closed and remembered that "discretion is the better part of valour" – especially where schoolboy humour was concerned. He was sure it had another translation.

A beautiful Russian Orthodox cathedral loomed above them. Gold leaf abounded on the wall friezes and the domes, making it look foreign in this land.

'You are Orthodox?' he asked.

'No, we are Lutheran.'

'Then who is this for?'

'*Russians.*'
'*But you are Estonian.*'
'*Yes, I know this.*'
He could see she was trying not to smile at his confusion.
'*Once, Russia ruled us. When they left, some of their people remained. It is always this way, as with Germans, Swedes and Danes before them. Come.*'

The top of the hill held a collection of very pretty buildings separated by narrow lanes. Maarja chose a path that took them along the town wall to a clearing from which they could look down on the rest of the town. Huw looked as best he could, with the cold wind blowing in his face. He wished for his goggles, but felt perhaps they would not be right in this company. The cold air pulverised the nerves of his face, making it feel like a mask.

The town below them was like a Christmas card. The maze of red-tiled roofs was intermingled with church towers and their beautiful spires. Not far beyond, the navy ships were berthed in the harbour, dark silhouettes against the grey Baltic.

'*This is my city,*' Maarja murmured. '*It is beautiful, is it not?*'
'*Yes,*' Huw breathed. '*I just wish I could see it through the cold.*'
She laughed at that. '*You are so... English.*'

He looked away from the city and into her eyes, dreaming of the warmth within. Then she turned to go and he stopped her.

'*I want to look at it one more time, if you don't mind.*'

He shielded his eyes, covering the pain throbbing between his eyebrows, and took a long hard look at the beautiful city.

'*Thank you, Maarja. It is a very special place.*'

She nodded and smiled. '*Yes, it is special. You are welcome. 'Perhaps we may find somewhere to have hot drink, for you look so cold.*'

She walked off, and for a second he felt rooted to the spot. Only his eyes followed her, and her words floated over the air, gently mocking him.

'*You are so cold that your legs are frozen, Huw.*'

His cheeks flushed hot as he followed her back to the street. It warmed up his face and felt good. They moved from the hill back inside the town walls and Maarja steered them into a small building, and a dimly candle-lit room. There was more illumination coming from the tiny fire in the hearth. The furniture was sparse, plain and battered. She spoke to the downcast barman and then made herself comfortable on a seat.

'You are cold. You need soup,' she said simply.

'So are you, perhaps you should join me.'

A slight inclination of the head and a smile was the reply, as she called out to the barman. There was no reply, but he returned soon with two bowls of a dilute broth.

'You have not prepared well for this cold,' she chided.

'I could have worn what I was wearing in the Baltic, but it's hardly flattering.' He replied and she snorted her scorn.

'Here, you wear what keeps you alive. Eat.'

The bread was dark, sour and moist, with a hint of yeast working towards alcohol. Huw felt he could get used to it in time.

'I am surprised you could find a restaurant open.'

'People will still try to make money when they can. In spring, country folk will come in with flowers, berries and mushrooms to sell as well as their crops.'

'But not today.'

Maarja shook her head. 'When the snow is down, people try and use what they have stored. If not, they starve.'

Huw detected an undertone of resentment, but could not think why.

'We are here to help, Maarja. And we will see the job through.'

She glared back. 'To you, it is a job. Here it is fight for our land and our people.'

'And the more I stay here, the less of a job it will be,' Huw said gently, her aggression knocking away his shyness. 'You should eat your soup also.'

He half expected the bowl on his head, but instead she sighed and picked up a spoon.

'This is not good soup. In Estonia, we make better soup in better times.'

She kept her eyes down, examined the bread.

'My brother is in army. He fights in forest. They use train as moving barracks to intercept enemy. We don't know where he is. I am sorry if I seem angry. My world is no longer what it was.'

It was as if the sun had returned, the conversation began to grow warmer. As she talked of her life and land, Huw realised it was the first time he had relaxed since coming to Tallinn. He was desperate to keep the conversation going. The soup had put colour back in Maarja's cheeks and she looked stronger, glowing before his eyes.

'Tell me of your land,' she asked.

'Where I come from is a small town on the west coast of Wales called Aberystwyth.'

He shook his head as she tried to repeat it.

'It's fine. It has a harbour, a ruined castle and a university. It has a long promenade, where you can walk on a summer's evening and watch the sea change colour from blue to green, as the sun sets behind it. There are hills and valleys, lakes and woodland. On a clear day, you can see the mountains, as you lie on the beach and enjoy the sound of the sea.'

'You miss this place?'

'Yes.'

'Why did you leave?'

'Many years ago, the fleet sailed into the bay. They let people visit the ships and at night, gave a display with their searchlights. I knew then the sailor's life was for me.'

'And now?'

Huw became aware of a faint whining sound outside. It was getting closer and as realisation dawned, his training cut in. He grabbed Maarja quickly and pulled her to the floor. An explosion followed that shook the building, sending plaster and dust down from the ceiling.

She looked at him in alarm. 'Russians!'

'They must have ships in the bay,' Huw replied. 'The ice must have broken sooner than expected. I must report back.'

He got up to leave and then stopped and looked at her.

'I will be alright,' she said. 'I will go to Russian cathedral on Toompea. Even Reds still believe and they will not harm their own.'

On impulse, he drew her close and kissed her. The world stopped as a small smile crept on her lips.

'I still want to dance,' was all she said.

Chapter Seven

Kadrina

'You come.'

Märt had not had much to say at the best of times, like so many Estonians that Huw had met in twenty years. Why speak a hundred words when one can do?

Huw opened his hand to gaze at the small flower he was holding. Its leaves at the top flushed violet, opening out like a star. Below them a yellow, horn-shaped flower pointed straight with pride. Huw had never seen its like before in the forests of Märjamaa and he marvelled at the delicate beauty.

'To where?'

'Kadrina, with Smiler.'

'Young Juhan seems to have a smile for every occasion.' Huw agreed. 'It's a rare trait.'

'He is fool, Märt replied. 'He does not know when to laugh and when to cry.'

'Why Kadrina?' Huw asked.

'Reds are close. We check. Report back. Nothing more.'

'Why me?'

'I too am asked this question,' came the reply and a rifle was shoved in Huw's hands. He never knew if Märt was joking. Somehow, the land's conflict appeared private to the man. There was no further discussion, Huw slung the rifle on his shoulder and followed into the forest.

'How do we get there?' Huw asked.

'We walk,' Märt said simply.

Juhan smiled like it was a joke.

All was quiet, as if the birds had left for saner shores. The path through the slim, tall trees was clear to Märt. Even in the gloom, he could tell which way to turn from the shapes of the land and the trees. Huw wished he had the woodcraft.

'How many midge bites now?' Juhan asked casually.

'About seventy.' Huw cursed, as he was reminded of the bugs. He started to itch everywhere again.

Juhan chuckled. 'So much choice – which to scratch first?'

'Now I'm covered in vodka.'

'Yes, vodka is good for swelling.'

'I smell like a drunk.'

The trek took most of the day. Huw wondered how their boots would bear up to this continual punishment. Where they would find repair or replacement in the forest? Perhaps he should radio for a parachute drop of new boots. Stranger things had been known in war.

Kadrina was like every other town Huw had seen. A group of small dwellings lining roads converging on a church with a tall steeple, standing proud in the centre. The surrounding fields still showed signs of being worked. However, many were overgrown or damaged – a legacy of the years of conflict, and the drain of men who worked them.

Märt made for the outskirts, and led them to a sturdy farmhouse with a lean-to barn. There was a well close by and the ubiquitous smoke sauna lodge that always had Huw thinking of stout garden sheds.

A woman came out of the house to greet them. Old beyond her years, she carried a potato and a knife. Casual though she was, there was hardly a chance that she would begin to peel the potato.

Märt hailed her and she nodded in reply, the knife lowering as she recognised him. He followed her inside, whilst Huw and Juhan hid in the barn. There was a strange silence in the air that made them all uneasy. Soon, Märt returned.

'It's worse than we thought. Tanks are here.'

'What now?' Juhan asked.

'We wait.'

Then an unmistakable rat-tat-tat of machine guns and engines began to cough to life.

'They're coming,' Huw muttered.

Sweat dripped down his face, smearing the mud camouflaging his pale skin. Märt placed his hand on Huw's wrist and motioned him to be quiet.

'They are busy in Kadrina,' he said. The tension made his voice taut, his words clipped.

They listened to the noise of the tanks, holding their breath, waiting for more gunfire. There was none.

'This is not good,' muttered Juhan.

'There are Metsavennad there,' Märt said. 'They should hide or surrender, you can't fight tanks.'

A movement caught Huw's attention. It was a motorcycle and sidecar. The passenger was holding a machine gun.

'Company!' Huw hissed, pointing ahead. They moved into shadow.

'What shall we do?' Juhan said.

'Hide,' Märt replied. 'In long grass.'

'And the woman?'

For once, Märt hesitated. Juhan pushed him away.

'Go, I will stay.'

'What?'

'Go,' Juhan smiled and gave up his rifle. 'You would let your heart take over.'

Huw dragged Märt away. 'There's no time to argue.'

Crouching low, the two partisans ran to safety, dropping to the ground, rifles ready and cocked. Huw looked up and through the grass he watched Juhan stride out towards the approaching motorcycle.

Huw's heart missed a beat as the passenger raised his gun. Then he realised the man had only shifted to keep his balance. He prayed Märt would not shoot. He prayed they would all stay alive. He apologised for being such an atheist bastard in the past and promised he would change. Anything, anything for them to get through this.

Juhan waved at the soldiers and stood calmly as the bike came to a stop. Huw cursed the wind for not letting him hear the words. Then it gently changed direction and he listened. The language was harsh to his ears, although Juhan spoke with confidence.

The soldier's tone became aggressive, but Juhan answered with his lazy smile, spreading his arms to indicate the land and pointing at the sauna. The Russian nodded and Juhan called out for the woman to come out.

'Bring glasses!'

Huw was not sure what Juhan was up to, so he kept his rifle ready, in case the passenger made a move that would threaten his friend. There was no doubt in his mind, Huw would shoot if needed. Then the three would have to make the best of it, the old woman also. That was war. Huw accepted it, though he knew in his heart it was wrong.

The woman came out with a bottle and three glasses. Juhan poured out the vodka and took a quick swig. Then he opened his mouth to laugh.

'Good stuff!'

He poured three glasses and offered two to the soldiers. The passenger refused to acknowledge, but the rider took it with a nod, offering harsh words to his comrade. The man was trying to smile, but stopped short. That was Russians for you, Huw thought, remembering the submarine.

Juhan and the rider clicked their glasses and downed the vodka. The rider nodded again and Juhan offered the bottle. Again there was that half smile from the Russian and a nod. He stowed the bottle and kick-started the motor. With a hand raised in farewell, he rode away.

The tanks were mobile again. The monsters ambled slowly down the road, throwing up dust like a storm. Huw watched them, heart in mouth. With a rustle of the reeds, Märt was at his side, gently pushing down the rifle that Huw was raising by instinct.

'What the hell did he do?' Huw hissed.

'Act Red. He's good. Everyone loves Smiler.'

Juhan crouched down with them.

'Vodka cures all ills,' he chuckled.

'What now?' Huw asked.

'I go to Kadrina,' Märt replied.

'They may have men there,' Huw replied.

'I go to Kadrina,' Märt repeated with an edge to his voice. 'I must see everything.'

He got up and walked off. Juhan shrugged and the other two followed, trying to blend in with shadows wherever they could. They walked to the centre, looking for life.

They found a group of women. One had her hands at her mouth. Another was on her knees, reaching out as if to grab the ground, yet not touching it. She appeared in torment. There was a gentle sobbing. The woman on the ground started to wail. She was grabbed in a hug by another. It didn't stop her. The men reached the group and Märt spoke to one who just looked on in silence.

'What happened here, Airi?'

She kept staring and Märt had to ask again, gently shaking her arm. Slowly, her head rose to stare at him. Tears fell from her face.

'They were unarmed. They had come out without fight, to surrender.'

Huw's gaze took in shapes in the road. A rainbow of colours. Stretched shapes, no form. Like, no... surely not? *Please God no...*

'After the Reds shot them,' Airi whispered. 'They laid them out in a line. Then the tanks...' She swallowed hard. 'They drove back and forward until there was nothing left. How do we bury our dead? They have left us nothing.'

'Where were you?' The hysterical woman grabbed Huw shaking his tunic. 'Where were you? You could have saved them. Where were you?' Her last words came as a screech. Airi gently led the woman away, but the question still shouted over and over in Huw's mind. *Where were you?*

Huw found Märt on the road, looking where the tanks had gone. Märt's eyes were raw, his face white with fury.

'You go back, take Smiler.'

'What?'

'I go. To kill, I will kill them all.'

'You can't.'

Märt turned; he was shaking now.

'You do not tell me this.'

'You said yourself, we can't fight tanks.'

'I must... I must do something.'

'We can, but not like this. We must find a way to our strength, not to theirs.'

'This is my home,' Märt said quietly. His eyes looked around. 'These are my people.'

Huw grabbed Märt then and shook him roughly. 'You go after them and they will kill you. We will go back and we will get them when they don't expect.' Märt was struggling now. Huw hung on and shouted, 'How do you want revenge, by walking into their bullets?'

Märt shook himself free, with a backward slap that sent Huw to the floor. He looked away again. 'We should have killed them at farm.'

'I would not wish it,' Juhan said quietly. 'I drank with soldier and we talked. He asked questions. His last words to me were. *Please remember this, friend. We are not all animals.* He knew what had happened, he knew I was false but he wanted no part of here. I judge this man by his humanity, not his badge.'

'There is no humanity,' Märt muttered. 'War has taken humanity.'

He shouldered his rifle and walked out of the village.

Huw stood up stiffly and something fell out of his pocket. He bent to pick up the small flower he had kept without thinking. In his eyes, it was still beautiful, but now it had changed. The top was a purple star, open in sorrow. The yellow petals were a bell, tolling in grief. He gazed at the flower and marvelled how something so wonderful could still exist. Perhaps if such a thing could, there was still hope. Perhaps there would always be hope, whilst people like Juhan survived. Whilst there were still people ready to see someone for who they were, not what they wore.

Huw gently put the flower back in his pocket, to remind him of the light beyond the dark clouds. He looked at Juhan with his warm smile and finally acknowledged the wisdom in his eyes.

Huw sprinted to the harbour with the other crewmen. Wakeful *was already leaving by the time they arrived. Ratings were preparing to raise the* Caradoc *gangplank, but Huw managed to launch himself up it in the nick of time. For a moment, he was convinced the commander would throw him off, but the man paused, then with a wry smile said 'Welcome aboard, son.' Then they were off towards the grey Baltic horizon.*

It was most of the day before they returned, but all the ships made port intact. Their hosts were still keen to show their gratitude and the banquet in honour of the Royal Navy squadron had been rescheduled for the evening. The promise of a dance, however, was now a distant memory, lost to the engagement of the Russian ships. It was as well, perhaps, that the ladies had not been present, for in their euphoric state, many of the men may have taken the thought of hiring them too literally.

Whilst they steamed back, Huw had been desperate to make port and by the time he arrived at the banquet he was in a tormented state of hope and anxiety. Hope that he would see Maarja was safe and yet a great anxiety that he might not. To his dismay he saw no women there save the serving staff. His heart felt heavy; he would be left none the wiser as to her fate that night.

The initial joy of having the chance to prove himself in battle was now replaced by emptiness and fatigue. Huw had been there and seen it happen. He'd done his bit and more besides – all the time with one eye on the ever-receding coastline, and the Orthodox cathedral on Toompea hill. He looked desperately for faces he had seen from the Estonian government, those who could speak English and might have known of her fate. But as he cast his gaze around the banquet, it was as if he had walked into a room full of strangers.

It was a long-drawn-out affair. Many Estonian notaries were present, showing their appreciation for the force. The speeches were long, the food courses longer. The arrival of the crews had caused such a stir. The British that had been left in port and the Estonians present were keen to ask questions about the action. Huw ached to get away from it all and find Maarja, even though he had no idea where to begin to look in the city. The banquet began to break up, and an Estonian delegate caught up with him as he stood with Taylor, at the back of the hall.

'We thank you for saving us tonight,' the Estonian said. 'And you capture Red battleship, no?'

'A destroyer, Spartak,' Huw replied, more embarrassed than gratified.

'And Russian sea lord on board also? This is great event! Thank you friend, thank you.' The Estonian moved off to thank others and Huw turned to Taylor.

'It's nice to be thanked, though I feel he was just practising his English.'

Taylor just shrugged. He was slightly younger than Huw, though he looked a veteran. He'd been a good friend for years and they had a lot of things in common. Tonight though, he lived and breathed the excitement of the moment. It irked Huw for at this point all he wanted to do was be alone and nurse his black mood.

'Tell you what, Williams. I wish I'd been on Wakeful. We're all heroes, but they're the only ones who fired a bloody shot! Do you think they hit her? The Russians claim they turned their own guns too far round and shot their own chart room. What do you make of that?'

'Saving face by claiming incompetence? Either way, it did it for them. They wobbled like a drunk across the bay and holed themselves on the shoals.'

'Still, we got a bit of action in an engagement.'

53

'What? Rushing out to watch Wakeful get off one shot is hardly enough to get in the line for medals, John.'

'You're a bit glum, Huw, on a night to celebrate.'

Huw grimaced. 'I spent all that engagement below deck and all for nothing.'

'Damage control parties are key, Sub-lieutenant, and by all comments, your lot were as keen as mustard and ready for anything, all credit to you. And you got on that boarding party; I never got to see what she was like.'

'I'll never complain about cleanliness on a British ship again,' Huw replied. 'I felt greasy just going there. The sailors looked almost happy to surrender to us. Bloody Russkis. You know when we told them to man their pumps? The whole crew had to call a meeting to vote on whether they should or not.'

'That's Bolsheviks for you,' Taylor said, snagging a cake from the table. 'Good spread this.'

'Yes, I feel embarrassed,' Huw replied. 'Damn town's starving and they lay this on for us. I wonder how the other ships are faring in Libau.'

'Probably the same, if not worse. What about that man Krasalnikov, the First Sea Lord of the Russian Navy? And you found him hiding under a bag of potatoes?'

'Sixteen bags, Taylor. But then, if you were that important, would you come quietly?'

Taylor gave him a sly grin. 'I know why you're so glum, my friend. It's that girl, isn't it? You didn't get the chance of getting your hands around her.'

'Nothing of the sort,' Huw lied.

'Well, you wouldn't be interested to know she's outside now then.'

'What? How do you even know what she looks like?'

'Because I just went out for a few minutes to get some air. There was a girl there, pretty blonde thing, she was asking after you. I could watch her just talk all day, that one. No wonder you've been so secretive about her; I wouldn't let out how damn gorgeous she is to anyone. Has she got a sister?'

A slight cough behind them made them realise their conversation was not exclusive. Caradoc's commander was standing close by.

'Now you've had your fun, gentlemen, make ready. We're casting off pretty soon.'

'Are there more ships out there, sir?' Taylor asked.

'We think so. The Estonians have translated papers found on the Spartak. We think the cruiser Oleg may be out there and our captain fancies bagging that before she comes into the bay – or makes a run for it.'

Huw began to get ready, but was pulled sharp by his commander's words.

'Not you, Williams. You did a sterling job today, but the captain has spoken. You're assigned to shore duty and until that changes, that's where you remain.'

'Sir.' Huw tried not to sigh out his disappointment.

'Off you go then, Taylor.' Taylor saluted and left, not missing the opportunity to wink at Huw in passing.

'Another thing, Williams. A friendly warning.'

'Sir?'

'If you are messing with a woman, a word of advice. We've not long left here. We leave as soon as the ice begins to set in and the locals reckon that's only about a week away. Don't get too friendly, you're not staying.'

Huw left quickly, crushed by the double blow of not being allowed on ship for the engagement and the sudden news of their departure. He heard his name called out, but jammed his hands in his pockets and began to walk down the road to his digs. He knew it was Maarja, but he couldn't face her, not now. She rushed out to him as quickly as the snowy path let her and caught up with him away from the throng.

'Huw, what is wrong? I call to you and you ignore this?'

He turned and met her eyes, making her smile. The warmth was tinged with sadness at his rebuff.

'Huw, I was so worried. Thank God you are safe.'

Huw was anxious to leave, his delight at knowing she was safe had become pain with the knowledge of his imminent departure. He tried a weak smile.

'I am relieved that you are safe. I was worried that you may have been caught up in the attack.'

She laughed and straightened a wayward lock of her fair hair.

'*I was always safe. Then I watched your ships leave and they switched off their lights. Then there was a fire on horizon and I feared...*'

'*I'm afraid it wasn't as exciting as that, Maarja. Now the ships are going out again and they are leaving me on shore.*'

She looked deeply into his sad eyes and frowned. '*Come with me.*'

It was a simple command that left him in a delicious purgatory. Part of him felt he did not want to be there and yet he was desperate for her presence.

'*Where to?*'

'*Where we went before, I think you are dressed for it today, even your scarf.*'

Huw looked at the banquet hall wistfully. The cheerful bunting added to the warmth of the welcome they had received that night.

'*You really wanted us here,*'

Maarja smiled. '*For sure, you are welcome. You have protected our rear while we fight on the ground. Come, let's walk.*'

They moved in silence for a while, arms linked, towards the old town and Toompea hill.

'*How did you learn English?*' He finally asked.

'*My father was lawyer,*' she replied. '*He sent me to be educated, so I speak English, French, German and Russian.*'

'*And Estonian,*' he had to add, and she squeezed his arm in reply.

'*Okay, I also speak some Finnish and Lettish. How many languages do you have?*'

'*Two.*'

'*This is good, one more than I expected.*'

This made him smile. '*Yes, we are a lazy race.*'

My father was from poor family, he had scholarship. My family is from south.'

'*So, a farmer's girl?*' Huw tried to tease her, but she missed the dig.

'*This is nothing to be ashamed of.*'

'*No, my parents ran a café in the town in Wales. He was a lead miner of old and her family had a farm, which I worked on as a boy. I too got a scholarship. Only reason I went to school. Bloody hard work, if you pardon the language.*'

'We have something to share?'

'Yes.'

They had reached the platform once again that looked out to the harbour and beyond. He could see the lights of two ships moving out of harbour. From the vantage point, the ships appeared to glide effortlessly along. Then the lights went out and they disappeared from view.

'What has happened?' Maarja asked.

'As they are chasing ships, they do not wish to advertise their arrival,' Huw replied. He knew one of them was Caradoc and his heart felt heavy with the commander's words once more.

'I cannot see them,' she said.

'I can't see anything in this damn cold wind.'

'You are sad for not being there, friend Huw.'

'I am sad for that, Maarja. But also when the ice comes in a week, we will be gone and when the spring thaws it, a new squadron will arrive with different ships.'

She stared long into the night. 'Estonian government will want some contact, perhaps they will need navy officer to do this.'

Huw sighed. 'Perhaps.'

He felt the warmth of her hand on his in his pocket and suddenly grinned.

'I know what I can do.'

He rummaged in his coat and produced a pair of goggles.

'Now we can watch.'

'You have another pair?'

'No, but here,' he placed the left lens over his right eye and drew her closer. She pressed the right lens to her left eye and giggled as their heads touched.

'There they are!' He said triumphantly.

'Where?'

'Look, there is a faint shadow moving on the sea there.'

'Yes, yes, I see it! She is so graceful.'

'Yes she is,' Huw whispered.

He turned to face her and in their closeness he knew there was no turning back. He moved to feel the warmth of her lips on his.

Chapter Eight

Rabbit stew

The longer he stayed in this land, the more closely the ghosts of his Estonian past gathered around him. Even after the horror he had witnessed, Huw could not escape the memories of a life and a love lost. He wished it were different. The anger and bitterness that stirred within him made him feel the land itself was laughing at his loss.

Märt offered no conversation and even Juhan's face had settled into a permanent frown. Huw had far too much time for his own thoughts as they travelled back though the forest from Kadrina to the camp. He knew he had to get his companions talking before the shock borne of anger affected their judgement. It was for his own good also, past experiences made him fully aware of the consequences of a long silence.

'How are you, Juhan?' He asked.

'I am sad,' came the simple reply.

'They were already dead, my friend. They did not suffer the tanks.'

'No, but what was done was not right.'

'It never is. War makes people do things that they would not even dream about in better times.'

Märt cursed softly, but otherwise kept his counsel.

'Märt, we must rest soon,' Huw said.

'I hear you Englishman,' Märt replied. 'But I want to cross Tallinn road first.'

'Come on, Juhan,' Huw said. 'We'll get back in time for one of Raio's rabbit stews.'

'Ah yes, rabbit stew,' Juhan replied, though his voice betrayed the lack of enthusiasm for eating it.

The road from Kadrina was quiet, but as a precaution, they still kept within the shadows of the trees. When they got closer to the main road, Märt chose a path that moved away from the junction and its potential roadblocks. As they approached, they became aware of the sound of moving vehicles, Märt signalled them to approach the Tallinn road with more caution. It was now a hive of activity.

Trucks, guns and lorries headed west in what seemed a never-ending procession.

'Red Army moves faster than I feared,' Märt said, as they lay down on the needle-strewn sandy ground and watched the convoy. He kept them well away from the arc of sunlight at the forest perimeter, away from hostile eyes. 'Now is our time to rest, road is too straight here to avoid being seen. We cannot cross before dark.'

'You are still angry, Märt,' Huw said.

'For sure, how can I be otherwise? These people, my people, were cut down when they had no chance to fight. They survived when Reds came first time, they suffered for four years in war – then to be killed as revenge? For sure, there is no justice in this world.'

'What do you mean by that?'

'German Army held Reds back at Narva for five months, and then they fell back to the hills and held Reds for longer. Now Reds are through and they want to hurt people for all their comrades who died. German Army must be moving back fast, so Reds look to kill anyone with pulse. They have no honour, those who would do this.'

'Märt, I wish to go home, to Märjamaa,' Juhan said softly.

'I also think of this, Juhan,' Märt said. 'Perhaps soon it is time we looked to protect our own. No-one is safe.'

'Who is waiting for you, Juhan?' Huw asked, fearing he already knew the answer.

'My mother, Maarja,' Juhan replied. 'Did you know her?'

Märt looked straight ahead and made no sign of wishing to take any further part in the conversation. Huw took a deep breath.

'I may know the name.'

'You would like her, she is nice person.'

Lorries filed past carrying grey-clad troops and for a moment, Huw wanted to take a machine gun to them all. It's amazing what war does to a man, Huw thought. In another time, he would be deemed psychopathic.

'I should come with you,' he said, as calmly as he could manage. 'I will report back to base, we need intelligence at the front – and the front has passed us by.'

Märt nodded. 'We will explain to Metsavennad when we return, Raio is calm enough and good leader. He will keep them safe.'

'How will we travel?'

'Who knows? Walk, steal ride on train. Whatever we can find.'

'We may steal lorry,' said Juhan. Märt cursed again quietly.

'It has merit,' Huw said in the young man's defence. 'If we keep off the main road.'

Märt shrugged, it was the only concession Huw was going to get in reply.

After a while, Märt sighed. 'Whatever we do, we must be doing it before winter, so now is our time to leave.'

The door of the GAZ jeep opened and Oleg climbed inside with a grunt. He handed his lieutenant some black bread and they both chewed in silence for a while, watching the columns drive past them.

'There have been reports of killing in the villages, Yuri.'

'Yes, the soldiers are angry. The way the Nazis have got in the way of us, when all around is falling. They think there was help from the locals for this so-called German force.'

'Why is it "so-called"?'

'It is a force of foreigners blinded by Hitler. Norskis, Nederlanders, Flemish, even some Estonians. They have held us up for so long, it is inevitable someone would suffer for it in the end, Comrade Oleg. Those who are left behind always suffer.'

'These people were not fighters, they were villagers caught in this shit. If we keep on killing people, there will be nobody left to farm the land and feed us all, while an army of partisans will be waiting in every forest.'

'They would be no match for our army in the battlefield.'

'They would not be found on your battlefield. The forest would be their battlefield and we would be worn down by a war of attrition, armed by the Americans. What we need is these people on our side, so we can root out the traitors and spies.'

'So, to help us find foreign agents?'

'Yes, the West hopes we will leave here when Germany falls, but this is our land from times of old. The longer the West waits to learn the truth, the more we will be ready – should they decide they have not had enough of fighting.'

'So, I get word to the commanders?'

'Yes and find that tank commander. Mention if he does that again, he will be in charge of a guard post in a gulag in Siberia. I have a spy to catch and I don't need distractions. I need help.'

'For the spy?' Yuri asked, but Oleg ignored the question.

'We have been asked for some corpses, for a monument in Tallinn to the fallen comrades. When we liberate the city, we will need something to remind everyone of the struggle.'

'Perhaps you want this tank commander to volunteer to be one of them?'

'I'll leave it to your judgement, Yuri. Bring the bodies to the city; I don't care where you get them from. They will be heroes of the liberation, but they will be dead. Nobody will get in the way of my mission.'

For a moment, the room felt darker, then Yuri felt the light flood back as his colleague began to smile once more.

The traffic started to ease as dusk fell and the three men scooted across the road in the dusk without any alarm. Moonlight from behind a thin covering of cloud was just enough for them to find the side road leading to the coast. Millions of stars flooded the dark sky through the small gaps in the cloud, more stars than Huw had ever imagined were up there.

Märt cursed. 'There is heavy cloud on horizon, thick and unbroken. I do not feel we will reach camp tonight. It will soon be too dark and I do not know this forest well enough. We may need to shelter and move in morning.'

'Sure,' Huw agreed. 'But we can keep to the road until the first village and see?'

'Agreed.'

Huw could not remember what happened next. He was woken later by someone shaking his shoulder. He looked up to Juhan's cheerful smile.

'Come, before the mosquitoes eat you.'

Huw's shoulders ached from lying on the uneven ground and his neck burned with stiffness. The dreamless night had made him realise how exhausted he actually was. Perhaps he could snatch some more rest before his next radio report?

It was going to be a warm day, the sun streamed through the canopy to light up patches of the ground below. Huw enjoyed the relative warmth of the morning, the gentle breeze making the branches above sway in a lazy rhythm. Most of all, he enjoyed the silence around him; it told of a freedom from outsiders and a chance to move away from the horrors at Kadrina.

There was a nagging thought playing on his mind now. If Maarja had a son, it stood to reason she had a man. Whilst the practical side of him knew this would probably have been the case anyway, his stomach had still plummeted at the indirect news. Why was he still eager to run back to Märjamaa on a fool's errand? He knew the answer only too well. He had to see the evidence with his own eyes, before he would let go the gossamer thread of hope and tumble into the abyss.

He started observing Juhan from afar, looking for mannerisms that he recognised from his lost love. He could see Maarja's smile in the broad beaming one presented to him at almost every occasion. He could look into the man's eyes and be shocked to the core, seeing Juhan's mother from long ago. There were other things that felt familiar, but when he tried to imagine them associated with Maarja, it was like a wrong note on a piano. He was at a loss to explain why.

As they approached the camp, Huw listened for the warning bird-call in the air. His foot dragged over a stump and he stumbled, cursing himself softly. Looking back, he saw a metallic glint and quickly bent to retrieve the offending object. It was a knife: one he recognised.

'Märt,' he called. 'We have a problem.'

'Toomas' knife,' Juhan said when they convened. 'But where is Toomas?'

'There is blood on the blade,' Märt said. 'Toomas would not be so clumsy when hunting. Spread out.'

The answer to the riddle became clear as Huw approached a fallen bough. Toomas' body lay as if casually tossed aside. His tunic was thick with coagulated blood. Huw waved the others over and they looked at how Toomas was left.

'He died facing them,' Juhan said.

'Yes, but he is dead,' Märt snapped. 'And shot, so we have enemies with guns. Take what is needed from him; we will bury him later. First, I wish to find if we still have camp.'

A few paces on, Märt found his answer. Another body lay in the grass, clad in a German uniform. The jacket lapels bore the death's head with two crossed bones. Flying insects had already discovered the sweetness of the freshly spilled blood.

'Ambush,' Märt said. 'Keep low, keep in sight of each other and keep away from any path. We must come to camp through trees. No more talk.'

They crept on towards the camp, moving from tree to tree. Märt led the trio, and as he moved to a new spot, his place was taken by Juhan and then Huw. The feeling they were walking into a trap, one with machine guns and grenades, was overpowering.

There was silence, save the rustle of leaves and a chirping of a bird in the canopy: the atmosphere felt threatening and oppressive to Huw. Within the realm of the camp, there should have been signs of activity by now. In the scrub, Huw could make out a pair of jackboots. The grey uniform of the wearer was faintly visible amid the bushes. He waved to Märt and they moved over to check. The way the boots lay, pointed upward and apart, gave the indication that there was no danger. The corpse showed signs of damage from an explosion.

'Don't move him, he may be booby-trapped,' Märt warned the others.

Huw heard a metallic click nearby. It repeated again and again, like something swinging loose in the breeze. He checked for the source and spied a faint wisp of smoke further on. Signalling for the others to follow, Huw made his way cautiously towards the centre of the camp. Hiding behind a bush, he scanned the area for any signs of life. Then he rolled into the hollow and, crouching, made his way to the camouflaged dugout. Trying not to gasp for breath, he waited, listening for sounds in the bunker, then gingerly lifted the flap.

Märt and Juhan found him a few moments later, attaching the loose chain of the iron cauldron to its tripod over a doused fire. At least one bullet had hit the pot and the contents now lay in the ashes. All around lay bodies of the Forest Brothers. They had been shown no mercy.

'You were right about the ambush,' Huw said. 'The area is clear now. They have taken what they wanted.'

'Which is?' Märt asked.

'Food. This was no Destroyer squad. A foraging party for the German forces, more than likely. They left all our weapons.'

Märt made a face as if to spit the bad taste from his mouth. 'Where are Raio and Peetr?'

Huw grimaced. 'Raio is over on the ridge, Peetr is in here. He's alive, but barely.'

He lifted the flap and they stepped inside, leaving Juhan to keep watch. Peetr was seated on the floor, quivering with pain. A bottle of vodka was clutched in one hand. A damp patch on his clothing told of a large stomach wound.

'Märt.' His voice was now a rasping whisper. 'I knew you would come back to us.'

'Too late to help fight,' Märt replied.

'It would have been no use… too many.'

'Do you think the deserters talked when they raided Siim's place?' Huw asked.

A bubbling response came from Peetr. 'No, you are safe there. That army is all running away now, leaderless and scared. I think Mother Russia finally broke them.'

'Are you sure?' Huw asked.

Peetr waved his hand weakly in dismissal. 'I lay and listened to their talk. They were only after food. I just think we were unlucky.' He laughed, which brought on a fit of desperate coughing. 'As if Estonians are ever lucky.'

'Huw, take Juhan. Check all bodies,' Märt said. 'Weapons, ammunition, anything of use. Watch out for traps.'

'They set none,' Peetr muttered.

'We will be careful even so,' Juhan said from outside the dugout.

'He is good boy,' Peetr whispered. 'I try to make him think too hard, perhaps.'

'It is fine,' Märt replied. 'We are leaving, my friend, there is nothing left here. Perhaps I should go back and try and help my village.'

'Yes, though you have been away for so long, I hope they don't take you for Destroyer,' Peetr said. 'But will it be wise, taking Englishman with you?'

Märt shrugged. 'Who knows? I have debts to pay, he will not add to my burden.'

Peetr gently moved his head. 'Perhaps you are right. I wish I could come. I wish I had gone to Finland with you, to fight.'

'Someone had to stay, friend. And you were there when we needed you.'

'Yes, yes. We bloodied their nose that day. I bet Stalin wasn't smiling so much then, but now…'

'There is still hope, my friend. There is always hope.'

'Perhaps, I will do my best to spit at the face of every soldier I meet up there. They will get my phlegm straight between their eyes.'

'I don't know, Peetr. Perhaps I should stay. These people, they have grown to trust us. I want them kept safe.'

'Oh my friend, even you cannot keep them safe with a boy and an English spy. Maybe stay a while, until you are sure, hey?' Peetr watched his friend's face, though his eyes were less bright, then he added. 'My friend, you speak of debt. Only you know if this still needs paying. Think on it, do not rush.'

Märt nodded, his smile failing to hide his anguish. 'But I tell you, I feel with Huw that Estonia has a chance. He is stronger than you know. I must keep him safe. Perhaps deeper south is the answer.'

Peetr seemed to relax a bit and Märt tried to think of words to keep him from slipping away. 'Do you remember first Red invasion? When Russians came and we had visitor?'

Peetr nodded, his smile fixed now with the pain. 'Fool of a man! Made up to commissar and he thought he was God. Tell me his tale.'

'You were there, Peetr.'

'I know, but I want to hear it and my jaw hurts.'

Märt took a breath and began. 'He was local and he was made commissar when Reds first came here. One evening, he thought of walking home through our forest, as if nothing could touch him. It was good day. Raio had found some vodka and we had killed boar. We had girls come visit from village. Ah, they liked you, Peetr, especially Kaia. You had good voice, good songs.'

Peetr's breath was rasping, but he waved his hand to continue.

'Raio saw him come and gave him vodka. He took it and sang with us. Oh, that gleam in your eye, Peetr, when you sang Metsavennad song. Then fool knew who we were and he thought to run, but Toomas caught him. We took his gun and sent him on his way. When he got back, his masters demoted him for not arresting us. I would have loved to watch him try.'

'Good tale,' Peetr whispered. 'I like it with singing and girls. Perhaps I remember she liked you.'

'Peetr, you know this is not true.'

'And Reds took her on lorry with others, then on train to Siberia. I wish I had strength to go and kill those men who did it.'

'You did, Peetr, and afterwards you cried for them. Please rest now, I will watch over you.'

'Yes, yes, I am tired now. Soon, I will be watching over you, Märt. Soon.'

Later, with their tasks done, Juhan and Huw returned to find Märt dragging bodies into the bunker.

'We take what we need, no more,' he said quietly. 'Then we put all boys in here and collapse it. Forest can have its soldiers.'

'Do you wish to burn it?' Juhan asked.

'No, I do not wish to attract attention. If we take supports from the front, it will go.' Märt replied.

'Where then do we go?' Huw asked.

'Siim's farm first, I'll make sure they are safe. Then we will think about what to do next. We cannot stay in this forest. I will not stay here. This is dead to me. You two can still choose, but I am going to Märjamaa.'

'I will follow you, Märt,' Juhan said quietly.

'Then we have work to do,' Märt said, carrying on with his gruesome task.

Huw turned away. The dead faces of people he had begun to know all became unbearable.

Huw awoke in the most comfortable bed he had lain in for years. He felt he had fallen into the softness of the mattress and pillows. His body ached to stay and drift in and out of sleep, but his mind was actively trying to remember how he had got there.

A door opened and Maarja walked in, carrying a tray.

'Black bread, smoked fish and coffee. Easiest way to wake up.'

'You are so rich,' Huw said, as she came to sit on the bed.

'We were, perhaps,' she replied. 'Though having this house is one thing. If guns hit it tomorrow, we would have nothing and would be forced to live in tent.' She giggled at the thought. 'You must eat and then we must see if we can get you out without anybody seeing.'

'Where are we?'

'In my house, do you remember nothing of last night?'

Huw remembered quite a lot, he felt aroused as he dwelt on the finer points. He gently reached over and drew her to him for a kiss.

67

'What time is it?'

'Not late enough to worry, kallis. They won't miss you.'

'I think they expected me to bunk on one of the other boats.'

'Did they say which one?' Huw shook his head. 'This is no problem, nobody will ask. They will all have been happy to know that you were not their problem.'

She lay on her back and smiled.

'Come to me again, there is still time.'

'Won't the coffee get cold?'

'I like cold coffee,' she replied, her lips searching for his.

'What on earth have you been up to?' Taylor asked Huw on his next visit to Caradoc.

Huw flushed. 'What do you mean? I should be asking the same question. You bagged another destroyer last night, I see. Or did she just sail into the harbour on her own?'

Taylor grinned. 'The Avotril? Easy one, she was lurking out there, lights out, playing dead. Waiting for the cruiser, Oleg, to come back from refuelling, I believe.'

'There's no damage to her.'

'No, brilliant piece of work by the skipper. He got her boxed in by four of us when she tried to make a run for it.'

'Any Russian admirals this time?'

Taylor laughed and clapped Huw on the shoulder. 'Not this time, anyway, you're distracting me. What the hell have you been up to, you sly old sea dog?'

Huw shrugged. 'Nothing criminal, Taylor, you know me.'

'Well, I just overheard a discussion that the captain had with the Estonians. It seems as though we're leaving you behind, chained to a desk for His Majesty's Navy. Have you been busy?'

Taylor's enquiring glance did not get an answer from Huw, although he felt his face glow with embarrassment. 'Don't know what you mean, old son.'

'Have it your way. I just hope you are establishing good cultural relations with the Estonians.' Taylor stopped at the door, turning for one last comment. 'Look on the bright side, I'm sure she doesn't snore like I do.'

Chapter Nine

Forest ambush

'Papa! Papa! Juhan comes!'

'Thank God,' Märt whispered, seeing the farmer striding towards them in delight. Märt was caught in a fierce hug.

'Märt, Juhan! Wonderful! I thought you were all dead.' Siim shouted.

Anna came out of the house, shrieked and ran to them. 'Alive, alive!'

Märt became quite self-conscious. 'Thank you, thank you, but can we move from edge of forest? My friend gets eaten by bugs.'

They moved towards the farm and Huw was relieved to see there was little damage. The dark log buildings seemed untouched by the madness that had occurred in the past few days.

'Siim Kask, Anna Kask – Huw Williams,' Märt made the introduction and the farmer grabbed Huw's hand in welcome. Juhan had arrived with the young Piret giggling happily on his shoulders.

'So, you survived, Siim,' said Märt.

'Yes, yes. The Germans came through and we hid in cellar. They were after food, money, valuables. We left them to do what they wanted to. They did not stay long, they sounded scared.'

'It would seem our luck was not so good,' Märt replied. 'They found our camp.'

'Yes, I know, I know. We found out soon after. Are you all that are left?'

'Yes, my friend. We were lucky.'

'Come and eat,' Anna called. 'There is not much now, but what we have, we can share.'

'Juhan, can Uncle Peetr come and do magic after?' Piret begged. Juhan tried to smile.

'No, my little one. Peetr has gone away.'

'Why? Was it soldiers?'

Juhan couldn't speak. He gave a curt nod and looked away.

'Piret, kallis. Go bring some water.'

Anna hushed her daughter away and put her arm around Juhan. 'Perhaps hot drink might ease pain.'

69

Juhan's tears were flowing now and he could only nod.

'Anna will take care of him, Märt,' Siim said as they followed. 'You three can stay with us for now. We have room and between us all, we can find food and get by. You were hiding from Germans, I don't believe that Reds will know of this. You should be safe – or as safe as you can be in Estonia.'

'Thank you Siim, I think we will. There is nothing left for us in this forest,' Märt replied.

Siim laughed and slapped Märt's shoulder. 'Perhaps some wild boar, eh?'

Huw frowned. He was endangering these people by being with them. In time, the more he used the radio, the more perilous it would be for his hosts. His mind raced for a while, then he grimaced and followed the rest. This was the way of the world. These people already knew the dangers, Märt especially. Having a British spy on their doorstep was one more of the problems that had been thrust upon them by two invading armies.

He took Märt aside. 'Shall we move the radio?'

Märt shook his head. 'It is watertight where it is. Better to keep it out of here for now, in case of visitors.'

'What can we do here?'

'Plant, harvest what we can and hunt. Repair and make this farm good once more. I think I owe it to these people to make them as secure as I can. But we keep an eye out for Reds. If they come, we will need to hide.'

'How long are we staying?' Huw asked. He was surprised by Märt's apparent lack of urgency to return to the village.

'A week, perhaps more. I want to make sure it is right decision and some hard work will focus my mind.'

'I will need to send a radio report.'

'Yes and I will need to get battery cells charged also. Come on, let's eat first.'

Huw's message was hard to compose. He desperately wanted to tell the full horror of Kadrina. The best he could manage was "locals being murdered." Quickly he added "Many" to the message. The acknowledgement was too clinical for the intensity of the images still playing in Huw's mind. He signed off tersely and walked back.

'What can you say?' Märt asked 'What can they do to change things now?'

'They can talk to Stalin. They can stop supplying him.'

Märt shrugged. 'They talk to Stalin and he says it is lies. Hah! Next thing you tell me is he listens to your Churchill. If they stopped supplying Reds, all it would do is make the Germans strong again. The best we can do for now is to keep English informed and when Germans fall, make sure Western Allies fulfil their promise of Atlantic Accord – and come to our aid.'

'Like they did before?'

'Yes, my friend. And you are crucial to this, for you still remember. You can tell this to those that refuse to see the world for what it is in my land.'

The days passed and the three men settled into helping on the farm. The remaining fields were harvested, the buildings were repaired. Märt and Huw looked at where the defences could be strengthened, where they could hide; most of all, how they all could escape unseen back to the forest. Juhan spent his spare time teaching Piret folk songs, as if the war was far away.

Huw gave occasional radio reports, though there was not much to tell. The Reds had moved west and southwest, he had heard. Tallinn was under siege.

Märt and Huw sat in the barn one evening, discussing the replies from the British.

'They are pushing me for answers, Märt. How ready are the people? What is the mood?'

Märt slammed his fist into his other hand. 'People are tired, they are more than ready for change, but it will not happen unless we have help. Tell them.'

'I cannot seem to get the point over,' Huw replied.

'Tell them without their help, we will die,' Märt shouted.

The barn door rattled as it was dragged open and Siim appeared. He looked troubled, as he removed his cap and took the pipe from his mouth, using it to scratch above his ear.

'My friends, I have grave news. Tallinn has fallen. They say our land is mostly taken and soon islands will fall.'

Märt swore softly. 'I suppose they cut through so fast. It was only matter of time.'

'Perhaps now we will get an answer,' Huw said, but Märt still looked unconvinced, so Huw took a deep breath and continued. 'I think I need to move, Märt. I have been here a month and we hear little. I may need to get closer to the war.'

'Yes, I see this.'

'Perhaps we should go south, like you said.' Huw paused. 'Will you help me?'

Märt was quiet for a long time and then his face changed. For a fleeting moment, it bore a contrary mixture of both relief and pain. He looked over to Huw and nodded slowly.

'I will, Huw. Juhan was right, when he talked about going home. I have been away for too long. Perhaps it would be better for you to set up your base from there?'

So you can find Maarja. The words were unspoken, but hung between them. They still could not discuss her. Something in the air made Huw hesitate, a tension, adding to his nervousness. Maarja had obviously moved on years ago, but he knew he could not refuse the chance to find her once more. He tried to make his voice sound casual, though he felt a fool for doing so.

'You are right, Märt, it is my home too. Perhaps it will be easier to operate among familiar surroundings, closer to the main road between Tallinn and Pärnu also. But Siim and his family, will they be safe?'

Märt shrugged. 'We would not be able to protect them against strong force. They are Estonians, they will do what they can.'

'Juhan might stay.' Huw ventured, knowing in his heart that he did not wish it

'Juhan will do what he wishes, but I know he will come. We will clear up here, have our words with Siim and Anna and then you make your last report tomorrow on our way south.'

The radio was still intact and Huw made contact with his control.

'Party disrupted. Moving inland to new party,' he said.

'Stay with party,' came the reply.

'Party broken up, nowhere to stay. Am moving to new party,' Huw tried.

There was a long pause before finally: 'Make contact with bea…' A burst of static drowned out the message.

'It sounded like make contact with bear,' Huw muttered. 'What the hell are they thinking?'

'We must go, signal has been jammed,' Märt said. 'We do not wish to draw them here.'

Huw stood back and turned to go. He jumped in shock at the sound of a rifle and looked back to find Märt had shot into the radio set, and was following it up with a few bashes with the rifle butt.

'What the hell?' Huw cried as Märt looked impassively back at him.

'They know you move camp and we cannot take this with us, so we leave it broken here and perhaps they will not look for us.'

'But how are we to stay in touch?' Huw asked.

'I do not know, but we will not travel through Estonia with radio. It would be suicide.'

'I could have saved some parts…'

'Too great risk, if you were caught with them, you would be dead. Trust nothing here; it is only way to stay alive.'

Huw mulled over the scene as they carried on their journey. That last broken message, were they asking him to go to the Reds? Was that why Märt shot the radio, because he thought the same also? After Kadrina, Huw doubted he would want to follow such orders. His concern now was what Märt thought of him, an ally or a Russian mole?

Märt had argued it was better that people thought the whole camp had been wiped out, and it was hard not to agree. There would be less trouble for Siim when the Red Army finally came or, judging by the first invasion three years before, at least no additional trouble.

They made rapid progress through the forest and Juhan soon felt the need to talk. 'Why use train?' he asked. 'It is far to get to, almost back to Kadrina itself.'

'We need to move fast. Roads will be watched,' said Märt.

He sounded more subdued to Huw – less angry, not even resentful. As if he had resigned himself to his lot.

'Most people are trying to escape war, nobody will expect us to move towards it,' Märt said. 'We cannot stay for long on train, if we reach Tallinn, we will have gone too far.'

They moved on through the forest, Märt checking the sky when he was able to see through the canopy.

'If clouds keep away, we will find railway by dusk.'

'And if you cannot see sun, we will be walking in circles,' said Juhan.

This time, crossing the main road was no challenge. The traffic westwards had gone and they were across well before they heard an approaching vehicle.

'We have luck,' Juhan said, but Huw shook his head.

'It means the line has moved further forward.'

'You are right,' said Märt. 'They probably camp past Tallinn now.'

'They will not look for you then?' Juhan asked.

'Why would they?' Huw asked.

'Juhan is wrong,' said Märt. 'Reds brought you here and they will not wish for anyone to stay in Estonia who can report back to British when they have finished with German Army. They know where you landed, and this is where they will start to look.'

'They would kill him?' Juhan asked.

'In time, possibly,' came the grim reply. 'Or turn him.'

'And how do we know which train to take?' Huw asked.

'We will work that out when we get there,' Märt replied over his shoulder, as he reached for his pack.

They kept to the edge of the forest, letting the gloom mask their presence. On a sunny day, the contrast between the dark forest and the bright light shining on the road was great. Huw winced every time he looked out at the bleached vista beyond the treeline.

There was little conversation now. Their world and thoughts, were swept up in the "pad, pad, pad" of their feet as they tramped through the sandy forest base. The laboured breathing of tired men, the occasional clink of metal from their packs or the buckle of a rifle strap, all commanded their attention as they tried to move with stealth, whilst looking for signs of danger.

They had been hours on this path when Märt stopped them. He was listening keenly to the air. At first Huw heard nothing. Then he heard a faint noise. Was it voices? Russian voices, perhaps? Märt made some urgent hand signals to get his colleagues to follow, but with caution.

As they crept forward, the scene began to unravel. A khaki-covered lorry parked on the roadside came into view as they rounded a bend. A stream could be heard babbling nearby. They moved towards the sound.

The dense woodland gave way to a clearing, where three soldiers could be seen washing in their undergarments. Their uniforms lay drying on bushes further up towards the road. One was scrubbing his boots as they sat, feet in the water. From the tone of their voices, they were unhappy with the world and Huw found confirmation of that when Märt whispered next to him.

'Then perhaps you should not have come.'

Märt quickly signalled a plan of action and they split up. Huw made his way slowly back and round to the road. Seeing no people at the vehicle, he crept quickly to it, keeping low and avoiding treading on the loose gravel of the road surface. He glanced back at the scene by the river. Juhan had managed to reach the bushes unannounced and was stealthily picking the clothes off one by one. Märt, still hidden from the soldiers, had his rifle at the ready.

The complaining tone of the soldiers had turned to cynical laughter. Two had started smoking cigarettes; one had produced a small bottle of vodka as if they were on a picnic. Huw found this bizarre, after the impersonal nature of the soldiers he had met on his journey. He crept around the vehicle and edged his way along the dusty bodywork, to look into the cab. He could not believe he could see the key in the ignition. The door latch was smooth, but as he slowly lifted it and began to pull the door open, he knew it was going to be so stiff that soon it would sing its woe to the world. He looked back to find that Juhan had managed to steal all the clothes and was even trying for the two pairs of boots lying under the bushes.

Huw was mesmerised by the crazy scene. There was surely no way that Juhan could carry all this kit but it became obvious he would have a damn good try. Märt had moved to his side, looking to cover the escape. Even so, their luck was not going to hold forever.

Sure enough, as Juhan reached for the last boot, its twin gave up the fight and slipped from his grasp, falling to the floor with a thump that attracted the attention of one of the soldiers. The spell broke and the soldiers scrambled for the bank. Märt fired a warning shot, which sent them to their bellies, giving Juhan enough time to gather the remaining boot and run.

Huw needed no further hint. The door groaned in complaint as he yanked it open. He jumped into the seat and tried the ignition. The lorry spluttered and fell silent. Huw cursed it as he tried again. It responded sullenly, firing tentatively, but enough for Huw to save the engine with the clutch. He kicked the accelerator and the engine roared in approval. Juhan threw the clothes into the back and dived in. Märt reached the lorry as Huw leant across to open the door, but found he couldn't reach.

Märt yelled him to drive and Huw was quite happy to oblige. Märt stood on the cab step, holding the wing mirror with one hand. With the other, he held out the rifle and fired another shot at the madly pursuing, under-dressed soldiers. As the men became smaller and smaller in the wing mirrors, Märt opened the door and swung into the cab, slamming it shut.

'Don't you know anything about Russian lorries? You don't treat them with respect. They only understand violence.'

'If this bastard doesn't move any faster, I'll pull its bloody doors off by hand,' Huw shouted back.

'We will drive for few miles down towards main road,' Märt shouted. 'Then we use their uniform and become soldiers.'

The canvas flap on the back of the cab opened and Juhan appeared.

'God shines on us today, for they appear to have stashed some food. There are weapons also, pistol and ammunition.'

'What cargo were they carrying?' Huw asked.

'Not much,' Juhan replied, 'but there are things we may use.'

'Like food!'

'Yes, do you like beetroot, comrade?'

Huw laughed. 'I'll take anything you have, my friend.'

'Fools,' said Märt. 'They walk into hostile land and treat it like playground. They think they are invincible.'

'Not now,' came Juhan's chirpy reply.

After a few miles, Märt called a halt to the journey.

'I must admit, travelling on truck may be better for us, now we have it. I was not expecting road to be so quiet. We can always go to ground if it gets too dangerous. Certainly better than waiting for train.'

'Fair enough,' said Huw. 'You know the country better than I.'

Märt shrugged as an acknowledgment. 'We are close to main road and will soon meet other vehicles. I will talk. Huw, you can pass as Estonian, to outsider, but there may be those who know our accent. You think too much in English way, they will know you are not of here very quickly.' Huw nodded, and Märt continued: 'We must change into these uniforms now also. We need to head for Tallinn and break towards south road when we are able.'

'We have time before our pursuers limp into view,' said Juhan.

'They will be in Siberia for this, as prison guards if they are lucky,' said Märt. 'Mother Russia does not understand failure.'

The boots were useful for Märt and Juhan, replacing their aging footwear.

'Are there socks?' Märt asked. 'Wear two pairs, Juhan, and your feet will not blister.'

Trousers were a different matter. 'Huw nothing seems to fit you,' Juhan said.

'My people have short legs,' Huw replied. 'I cannot help this.'

'Märt has a perfect fit,' said Juhan, 'but for you? The best are these and they are too long. It also leaves me wearing these.'

He quickly donned a pair of trousers and opened his hands to show the fit. The trousers were too short and finished a full inch above the ankle. In terms of fitting, it made Juhan look ridiculous and Huw could not stop himself laughing, which brought back Juhan's broad grin. Märt looked impassively on the scene and then he snorted. It soon grew to a chuckle and then they were all roaring with laughter.

Märt began to change and slowly his laughter took on a harder edge. His face clouded, as if he was in pain. His pent-up emotions flooded out, his shoulders heaved with great sobs. Tears streamed down his face and he wept uncontrollably. Huw reached out to grip his shoulder, desperate to provide solace. Juhan looked on quietly, no longer laughing. He understood why Märt whispered the same words again and again.

'Raio, Peetr.'

'Raio, Peetr.'

Chapter Ten

Redemption or revenge?

The navy had left and winter was now encasing the old city. The temperature was well below anything Huw had experienced before on land. He had found lodgings with people that were ignorant of, or at least discreet about, his regular visitor.

Maarja had become his life and he spent all his spare time with her. She began to teach him basic Estonian and they talked of the differences between their cultures – food, music or the way that Tallinn and London differed, each point was a new revelation to them both. In the time before the arrival of the new squadron, there was time to indulge in his romance and he did not need encouragement.

At night with her in his arms, he felt complete. Yet every day he would walk out of the city gates, head up and around to the top of the Toompea and gaze out on the horizon. He looked for what he hoped he would never see again, the tell-tale silhouettes of warships.

'What is wrong tonight?' she asked.

'I am thinking of the navy,' he said. 'They will come.'

'I know this, Huw. In time ice will thaw and Russia will once again try to reclaim us for its own. Either your navy comes or they leave us to die.'

'Our government will not want the Bolsheviks to be so strong in the Baltic. Once here, where next for the Reds? Sweden? Poland? They will come.'

'And what then? A new master, but same job.'

'Perhaps. I hope so.'

She reached to embrace his neck and kissed his eyelids.

'Come to sleep, kallis. I think you worry too much. What will happen, will happen, but we will endure.'

At the end of February 1919, four ships appeared on the horizon and Huw was called to the headquarters of the Estonian Navy to give advice.

'We have concern,' said his Estonian colleague, as Huw gazed across the water with binoculars. 'Sea ice is thinning. If it melts

early, Russians will be here quicker and they will attack us with none of your ships to defend.'

'Well, we will just have to teach them to stay away,' Huw said. 'Don't worry, the fleet will come.'

'As you say,' the man agreed. 'It is hard, for even our supposed allies, in White Army, believe we are part of Russia. We have long, difficult road ahead of us.'

'Well, these little beasts mean no harm to us,' Huw replied, handing back the binoculars. 'They are not Russians. They don't fart coal smoke from their chimneys.'

His colleague looked puzzled, so Huw smiled an apology.

'There are two merchant ships and two warships, destroyers. They look British and I think I can see the white ensign. The merchants are fat enough to be colliers. Looks like His Majesty's Navy has returned, bearing coal.'

'Only two destroyers?'

'Reconnaissance, my friend. I need to polish the buttons on my uniform, for they will want me to make a formal report.'

'Tell them we are starving and cold, but apart from this, life is good.'

'I will.'

Huw sought out the captain of the lead destroyer as soon as they berthed and became engaged in a lengthy meeting. When Maarja caught up with him he could only manage a weary smile of greeting.

'Huw, what is wrong?' she asked gently.

'Oh, nothing. Well, something. Everything really, if truth be told.'

'My love,' she reached to relax his neck and he smiled sadly.

'I had a long talk with the captain and there is some good news for Estonia. They have brought in two colliers laden with coal for the city. We will be able to sit by a fire once more. The squadron arrives in a few days also, before the thaw and before the Russians can break out.'

'There was something else, I think.'

'The navy has decided to change the squadrons every six weeks. After this time, each will be relieved by a new squadron and their crew. I am to go back also.'

'So, we have six weeks?'

Huw nodded. 'Perhaps less.'

'Then we have six weeks to change their minds.'

'It is late September and I really should be swimming in the Black Sea,' Oleg muttered to himself. 'Not sitting in this northern pigsty.'

He'd had enough of the constant moving from rough billet to rough billet. He craved release from the niggling pain in his right shoulder, but he had a mission and he would not fail. He could not fail.

He had managed to commandeer a vehicle, at the time when most troops were arriving, packed like sardines in cattle trucks. It was fate that he wasn't an ordinary soldier, charging forward into the enemy with a handful of bullets, the guns of his comrade commissars pointed at his back to stop him retreating. It was luck that unlike many of his comrades, he had a weapon, even.

Oleg smiled to himself. Luck had nothing to do with it. It was sheer willpower and ambition that had pushed him to where he wanted to be. Now he could begin his personal crusade.

His trusty assistant, Yuri, returned to the GAZ jeep to report. They had sped across Estonia now the German army was in retreat and he wanted news. 'Some good tidings, comrade. The Soviet army has control of the city. Tallinn will fall to us and we will move south and west.'

'At last! Now get me an office to work in and a nice bed to sleep in,' Oleg grinned. 'We can start rooting out the western spies.'

'You want this man Williams?'

'Very much, Yuri. He is the newest arrival and the one who will know the most about how the British think and their tactics. He won't be some peasant farmer trying to liberate this land. He will know how London works and in the end he will happily tell us. Then he will happily tell London what we want them to hear.'

Yuri had an instinct that somehow there was more, but he knew better than to ask. He trusted Oleg with his life, ever since the man had rescued him from trial in the courts and exile. He would die for the man.

'I have more news, Oleg. They have been through the German government offices already. The Nazi scum were so much in a hurry to leave, they did not destroy anything. We have much intelligence, including something of great value.' He beamed. 'The Germans made a list of all known partisans in the country and their leanings. Who they are, where they are and where their friends and family are.'

'This is of great value indeed! Our work is made the easier for it. Go and retrieve the papers for this region. Get a German speaker also and we can start straight away.'

'Comrade, I have some knowledge of German. I never mention it, in case it is seen as being for the wrong reason.'

'Not here, my friend. Go and stay alive. You are so essential to this operation. We have much work to do and soon much to report to the boss. This is a good day, Yuri. All we need now is some vodka. One of these stinking hovels is bound to have some.'

'We have time, Märt; we can rest here. Those soldiers would be fools to follow us,' Juhan said.

'You do not understand, Juhan. We have no time at all. We must get south to safer forests. We must find your mother.'

Huw had gone to find kindling for a fire, only coming back to the enigmatic words about Maarja. Märt was so wound up, he looked ready to snap.

'We must make time to eat, gentlemen, or we will have no energy for anything,' Huw said firmly.

Märt glared at the branches in Huw's arms, as if it was a betrayal, but he gave a sullen nod and looked away. They had moved off the road into the forest on a dirt track, hidden from prying eyes. Märt looked ready to sleep for a week, but he still wanted to move. Huw also noticed the pain he still showed for his dead friends.

'Märt, it will be better if you talk of your friends, whilst we eat,' he said. 'You need to pay them tribute and it will ease your burden. It will also tell me why you are in the north.'

Märt sighed, and as Juhan worked on heating the open tins over the small fire, he began, 'When Reds came, we had little warning. We certainly had no weaponry. Reds came quickly and started rounding up people to take away on trains.'

'To Siberia,' Juhan said.

'Well, that is the normal place for undesirables,' Märt replied, his attention apparently focussed on feeding the tiny fire. 'They had list. First, government officials, politicians, military. Then they just wanted numbers, quotas. Many of us went to forest. Some of us wanted to fight back, so we escaped.' Juhan came over holding a can between two sticks for Märt, who nodded thanks.

'We headed north, for Finland, where they trained us as soldiers. Finnish boys, we called ourselves and we were strong. Raio was my sword brother. We fought together many times.' He looked at the grey stew in the tin, levered a lump out with a knife and chewed thoughtfully for a while before continuing.

'Did you hear about Kautla? I was in Erna unit. We went in to rescue people who were trapped there by Red Army. We were surrounded, but we fought our way out. Peetr was farmer in the region. He grabbed his rifle and joined us. He saved my life then, although this raid killed his woman and child. Reds shot them for no reason.'

'And Juhan?' Huw asked.

'Heard of Kautla and went to find them,' Juhan replied with a grin.

'How could you go so far and just find them?'

'Because Juhan could fall into cess pit and still climb out smelling of cologne.' Märt snapped.

Juhan brought another tin over to Huw. It was like bully beef and Huw wolfed it down gratefully.

'Why do you say that people will expect Estonians in the Red Army?' Huw asked between mouthfuls.

'You know why,' Märt replied. 'Even in your time, Estonia had Reds and there were Russian villages. There are also those who were not sent to Siberia, but sent to fight instead. When they retreated, they grabbed every working man with pulse. An Estonian in Red Army will be no surprise, Estonians driving lorries will be even less so. Reds think little of us. We are not good for much in their eyes.'

'Was it not easier under the Germans?' Huw asked, staring at the glowing embers in the fire. He thought about dropping the empty tin on it, but then decided against it. The remains of a fire would be easier to hide than a burnt-out can. They would have to take their rubbish with them.

'German army drove Reds away in 1940,' Märt replied. 'We came back from Finland thinking we were free. We flew our flags and sang our songs, some even joined Germans; our prime minister encouraged it. All for our freedom, but it was not to be. We were nothing more than another conquered land. Landlords of old had returned. When we realised this, many went back to our forests and waited for Germans and Reds to kill each other. Toomas came south from Eisma to join us, others followed. It was hard life, but we are free.'

Questions were burning inside Huw, but he could only face asking the one which had the least potential to crush his hopes.

'Why are you going south now, Märt? It has been a long time since you left.'

'I left my people in south to fight for Estonia, I did great wrong, for I should have remained there and fought. There is nothing left here in north, it has all been destroyed, but in south – I may still have chance to redeem myself.'

Huw looked at Märt and remembered once again the young smiling baker. He had been a bit like Juhan in his manner, someone who accepted a man for who he was, as Huw had found when he arrived all those years back. The man was less warm now, the bitter years had hardened his face and he never seemed far from violence. There was something in his words which sent a sudden thrill of fear into Huw's heart. The fear of uncovering the truth, and finding it every bit as bad as expected.

'Märt, you know I have to ask,' he asked hesitantly. 'I have tried to avoid it for so long, but... Juhan says his mother is Maarja, is this...?'

'Maarja who bewitched you when you came here? Yes.'

'What happened?'

'It is no good to stir things of past. I made that mistake when I left. I believed I could make difference, to keep my country alive. I was so proud, I forgot my family. If I can have second chance, I will not make that mistake again.'

'Märt,' said Huw slowly. 'I did not ask that, what are you telling me?'

Märt gazed for a long time in the fire, looking for answers, playing with ghosts. In the end, he gave a long sigh. 'Maarja is my wife, and I left her to fight in Finland.'

'Why did you marry?' Huw exclaimed in shock.
'Because I was there and you were not,' Märt snapped in reply.

A million questions washed on the shore of Huw's imagination, to disappear in the cold silence that followed the words. Eventually, Märt placed his hand on Huw's arm and pointed to Juhan, just out of earshot.

'You have many questions and you deserve to hear much more, Huw. I will answer these in time, but not here, not with Juhan near. I do not say you have to come south with us, even though you wish it. You must do what your orders are.'

Huw felt as if he had been smacked. He watched Juhan and beneath the traits inherited from Maarja, he began to see Märt in the young man's manner. He bitterly cursed his mind for not seeing them before. He had been so obsessed with finding Maarja, he had let his heart over-rule the signs that were staring him in the face, in the hope that they were imagined. The reality was sobering. He was watching his dream die.

'To hell with orders,' he snapped. 'I want answers, then I will do what I think is right.'

'Then you travel with us and I will give you those answers.'

'And a bloody radio would be nice also.'

'We will see what we can do, perhaps we can get RAF to drop one by parachute when we get to Rapla.'

Huw cursed, but he knew that was all the information he would get.

85

Chapter Eleven

A curtain of water

'You know, I could stay here forever,' Huw said as he lay on the grass in the local park. 'The sun is so warm as to make my toes begin to melt. The breeze is gentle and it makes me want to sleep. And then there is this beautiful Estonian girl lying on my chest, squeezing the life out of me.'

Maarja laughed and gently made to slap his face.

'Are you suggesting I am fat?'

'No, I am saying you are trying to stop me breathing.'

'I can start you breathing,' she said and tickled his ribs. He gulped and grabbed her arms, whilst she leant forward and kissed him.

'I cannot leave you, Maarja,' Huw gasped.

She grinned. 'Perhaps you should stay and become Estonian. Do you think they would notice if you stayed?'

'I think they would turn the city upside down looking for me. His Majesty's Navy doesn't like losing its boys.'

'Then we will go south where my family farms, hide in forest and live off berries and mushrooms.'

'Sounds marvellous, but I think they would still find me.'

Maarja sat up indignantly and straightened her hair 'Pah, your navy does not know anything about forest. They would not even find Märjamaa on the map.'

'Is that where you get your name from?'

She smiled. 'It is simple place, away from the sea. Lots of good farming land, next to clean river, good if you need to get cool swim in summer after long day of work.'

'Ah well, then to Märjamaa we must go, my love.'

'If that is what it takes to keep you, kallis.'

'My God, you are serious!'

She pressed her forehead to his and then kissed him. 'Of course, what else?'

A few nights later Huw stood outside the town house, gently lobbing small stones at Maarja's window. He saw a dim light and then Maarja's head peered through the curtains. She quickly disappeared, rushing to the door. Huw stood at the threshold, looking distraught.

'It's time, Maarja,' he stumbled. Maarja had never seen him look so uneasy. 'I have been given my orders. The new admiral...'

'Come in, come in,' she whispered, pulling him across the doorstep. 'It's unlucky at door-step.'

She took him into a living room and drew him to a sofa, where she embraced him and kissed him until the cold of the night disappeared from his lips.

'Now, tell me what has happened.'

'We have a new admiral, Cowan. He's a bit of a tiger and talks of taking the fight to the Russians. He wants to move us out to Biorko in Finland, so we can be closer to the enemy base at Kronstadt. We'll be faster to react to the Russian fleet when they sail. He doesn't see the need for a presence in Tallinn and he thinks it's time I went home. Caledon sails tomorrow for Copenhagen and I am to be on it. I...' Huw faltered and Maarja embraced him.

'Kallis,' she whispered.

'I don't want to go,' was all he could manage to say.

'You can stay,' she said. He looked deep into her eyes, seeing the iron glint of her resolve as she said, 'we can still go to land.'

'We cannot just leave here?' he gasped and she shook her head.

'We can do what we want and if it means keeping you, I will do what I must.'

He took a deep breath. 'Do you know what you are saying?'

'I know what I am offering. There is one way for us, if that is what you wish.'

He hesitated and looked away and she flushed.

'Or what did you come for tonight? Sympathy?'

'Alright, steady on girl, let me gather myself. I don't know the language and I have to find a way of saying goodbye to my family back in Wales, perhaps I can get a message.'

She pulled his arms around her and placed a finger on his lips. 'You will have me, these other things we can work out.'

Huw's heart leapt, as it always did, when he gazed into her eyes. The price was high but the loss of her would be worse. There were times for moments of great courage, times when you had to face *down your demons, defy the world and take the battle forward. Huw knew his time was now.*

'I cannot lose you, Maarja. I would die without you.'

The tension of the moment reached explosion point as they came together, only their clothes providing a temporary barrier to their passion. Oblivious to anyone in the house who might hear or discover them, their love became a magnesium flare to the darkness of the world. As Huw lay back panting, he knew his fate was forever bound to hers. Whatever the world might bring, she would always be a part of him.

The rain had begun to fall as they drove for the Tallinn Road. Though the uniforms were ill-fitting, they would serve. Huw drove steadily, despite his body being sapped of energy from the latest flashback.

He knew Märt was keeping things from him and that he was being manipulated. He also knew he had no choice but to carry on with the dance to see where it would end.

They stopped before the main road and Juhan got out and ran, crouched low, to the junction. He gave a quick wave and Huw kicked the accelerator to lurch the vehicle forward and onto the main road. Juhan leapt onto the moving vehicle and then they were ready.

'Don't forget, we drive on right hand side.' Märt said dryly.

'No my friend, you drive on the wrong side,' Huw muttered in English.

Juhan grinned amiably, and Huw felt better for it, even though he knew the attempt at a joke didn't translate. It would be a long journey if a lack of humour travelled with them, reflecting the bleakness of the country's plight. They managed many miles without distraction. A few small villages were on the route and Huw gazed upon the sorry state of the wooden houses as they passed by. Many were now abandoned with their doors hanging open, a clear indication of the sudden flight of occupants. A cart stood jutting into the road. Parked in a rush – perhaps someone had taken the horse and abandoned it.

It was an hour before they made their first contact with the invading army. A motorcycle and sidecar sped past them, the passenger paying particular attention to the lorry as they passed. Juhan waved and received a nod in reply.

'They will stop us further down this road,' Märt said. 'You let me do talking; there are enough Estonians in Red Army who do not speak Russian well. You can be one of unlucky ones.'

Huw shook his head. 'You have a crazy country, Märt.'

'Yes, but it is my country, not Hitler's or Stalin's.'

Märt was right about the welcome. The motorcycle had halted round the next bend. The rider had got off and was waving for them to stop.

'Do you think they know this lorry is stolen?' Juhan asked.

Märt shook his head. 'No, as we left owners in forest with no clothes or way of getting help.'

They stopped and watched the rider walk up to the lorry, brandishing a pistol. Huw noticed the sidecar had a machine gun fitted and the passenger's trigger finger was poised and ready. Although the soldiers were in Russian uniform, the motorcycle was clearly of German origin. Huw's grip tightened on the steering wheel. He mentally measured the distance to the forest and looked for potential means of defence.

The soldier stepped onto the running board and shouted in Russian. Märt gave a reply, affecting a heavy Russian accent. Juhan sat impassively at his side, while Huw stared straight ahead. The conversation carried on, the soldier sounding aggressive, while Märt replied evenly. At one point, Juhan laughed, which generated a snarling response from the soldier. Juhan replied amicably and the soldier grunted and gave a nod. He then stepped off the lorry and waved them through. Huw needed no second invitation.

'What did he say?' Huw asked Märt, as they sped away.

'There is convoy some miles ahead and we should join it. There are partisans active in these forests and we should be more careful.'

'Is that what you were laughing at?'

'No,' replied Juhan. 'Märt was asked why we were not in convoy and he said we had broken down. The soldier said he was surprised we were going anywhere with an Estonian driving. I told him that I had lived on Russian border and we got Estonians to drive when we wanted vehicle scrapped.'

'When did you live on the border?'

Juhan shrugged. 'Never, why should I tell him that, though?'

A few miles on, they saw the tail-lights of the convoy and moved towards it. Märt noted the lack of security at the back.

'This is arrogance.'

'Perhaps there is not enough armour around here,' Huw said.

'No, they are arrogant to believe there is nothing there to stop them.'

'Is there anything?'

Märt looked away and his reply was lost to the sound of the engine. The convoy made steady progress, but the journey was becoming more uncomfortable. The winding road was rutted and pitted, whilst the clouds of dust meant the windows had to remain shut.

'They have tanks in front,' Märt said, 'and tanks chew up road that we travel on.'

'Perhaps tank men should try a go driving lorries,' Juhan replied, but Märt waved his hand dismissively.

'Tank men think their manhood is size of their gun barrels.'

'The engine is getting too hot, Märt.' Huw warned. 'We will need to find water soon or we really will break down.'

'I understand.'

'No you don't. Next stream you see, we need to fill the radiator or we go no further. An egg would also be handy for it leaks like bloody sieve.'

'There,' shouted Juhan, and Huw pulled over close to a stream. They quickly made for the water, using their helmets as vessels. As they quenched the thirst of the radiator, a small Russian jeep appeared, complete with officer and driver.

'Radiator is empty,' Huw said to the officer, as he approached them.

'You speak Estonian?' The officer replied, and Huw cursed himself for a fool.

'Yes, I am from the borders region of Võru. We have no water in the radiator and the engine will blow up otherwise.'

'I have not seen you before,' the man replied, with a frown.

'No, we were from an earlier convoy but we broke down, this truck is useless.'

'That's fine, don't stay too long, Forest Brothers are active around Jägala and there are still German stragglers here.'

'Yes sir,' Huw started to walk away, but the officer quickly shouted for him to stop.

'What is going on here? You are not wearing Russian boots?'

'No, they did not fit. I took these from a dead German.'

'Those are no German boots,' the man replied, reaching for his pistol.

Juhan appeared behind the man, causing him to whip round and aim the gun. Huw rushed at the man, stamped on his calf, then wrenched and twisted his neck until there was a sickening crunch. The man dropped to the floor without a word. Juhan was left staring straight at Huw, mouth open. Huw looked across to the jeep to find Märt behind the driver, who was now slumped over the wheel. He pushed Juhan forward to help Märt carry the driver into the back of the truck, returning for the dead officer.

'The driver is unconscious?' Huw asked.

'Yes,' Märt hissed. 'Unlike you I have no need for killing first.'

Huw looked up. The convoy had now reached close to the horizon, too far for him to be able to gauge if it had stopped or not. He sighed.

'I had no choice, Märt. He knew I was an impostor.'

'Perhaps, but if you had kept your mouth closed, like I told you to, things might have been different.'

'I think someone is coming, though I'm not sure,' Juhan said, from the front of the truck.

'There's no time, we need to take jeep now.' Märt shouted.

They threw their weapons into the jeep. Märt took the wheel. He pulled the vehicle onto a side road heading north. The road was no more than a dirt track, yet Märt showed no desire to cut his speed. Clouds of dust bloomed behind them.

'You have to slow,' Huw shouted.

'No, we have to run,' Märt replied.

'If you are slower, you won't throw up so much dust, and we will be less obvious.'

Märt nodded. 'You are right, keep a lookout for pursuers behind.'

Huw found it hard to keep a hold on the jeep and look back, not knowing the contours that lay ahead. To calm his mind, he likened the journey to riding the waves of a heavy sea. It made it feel easier.

'Anything?' Märt shouted.

'Nothing!'

'In that case we hide now, before they see our dust trail. They will come.'

Märt was following large tyre tracks, to camouflage their trail. He suddenly slowed and took the vehicle off the road. Aiming for a group of bushes, he circled before edging slowly into them from the blind side of the road. Huw looked back and saw clouds of dust in the distance.

'Get branches for camouflage. Let's move,' Märt shouted.

'What do you plan?' Juhan asked.

'Jägala. We hide then we go back. Reds will not expect this.'

They covered the jeep in brushwood and then moved quickly towards the river. Märt led, picking his way alongside the bank. In the distance, they could faintly hear the straining notes of vehicles being driven at speed, which sparked their efforts to move on. The river was wide and disappeared behind a ridge. The roar of rushing water drowned out any other noise. Good for hiding, but bad for giving them warning of pursuit. At the ridge, the river pulsed with increased power, white plumes forming as it swept over rocks to the edge. They were nearing the edge of a cliff.

'This way,' Märt shouted, disappearing past the ridge. He made his way down to the lower course of the river and then started edging back to the fall.

For a second Huw's mind spun at the drop and the size of the horseshoe next to him. A curtain of water cascaded down. Thick brown tresses of water, tinged with white foam, hammered into the rocks below. Märt was making his way along the cliff side towards a gap behind the curtain.

'You're joking,' Huw muttered, but he followed, fearing imminent pursuit. Märt disappeared behind the cascade. They would be trapped!

'An excellent place to hide,' Juhan said, at his side.

'Yes, but one without a back door,' Huw replied.

They followed Märt in and moved to the centre of the falls, where Märt wearily sat down.

'As long as our camouflage is good enough, they should drive on past to north coast. It will be dusk soon and a dark night. We will be too obvious, traveling with headlights. We can return to jeep at first light, to make our way south. If we are challenged we say we are searching for deserters. We need rest and food,' He made a face. 'But at least we have rest.'

Juhan pulled his pack open and handed out strips of dried meat.

'I didn't leave it all behind. I thought we would need to be ready. We want water?' he stuck his hand out towards the fall. 'It is good, pure and clean.'

'I'll argue about the clean,' Huw grumbled.

They chewed the meat slowly, their limbs grateful for the respite. Juhan settled his pack as a pillow on some rocks that were fairly dry and relatively flat.

'We leave at first light,' Märt said. 'I will take first watch.'

Huw felt exhaustion creep over him, like fingers firmly pressed on his shoulders. He knew he could not sleep for too long, but he needed some rest and the thunder of the water nearby was soothing. He closed his eyes until the roar became a dull echo in his mind. He was woken by a shake on his shoulder.

'We must get ready.' Juhan's voice came out of the gloom.

'Come,' Märt said. 'We must take great care as we move, we will be very exposed.'

'There is nothing ahead,' Juhan said happily.

'How do you know?' Märt asked.

'I just checked.'

Märt closed his eyes and mouthed a silent curse.

'We must be careful as we leave this area also,' Huw said gently to Juhan.

'I also checked, there are no footsteps in dew. We have not been found.'

'God's sake Juhan, do you ever think about what you are doing?' Märt thundered.

Juhan shrugged. 'You were going to do this anyway but you were busy adding water to Jägala.'

'You should know you will never win with Juhan by now,' Huw reasoned.

Märt sighed. 'Yes, you are right and yet I am still surprised.'

As they made their way up the path, Juhan's words proved true. Huw scanned the path for signs of movement, but although the dew had been heavy, only Juhan's two sets of footprints could be seen on the grass, going from and then back to the falls. The jeep remained hidden in the brush and after carefully removing the branches, and with a bit of persuasion, it coughed to life. They headed south, into the oncoming strife.

Oleg looked at the row of carcasses laid out on the forest floor. The stench was bearable to him, just. All had died by the bullet. He picked up the cauldron hanging on its tripod and turned it around to look at the damage. 'And these were all found in the bunker?'

'Yes comrade,' Yuri replied.

'Are there others?'

'German soldiers lie around here. There has been a skirmish.'

'Bring them.'

As more were brought in, Oleg had their helmets removed and added to the line. He turned to face the farmer, who stood under guard. 'Ask the man if he recognises the spy.'

The farmer shook his head.

'Oleg smiled. 'He would not tell me if he was there.'

'What do you wish to do?' Yuri asked.

'Let him go, Yuri. I can see in his eyes he tells the truth.'

'Surely we should punish him? He obviously helped the partisans.'

'Who held out against the Nazis? We can leave him in what peace is left in this world.'

'Comrade Oleg, I must say this. Your methods are... strange. I fear that if we appear too generous we may lose the respect of the men and the people will feed from it.'

Oleg smiled, but his eyes were cold fire. 'I thank you for your concern, lieutenant. I will bear this in mind.'

Yuri hesitated. He knew he had crossed the line.

'What are your orders, sir?'

'Release the farmer and keep listening out for any reports of disruption to the convoys or trains. Anything – sabotage, vagrants, the slightest problem.'

'Attacks?'

'Not as such, small acts like robbery, single killings. Bring me the files of our man, I want to know what he ate, who he kissed, everything.'

Chapter Twelve

To catch a baker

The watch on Caledon *was surprised to see a woman striding purposefully up the gangplank. He admired her figure and the graceful way that she moved. He was so taken with her that he did not appreciate at first that she was speaking English.*

'I am from the Estonian government,' she said, producing papers. 'This is my warrant. I need to speak with your captain.'

'I'll get the commander,' one of the sailors grunted, returning quickly with an officer.

'Your Sub-Lieutenant Williams has been arrested and detained in our prison.'

'What for, madam?'

'He is accused of robbery of our bank.'

'Madam, we are about to set sail. Can you not release him into our custody? We will ensure that he serves penance in England on his return.'

She shook her head. 'This is not possible.'

'This is highly irregular, madam and embarrassing. We do not have time to delay, are you sure there is nothing you can do?'

The woman smiled apologetically. 'I must say, I believe him innocent. I work in the Justice Office and I believe it is – you say a misunderstanding, no? But the judge has had to go to Pärnu. We can sort this out, but it will take days. We will do what we can.' She smiled at him, but beneath the warmth was a direct challenge, daring him to cry foul.

'We do not have days,' he sighed. 'Can you vouch he will be safe for a few weeks?'

'He will be free in a few weeks, Captain,' her smile dripped honey, making the man soften his tone.

'That's "Commander", my dear. Look, we have to leave today, but the remaining squadron will be replaced in six weeks or so. I will inform the captain that Sub-Lieutenant Williams is going back with the next squadron. I hope your government will do what they can in the meantime.'

'For sure, thank you Commander. I will go back and report this.'

Maarja headed back to the house, where Huw waited. He had his coat on, bags packed and the look of a haunted man. She swept into the room and took her coat off, shaking the cold from her shoulders.

'A nice day, I think.'

'What happened?' Huw asked.

'I explained you were delayed by government,' she replied flouncing down on the sofa next to him. 'They agreed you could remain at this time.'

'Agreed?' He caught the glint in her eye.

'They did not argue and by the time they know, you will have disappeared into forests.'

The forests – Huw watched the lines of evergreens flick past as he drove along the road. They were the one constant in a volatile land churning with anger, pain and conflict. He hated himself for the lost years. He cursed himself for not coming back earlier. There must have been a way, nothing should have been impossible with a love that strong. He could have got a berth on a steamer as a deck-hand, but he hadn't. Instead, he had spent his years thinking of what had been and what never would occur. And Märt had married Maarja. Juhan was their son. He knew he had to find her, but he was sure it would only feed the pain, not cure it.

Märt was asleep in the back and Juhan was in the front passenger seat, looking strangely across at Huw.

'What is wrong, Juhan?'

'Nothing,' came the reply, with a shrug.

They continued in silence for a long time before Juhan spoke again. 'You killed this man.'

'Yes, but this is not a surprise, surely? You were in danger, Juhan.'

'Yes, but you just killed him, right in front of my eyes, like machine. Just like this,' he clicked his fingers. 'You are dangerous man.'

Huw thought for a while before responding. Juhan had a new respect for him, but one based on fear.

'Juhan, the man was reaching for his gun. He would have exposed us; we would have been captured. He could have shot you and I had a moment to think of an action. That was all...' He searched Juhan's face. 'In my training, they showed me how to do this. I had no choice, Juhan. It was him or us.' Juhan chewed his lip thoughtfully. Huw continued: 'He was the first person I've killed by hand, Juhan and believe me, I will see his face a lot in my thoughts now. But if I had to do this again, I would not hesitate. It was him or us.' Huw gazed at the forest. The trees were a barrier, closing him in. 'I do not have any friends in this land, Juhan, perhaps not anywhere. I don't want to lose any. I had to do this, surely there have been times the Forest Brothers have faced this before?'

Juhan nodded and continued to think for a while as the jeep bounced along the pitted road, then he spoke and Huw just caught the words above the engine note.

'I will not kill.'

Oleg had a map spread out on the table of his makeshift billet, a farmhouse near the roadside. He had marked points on it and sat back, chin in hand, trying to think of his next move.

Yuri came into the room shaking rain from his coat, glad of the respite from the elements.

'You have news, Yuri?' Oleg said without looking up.

'Yes, comrade.' Yuri always knew better than to provide more than the desired answer when his commanding officer was deep in thought.

'A sighting?'

'An event, comrade Oleg, a convoy leader was found dead in the back of a truck. His driver was knocked unconscious by his side. They suspect partisans.' He pointed to the map. 'Jägala. They escaped northwards past the waterfall and then were lost.'

'And did we search the waterfall area?' Oleg still sounded dispassionate, as he continued to stare at the map, chin in his hands.

'I doubt it, comrade Oleg. Convoy guards are hardly the elite. The driver said there were six men.'

'And you believe him?'

'No, I got a description of these men, but I think we can discount all the vague ones. He was afraid of being punished – or blamed. I talked to him about transfers and he decided there were two or three. He has not spoken to others.'

'Hmm. So our prey will have double-backed and I wouldn't be surprised if they are back in the convoy. Let's look at the old reports the Germans made. I want names of the partisans and their history. These men are going somewhere, their movements are so random I wonder if it's actually a military target.'

Oleg stood and Yuri heard the man mutter faintly to himself. 'The battle is not yet over.'

'They may go to Tallinn.' Yuri ventured and Oleg pursed his lips.

'Yes they may. Even so, I would like to know if any of these men are not from the forests we have just traipsed through. It may be a clue, if we know where they are from.'

He looked at the map and sighed.

'Eisma, Kadrina, Jägala. It all looks so random, but perhaps there is a connection. It depends on where the next sighting is.'

Maarja had managed to get them a lift in an army truck moving southward. One donated by the British, Huw had pointed out. 'See, the steering wheel is on the right side of the road.'

'No, it is wrong,' *she had replied.*

'Huh, you drive on the wrong side, it is the tragedy of Europe so many do.''

Her laugh was carefree, a relief from the endless drone of the Rover engine. The rigid suspension bruised and battered them as they moved alongside the rough road. Their one attempt at a kiss had seen Huw close to obtaining a broken nose. Despite the punishment, they were in each other's arms and revelled in their closeness.

They arrived late at night in the village.

'I think we need to walk now,' Huw said, as the lorry screeched to a halt. 'I need to remember how my legs are connected to my body. Where are we now?'

'This is Märjamaa,' she said with a contented sigh.

'I can't see anything in the dark,' Huw muttered.

'Imagine this small village with pretty houses and lovely church, proud in centre.'
'Yes I can,'
'So, you are in Märjamaa.'
'No, I'm in Llanilar.'
'Well, you should be in Märjamaa!'
'How far is it to go?'
'Few kilometres, nothing more.'

Huw kissed her gently. *'Tell me this though, how will I know where the road is in this light?'*

'It is simple, kallis. You follow me, if you don't, you fall into ditch. Then you know you have left road.'

'Will they be waiting for us?'

'No, they do not know we are coming. Don't worry, this is Estonia and besides, soon they will need help with farm.'

'Doing what?'

'Everything!'

Huw's mind focussed again, and he quickly checked the sleeping Märt. He lay motionless, as if catching up on four years of lost rest. Huw thought of their first meeting.

'You are the baker?'

'Yes, you are Englishman, no?'

Huw smiled at the apparent label cast on him. It wouldn't matter if he was a doctor or a scientist, to many he would always just be the Englishman.

'Your bread is different, it must be difficult to make.'

'Thank you, it is perhaps just different.'

'No, I have tasted black bread many times, yours is really good.'

Märt flushed. *'We try to keep same recipe, it is important to ferment dough correctly.'* there was a pause, as Huw struggled for something to add.

'You speak good Estonian,' Märt finally said.

Huw waved disarmingly. *'No, I am still learning. There is no choice but to learn in this village, but that is good.'*

Another nervous smile followed and then Huw ventured, *'So, if we bring our crop to your mill, there will be enough.'*

'Yes, yes, this is fine.'

'Good,' Huw said. 'The quicker I do this, the quicker I get fishing.'
'Ah yes, I too like fishing and river here is good, fish are many.'
'I go to the river near Sipa, come and join us if you wish.'
'Yes, I will try.'
Maarja walked up, carrying a basket of supplies.
'We must go, Huw. We have much to do.'
'Perhaps we fish,' Märt said, as they left.
'You are kind man,' Maarja said as they walked down the road.
'Why is this, kallis? I have no friends here; I think these people are not so keen on foreigners. They feel I have nothing in common with them, why am I kind?'
'Märt is shy man, he speaks little and people avoid him.'
'But they eat his bread? Well, at least he and I have something in common. We like to fish.'
'And now you go fishing, I am sure vodka will be involved. You are good man and you will make good friend. Estonians are slow to like people, but when they do, you will have true friend. Now, we must be ready for dance. Tonight, I will be teaching you in barn.'
'I can think of many other things we could do in the barn.'
She punched his arm. 'Stop it! When harvest ends we shall celebrate at dance. You will have to try to dance or one of our pretty boys in village will take me up in their arms and then where will you be?'
'You mean like this?'
He picked her up and she squealed with laughter.
'Put me down, you fool.'
He slid her down and gently kissed her on the lips. 'If the pretty boys want you, they will need to get up very early.'
Huw began to walk off then stopped. 'Hang on, he didn't think I was trying to date him?'
She erupted with laughter and patted his flushed cheeks. 'Personally, I don't think he is that way, but you never know with these pretty boys.'

'Huw, roadblock! Märt, wake up!'
Juhan's voice broke through the dream.

Märt quickly moved to sit up, closing his eyes briefly and shaking his head, as the blood flowed back from it.

'Some notice next time, Juhan,' he grumbled.

'Sorry, it wasn't obvious.'

'Fine, just act normally. We should all be thinking we are part of this army, so why is there problem? 'Juhan, look natural. Juhan!'

Märt reached out and shook his shoulder, breaking his apparent paralysis.

'Just relax everyone, we are Reds. We are here for reason and we are busy. Let me do talking and don't let anyone bully you.'

As they got closer, they made out about half a dozen soldiers near a couple of trucks. A machine gun on a tripod stood nearby, unmanned. The soldiers lounged around apathetically by a small fire on which a pot boiled. A few looked up as the jeep got closer and Huw raised his hand in greeting. One of the men nodded a sullen response and then jerked his thumb in the direction of the roadway.

'That's fine by me, pal,' Huw muttered, and carried on slowly accelerating away. The soldiers remained disinterested and the jeep continued without delay.

'Juhan my friend, you can start breathing again.'

Juhan gasped and smiled. 'Yes you are right, air is good.'

Märt leant over from the back. 'Let's make distance. I want to be heading south before we meet anyone else.'

'I hear you, Märt,' Huw replied. 'But this tank of diesel will not get us to where you want to go. If I don't push the speed it will help. It may also be that the Reds have not got to Märjamaa yet and that means we have to cross the front line – in a Russian GAZ.'

'Agreed, so this journey will forever be open to change.'

They fell silent. Huw's mind had already drifted to long summer days of harvesting hay and long summer evenings rolling about in it with his beloved Maarja.

'They did what? Bring me that man now!' Oleg shouted.

A sergeant was wheeled in under escort by Yuri. He looked nervous, guilty even. Oleg knew this man was expecting trouble and he was in no mood to disappoint him.

'My man tells me you were in charge of a roadblock?'
'Yes comrade, more of a checkpoint really.'
'And you were charged to do what exactly?'
'To observe all vehicles coming through.'
'And check them?'
'Yes, comrade.'

The terror in the man's face told Oleg would have no trouble extracting the truth from him.

'How do you check them?'
'I... I...'
'How, comrade?'

Oleg smiled and sat down. He took out a silver cigarette case and opened it, offering one to the soldier. The man reached out a trembling hand, noticing the German Reich eagle on the casing. Oleg was satisfied with the beads of sweat now on the man's forehead.

'It's been a long march, hasn't it, Sergeant? Here, have a light.'

The man gratefully drew in the smoke and exhaled in relief.

'How long have you been on the road now?'
'Over a week, comrade, but we are fighting ready.'
'I do not doubt it, comrade. I do not doubt it. But you must be tired, no?'

The man hesitated and Oleg persevered. 'Well, I'm tired, so you must be exhausted.'

'It has been hard sir, yes.'
'And have you encountered many Nazis?'
'No sir, we have been support troops up to now.'
'So you have to stop vehicles on the road and check their credentials – papers, personnel and so on, no?'
'That is correct, comrade.'

Oleg opened his hands. 'My God, man. That must be hard to keep up with all the traffic. I'm sure that if anything looks the part, you can just wave it through?'

'Comrade, I...'

The man was turning white. Oleg held up his hand in defence.

'Well that is what I would do, anyhow.' Oleg winked. 'We can't all be square bashers, eh? Tell me, have you seen many trucks and tanks?'

The man nodded.

'But all in a convoy, yes? The occasional straggler though. Things break down, people need to relieve themselves. It's natural.'

The man took a long drag on his cigarette and nodded.

'Yes sir, just that. A GAZ jeep we had today.'

'A jeep? Well that's a rare one, what was it like?'

'Three men, sir. Officer in the back.'

'Oh really? What rank?'

'I do not know, Comrade, your rank perhaps, the roof was covered. The rain was terrible.'

'Tell me about it! And those officers won't be so appreciative of being delayed as they try to catch up. They can be really vindictive.' Oleg smiled, picked out a cigarette and slowly lit it. 'Why do we want this bloody country anyway? Muddy shithole.'

The man nodded and smiled nervously. Yuri wondered if he would see the face crack, so eager was the man to please Oleg.

'This jeep must have been a straggler, Sergeant. And you don't want to stop them, so you wave them through, surely?'

'Yes,' the man replied agreeably.

'When?'

'Six hours ago now, sir.'

'That's alright then, they'll have caught up with their convoy by now. Thank you, Comrade. I now know where to look for them.'

Oleg stood up and shook the man's hand.

'I hope you get some rest soon. Here, take some more cigarettes and thank you for the information.'

'Comrade, you are generous!'

He grabbed a handful of cigarettes and scurried out of the door held open by Yuri, who then looked back at his commander.

'A fat, lazy layabout. What is to be done? Send him back to the roadblocks?'

'Send them all to the front. You heard the man, they are all fighting ready. It is what Comrade Stalin asks of his men.'

'And the jeep?'

Oleg moved to a map laid out on a table and started tracing his finger down the eastern main road. We're off to the south, Yuri, to Märjamaa. According to the German files, the Estonian bandits near Rakvere had two members from there. Perhaps they would have been with the spy. I need the files of all government officials who were in

Estonia before we liberated them. Everyone, right down to the typist and cleaner.'

'It is done – and should I put out calls to apprehend a GAZ jeep with an officer and two men?'

'I doubt he was dressed as such, that arse would have told me he was Tsar Nicolas if he thought that is what I wanted to hear. Make sure they see a lot of action, Yuri. How fares the front line now, anyway?'

'We are at the coast and moving south, comrade Oleg.'

'Good, plenty of time for us to go visit Märjamaa then. I fancy we will be catching a baker.'

Chapter Thirteen

He swears in a different language

'How dare you laugh at my parents!'

''I did nothing of the sort,' Huw protested.

Under a bombardment of angry Estonian, too fast for his total comprehension, he grabbed her in an embrace.

'You forget, I know what you say these days.'

'This is good, for you should know what I think.'

'Alright, I didn't laugh at your parents. When you said you would have been disciplined for talking to me so early on, it just sounded funny.'

'So, now you mock how we bring up our children?'

'No, but you are so defensive about it all.'

The fire died a bit in her eyes, and she stopped trying to break free.

'I don't know why, it is our way. Perhaps many centuries of having one nation or another trying to own us? We take some time getting to know people. They have to earn our trust.'

'Why so flighty today? Today was a good day. We got a lot done in the fields. There will be marrow for pancakes and berries and currants for jam.'

She frowned and looked away.

'I heard British Navy are visiting Tallinn.'

'So? Tallinn is a million miles from here.'

'Even so.'

'It has been years, kallis. The war is finished, why would they bother with me? And how would they know where to find me anyway?'

'Tühista, tühista, tühista,' she muttered to herself. *'Perhaps we need to move on, go to islands, where no-one will find us?'*

'I think you are far too nervous. There's too much going on with the world for them to worry about me.'

'I hope so, kallis. Part of me would die without you.'

Huw brought the jeep to a stop at the roadside, where a gravel patch covered sparsely in tufts of grass separated the raised road from the

107

sandy forest ground. He stretched and then swung out of the vehicle. Away from the yellow patches of flat farmland, the forest was almost cool and refreshing to look at. A telegraph pole stood as a sentinel nearby, the line severed long ago, useless to all but the local stork, who had built a massive basket of a nest on its peak.

'What is wrong?' Märt asked, rousing from the back.

'Two things,' Huw replied. 'One, I have been driving for two hours since the roadblock and two, I need a piss and have waited a long time for a decent place to stop.'

He turned his back and started adding his own irrigation to the land.

Juhan laughed. 'Huw, I think you are true Estonian man already.'

'This is not good time to stop,' Märt said. 'We must carry on.'

'We have made good time in this vehicle – where are we now?'

'Twenty five kilometres from Märjamaa?' Märt replied. 'And remarkable for this GAZ.'

'I think we need to start talking of our plans,' Huw continued. 'We can't just drive into Märjamaa with this; we will need to ditch it nearby.'

'Yes, I know this,' said Märt. 'But we can get closer still and then hide it. We need to do something so that we can use it again.'

'Especially if we can find fuel,' Juhan shouted from the jeep.

Huw made a face. 'He's right, we've been lucky so far, let's hope it stays.'

Märt climbed into the driver's seat from the back and made himself comfortable, before declaring, 'Well, we can still go further. According to this gauge, we should have enough to get home if we are careful. Keep an eye out for good place to hide it in forest.'

Juhan looked back down the road wistfully; the farming land and forest could not hide the twin spires of Rapla's church of Maria Magdalena in the distance.

'It is a shame we have need to avoid this town. I would like to visit that church some day.'

'To do what? Pray?'

Juhan shrugged off the rough response. 'Why not? We need all help we can get. Perhaps one day I will become minister.'

'Well you have good temper for it,' Märt conceded. 'Come on, I want to try and get us past Kuusikuu before we stop. We cannot afford to stick around here. Rapla will be crawling with Reds now –

and some will have crept out of their rat holes to embrace our invaders also. They would try to impress their new masters by catching people like us.'

'Why would the Reds want to bother with Rapla?' Huw asked.

'Railway runs through it to Viljandi, makes it an ideal garrison town for this area.'

'I would have thought all the Estonian Reds would have been driven out when the Germans came.'

Märt grunted. 'With all infestations, you clear them out and if you are not careful they come back – slowly, then faster. It is shame, for in Rapla, they liked my bread.'

He gunned the engine and they set off westwards. Farther down the road, Juhan shouted to stop.

'What now?' Märt snapped, his mood worsening the closer they got to their target.

'I saw vehicle in ditch. Wrecked car – German, I am sure.'

'And what?'

'What if there is diesel in tank?'

'It's worth a try,' Huw said quickly, and Juhan was out and unfixing the jerry can before Märt could reply.

Märt settled for a dirty look at Huw in place of many minutes of harsh conversation. Huw had to turn away, lest his smile made it worse. He walked over to the spot where Juhan had disappeared from the road and sure enough, the young man's keen sight had picked up the wreck of a canvas-topped Kubelwagen lying on its side in the ditch. It was partly submerged in the mud. The long grass, together with its camouflage markings, had covered it sufficiently to hide it from all but the keen eyed.

The sickly-sweet smell of death was all around and Huw hoped that they could limit the contact with the remains of the occupants that would be rotting inside or nearby. Juhan was ankle deep in mud, standing with the underside of the car above him like a wall of metal. Together, they pushed it to a more vertical position. Juhan found the fuel tank and gave it a tap with a knife. The dull echo of liquid sloshing around could be heard.

'She is going to help us out, I think,' he said with a grin.

Huw traced the fuel line and began to work it free. Satisfied he had enough slack, he sliced it with his knife and held it up until Juhan could bring the jerry can close enough to transfer the fuel. As

Juhan stood happily collecting the diesel, Huw went around checking the vehicle, looking through the cracked windscreen first.

The view made him glad he had an empty stomach but he was reluctant to leave without checking for anything else of use first. Grabbing the bonnet he manoeuvred himself into a position to provide maximum leverage to kick through the windscreen. It didn't take long to realise it wasn't going to give. The back window was too small to wriggle through. Anyway, the thought of crawling around dead bodies was repulsive, so he checked the state of the soft top to see if it was easily sliced.

He became aware of the sound of approaching engines. Peering over the long grass, he spied a line of trucks in the distance, and knew they would pass them by in minutes. He cursed and shouted for Juhan to come around. Grinning, the young man appeared with a jerry can of sloshing diesel. His smile faded when Huw pointed out the trucks.

'It's too late to get back now. We are fairly out of sight here, so keep low.'

'And Märt?'

'I don't know, Juhan. He'll have to make do by himself.'

The column came closer, comprising three trucks and a GAZ jeep. Huw crouched lower and cursed again as he heard them stopping. There was a crunch of boots on the loose stones of the roadside, followed by voices shouting questions in Russian. Huw looked at Juhan, who made a face. The guns had been left with Märt. Huw had confidence in his training, but knife work in this exposed area would be awkward and certainly impossible to do without alerting the rest of the convoy. Still, he noted, it wasn't raining. Perhaps it was a good day to die after all.

Men began to walk through the long grass. Flies congregated on Huw, as if they had just sensed fresh meat. He didn't dare brush them away. Voices and footfalls on the other side of the Kubelwagen were getting nearer – too near. A bit more conversation, then the vehicle started rocking. The soldiers were trying to right it, but the mud held it in its slimy embrace. Desperately, Juhan tried to hold it still.

There came a shout from above and a discussion followed, with a lot of cursing. The boots moved on. Huw was sure they were climbing back up the bank of long grass. His calf muscles were on fire. He could hear the shouts growing fainter, but dare not move his now trembling legs. The twin steeples of the church were still prominent on the horizon. He imagined what it might be like inside the building, a sanctuary from madness.

At last the trucks revved and started to move off. Huw waited until they were a faint noise before he risked standing up.

'Did you piss yourself?' Juhan's voice cut through the agony, as he stamped furiously to renew circulation in his legs.

'No, you?'

'Damn nearly,' was Juhan's cheerful reply. Soon the sound of urination could be heard accompanied by the humming of a jolly Estonian folk song.

The jeep was still there, and Märt was moving, much to Huw's relief. He turned once more to the Kubelwagen. 'Now, let's take what we can and get out of it,' he said. He sliced open the soft roof and stepped back, repulsed by the wave of putridity. He scanned the inside, Juhan's chatter assaulting his ears all the while.

'You know, it was funny to hear their talk. One said this smell of death was enough to tell him there was nothing of worth, except to bears. One noticed fuel pipe had been cut and said Estonian vultures had already been here. Then when they were called back, they did not delay.'

Huw snatched what he could, then they slithered hastily back to the road, to find Märt sitting impatiently, tapping his fingers on the steering wheel.

'You took your time,' Märt snapped.

'A Luger, with rounds, a map not covered in blood and a spare tank of diesel,' Huw responded. 'What did you get?'

'I have no need for diesel,' Märt replied. 'My new comrades believed my story and gave me fuel. I told them I had sent you back to Rapla for some. They told me we should catch up with them, down this road, just north of Märjamaa.'

'That's nice, I take it we shall disappoint them.'

The only reply was the engine roaring to life. Märt took them slowly down the road, keeping his distance from the dust cloud ahead that marked the convoy's progress.

A few miles on and without warning, he turned off the road and down a gravel track. They sped past fields and down towards a small farm. Huw remembered knowing the family that worked this land, but had never visited the place in his past. Now, he admired the diagonal struts of the wooden fence flanking the track. It appeared unbroken from the years of strife, a testament to the brief past of calm, now idyllic in memory. The buildings looked robust, albeit repaired. The dark wooden planks rose up from the ground to form their sturdy walls. The thatched roof of large reeds set diagonally down the rafters made it look homely.

A grey-haired man stood at the farm gate, watching the jeep's approach. He held a scythe, but it seemed to be more of a support than a defensive weapon. A group of women worked hard in the fields near the barns, their faces hidden by shawls as they looked down at the ground they worked on. Their woollen garments were the colour of the earth.

A large swing hung in a clearing nearby: a square of four planks supported vertically by struts attached to the frame, designed for many to use in one go. Huw's mind raced back to a similar contraption – he standing on one side and Maarja on the other. The speed and the height they reached sent her off in squeals of delight. Huw had worried they would break the swing, but he didn't want to end the moment. He basked in her joy, the way she touched the tip of her tongue to her front teeth each time she added power to the swing. Her eyes sparkled with delight. Looking back at the scene, Huw felt the pain of loss more heavily than ever.

'We must find if Maarja is still alive,' he said out loud.

Märt nodded. 'Yes, we must. Hai! Andrus. Andrus Ots! Tere, tere!'

Huw cursed his indiscretion, as Märt drove the vehicle into the farm courtyard, parking it out of view of the track they had travelled up.

'Tervist,' the farmer said in greeting. 'Märt? Märt, is this you?'

'Yes,' Märt gave a slight smile. 'It is good to see you in health. These two are from Märjamaa also.'

'Is this true? You fight in Russian army now?'

'I would like to talk, Andrus – if there is somewhere quiet we can go? Your barn, perhaps?'

Huw froze. Something wasn't quite right, as if the world had suddenly changed. It was too quiet. He looked around the farm. It was completely deserted, save the farmer and themselves. It was strange, for there should have been more people. Where...?'

'The women in the field,' he gasped to Juhan. 'Where have they gone?'

'They are here,' a man's voice replied, and Huw turned to look straight down a gun barrel.

The holder of the gun wore a woollen skirt, shawl and headscarf – and a pronounced moustache, and a pipe jutted out of his mouth.

'It is strange when men dress as women to work in these fields,' Juhan said.

'Strange, but necessary,' the man replied. 'There are many prying eyes around. Many foes who would wish harm upon simple farm folk. We have to be careful and look after our own.'

'We are friends,' Huw said.

'Let's go into forest and find out,' the man said, indicating for them to walk. 'Keep your hands open and don't try anything stupid. I have plenty of reasons to shoot Reds.'

'We are not Reds,' Huw said.

'All the more reason for you not to make mistakes,' the man replied.

'We will hand you our weapons and come with you,' Märt said. 'We will convince you of who we are. Some of you will know me from before.'

'Many things have changed since then. Your weapons, then we can talk.'

'Huw, your knife also,' Märt said, and Huw slowly drew it from the sheath around his lower leg, handing it over hilt first to another of the "farming women".

'Do not worry,' the man said. 'If you prove true, we will return it.'

'If not?'

'You will not leave forest. Andrus, you do not need to come.'

'Well, this is true,' the old man said. 'But I knew Märt when he was our baker. If he is patriot, I wish to defend him. If not, I wish to shoot him myself.'

They started to move deep inside the forest.

'All this effort for nothing,' Huw said to Juhan.

'It will be, if you don't shut up,' his captor warned him from behind.

113

The journey reminded Huw of his trip to the Forest Brothers camp in the north. The forest looked featureless, the evergreens providing limited landmarks as they went. Huw tried to sharpen his thinking and look for small landmarks: an exposed root or a prominent branch, a fallen bough riddled with fungi – anything to help, should he try to escape.

'You are very observant,' said his captor. 'But my trigger finger is sharp, even for trained man like you.'

They walked a few miles before they reached a clearing where the captors left Huw, Märt and Juhan standing alone. Others rushed out from a dugout and over ridges. The men spread out, some taking up defensive positions on the corners of the camp. Huw became aware of a large man wearing a leather jerkin and sporting a thick beard, who appeared to be the leader.

'So what have we here?' the man said, his deep voice cutting through the chatter.

'Destroyers come to Andrus to cause trouble,' the moustachioed partisan replied.

'We are not Destroyers,' Märt said quietly. We are Metsavennad from near Rakvere. Many of you knew me, for at one time I was baker near Märjamaa.'

'Yes, you are known here,' the leader replied slowly. 'Baker who ran away to war before Red terror and now you are here, claiming to be one of Virumaa's Metsavennad. One who has come home and for what?'

'My wife, I left her here on farm near Sipa.'

'Is it not late now? The Reds came through here in '41, took hundreds of folk away in their cattle trucks.'

'I do not feel it so, here,' Märt tapped his chest.

'Ah,' the man smiled too sweetly. 'So you missed your warm bed – and what made you leave it so quickly?'

Märt's expression did not change, nor did his body language, but Huw felt as if the temperature had dropped in the glade.

'I went to Finland to fight for Estonia,' Märt said.

'And?'

'There is nothing more to tell, this is so.'

'I went to Finland also, August,' said one of the Forest Brothers. 'Yet I do not remember him.'

'There were over two thousand of us,' Märt replied. 'So I certainly do not remember all faces. I was one of Haukka men and went to join Erna. I fought at Kautla Wald.

August nodded his head and tugged his beard. His arms were folded as he sat on a fallen bough as if in judgement.

'You are noble patriot indeed. So, I too heard of baker who went to be Finnish Boy. Erna? A noble cause.'

Märt shrugged. 'If you say so, we broke through Reds encirclement and got villagers out. It was what we were trained for.'

'And people of Kautla were grateful, no?'

'Those who did not escape or chose to stay behind were murdered by Destroyer battalions after. I feel I condemned as many as I saved.'

'Is that why you went north?'

Märt made a face. 'Perhaps. Up there, Metsavennad needed organising, we did not know if Germans would turn out to be as bad as Reds - or if Reds would return.'

August started to pace up and down, still stroking his chin.

'Why then did you leave?'

'My unit was wiped out and I decided to come home.'

'Indeed, late nonetheless.'

August walked over to Huw. 'What of this man?'

'He is an agent for English,'

'English?' Without warning, August lashed out and slapped Huw's face.

'Twll-du,' Huw gasped, without thinking. August moved back to sit.

'Inglismaa, hey? He swears in different language.'

Huw made no attempt to give any reply, but Märt calmly replied.

'He is from part called Wales, they have their own language.'

'Indeed, how convenient.'

Huw snorted in derision and sat down on the ground.

'You have not been told to sit,' his guard hissed.

'Well, I've heard enough of this farce and besides your man in the hollowed out tree stump has a rifle pointed at me.'

There was a silence in the glade. August smiled the slim smile of a wolf.

'These two with me are of this land,' Märt continued. 'This Welshman moved here at time of independence.'

'Oh this is nonsense,' Huw raged. 'I can tell you know this already. You know Märt; some of you know Juhan, perhaps even me. Stop wasting time.'

August's eyes narrowed, it was the closest he appeared to get to anger.

'You are impatient Englishman. Yes, we know of you, but perhaps not of what you represent. Reds have brought many problems here. They infiltrate our bands, posing as refugees. Destroyer patrols rape, kill and damage as they see fit. Many things are not what they seem.'

'And why would we be like this?' Huw asked.

'You wear clothes of Destroyers.'

Huw was thrown by the reply. He looked across to Märt for guidance, but received a shrug in reply.

'It was all we could take.'

'We stole these from patrol near Kadrina,' Juhan said. 'They had stopped to wash their clothes in river.'

August's brows furrowed and he slapped the bough.

'Did you not shoot them when you saw their badges? You do read, don't you?'

'I cannot read,' Juhan replied.

'Are you simple?'

'No, I don't think so, but words are difficult for me to see properly in my mind.'

'It makes little difference,' Huw said, tapping his temple. 'Juhan has broader vision than all of us in here.'

August paused and took a small tobacco tin from his pocket, inside were small cigarettes with a flint. He removed one, lit it with difficulty, then said, 'When Mother Russia came, local Reds flocked to cause and took out their petty revenges here. They took what they coveted, they harried whom they hated and they killed who they feared. Then Destroyer battalions were brought in to cause trouble and more besides. They were different; they did it because they could and because they enjoyed it. When trucks came to take people away, I think some even were glad to go, their lives had been made hell. So you see, we have no love for Destroyers and would treat them as they would treat us – like rats.'

August took a deep drag and threw the butt away.

'So, I accept that you are these men who you say. But what brings an English spy to middle of Estonia, away from battlefield, flanked by two Metsavennad from north?'

There was no reply for a long time, as Märt and Huw weighed up the question. August finally held out his hands.

'Truth now, you must give me something more. Why are you here?'

'I was ordered to establish a base and report back intelligence…' Huw began, but August waved his hands with irritation.

'No, no, no. this is not enough.'

'I…' Huw began to speak, but Märt spoke over him.

'I am here to find my wife, Maarja and keep her safe. She is only woman I ever loved.'

August nodded slowly and resumed his seat. Huw took a deep breath.

'I am here to find and protect Maarja, the woman whom I loved and ran away from the Royal Navy to be with.'

Somebody took a sharp intake of breath. August raised his eyebrows and said nothing again. Juhan's eyes were wide, but he still managed to speak.

'Maarja is my mother.'

Huw could hear the wind rustle the leaves in the trees. A bird sang in the canopy, otherwise time seemed to stand still.

'She is formidable woman, August,' one of the Forest Brothers said and some grunts of agreement followed.

August scratched the back of his head and blew out a huge breath. 'Stand down boys and let's get them some food. These men are hungry and it seems they already have troubles enough.'

The partisans laughed and the tension eased. August held out his hand to help Huw up.

'Thank you, August. Do you know of any news west of Märjamaa? Do you know if Maarja lives?'

'The last time I heard, it was so. Some families moved into forest when Reds came, but they stayed until deportations, then they hid. They returned when Germans arrived. Rest now and we will go over in morning.'

Huw looked across as Märt was embraced by Andrus, as if a long lost son. For the first time in months, perhaps years, he began to feel he was amongst friends. He certainly hoped it was so.

Chapter Fourteen

The promise

Huw woke up in the middle of the night in a cold sweat. The warmth of Maarja's body was reassuring, but something wasn't at all right. In the dim light he could make out her form and he gazed down at her. A desire to caress her hair came upon him, but he knew it would not be welcome if it woke her at this hour.

Then he heard a rapid knocking at the door. He climbed out of bed and slipped on his trousers, moving to the landing as quietly as the complaining floorboards would let him. He reached the door and opened it to find his friend Märt standing there. In the faint moonlight, he could see the concern on the man's face.

'Huw, you must leave, now.'

'What? What's wrong? What's going on?' *Huw was stunned by the unexpected words.*

'The navy are here from Tallinn, they have come to look for you.'

'What? How do you know?'

Huw let Märt in and lit a lamp.

'No. No lamps, they will see. Their vehicles woke me up and I heard them talking as they met policeman in front of my shop. I do not know why they do this, but they look as if they mean to take you. You are good man, so I give you chance to leave if you need, before they come.'

There was a sound above them and a glimmer of light, as Maarja appeared on the stairs. She was dressed in silk pyjamas and dressing gown – one of the few luxuries she had insisted on keeping from her comfortable life in the city. She was still only half-awake and had not stopped to think of her appearance.

'Märt? Is that you? At this hour?'

'Yes, Maarja, it is me. English navy are coming for Huw, he must escape now.'

Maarja gave out a low moan of dread.

'We must leave!'

They all stopped as they heard the sound of a truck approaching, labouring on the uneven road.

'Oh God, Huw! You must leave now!' *Maarja shouted.*

119

Huw raced upstairs and grabbed a shirt and jerkin.

'You know where to go, towards Kasari River,' said Maarja, thrusting his boots into his hands. 'Hide in reeds; I will follow when I can. We will go to Hiiumaa and they will not find us.'

Huw paused to kiss her, their passion holding them together as if their lives depended on it.

'I love you,' she whispered.

'I know, I love you like no one else. I will return, they will not stop me.'

'Later then.' she gave a brave smile and brushed his cheek.

'Huw, they have arrived in yard,' Märt shouted from the stairs. 'Leave through window at back. Quickly now.'

'Märt, I am grateful for this.' Huw said.

'Go, friend. Be lucky now.' Märt said. 'I will answer door and slow them.'

Huw scrambled through the window and slid down the thatch. He hit the ground and looked around. It was pitch black and quiet. If he ran to the smoke sauna, then to the barn, he would have cover to the edge of the forest and then they would never find him. Taking a deep breath he launched himself forward and reached the sauna unscathed.

Sounds of a struggle erupted from the front of the house. He had seconds at most and chose to run for the barn. Then the ground ahead was flooded with blinding torchlight. Voices and the sounds of running boots followed him. He broke cover and sprinted headlong. He knew capture would mean being taken back to the Royal Navy, to prison in Portsmouth. Huw had no desire for British justice, he had been away too long and was a different man from the youthful cadet of long ago. He had to escape.

He sensed someone was close and darted to the side. Hands tried to grab him and he fended them off with a stiff-arm to the man's face. Then he was knocked to his knees by a charge from the side. He threw the man off and tried to stand, but another grabbed him, then another. He was pressed down to the ground and they secured his hands. Then he felt the cold metal of a gun barrel on his neck and he lay still.

Maarja screamed as Huw was led away. He could hear her struggles as she tried to break through to him. He wished he could touch her once more, but his captors had covered his head with a coat and were frogmarching him away.

'I will come back, Maarja. Do you hear me? I will come back for you,' he screamed.

He was roughly dragged into the truck, which sped away, leaving Huw with nothing but the echo of his own words. 'I will come back, I will come back.'

Huw was now so used to snatching sleep when able to. His body quickly replaced the fog of drowsiness with an adrenalin push when Märt roused him late in the night.

'Huw, we have word, trucks are heading for Märjamaa. I think they have started deporting again.'

'What? Did they not take enough last time? Between Siberia and the Red Army, I thought they must have just about bled the country dry of its people.'

'This is worse, my friend,' August's deep voice boomed in the darkness. 'Our German friends compiled lists of Forest Brothers, who they are, their families and friends. The fools left papers behind and Reds now have all this.'

Huw gasped. 'Maarja?'

Märt nodded. 'She is in danger. She will be wanted because she will be listed as my wife.'

'Then we need to go.'

'Yes, Juhan is taking weapons to our jeep. August will send man with us – others will make their way through forest.'

'Well, what are we waiting for?' Huw asked.

'I come with you, friend,' August said, offering Huw his knife back.

Huw took it, nodded and put it back in its ankle sheath. 'Now we get to show you our worth, August.'

They moved as fast as the forest allowed. Huw tried to regulate his breathing, to force down the fear that climbed up his throat. After coming so far and waiting so long, it was unbearable that anything should stand in his way.

A rifle shot interrupted his thoughts, followed by a burst of automatic fire. Märt glanced at Huw and they both broke into a sprint. Huw was the faster and soon reached the edge of the clearing.

Märt was not that far behind and a breathless August joined them to survey the scene. Two vehicles stood at the farm gate, a truck and a jeep with a machine gun. A group of soldiers lay on the ground, another stood behind the truck. The machine gunner lay over his weapon, motionless. Another shot rang out, seemingly from the vicinity of the barn.

'Juhan appears to be holding up Red Army with nothing more than his rifle,' August panted.

'Yes, he is accurate and they are less than bold,' Märt replied.

'This will not last forever,' Huw said. 'That one is creeping forward with a grenade. I am going to circle round and attack from the rear, keep them busy.'

Märt bared a wolf smile. 'Good hunting.'

As the man stood to throw, Märt shot him. The grenade dropped from his hands and a few seconds later, the nearest soldiers were peppered with shrapnel. The Reds turned to face this new threat and fired wildly into the forest.

Huw had begun his sweep around the back of the vehicles and he braved a quick glance back. To his surprise, Märt appeared to be walking forward firing into the soldiers. He looked like a giant and the troops were further confused by August firing from a position closer to the farm. Huw needed no more incentive and ran to outflank the troops. Nobody noticed him; their attention was brought to bear on the attack from three fronts.

The leading officer urged his men to regroup, but fell. The shot came from the barn. His sudden death unnerved the soldiers and two broke, running back towards Huw's position. He rose up to meet them and in one quick movement stepped to the side and slashed the throat of the first. The other saw this and raised his gun. Huw threw the knife, hitting the man in the centre of his chest.

Huw's head was pounding now, his breath coming in short bursts, but he crouched again, remaining alert for more trouble. There seemed none; those that had not been killed had run off. The farm was eerily silent. The remaining soldiers lay dead.

Huw started to shake as the adrenalin left him. He was afraid, and angry, that this action had delayed them reaching Maarja. Whereas before it was a whisper of desire in Huw's mind, now his body screamed for her to be with him again.

Märt was walking towards him with Juhan at his side. They both bore rifles. Huw watched their slow-motion approach. He could not understand their distant, echoing words.

Märt grabbed Huw's arm. 'Huw, are you well?'

'Yes, yes,' Huw shook his head and retrieved his knife from the now-dead soldier. 'It's just no longer the training ground, that's all. We need to go.'

'We will go my friend, I take one jeep – you take other. August will take his men across to try and reach junction with main road. Juhan, are you good also?'

'For sure.'

'Are you certain,' Huw asked.

'Yes, why?'

'You said you would never kill,' Huw replied.

Juhan shrugged. 'I did not kill. Andrus aimed to kill, I aimed to injure.'

Huw sighed. 'You are a dangerous man, Juhan – to yourself.'

'Quickly now, we have little time. Gather what weapons are of use,' Märt hissed.

'Andrus?' Huw asked.

'He will move his family to forest. August's men will look after them. Andrus has no choice now, they are marked for deportation.'

They piled into the vehicles, turned around and headed off back down to the main road. It wasn't fast enough for Huw, but he grudgingly let Märt go in front. He knew it was better for the calmer head to lead. They found the main road and raced towards Märjamaa. The night was pitch black now, the clouds thick enough to stifle the lunar glow. The narrow bands of light from the headlights and brake lights of Märt's jeep were all Huw had to ensure his own did not slip from the road and end up like the Kubelwagen. Although it felt like hours to Huw, they soon crossed the Tallinn Road and swept into Märjamaa.

The small groups of houses looked unfamiliar to Huw in the limited light, but as they slid across a road junction, he could vaguely make out the silhouette of the tower of the church. Huw believed he glimpsed people opening their doors very briefly, but perhaps it was just his imagination. Certainly, if they did, they closed them as fast. At the speed they were going, Huw felt the jeeps stood a good chance of being unimpeded by any soldiers in town. Perhaps they would assume that the two vehicles were on urgent business.

They sped off west towards Koluvere, hoping the Russian uniform they still wore would be enough to pass them off as Reds if they were seen. Huw was ready to face a hundred Reds, if it meant saving Maarja. His doubts were still there about what he would or even could do, but he was overcoming his nervousness through cursing.

Ahead, Märt's jeep had shot up another track and soon a set of familiar wooden farm buildings came into view. They sped to the house and halted outside. Märt and Huw jumped out and ran for the door, which was wide open. There was no activity inside. As they entered, the faint illumination from the jeep headlights gave the impression that things had been gathered in a hurry. There was no sign of violence or a struggle.

'Damn!' Huw ran to switch the jeep engines off. 'Maarja, Maarja!' he called desperately, holding up his hand for silence, hoping without hope for a reply.

'Huw,' Märt shouted. 'Calm down.'

'Do you think they made the forest?' Huw shouted back.

'No,' Märt replied. 'No I do not. If snatch squad came to Andrus, Reds may well have sent one here. If farm folk had fled to forest, I feel sure they would have closed door to make place look normal.'

Huw screamed. 'We're too late; this is all my damn fault!'

'Can we catch them?' Juhan asked. 'They cannot be far; table was wet with something spilt on it. We have jeeps, they are faster than trucks.'

'Which way, Juhan?' Märt shouted, suddenly losing his composure. 'West or east? Then at end of that road, where next?'

'Where will they take them?' Juhan asked calmly.

Märt took a deep breath and held up his hand in apology. 'You are right, they will go east. To railway. Junction in Rapla will be quickest route. Then they take them on trains to Siberia.'

'But then we would have passed them, surely by now?' Huw asked.

'What if they went to other farms?' Juhan asked, and Huw smacked his hand on the side of the jeep.

'Stupid of me, we probably passed them when they went to another farm – or they may have passed when we were fighting at Andrus's – but what if we are wrong and they go to Tallinn?'

'We cannot be wrong,' Märt replied. 'That is all they would do. Juhan, you drive.'

Huw stared. Märt raised a grim smile.

'If we catch them, I want someone with machine gun who won't hesitate to use it, so Juhan must drive. Let's go, look for headlights in distance and don't forget to be careful. They may not expect us, but they will be armed.'

The jeeps sped off once more. Huw scanned the gloom for signs of movement. He tapped Juhan's shoulder and pointed. 'Look, beyond the village. Tracer fire.'

Unmistakeable streaks of red lit the sky intermittently. Juhan flashed his lights at Märt and then overtook as the other jeep slowed.

'Crazy boy,' Huw shouted.

In the dashboard glow, he saw Juhan's grin, almost demonic in the pleasure of the chase. They raced back to Märjamaa, which still looked completely deserted. Huw was sure that more than a few people would be looking from behind their curtains, wondering what was going on – fearing the worst. A Russian guard ran out and shouted. Huw waved and looked away.

They headed north and Huw noticed flashes of yellow light to the east of the Tallinn road. The Rapla road was only a mile further on and Juhan switched to it without hesitation. It didn't take too long to find the source of the flashes.

'Kill the lights!' Huw shouted. Juhan did so, Märt copying as he came to park at their side. The scene ahead was desperate. The road was blocked by a truck that had come to a stop sideways. A small crowd sheltered behind the truck. The flare of an explosion picked out August leading another group away from the fight towards the forest. The army vehicles had parked on the road close by and soldiers were raining fire on the scene.

'Any thoughts?' Huw shouted to Märt.

'Hit them from behind, it will draw their fire.'

'Right then,' yelled Huw. 'Let's go in all guns blazing, true cowboy style. Remember the Alamo.' The others paused and Märt raised a quizzical eyebrow.

'Another time, perhaps,' Huw muttered.

125

The tyres screeched as the two jeeps leapt forward into action. Huw held onto the gun in a futile effort to keep it steady. When they were a stone's throw from the battle, Märt jammed on his brakes and Juhan followed suit.

'Lights. Full beam. Now!' Huw yelled, and set off a torrent of fire at the soldiers.

Blinded and bewildered by the sudden attack from the rear, the soldiers started firing wildly back. Outflanked as they were, the men quickly realised how hopeless their position was and made a run for the forest.

'Twice in one night,' Juhan remarked.

'Two too many,' Huw muttered under his breath. 'Where now, Märt?'

'To farm of Andrus,' came the reply. 'We take jeeps into forest as far as we can, to hide them from patrols. I know how we get to Metsavennad camp. Juhan! Back here, now!'

Juhan came running back with a rifle and what looked like a stone in his hand.

'We need to get supplies, no?' He asked, and Märt shook his head.

'No, some soldiers may escape to forest and may regroup to reclaim their vehicle. There may be reinforcements coming also. You don't know and we don't have time to find out. Let's get out of here.'

The jeeps negotiated their way round the army vehicles via a gap at the verge barely wide enough. All the while, Huw trained his machine gun on the truck. There was no sign of life. He breathed a sigh of relief as they sped away.

On arrival at the farm, they looked for the best way to hide the vehicles. The path was just wide enough to drive for about a hundred metres, then it forked and narrowed around a tree and they had to stop.

'That's far enough in to avoid immediate discovery,' Huw said.

'Agreed, we will come back in the morning and tidy it up. At day, we will make sure these are covered in branches.'

'Can we keep them?' Juhan asked eagerly.

'We will ask August,' Märt replied. 'It may be he will not want them so close to camp.'

The journey back to camp on foot became a problem. The long trek to the south had taken its toll. The adrenalin from the rescues was spent and soon, wrong decisions by exhausted minds got them lost in the dark forest. Eventually, even Märt had to admit that he didn't know where they were. He cursed and sat down against the base of a tree.

'It would appear this is as far as we go.'

'Yes, soft bed tomorrow,' Huw wheezed.

There was no answer save Märt's breathing, so Huw settled down for a rough night.

'If we are lost in such a dense part of the forest, I doubt others will find us so easily, so we don't need a guard,' he said.

'You are keeping foxes awake,' Märt muttered.

'But we did well, Märt.'

'Yes, so now we rest.'

Huw felt cold, he could hear the calling of birds, feel the gentle breeze that rustled the leaves nearby. His mind raced away *and he wondered if he could close the curtains and get a few more minutes in bed. He reached out to the blond woman lying by his side, he reached...*

His hands touched leaves in the mud and he woke with a start. It was morning and the sun had already cast its light as best it could through the forest. He shivered and stood up stretching, rubbing the side that had taken all the weight during his slumber. Looking around, he spied Märt lying by a tall tree nearby. It was just the two of them. Huw went over to rouse Märt.

'Do you remember Juhan being with us when we stopped?' He asked.

Märt shook his head and sighed. 'I don't remember much after we left jeeps. Perhaps we should retrace our steps to Andrus' farm and then try to find camp. With luck, we will find Juhan somewhere.'

'Perhaps we can kill a wild boar on the way,' Huw said, his stomach rumbling at the thought.

They carefully retraced their steps back a few miles. Then Märt stopped and cursed.

'He is unbelievable.'

Juhan was walking towards them with his hands full of berries.

'Where have you been?' Märt demanded.

'To camp,' Juhan replied, surprised at the question. 'It was where you said we were going.'

'You know it's too late to get angry,' Huw said to Märt. 'He will never change.'

Märt gave a rare smile. 'I suppose there is truth in what you say.'

Juhan's good humour could not be quenched. 'You have to see this. Someone in camp is trying to make bread. They have made kind of oven.'

'Perhaps I should not see this,' Märt replied. 'Or indeed, perhaps I should go to stop them poisoning themselves.'

Juhan led them back through the forest to the camp. Huw had a first real chance to study it and noticed that it was set in a hollow, flanked by trees at regular intervals. The stout trunks provided good cover for the pickets and the hollow hid all activity from prying eyes. A sturdy place to defend, but an easy place to surround, Huw thought. There seemed to be no back door.

As they moved over the rise, the camp seemed to come alive. The noise of the camp, suppressed within the hollow, hit them full on as they breasted the edge, like a wave. People were busy everywhere; cleaning weapons, clearing space for the refugees, cooking and repairing. Branches had been brought in to fashion shelters. Huw leant against one of the trees and looked down with a heavy heart.

'How many more? Fifteen, twenty? They are less of a fighting force and more of a village now. How will they keep safe from the Red Army?'

'By woodcraft, by guile and by necessity,' Märt replied. 'They have no choice. As long as they keep hidden, perhaps Red Army will leave them alone.'

'Perhaps, but rescuing people from snatch squads isn't very low profile.'

'Groups like this will unite. One network of Forest Brothers will be unstoppable.'

'Perhaps, my friend. First I think you and I should put our experience to good use in this camp. It needs greater defence and cover for the families also.'

Märt looked around wistfully. 'This will not suffice, we would be better looking deeper in forest for better place to make camp.'

Huw looked on and breathed in the heady atmosphere. There was an air of fulfilment today, as if the rescue had made the men wake up for the first time for years. Smiles could be seen all around, jokes were being bantered between the folk and there was much backslapping. The Forest Brothers were proud of the work they had done the previous night.

Someone started to sing a folk song and others joined in. Juhan walked into the throng with a broad smile. He hoisted his rifle onto his shoulder and braced himself as a woman ran to hug him. She clung onto him as if she could never leave his side, her body racked with sobs.

Juhan gently stroked her hair and talked to her, smiling fondly. She wiped her tears and then hugged him once more. Juhan then spoke and indicated to where Huw and Märt stood. The woman looked up and the blood rushed to Huw's face as her gaze met his. It was Maarja. He grabbed the tree for support.

She had changed. Age had filled out her girlish frame and while Huw was sure her face had grown older, he could not swear to it. It made no difference; he was still captivated by her and had difficulty suppressing the desire to rush to her side.

The moment passed. Maarja turned her back and led Juhan away. Huw looked at Märt, who was biting his lip. Then his friend moved off towards a group of people trying to prepare bread and fire a rudimentary oven. Huw stood alone.

Oleg cursed. It was bad enough that the truck had been ambushed, but that they had let the peasants escape was intolerable. He gazed with contempt at the group of soldiers trying to move the truck to the roadside.

'Perhaps they should take the handbrake off first,' he snapped.

He wondered how he was going to get through the day without shooting someone.

'Do you wish me to suggest it?' faithful Yuri, always at his side, asked meekly.

Oleg reached for his cigarette case.

'I think you would be more diplomatic than I.'

'You have said before, Comrade Oleg. If they had a gram of intelligence…'

'...They would not be doing this job. True, Yuri, true. We are very close now. It would help if these men did their jobs properly. Are there many killed?'

'Not really comrade. One or two bandits, no markings on them. All our soldiers survived.'

'Pity. Bring me the officer in charge.'

Yuri returned with the man, who looked rather frustrated at being dragged away.

'Comrade, I have a road to clear,' he snapped.

'Indeed,' Oleg replied. 'But you have a lot more to do. Have you started searching the area for bandits?'

The man whispered a curse. 'Look, I don't know who you are, but our brief is to clear this road. That's all we're going to do.'

Oleg nodded slowly. 'Indeed, this is true. You do not know who I am. Here.'

He produced a document and handed it over. The officer's face paled.

'NKVD[1]? I mean, comrade, I...'

He pulled himself together and saluted. Oleg smiled coldly.

'That's better. Now, I am taking charge of this operation. I want your men to move the vehicles. I want your guards to search the area for signs of where the bandits went.'

A look of disgust passed over Oleg's face, as he saw the man's confusion and he pointed, making his words crisp to emphasise each one. 'You start with that side of the truck. It's the only way they could escape and not be exposed to fire. Then let's see if the jeeps left any tyre tracks. I want anything you find reported immediately. Understood?'

The officer saluted and walked swiftly away, screaming orders to his men.

'Did he just shit his pants?' Yuri asked. Oleg gave no sign of hearing.

'We had the woman in our grasp and the fools let her go. The English spy must have been involved. Soon, we will get them. Soon.'

The terrified young boy lay in the ditch, his breathing shallow for fear of discovery. He was one of three youths who came secretly to

---

[1] Soviet law enforcement egancy. Worked with KGB.

loot the debris, hoping to make a name for themselves. When the army arrived he had dived into the reeds. The other two hid in the fields opposite. Thankfully, the soldiers had paid little attention. They just appeared keen to move the truck and leave. The boy-partisan knew some Russian and could hear the complaining. They hated Estonia as much as their work.

He hated soldiers; he hated all Reds. He remembered the words of his teacher, years ago: *You should never judge any man by his nationality, religion or race.* 'Everyone is an individual, Tõnis. *Everyone is capable of carving their own path in life.*'

The words echoed in his mind. He had tried to live his life by those rules but it was hard, so hard for him.

They had come for his family in the early hours of a morning. The commissar made sport of them.

'*You are unlucky tonight, undesirables on my list are not home, but we need the numbers, so you will have to go in their place for holiday in Siberia. Pack your things, but don't take too much.*'

As they had been taken to the truck, his mother had fallen to her knees and pleaded for her children. She grabbed at the leg of the commissar and screamed for mercy. The soldiers bayoneted her. In his anguish, his father launched himself at the soldiers in a futile attack. '*Run children, run!*'

Tõnis ran for his life. His sister stayed frozen to the spot. He found his way to the forest and hid until the men had gone. Later he found out what he had left. His mother was dead, his father also, shot in the head. His sister had been given to the army for their pleasure.

The soldiers had taken the family next door instead. It was the house of the teacher who had given Tõnis the benefit of his wisdom years back. When they finished beating the man, they threw him in a cattle truck. Tõnis doubted he had lasted to Siberia.

It was hard to believe the creed, given to him all those years ago, but Tõnis hoped he would be able to someday. For now, the memory was too much like an open sore.

A jeep had pulled up by his patch of reeds. Tõnis lay as still as he could. The officer looked kind. Tõnis had almost forgotten people could look that way, until the soldier with him had brought news. Tõnis had never seen so much hate. He closed his eyes and prayed.

Dear God, he thought. All my suffering and pain, just to end like this? Please God, no.

A local family had given him food and shelter after the massacre. When the Reds had found out, that family was also taken away. From then on nobody had helped, for fear of their lives. But the Reds couldn't catch him and soon he found other outcasts, living hand to mouth in the forest.

But now to die like this?

He listened to the conversations and it set his mind racing. He had to survive and get word back to the camp. He prayed, 'Please God, let me do one good thing in my life.'

He lay in the reeds and tried to be part of the land. He reached out to the sounds of nature to keep his mind occupied. He became absorbed by the embrace of the earth and the coolness of the ground. It worked so well that when the shots rang out, he hardly heard them.

'Who gave the order to fire?' Oleg screamed.

'Comrade, we have instructions. Any bandit or anyone seen to aid a bandit is to be shot forthwith.'

Oleg slammed his hand down on the bonnet of the jeep.

'Idiots! We need them alive. They can tell us where the camp is and who helps them. Don't you understand anything? Check the bodies now.'

There was a delay and then the officer called across to Oleg.

'They are both dead, Comrade.'

'They may be on our list,' said Yuri.

'In time, we may join them if they are not,' muttered Oleg. 'Bring the file and let's see what we have.'

Tõnis heard the two men depart, leaving only the whisper of the wind through the reeds. A bird sang in the trees of the forest he desperately yearned to get to.

Tension gripped him. He knew this was the moment to act. There was no time for fear. He would only have one chance. It was now.

His body refused to move. He had lain still for too long. Tears blurred his vision. It did not seem fair. Then he heard a voice that he thought he would never hear again.

So, what are you waiting for?

His father had always teased him so on the hot days, when Tõnis would stand at the river side, not wanting to feel the cold waters on his clammy skin. The words washed over him now like a cool wave and slowly, he rolled to the side, leaving the mud's caress. Then he looked up and moved into a crouch.

With an unsteady gait, he crept to the first tree. It was so close he could almost smell it. He chanced a look back and, blessing the foresight of the engineers who raised the road, he made a loping run towards the woodland beyond.

There was a shout and a hail of gunfire, but it was all too late. Tõnis laughed for the first time in years. He was going the wrong way, but then perhaps it would make the soldiers think that the camp was over there. He would lead them a dance, then double back to home. For the first time in years, he felt something good was happening to him.

'Shall I call them back?' Yuri asked.

'No, leave them,' Oleg snapped. 'Let them go off and play soldiers. With luck, they'll all get lost and do us a favour. Bring me the exclusion list that truck was working from. We will work back from there and see where it leads us.'

Chapter Fifteen

Dirty linen

Huw was finding it impossible to get to Maarja. Obstacles kept on being planted in the way. In the busy camp there was no private space, and Maarja appeared to be keeping him at a distance. He also felt awkward. That Maarja and Märt were acting like strangers added to the general confusion in his mind.

Above all, he didn't know what he was going to say. After all the years of hurt, to be facing the woman he had yearned for was beyond his dreams but so much had happened since they last spoke that he didn't know what, if anything, was left between them.

A woman of the camp handed him a canvas bag of laundry and told him to take it to the river. He started at the command, for it had broken through his reverie. He looked towards Juhan, who was cleaning his rifle and got an encouraging grin in return.

'I will take it for him, mother.'

'No,' the woman replied. 'Englishman can do it. Everybody gets to help and he is not busy.'

'It's fine, Juhan,' Huw replied, taking the bag and slinging it over his shoulder. 'Just point me in the direction of the river.'

The woman jerked her thumb to the side. 'Follow your nose.'

Huw set off in the direction vaguely indicated. Ahead, the foliage faded into a gloom and he wondered how he would pick up any clues for the river. Thankfully, the trees grew tall and thin, the branches did not come down to ground level. He would not have to hack his way through. He guessed the lighter line of sand in the needle-strewn floor was a path and made for it, keeping his senses focussed for clues.

The path was easy to follow, but after a while Huw knew it was not right. He could understand the logic of the camp not being too close to a river. It provided a clear path, an easy way for hostile forces to make their way through the dense forest and their approach would have been partly masked by the sound of running water. Even so, Huw felt the camp could not survive this far from the river. He looked around at the lie of the land.

To his right, the forest appeared to brighten, hinting at a clearing. He made his way towards it and was happy when his judgement proved correct. Even though it was still not in sight, he smelled the cool presence of the river. He carried on until he could see the water and hear the flow. There was an incongruous splashing ahead and Huw made for the sound, to find a woman washing clothes. She was beating them on a smoothed, bark-free tree trunk. By her side were two buckets of water. Huw did not need her to turn around. He knew it was Maarja and she was alone.

He walked up and gently put the bag by her.

'More clothes.'

Not the most original words, but all he could think of saying. Maarja looked up briefly and nodded her thanks and then continued working on a shirt with a flat stone. Huw stood by, wondering what his next move should be.

'Do you need help?'

She nodded, so he took up a shirt and wetted it, rubbing in a small amount of her precious soap, and found himself a stone. He watched her actions and tried to copy, rubbing the shirt in broad strokes with the stone. He needed to break the stifling tension.

'This seems a luxury for where we are,' he tried.

She continued to work on the clothes and barely looked at him as she replied: 'Where possible perhaps, life without rotting clothes and lice is good.'

They worked on together in silence until Maarja stopped and grabbed his hand that was holding the stone.

'You hold stone and work like this. It is to move dirt away, not grind it into this shirt.'

'I'm sorry, Maarja,' was all that Huw could think of saying.

He meant for the washing, or at least he started as if to mean that, but they both knew the words went far deeper.

Maarja kept working at the washing. The stone went back and forth time and again. She seemed to be having difficulty removing a spot of dirt. She worked and worked it through and then stood up with a sigh.

'Please, I need cleaner water, could you get it?'

She looked exhausted. Huw gave her a reassuring smile and removed the dirty bucket.

'Do not throw water into river,' she added. 'Should anyone be downstream, they may notice the dirt in water or soap bubbles.'

Huw nodded and fed the water to a nearby tree. He filled the bucket and turned, not failing to notice Maarja wiping her eyes with her hand.

'Are you well?' Huw asked. He was desperate to keep the conversation going, if not to start a significant one.

She chuckled, but not out of good humour. 'You Welsh ask stupid questions.'

He closed his eyes and tried to bury his frustration. 'I meant to ask if you were injured, how you have been, anything really. But you are so closed to me.'

She sighed, moving to hang the shirt on a branch, and reached for another. 'I have no injuries. I have lost my farm, my house and any chance of leading normal life, but yes, I am well. How are you?'

The tension was becoming unbearable. Huw was frustrated by the cricket match of a conversation. He could all but taste the warmth they had had before. The want of it weighed on his chest like a boulder. 'Maarja, you must believe me, I tried to return.'

She slammed the rock on the shirt in anger. 'How long was it? Twenty years? You obviously tried hard.'

'No, you must understand, I tried.'

'But the soft living in England was too much, no?'

'No, no it was not. Just listen to me.' His voice took a harder edge, cutting short her reply and making her eyes blaze in anger.

'When I was captured and sent back to the navy, they took me back to England and sentenced me to prison for five years.'

'For what?'

'For desertion. I was lucky I suppose, for at first they wanted to shoot me.'

Maarja had one hand on her hip. 'But then you were free.'

He nodded. 'Then I was freed, without any money and in the middle of the Depression. Nobody wanted criminals to work, especially not disgraced navy officers. I had nowhere to live, I was even begging on the streets for a while. But I managed to get home to my family. When I got there, I found they were nearly bankrupt. My father was dying. My mother was ill and the café was failing. I had to help them, by then I was all they had left.'

137

He winced and moved to sit on the tree trunk. The stone dropped from his hand. He couldn't meet her eyes. He had made a choice and not returned. How to explain? He ran a hand through his hair and said, 'I felt so low, had no hope. I thought if I could go back to my family and regain myself, I would be the stronger for it. My parents both died after a few years and I sold the café. I thought now I had the confidence and the money to get to you and find out what had happened, if you were still there. I wrote a few letters to you, trying to explain. I don't think I did it very well.'

'I saw no letters,' Maarja replied.

'On God's honour, Maarja, I wrote. I made my plans and... I was a fool. I made arrangements to travel through Germany to get to you. I... They...' Huw stopped, as the pain took hold of him. He slammed his hand on the tree. '...I found a man who said he could organise my trip. He wanted money and I paid him up front, most of it. Then, when he knew he could get no more without being discovered for the fraud he was, he sold me to the authorities as a German spy. I was arrested and taken into custody for questioning. They took a long time, trying to catch me out, to prove I was what he had said. Then they let me go and I had lost my chance. I was poor again and the world had changed. Travelling to Europe was not as easy as it had been.'

Maarja watched Huw as he spoke, taking in every movement and every word, but she held her own counsel. He continued: 'Then I started to doubt myself again. It had been too long. You had never replied, nothing had gone right for me, why should you be waiting or wanting to see me again? So, I stopped trying and settled into a dark hatred of the world. The government had not finished with me. They decided I would be useful as a spy on the Reds. They trained me to come here and spy on the Germans. I was to provide information about the Germans to help the Red invasion and then keep an eye on the Soviet occupation. Much good that has done. They had left it too late anyway, you had already got tired of waiting.'

Maarja's expression did not change and Huw looked away in sorrow. He heard her step forward and took her slap to his face.

'I did not wait?' she cried. 'Is that what you say? How long did you expect me to wait, not knowing if you were alive or dead? What was I supposed to do, move into convent, keeping myself ready for your return and for world to become how it was?'

Huw groaned and picked up the stone to work on his shirt.

'I could not ask this of you,' he said softly. 'I would not, but today, I just wanted you to know why.'

She took up her stone and began to work on a new shirt herself with raw, angry strokes. 'As you say, but how do I know you do not have family back in Wales? Wife, children.'

'My family is dead, I never married. Who would have me? I have no one – why else do you think I would have taken this mission?'

He stopped and watched her work. Maarja finally glanced up and as their eyes met, he saw the pain within the anger.

Her eyes narrowed. 'So, what next? What do you want me to say?'

'What can I do, Maarja? You have a husband and son.'

She looked away and back. 'You said you would come back and I waited as long as I could, but you never came.'

There was a long silence before Huw spoke. There was regret in his voice, tinged with hurt. 'I did come back, Maarja. It's why you are here and not sitting in a cattle truck on the way to Siberia.'

He wanted to take back the words as soon as he had said them, but approaching footsteps behind them killed the moment. Märt's voice broke in. 'Huw, I need you to come. I believe I have found perfect new camp for August. We need to talk with him about it. One of his patrols was caught also and only one has returned. I think they need to move quickly to new place.'

Huw took a deep breath and put down the shirt. He looked to Maarja, but she was motionless and her eyes refused to meet his. He walked to Märt, who nodded to Maarja and without waiting for a reply turned to lead him back to rejoin the camp.

August looked up from where he sat as they arrived back at the hollow. Next to him lay an exhausted youth, being gently spoon-fed a broth by the woman who had sent Huw earlier to the river. The boy muttered and became more agitated as Huw approached.

August cursed out loud. 'This young fool and two of his friends went back to ambush to loot vehicles for weapons. No surprise, Reds turned up to spoil party. Now two of them are dead and Tõnis is sick from lying in ditch for most of day. Pah! These youngsters think they know everything.'

'Is he badly injured?' Märt asked.

'He'll live, after some rest – and my boot up his arse,' August snapped. 'However he tells me worse news. He could hear soldiers talking then NKVD man arrived, looking for "English spy" and one of women that was on lorry.'

'What?' Huw exclaimed. 'Which one?'

'It only makes sense that it is your woman, Maarja.'

There was a silence as they digested the words.

'We have problem,' muttered Märt.

Huw laughed bitterly. 'Perhaps I can understand my problem, for the Reds planted me for the British. But why to hunt Maarja?'

'German files?' August asked.

Huw shook his head. 'No, something else is going on here. Maarja would be listed as Märt's wife. I'm not in those files. The Reds might know my code name, but not my background.'

'Unless they spy in England,' August said.

Huw sighed. 'Yes, but surely they wouldn't know, I mean this guy has followed me from the north. How would he know where to go?'

'Where else would you go to, my friend?' Märt said. 'They have files, they know about Juhan and me and they know your history also. This is my fault, August. I am sorry I have brought it here. It seems to me that we should leave you before it becomes difficult. You need to move your camp also, I think. Huw and I talked and we do not think this can be defended well.'

August looked indignant as he spread his arms to indicate the hollow. 'We have this and bunker, no?'

'You have. But you have more people now, where do they all go?' Märt said.

Huw came to sit down and pulled out his knife to draw in the ground.

'August, this bunker is good as hideaway for small unit, when they are being searched for. You are not that far from Andrus' farm also. They know they had people going there, and it will be first place they look. There are two GAZ jeeps dumped nearby, they are not too difficult to find.'

'We will take one when we leave and you move other or destroy it,' Märt said. 'Mounted gun could be used in your defences.'

August looked around at the land, and the people gathered to listen.

'I think what you say is true, this is good for operations, but if we need another base to live in, where will it be?'

'I have looked and I think I have found place,' Märt said. 'I will show you.'

August nodded. 'That is good, but where will you go?'

Märt's next words hit Huw like a hammer blow. 'I want Huw and Maarja out of Estonia.'

'What?' Huw looked at Märt, but his face was unreadable.

'What are you saying?'

'Yes, what are you saying?'

Huw turned to find Maarja had returned to the hollow.

'You are being hunted by a Russian spy catcher,' Huw told her. 'Who also wants me.'

Her face clouded as she nodded understanding. 'Why is this?'

'I do not know if it is because of me or Märt,' Huw replied.

'Given that choice it is you,' Märt said. 'This man is operating alone. If he wanted Maarja only as family of Metsavend, he would send Destroyer unit.'

Huw turned to Maarja. 'Do you know why?'

Maarja shrugged. 'I cannot say. Perhaps they know I was working for government in old times. If he is searching for us, we are not good company to be with. So I agree, I will not stay.'

'I cannot leave Estonia, Märt,' Huw said. 'I have to keep telling the West what is going on here.'

August stood up and gently steered Huw and Märt away. 'We will continue this talk as you take me to place you have found for camp. Märt and Huw alone will take me. Then I will come back and explain what we will do.'

He grabbed his rifle and barked a few orders at his men. Without waiting to see if he was being followed, August started out following Märt's indication of the path to take. There was no conversation on the journey. August was busy looking for landmarks as they walked. Huw's mind was in turmoil. Whatever Märt's reasons, he decided they would not leave this new site until he knew what was going on. He'd had enough of Märt's constant secrets

The clearing was large, less of a bowl than the hollow. There were plenty of contours, which Märt indicated could be used for bunkers or shelters to be built. Huw scanned the area and nodded his approval.

'This is good. It is so far in the forest, any hostile force would have to be on foot to get here. It has good access to water and is easy to create shelters. It has a good low-lying escape route, with a lot of cover from outside.'

'Good for all except siege of army,' August agreed. 'I hear your argument and I will talk to my Metsavennad. Now we talk about your plans.'

'März is right,' Huw said. 'I am toxic. I've thought about it a lot on this walk. They have sent a specially trained man for me, that means they will search harder where they think I am. I will bring them to your camp, August, so I must go. März, you have to tell me though. Why Maarja and why to leave Estonia?'

März shrugged and sat down. He picked up a stick and started to sharpen it.

'Why it is Maarja? I do not know, but it is. She is toxic here also, so you must leave, for there is no hope of living here. You are compromised. You are not Estonian also. True, you have lived among us, but people still know you are not one of us and someone will tell.'

'So what? Nobody has ever caused a problem with this,' Huw replied.

'Times have changed. They take anyone who has opposed them. They take anyone who might. They take their friends and families.' He threw the stick away and walked to the edge of the clearing, fury burning in his eyes. 'We are already broken land, but they wish to crush us. To take away our identity. We have resistance, but little armed and not co-ordinated. I talked to August and he agrees with me. Here, as in north, Germans did not leave us prepared to fight, they left us to die.' März's voice was close to breaking. 'They have not listened in London. They do not *hear* you in your small messages. No, you must go and tell them to their faces. This is what happens, this is why you need to go. You must take Maarja away from this, safe from this hell.'

August nodded. 'We are but small band of people here, not army. If West came to help us, when Germans are beaten, we can rise and fight – and win – but we cannot do this alone. West must come; all this is inhuman. März is right, you must go and tell them.'

'How would we get away?' Huw asked. 'The Reds destroyed all the boats in Estonia when they first came here and we have no radio.'

'We will find way,' Märt replied. 'There will be Metsavennad near coast or on islands. We will find way of getting message and perhaps get British to fetch you or send you to Sweden.'

Huw winced at the thought of what they were proposing.

'I hate what has been done here. You are driven to the forest to scratch out an existence like animals. I feel I am running away, but if this is the best action, I will do it.'

Märt held out his hand to shake and Huw gripped the forearm. 'But you tell me this, my friend. You and Maarja, you act as if you are strangers or worse. What has happened?'

Märt shook his head. 'I did her great wrong. That is all I will say about it. Maarja will tell you rest if she wishes.'

'Then it is settled,' August said. 'We all have journeys to make and we must start them soon. We should return to camp.'

Huw felt it was far from settled, but again he had lost the moment, as Märt set off for the camp. They were faster on the path back, but once again in silence. Huw was still trying to fathom his two dilemmas – Why was Maarja being hunted by the spy catcher and what had passed between her and Märt? He was so absorbed that he nearly missed the movement up ahead.

He looked again. It was a man approaching. Huw ducked behind a tree and crouched down. His companions heard his movement and looked around. He gave frantic hand signals and they took cover.

Slowly the scene opened up. It was a patrol of Red Army soldiers. Why they had stretched this far into the forest Huw had no idea, but they appeared to be searching for something. Eight men were present, seven were armed and one was not, but had a radio pack on his back.

'They are searching for us,' Huw whispered. 'We must stop them radioing their position.'

Märt nodded and indicated with his hand for Huw and August to flank the party on either side. The soldiers halted and gathered round in a group. The radio operator crouched down, took the radio off his back, fished out the handset and prepared the aerial.

Märt aimed carefully and shot the man in the throat as he lifted the headset. The man spun round with a choking cry and fell still. The others crouched low and turned to fire in the direction of his shot. August immediately returned fire and the soldiers dived for whatever cover they could find.

The soldiers had managed to pick out Märt's position and concentrated their fire on it. Huw tried a sustained burst of fire to divert their attention. He realised it had worked far too well, when he saw to his horror a lobbed grenade flying through the air towards him. The tree he hid behind was not going to provide enough cover. Without any thought to the consequences, he reversed his rifle and as the grenade came into range, took one step forward and hit it back with the butt of his rifle, dropping quickly to the floor again.

Luck can appear when you least expect it and never be around when you most want it. Following the explosion and cries of pain that ensued, Huw noted that it was favouring him today. He rolled and lifted his head to view the scene. Three men were running away, directly at August's position. August had no problem despatching two of them and Märt shot the third.

Silence followed. Even the birds made no sound. Märt was the first to surface, very cautiously walking towards the bodies. August and Huw followed, all the time watching the soldiers for any signs of movement. No threat remained. The unfortunate soldiers lay dead where they fell. August looked over to Huw and shook his head.

'Explain to me what you just did again?' He held up his hands to stop him. 'No, no. I do not think I want to know. You could have shot yourself in leg or worse.'

'Or stayed where he was and dance with shrapnel,' Märt added checking the radio set. 'It actually looks as if it is still working.'

August looked around the forest for signs of life, but there were none. 'You were right, Märt. If Reds look to send men this far into forest, it will not be long before they threaten our camp.'

Märt was deep in thought. 'Sending eight in with light arms was suicide; what were they thinking?'

'Perhaps to pinpoint us when we use radio,' Huw replied grimly. 'These were expendable. If we take the radio away and use it far from the camp, it will throw them off. We can play them at their own game.'

Yuri came running over from the signal van, to the jeep where Oleg sat studying a map. They were at the edge of the forest. A truckload of troops waited impatiently for orders.

'We lost them.' Yuri reported. 'The men made contact with the enemy, but have gone quiet. I assume they were killed. It has been thirty minutes now.'

'Do we think the radio still works?' Oleg asked.

'We think so, but it's hard to tell,' Yuri replied.

'Then this part of the mission is a success, Yuri.'

'Do you think they will use the radio?'

'Undoubtedly, Comrade Yuri,' Oleg replied. 'But they will be fools if they use it at the bandit camp. It would send our moths to their flame. We wait for them, they will not be long, and the temptation is too great. They will move off: three, maybe four people. If we can get all three of our units to keep listening around this forest, we will pinpoint them.'

Yuri made a face. 'We know where the base is now. Perhaps not exactly, but enough to send in a unit to seek and destroy.'

'Not yet, Yuri. That will do for the bandits, yes, but I want this spy alive. We will need to bide our time. Besides, if we are close and they see us coming, they will scatter. No, let's keep listening and you make sure that any signals received are sent to the translator. I have already given him the English codes.'

Chapter Sixteen

Märt and Maarja

Huw sought out Maarja when he arrived back at the camp. He found her sitting in the shelter of a large tree whose roots had grown out and around the edge of the hollow before returning into the ground. One day the tree would fall, as its weight undermined the soil base and its roots further loosened the ground in its strife for security and nourishment. For now however, it formed a good shelter. Juhan calmly sat with his mother.

Maarja looked up at Huw's arrival, but showed little sign of warmth. The adrenalin following the skirmish had worn away any diplomacy that Huw may have held and he had no desire for a continuation of the confrontation they had had at the river. Abruptly, he moved off to deposit the weapons retrieved from the dead soldiers. He felt dog-tired, sank to the ground in a corner and let the strength drain from him. He awoke to the sound of approaching footsteps. His hand strayed to his knife by instinct, then relaxed. Maarja stood over him, holding a mess tin.

'It is water. Fresh.'

'Thank you,' Huw mumbled, sitting up and taking the tin. He sipped the water slowly and then wiped his mouth.

'Are you still angry with me?'

Maarja shrugged. 'I am angry with world. Nothing in my life is easy, no matter how much I wish it. So my husband wishes me to go with you to England.'

Huw nodded.

'And this makes *you* angry?'

Huw shook his head. 'What I have done here is minimal. I have arrived too late to help against the Germans. The Metsavennad I joined have been slaughtered and now I have a Russian spy catcher on my tail. I feel I will be leaving with nothing, having achieved nothing.'

'Perhaps this is not so. By explaining to English why this land makes you achieve nothing, you will provide information. They do not know of this now, but you will tell them.'

Her eyes followed his every move, looking for a reaction.

147

'He has spoken to you then?' Huw asked.

She smiled thinly. 'He and I do not speak. August explained what has passed.'

'And?'

Maarja sighed and looked away.

'I understand. I do not know why this man hunts me also, but I do not wish to draw him here. He will hurt others and they suffer enough.'

'I am coming too, Huw,' Juhan's voice rang out and he hovered into view behind Maarja, like a proverbial Cheshire cat. 'We can all go together. It will be fun.'

Huw cringed at the words. Was it always a game to the young man? Then a realisation hit him. 'You have had this conversation, so how long have I been asleep?'

Juhan made a face. 'Hours, camp has mostly moved out. You need to come now with us. You look troubled, what is wrong?'

Huw could only sigh and give a rueful smile. 'I have killed some men recently. Six – maybe seven. It does not sit well with me.'

'There is time when you do what you must to survive,' Maarja snapped. 'That time is now. Whatever happens, you do what you must.'

'Yes, but I can still regret.'

'So long as it does not stop you pulling trigger,' Maarja bit back as she turned to leave.

'What happened to you, Maarja?' Huw asked.

Maarja turned again and spread her arms. 'Look around you and don't ask stupid questions.'

'Come,' Juhan said. 'We must go also. Here is Märt.'

'We have hidden bodies,' Märt said. 'Though only necessity means they deserve burial. What happens here?'

Huw's teeth grated at the question. Too many secrets, too much bitterness, and a botched mission to boot. He was fed up of being polite. 'I will tell you how it is. I've gone along with your plans and all because of who you people were to me, once. The world seems to have changed and I haven't time for stories or half-truths. From this point on you don't hide anything from me, understood?'

He pointed at Märt and Maarja, but tried to ignore Juhan. He knew he would get a smile and a nod which could shatter his ill-humour. At this moment, he needed the energy of his anger, no

148

matter how negative it was. He stabbed a finger at them. 'Another thing, if we are talking of leaving this country, it's a hard road and a dangerous one. No room for childish antics. I don't care what has gone on with you two before. I really couldn't give a damn any more. But if you are travelling together, you damn well start talking to each other as of now. It's death for us all if we don't work together. Understood?'

It seemed to take an age, but through the looks of surprise and wounded pride came two reluctant nods.

'Good,' said Huw, dryly. 'It saves me knocking your bloody heads together. Let's go to the new camp and you tell me what you are planning, Märt.'

He stormed past Juhan without waiting for a reply. Juhan quickly fell into step with him and muttered two simple words. 'Thank you.'

Like a mist on a summer's morning, Huw's anger was fading away, leaving space for the old pain to flood in. He clapped Juhan's arm.

'Get some rest.'

Huw, Maarja and Juhan set off at first light, heading south. At the same time, a second party had set off towards Andrus' farm: Märt, two men and a woman. Both Märt and August had agreed that the numbers were not important, providing there was clearly a woman in the party. The plan was simple, Huw needed to find a place deep in the forest to send a message to the British. Märt would take one jeep to a given rendezvous, the other team would take a jeep northwards towards Tallinn as a decoy. It was important that they were seen to be going that way.

Their journey was possibly the more perilous, so Huw was not surprised that only three volunteers had been forthcoming. They risked much. Indeed, August's camp was risking everything and Huw was humbled by their generosity.

'We must succeed, Juhan,' he said. 'For these people.'

Juhan nodded soberly. Then his face sprouted the inevitable grin. 'We will succeed, Huw. Don't worry, coast is not far.'

Huw was flustered by Juhan's eagerness.

'Just find me a spot with a good signal, young man.'

'Always,' came the cheerful reply.

Maarja followed them in silence. She did not suffer, but looked troubled. Huw had no idea how to start any conversation with her. Every gambit had led him nowhere. Without warning, she stumbled and fell with a cry. Huw rushed to her side, but she shrugged off the proffered help.

'It is alright really, I'm just stupid city girl. I am fine,' she said.

Juhan had gone on ahead and now appeared just out of earshot. He turned and gave a grin before moving on.

'He is a good boy,' Huw said with a grin.

'Yes,' she agreed. 'But he sees world too simply. It means he has no fear, and we have to fear for him.'

They moved onto a boggier patch and their pace slowed down to respect the uneven ground.

'It's the same with the young all over,' Huw continued. 'They always see themselves as invincible. Just like that young boy who went back to the ambush. A few days rest and he's already up volunteering to be in the jeep.'

'He seems to have taken us under his wing,' Maarja agreed. 'I fear for them, they will not pass close inspection as prison escort for young woman.'

'No, but all they need to do is be seen and then run like hell.'

They carried on in silence, for fear of where speech might lead. Juhan found a patch of stable ground in the middle of the marsh, hidden by reeds. He had already set up the radio when they caught up with him.

'Here, we can see people approaching from a long way,' Huw remarked. 'And stay hidden from them.'

Juhan just shrugged and smiled away his ignorance.

'Who is going to see us here?' Maarja asked.

Huw ignored the question for a while, whilst he concentrated on the radio. He noticed she still watched his every move, but her eyes were tinged with sadness and regret. He flashed a wan smile in reply. He hated himself for not knowing how to make things right, how to change their world for the better.

'We know the man is looking for the two of us,' he said, 'and this patrol happens to bump into us in the forest with a radio? It's all too easy, too lucky. Are we being forced into a trap?'

'So what do we do?' she asked.

'We need to use this radio; it's our only contact. He knows this, but what he doesn't know is that Tõnis heard his conversation and so we know of him. That is our last ace to play. Hopefully with that we can spring the trap and jump clear in time.'

She nodded and reached out a hand. 'Give me your pistol. I will help guard whilst you do this.'

Huw passed it over without hesitation. He was not surprised by the thrill of her touch. He set to work immediately, trying his call-sign and waiting for a reply. It seemed to take forever until the very faint reply came back. He listened hard and then cursed.

'They tell me to stand by,' he fumed.

'It is as well we are not in hurry,' Juhan said softly.

'We have a rendezvous,' Huw snapped back.

Juhan was undaunted. 'We still have plenty of time.'

What seemed to be a burst of static broke through Huw's thoughts. It was his reply. He listened and then typed a quick response in Morse.

'Cover blown. Exposed to bears, request recovery.'

'Request confirmed. Rendezvous point Kappa Alpha Alpha. Call in three days to confirm details.'

'Three days? What do they think this is? A bloody holiday?' Huw growled, as he packed the headset and radio into its rucksack.

'Perhaps this is good, said Maarja. 'Three days will get us distance from here,'

'Yes and somehow they want us in Haapsalu. I'm sure the Reds haven't missed the town on their way to Berlin.'

He felt her hand on his arm and she smiled apologetically.

'We do what we must,' she said softly. He patted her hand and slung the radio pack across his shoulders.

It was a good two hours before Juhan led them to the point where they were due to meet Märt. He was nowhere to be seen. The jeep stood as if abandoned. Then as they approached, there was a low whistle and Märt dropped from his perch in a nearby tree.

He listened to the report and shrugged.

'There is nothing surprising here. We need to get to coast. We will get close and then call again. It is unlikely they will expect us to march into town. You are too cautious, Huw.'

Huw shook his head. 'There is a lot at stake.'

151

They remained hidden until dusk. What meagre rations they had, they consumed. There was no desire for conversation as they waited, with the spectre of the mission hanging over them.

As the light began to fade, they started loading up the jeep ready. Huw wondered how many more midge bites he had acquired to add to the itchy scabs already peppering his skin. He longed to get underway just to get his mind off the irritation. The GAZ jeep was ready when Märt suddenly hissed, 'Down, quick. I hear vehicle.'

Huw hit the ground and rolled into the long grass. The sound grew closer and closer. Then came a sight he had not expected. The other captured jeep shot past, with Tõnis standing behind the machine gun. He fired a warning burst back, before they were gone. After a few seconds, another jeep sped past, just out of range. Then a combination of motorcycles and a truck came past like a cavalcade.

'They are too damn early,' Märt shouted, rising from his hiding place.

'Yes, but they have given us a start,' Huw replied. 'Let's make the most of it and pray they are delivered safely.'

Oleg's patience appeared to be paying off. A radio message had finally been intercepted. He ran the message note from the radio operator personally to his code-breaker.

'Get working on this now, it will conform to the British codes given. I want to read it within the hour.'

He could hardly contain his wolfish grin, and when he saw the translation he could have danced with delight. 'Yuri, how are the roadblocks?'

'All set up, no way around them and not much notice as to their presence. The roads towards Tallinn, Rapla, Pärnu and Koluvere are all covered.'

'Take that last one further away from Märjamaa. Go west, closer to Sipa.'

'You are sure they will be driving, Comrade Oleg?'

Oleg punched the piece of paper he held.

'There is no other way. He has called for recovery and the only way in range of the allies is a boat. The nearest coast is seventy kilometres. How else do they get there, especially when they have two stolen GAZ jeeps?'

'Which way do you think they will go?'

'North or west, but I would prefer to be prepared for surprises.'

Yuri left, and Oleg removed a battered photograph from his wallet. In faded sepia, a group of people sat proudly in front of a farm. The photo had not fared well over the years. He brushed it gently with his fingertips, then sighed and placed it back in his wallet. It was always good to be reminded of what he was fighting for and what must be done.

A few hours later, Oleg settled down for a catnap, only to be woken as Yuri climbed into the jeep and started up the engine.

'A jeep was intercepted on the Tallinn Road. Bandits – two men and a woman. I have no word if any are alive.'

He set the jeep in motion and was soon at full acceleration. Yuri smiled towards his boss. Soon this sorry chase would end and the real work would begin.

Oleg looked straight ahead frowning. He made no indication of having heard Yuri. It was difficult to tell if his mind was concentrating on the present. Yuri knew there was something beyond orders that drove the man, but it didn't matter to him. He would follow Oleg to the gates of hell. He had already proven the fact in the ruins of Stalingrad. He was surprised seconds later when Oleg burst into life.

'No, west. Take the road to Kaluvere,' he shouted.

'What?'

'The jeep is a ruse, there are four of them now. Two bandits from the north are husband and son of the woman – those three plus the spy. Take the road west and keep your eyes open for them.'

'And what of the other jeep?'

'If there is any information to be had, they will tell us. One way or another.'

Chapter Seventeen

Captured

'Tõnis, Tõnis,'

The voice broke softly through his pain. Tõnis opened his eyes, but the world was a blur. He had been in the jeep, pretending to be a soldier guarding a female prisoner. They had been surprised by a roadblock and had elected to charge it, machine gun blazing at the back. It had happened years ago; his numbed brain even questioned if it had happened.

'Tõnis. Thank God you are alive. We were worried.'

The voice was familiar, but sounded so far away and echoing as if in a cave.

'Father?' Tõnis croaked.

'Yes, Tõnis. You have done well, you can rest here,' the voice's soothing words washed over him.

'Is Monika there?'

'Yes, yes she is. All is well.'

'Good,' Tõnis sighed. His shoulder burned and he felt a bit queasy. His head felt bound tightly in cotton wool.

'You are very brave, Tõnis,' the voice continued. 'I was so proud. They all escaped, you know. We helped them and now they are free.'

Tõnis' lips quivered into a smile, although it caused him pain. The voice continued its silky tone, washing over him like an ointment, gently relaxing him.

'British boat is trying to pick them up and cannot find them. Where shall they look? Do you know?'

The voice was gentle, but had grown excited and urgent. The smile on Tõnis' lips broadened, although his wound made it look like a lop-sided leer.

'Põltsamaa,' he whispered.

He felt a hand stroke his face and the gentle voice returned.

'Tõnis, how can this be true? Põltsamaa is nowhere near sea.'

Tõnis tried to sit up, but his broken body could not find the energy. His thighs felt warm and wet, he could not feel his toes.

'Yes, you are right,' he whispered softly. 'Põltsamaa is not by sea. Neither are you my father, you traitorous bastard!'

The blur was clearing. He could make out green clothing, like a uniform. The voice murmured over him.

'Tõnis, how can you say such things?'

Tõnis wished he could spit in the eye of his tormentor. He knew his body had no energy to get close, yet he still had the willpower to curse the man as his face came slowly into focus.

'Because you are weasel, Otto,' he snapped. 'You always were, and now coward and traitor also.'

Otto leant closer and Tõnis could smell the man's bad breath, or did he just imagine it? He wished he could smell lavender; he loved the smell of lavender.

'You had better rest now, Tõnis. Save your energy, for you will need it for talking later. When they have finished, you will tell them where bandits went, where your base is – and that night is day, if they ask you to.'

Tõnis sighed and slightly shook his head. It felt like lead. His body was more relaxed now and warm, perhaps warmer than he had felt for years.

'No, you Destroyer bastard. I'm going back to my family now. I've kept them waiting long enough.'

The vision faded and the smell receded. Tõnis was aware of a strange light-headedness, and a feeling of travel. He embraced it with joy.

'I have to say the roadblock is too far west,' Yuri shouted over the screaming of the jeep engine at full pelt. 'The map puts a road in front of it running back to the Tallinn road. They could easily double back on us.'

'No, it will be perfect,' Oleg replied. 'You will see.'

The road was empty as they set off. Märt unconsciously chewed his knuckles as he drove, Huw knew exactly what that meant. He had chided Märt in the past for the dead skin that would mix in the bread.

'There is trouble, Märt?' he asked.

Märt nodded. 'Yes, it is all too easy. No sign of enemy. We may have to change our plans.'

Huw turned to Maarja and Juhan in the back.

'Keep an eye out for any signs of life.'

A few kilometres on, Juhan shouted and pointed at the bend in the road ahead.

'I saw it there, headlight reflection through woods. Only for second, but definitely there ahead.'

Märt slowed the jeep down to a stop and killed the engine.

'I would rather not chance roadblock and if I was setting one, it would be somewhere like around this corner. Listen.'

For a long time there was nothing, then a metallic click rang faintly in the air. 'They've told us where they are,' Huw whispered.

Märt started the engine. 'We'll double back and go north.'

They set off at a reasonable rate but kept the headlights off. It wasn't too long before Huw's eyes adjusted to the darkness, although it was still a perilous decision to drive in such conditions at speed. Again Märt stopped and listened. This time they heard the sound of a racing engine and skidding tyres.

'Someone's after us,' Huw muttered. 'We won't reach the road in time.'

Märt looked across to Maarja. 'We will need to go to your farm and hide there or in forest until it is clear.'

Maarja nodded and smiled. 'Perhaps we will have clearer road at dawn.'

Märt pulled the jeep off the road and Huw once more found himself bouncing down the track to his former home. He was full of mixed emotions about this change of plan, but he could not think of an alternative. Not now at any rate.

They sped into the courtyard and the jeep screeched to a halt. Huw ran to the barn to open the great doors and hide the vehicle, whilst Juhan went to the house. As Huw reached the barn door, he was stopped by the sight of the bolt. It was not secure. Huw frowned, in old times, the door would always be bolted. The whole situation didn't feel at all right. What had it been like when they had visited here days before?

He turned to shout a word of caution to the others. Then his world was full of the clicks of cartridges loading into breeches. He looked round and into a forest of loaded rifles. He raised his hands and turned slowly to see Juhan being marched from the house. The others stood immobile at the jeep.

Märt's look said it all. The trap had been sprung and they had failed to jump clear.

The evening went on forever. The four were roughly thrown into the army truck and taken back to the police station in Märjamaa. They were dragged from the truck into the building and then separated. Huw lost count of the number of times he was hit by a man screaming at him in Russian. At one impasse, his bruised mouth managed to tell the man to engage in a nocturnal activity that was physically impossible. This brought the reward of more beating until his body gave up the fight and he slipped into unconsciousness.

Huw woke as he was dragged out of his cell. He was slung unceremoniously into the back of a vehicle, the door slammed shut and it set off rapidly. It was pitch black inside and Huw had to grope around to find a wall to prop his bruised body against. Above the rasping engine note, he heard a gentle sobbing.

'Maarja?' Huw whispered.

The sobbing ceased and a small voice answered. 'Yes, Huw.'

Huw found the floor with his hands and knees. He touched her leg, then felt her knee. By understanding the direction her leg was pointing, he moved to her side.

'Maarja, are you well?'

'I am tied. My hands behind my back, with wire. It hurts,' she whispered.

He set about freeing her. The wire was barbed and he had to work carefully. Long, painful minutes passed, until he had untwisted the end enough to start unwinding it from her wrists. She gasped when he slowly lifted a barb away that had dug into her flesh.

He managed to put an arm around her shoulder and gently brought her to him. She crumpled into his embrace and wept. Huw felt his own pain dull slightly, as he tried to absorb her sorrow. He tried to soothe her, telling her it would all be alright, but it felt like a lie.

He remembered the two of them hitching a lift to Märjamaa, escaping to a new life. So long ago and so far from the cruelty of the present. He could not stop crying.

'Courage, my love. Courage,' he whispered.

In time he felt her relax. Then out of the darkness, her fingers touched his face, retracting quickly when he grunted with pain.

'Huw, you are bleeding,' she whispered and Huw forced a smile.

'It is nothing, honestly. I will live.' Somewhere within came a feeling of inner strength. With Maarja so close, he began to revive. 'We will all live, my love. I promise you.'

'Where are they taking us?' she asked.

'I don't know, Tallinn I assume. If they are going towards Rapla, they are certainly taking the long way round, as they should have turned off right immediately. I'm assuming they already have prepared the old Gestapo headquarters.'

Huw shut up. This was a direction he did not want to take the conversation. Instead he asked, 'Do you know where Märt and Juhan are?'

'I don't,' she whispered. 'I never saw them after we were taken from farm.'

'It's alright, Maarja, we will find them again,' Huw promised, praying she would not ask how.

They clung to each other in silence, both lost in thoughts, memories and regrets. Finally, Huw knew he had to say what had been weighing him down for years.

'I should have come, Maarja. I should not have given in to my weakness and doubt. Even if it meant begging my way across Europe, I should have found a way. After all we had done to get to live together, I should not have let my courage leave me.'

She squeezed him tight until he grunted, as his bruised ribs and kidneys complained.

'I should have waited, Huw, I should have been stronger. I too was weak, I needed support and Märt was there. I am sorry also.'

The tears flowed down his face now, a testament to the lost years. He gently kissed her head.

'But you have a good son now, a strong one.' He felt her body stiffen and he repeated the promise. 'We will find him, Maarja. We will all come through this alive.'

Yet in his heart, he still didn't believe it. He looked around for some means of escape, but the darkness was all-encompassing. There seemed nothing left to do but conserve what energy they had. Instinct made him lean towards her and kiss her gently on the lips.

159

'For so long I had wanted to do that once again,' he whispered. 'But here I feel so sad.'

'It is no matter,' she replied. 'It was worth waiting for. And I believe you, we will prevail. Just believe this yourself.'

Huw could not remember when they drifted off to sleep. The sudden jolt of the truck coming to a stop reminded him of all the aches and bruises he was bearing. The engine was switched off and they heard a lot of shouting outside. Although unable to understand the Russian voices, Huw could hear the tell-tale signs of an argument. He could have sworn he heard a weapon being cocked. In the end, one of the shouting voices receded, throwing insults to the last.

Maarja gripped Huw's arm and whispered. 'Something strange has happened here. One was demanding we were taken to NKVD headquarters. Other man refused, he said his orders were from higher authority and he was quite happy to shoot anyone who stood in his way. This is strange, what do you think is happening?'

'I wish I knew Maarja, but I suppose we will find out soon enough.'

The truck continued on, but at a slower pace. Huw felt he could relax now he was not being thrown around the inside of the vehicle. His lower back felt detached from the rest of his body. The road became what felt like cobbled streets and then there was more shouting outside, before the truck came to a standstill and the engine once more came to a stop.

For a long time, there was no sound from outside. Huw made his way towards the door. He felt his way around the frame, but it was useless. There was no mechanism to spring it from the inside.

'It's like we've been put in a safe,' he muttered. A scrambling sound came from the door and with a complaining creak it swung open. Huw was blinded by the light flooding in. He screwed his eyes shut then cautiously opened them to focus on a rose-red sunrise. The pink clouds on the horizon caressed the buildings, before slowly fading upwards to the soft light blue of the morning sky. Huw cursed the fate that would make it the last one he ever saw, it was so beautiful and warm.

Ahead of him stood an army officer, the khaki uniform contrasted by the blue band around his hat. His fair hair and steel-grey eyes made Huw wonder if he would not look out of place in the

German army. The sound of footsteps made him turn and he saw Maarja being taken forcefully out of the truck by a dark-haired young subaltern. His slightly Slavic appearance was more what Huw imagined a Russian to look like. The officer smiled at his captives, waiting for them to adjust to their surroundings. He appeared to be in no hurry whatsoever. Huw ignored him and looked around. He had to be alert for any opportunities for escape. He knew it would be a very difficult thing for two people, but now he was with Maarja, there was no way he would leave without her.

They were on a quayside. In the distance, he could see Tallinn's spires and walls. Three or four ordinary soldiers stood guard, rifles at the ready. The ruins of the monastery of Pirita nestled in trees in the distance. If only he could reach there, he was sure he could find a way out for the two of them to the east.

'Welcome to Tallinn,' the officer said in perfect English. 'It seems a pity to waste such a beautiful morning. We shall go for a short boat ride.'

Huw's brain went blank at the words, making the officer smile.

'Come come, Huw Williams, former sub-lieutenant of the Royal Navy. There is no need for pretence. I will only speak to you in English for I know you will understand this. There is a journey we must make, you and I. A sightseeing tour, one you would never have had the chance to do on your *Caradoc*, hmm? Please.'

He indicated for them to climb on board a small launch and followed them onto the deck, drawing his pistol.

'So now please experience our hospitality. I apologise, for I would have used a stinking Estonian fishing boat, had I been able to find one. Unfortunately, we had to destroy them all to stop people running away from their destiny, as you have done until now. Please enjoy the view, Tallinn I am told is quite attractive from the bay. It is not far to our destination.'

Huw went to Maarja, who stood staring back at the stern, whilst the boat slowly made its way into the Baltic.

'This will be last time I set eyes on Tallinn,' she murmured. 'Perhaps it is best, for I could not bear to see what these people will do to my beloved city.'

'Where along the coast do you think he will go?' Huw asked.

Maarja sighed. 'I do not know, he seems to be heading out to sea. Will he take us to Russia? Will he use me to get to you?'

'It seems to be an awful long way of going about things,' Huw replied. 'He could have done that before we left the mainland. Do you know this man? Why is he so knowledgeable and so politely cruel?'

Maarja shook her head. 'I have no idea. Should we just jump in and drown ourselves?'

'The guards are waiting for that. We must look for opportunities to die only when there is no chance of freedom left.'

'Don't leave it too late.'

Huw tried to imagine the bay as he remembered it, teeming with British ships. He wished he could change it back to that scene, despite how impossible it was. All he could do for now was watch Tallinn growing smaller and smaller as it was taken from him one more time.

'Perhaps Märt and Juhan found a way out,' he said. 'You would be surprised how resourceful Märt can be. I certainly was, he's a different man to the one I knew.'

Maarja took a deep breath and grabbed his hand. She would not look at him, but kept her eyes fixed on the Tallinn skyline, as if it was the only thing left to cling to.

'Whatever happens, Huw, I am glad to have you with me. I just wish we had more time.'

Huw put his arm around her. 'I could murder a bacon sandwich. Do you think they might oblige me?'

She smiled and then her face clouded. 'Huw, there is something I must tell you, I think. Märt and I, what is between us? We swore to keep it secret, but....' She tailed off and smiled. 'You know in this situation, we may never have another chance.'

The soldiers were nonchalantly sitting around them and for a second, their closeness made Maarja hesitate, as if she was scared for the world to know – and the moment once again was lost.

'There is much to take in here,' the officer said from behind them. 'But we have just about reached our destination. Do you know the island of women, Mr Williams? Your good lady can tell you all about it, whilst we approach to land. Not too long now.'

Huw felt Maarja stiffen. He looked to her for an indication. She had gone pale, her jaw was tense and her eyes filled with tears.

'My love, what is it?'

'It is island we sent Bolsheviks to in 1919, when you brought ships in after battle. You know this place. Naissaar.'

Naissaar.

The word hung in Huw's mind. Then a flurry of images, voices and emotions came. He held onto Maarja for support as realisation grabbed him and dragged him down deeper.

There was a man with steel-grey eyes. An officer on board Spartak. *He didn't look like the enemy, and despite his predicament, Huw imagined him in better times, with a warm smile and a ready laugh. The men seemed to hold him in high esteem, even in the classless society that the ship and his nation had. He was a dynamic figure and Huw was certain he would be trouble.*

The man welcomed the boarding party with a crisp salute as they stepped onto the ship.

'My name is Commander Ivanovic,' he said. 'I surrender this vessel to the English navy.'

'Sub-Lieutenant Williams,' Huw replied, feeling the calibre of his salute was far below the one he had received. 'I accept your surrender. Please prepare your vessel to be taken in tow.'

Ivanovic barked a few orders and the men moved to obey, although there appeared no impetus to follow instructions other than because it was an order.

'My men are ready to comply. Please, we surrender to you, not Estonians. You must not give us to Estonians.'

Huw nodded, buoyed by the importance of the charge placed in him. The responsibility for these men, looking so downcast and beaten, made him feel powerful. He smiled sympathetically.

'Don't worry, we never give our prisoners to others. Now, please request your men to assess and repair the damage you have incurred by running aground. We don't need a sinking ship as well.'

Ivanovic held up his hand for patience. 'Please, this is a Soviet vessel. Such decisions must be made by all comrades. You must let us do this.'

Shocked by the statement and stuck for a formal answer, Huw found himself nodding dumbly. Ivanovic turned and spoke to the sailors with him and before Huw could think of what to say next, they turned and headed below decks. His heart sank, as he knew he had lost the moment. He turned to his small boarding party.

'Stand easy for now, this may take a while.'

He shouted at the back of Ivanovic's head as the man disappeared below deck, 'Don't take too long or you might notice your feet getting a bit wet.'

The chuckles from his party helped to bolster his flagging nerve. First command of a serious situation and the honour of leading a boarding of a captured vessel – he was desperate to gain a good reputation from it. He mouthed a silent prayer of relief when half an hour later, Ivanovic returned to report all was well.

'The crew are happy to be prisoners of the English and the pumps have begun to clear the sea from the ship. We are ready for towing to harbour.'

Huw's relief was must have shown on his face. 'Thank you,' he said. 'I wish to inspect the vessel now, if you don't mind.'

Months later, Huw was admitted into the Ministry of the Interior. The broad room seemed teeming with life as a sweet-smiling lady with her hair swept up showed him into the office, clutching a file to her chest as he passed. She called out for Maarja and followed up with a cheerful burst of Estonian, which caused a few of the other women in the room to giggle.

Huw was shown into a small room and presently the door opened as Maarja swept in. With a broad smile, she moved quickly to him and launched into a passionate kiss, which he could not resist.

'Huw, at work? How inappropriate,' she beamed.

'I have come here on formal business, my love,' Huw said, with a blush.

Maarja smiled back. 'But first we may...' she stopped. 'Huw, what is wrong?'

'I bring a message from Admiral Cowan. I need to convey it to the minister immediately.'

Maarja nodded and the warmth died. 'So, perhaps if admiral himself would avail himself of duties to attend, then minister would be available. However, as he sends junior attaché, it is only proper to be heard by same.'

He was surprised by her sudden chilly tone of formality and his smile froze in confusion. He coughed nervously and drew out of his inside pocket a letter.

'Admiral Cowan has written to the Estonian government, deploring the execution of prisoners on the island of Naissaar. He requests that all such activities cease and the men are accorded the rights of prisoners of war. I mean no disrespect by my being the postman and I certainly had no desire for you to think badly of me for being so formal, but this is serious. Lives are being spent here that could be saved.'

Maarja's eyes narrowed. 'Perhaps you should tell this to Red Army, who launch attack after attack on our land to bring us back under control. You should speak to White Army, who expect us to fall before them like peasants as they try to restore old order. Or Germans, as they try to re-establish new Weimar republic and return their landlords to bleed us dry. We may only be young nation, but tell me why you should judge us and not others.'

'Maarja, I don't come to debate politics with you. We are on your side, but you cannot kill prisoners. Not when they have surrendered. That is not the act of a nation with morals, one trying to establish itself in the world. Please do not be angry with me, but I have to make sure this message is heard. It may otherwise cause the admiral to re-appraise our role here. What then, if we're not watching your back?'

There was a silence while she scanned his face. 'Do you threaten us?'

Huw flushed and sighed. 'No, I am not clever with diplomatic words; I speak from a personal fear. These actions could make the navy ask questions as to whether it wishes to be involved in this campaign. It is a dangerous thought.'

Maarja looked at the envelope for a long time before taking it.

'There have been few executions Huw, and all were not angels. We have not taken lives of more than forty people, nor do we have plans for more.'

'Forty – that's one in ten! You are setting yourselves up to be as morally bad as those you stand up to.'

Her eyebrows gathered in an impending storm. 'And who are you to tell me this?'

165

In the impasse that followed, Huw stung with the rebuke. His brow hurt from frowning. He could think of no way of retreating without losing his temper or departing with barbed words that would kill the flame forever.

'I was told to deliver a message,' he said sourly. 'And that is what I have done.'

She gently caressed his cheek and gave an apologetic smile.

'I will see message is passed on and ministry is made aware of potential consequences. You will need to remain for an answer?'

Huw nodded. 'Thank you. I also brought you this.'

He reached back into his pocket and brought out a card. It was a sketch in pencil of a rose, standing proud from the vague outline of the ground. The leaves were symmetrical and drew the gaze to the beautiful spread of the petals. The flower was shaded, to leave no thought that it was white.

'I did not wish you to think this was an English rose,' he murmured. 'So I put a little Welsh dragon at the base to the left. Then as this is not only Welsh, I drew an Estonian lion. I had no colour, but the Welsh dragon is red, so perhaps you get the idea.'

Maarja gasped. 'It is beautiful and you have so great skill and ever gentleman in adversity. I am sorry for my harsh words, this decision for execution was not made easily and to some it is not right move for Estonia. Rest assured this will reach minister and I think we can get them to see reason.'

She gently held his face and drew him into a lingering kiss.

'Please do not let Naissaar come between us,' she whispered.

'No,' Huw replied. 'No it will not.'

Chapter Eighteen

The island of women

The boat docked at a small harbour on the island. Half the soldiers climbed out to secure the boat and the harbour area, the rest kept Huw and Maarja under close scrutiny. Oleg signalled with his pistol for them to leave, whilst his conversation continued in the same cheerful manner.

'Please, step ashore. The island has been a military base since the time of the tsar. There are many powerful guns here pointing out to greet hostile forces. This place, I am told, has beautiful sandy beaches and forests of slim silver birch trees. I tell you this, so you need not worry about it. We have so many other things to do here.'

Huw felt a gun prod his back, leaving him in no doubt that he should follow Oleg. They were marched into the forest, surrounded by enough soldiers to make escape a fool's dream. After a short walk, Oleg directed them towards an old building with a compound surrounded by rusting barbed wire. Huw and Maarja were unceremoniously brought into a large room in the building. Oleg moved towards a table where two pieces of paper were set out with a pen. A pot of ink sat neatly near to it. It was the only furniture in a cavernous room.

The captives were left standing in front of the table. Maarja could only stare at the paper, ashen faced. Huw felt vulnerable standing there, but at the same time, events were beginning to niggle him. He felt the anger born of helplessness and looked for the opportunity to express it.

'Maarja Tamm, you are charged with treason against the Soviet Union and collusion with their enemies. Your plea is entered on this, please sign.'

Maarja looked straight ahead and said nothing. The silence was claustrophobic.

'Huw Williams,' Oleg continued. 'You are charged with espionage against the Soviet people. Your plea is entered here. Please sign.'

'Go to hell,' Huw growled.

167

Oleg shrugged and picked up both papers. 'It is no matter. You both have crimes that need punishing.' He turned to Maarja. 'You helped organise the murder of forty of our brave Red Navy comrades. That was against the rules of war.'

Maarja's voice was tiny in the vast hall, but her words were clear.

'You helped organise the murder and kidnap of tens of thousands of Estonian citizens during the first illegal occupation of our country.'

Yuri stepped forward and struck her across the face. Huw bared his teeth and moved to strike the man, but Yuri had pulled out a pistol and nonchalantly waved him back. His smile was cold, inviting Huw to try.

'You can't hide behind a gun forever,' Huw spat.

The Russian reply was curt and unfriendly.

'Comrade Yuri casts doubt upon your parentage,' Oleg replied with a laugh.

'So you brought us here for something that happened twenty-five years ago. Some sort of personal revenge? What will your masters think?'

Oleg smiled his cold smile. 'They will understand as soon as they know of your capture. Tell me though, Mr Williams. What do you remember of your time here? I mean before you deserted your post and ran away with this woman?'

'I remember you, Ivanovic. I met you on board *Spartak*.' Huw said through gritted teeth. 'But you have changed, for then you were human.'

Oleg's eyes closed in satisfaction. 'From the mouths of babes and innocents,' he whispered. 'Is that not what you say? For my part, I should feel honoured that you remember the name. Do you remember what else you said?'

'I remember you,' Huw repeated.

'Is that so?' Oleg said softly, reaching for a photograph from his top pocket. 'Or is it perhaps you are mistaken?'

He walked over to stand in front of Huw, holding up a photograph.

'This is the man you met. This is the man to whom you promised security. And then you handed him over to these barbarians to die. You told him lies. I know, for he wrote to me, when I was a child in

Russia, and told me how a Lieutenant Williams had looked after his men. How you had shown honour and respect and promised them safety. Then we heard how you had led them all off to be slaughtered by these Estonian animals.'

'I told him what I believed was true,' Huw answered.

'You promised,' Oleg shouted, his face contorting with rage, 'and you lied. For years I have waited for this day, I knew I would have this moment. I studied hard, to learn your appalling language. I worked the system, to get into NKVD, for a chance to get to England and avenge the murder of my brother. The war pushed me here, but the lady smiles on me, for she knows I am right and I will have my revenge. And it will be quite beautiful.'

He moved to Maarja and grabbed her chin roughly. 'What do you say to that, bitch?'

'Get out of my country, bastard,' she hissed through gritted teeth.

Oleg pushed her away nonchalantly. Huw launched himself at Oleg, but Yuri was ready and brought him crashing down with a blow to the back of the head with his pistol.

'You think you are freedom fighters?' Oleg snarled. 'Woman, to us we are reclaiming our land. The land of Peter the Great; you are bandits trying to stop us get what is rightfully ours. Every killing you do is murder and you pay accordingly. Tomorrow, you will sing a different tune. You will beg for mercy and you will have none. We will serve you just as you did my brother twenty-five years ago.'

Huw and Maarja were dragged away by guards and thrown in separate cells. Oleg followed. He seemed to want to observe everything on this day. As Huw stumbled in, he turned and asked that he remain with Maarja.

'Touching,' replied Oleg. 'But not possible. A luxury I am not going to grant you, I'm afraid, Mr Williams.'

The door slammed, killing off any hope of further discussion.

'So, now you have achieved your goal, Comrade Oleg.

Oleg gave a grim smile and a nod as they returned to the courtyard. 'Today I should feel rich, comrade and yet my heart is empty. Perhaps tomorrow, when the woman dies, I will feel better.'

'What of the Englishman?' Yuri asked, a bit surprised by the reply.

Oleg's smile disappeared and a thoughtful expression came over his face. 'When he has watched his woman die, I will feed him to the NKVD wolves. They want to turn him and use him against the English.'

'Surely he will not turn after we kill his woman?'

Oleg shrugged. 'It is no matter. If they turn him, he will live his life in hell. If they do not, he will die in the torture chambers. Either way, I have settled my blood debt that I swore twenty-five years ago. Yes, comrade Yuri, perhaps today is a good day after all. I think we should have some spirit and rest tonight. Tomorrow will be a busy day. Perhaps even the sun will shine.'

Chapter Nineteen

One of the Finnish boys

The cell was devoid of furniture or blankets. There was a small hole in the corner for sanitation but it appeared to be blocked. The light was on permanently, flickering away with a faint hum. Huw assumed it was all part of the softening up process. Sleep deprivation, with a bit of fear and uncertainty thrown in. He cursed Oleg for trying to tease out as much pain as possible.

The door had a tiny, hatched window which was locked shut. Huw tried calling Maarja's name, but heard no response. There was no noise through the solid stone walls of the cell or the steel door. He pressed his ear against the door, hoping that the steel would transfer the noise from outside.

He could faintly make out what he took to be the footsteps of a patrolling guard. The coldness of the steel against the side of his face was nothing to the pain he felt for the predicament he found himself in, especially with Maarja's life in grave danger. His misery was now complete. His friends were dead and his love taken from him. All he could think of was the brother of his gaoler on that day aboard *Spartak*. Had Huw really caused this or did fate once more laugh in his face?

He drifted into a half-sleep, even though his cheek felt cold enough to freeze to the door. In time, he realised that the noise outside had changed. The rhythmic walk of the sentry had been replaced by rapid shuffles, then a few thuds. He was terrified something had been done to Maarja. Then he heard the key turn in the lock of his cell door.

He staggered to his feet and stood against the wall, waiting for the single opportunity he might get of forcing an escape. Probably it would only be possible by overpowering the guard and taking him hostage, but knowing Oleg that would not be enough. He hated Huw enough to shoot his own soldiers if it meant getting his revenge. Still, as Märt would say, it was a start.

The door opened and Huw prepared to spring forward. He hesitated – the man stepping in was not dressed in uniform, and spoke in Estonian as he firmly pushed back Huw's confused efforts at the end of his rifle. Their eyes met and Huw froze.

'You look tired, friend Huw.'

Märt stood at the door, grey with fatigue and covered in mud. The bruises around his face had grown yellow and purple with their slow healing. A large cut on one hand was an angry red, but Huw saw unbroken resolve in his eyes. His usual shy, sad smile remained. Huw staggered forward and caught his friend in an embrace.

'What kept you?' He managed.

'I was detained elsewhere,' Märt said, grinning at his poor joke. 'Come, we need to go quickly. There will be time to talk on boat.' He picked up a rifle lying next to what Huw now realised was the crumpled, still form of the guard. 'Here, take this and watch my back.'

Huw stepped gingerly into the corridor to find Juhan, who looked weary and dirty, but still managed a friendly wave. Huw heard Märt curse the young and the foolish, but he didn't care. He reached out and grabbed Juhan's arm in greeting and received a huge smile in response.

'I think Maarja is in there,' Huw said, pointing to the last but one cell. Märt frowned and cursed as he struggled through the bunch of keys he held. Each one proved a false dawn and Märt's language grew bleaker. Finally the lock turned and the door sprung open.

Maarja staggered out, blinking in incomprehension of it all. Her lips moved soundlessly and her head shook in wonder at the scene. She stepped quickly to hug Juhan and then looked around. On seeing Huw, she reached out to kiss his cheek. Then her gaze fell on Märt. She shook her head and gently caressed his face. Tears flowed down her cheeks as she whispered, 'thank you.'

'We must go,' Märt whispered. 'Quickly and quiet, there are still soldiers about here. Maarja, take this pistol. Can you use it?'

Maarja nodded. 'I will not hesitate.'

Märt gave a curt nod and swiftly moved to the end of the corridor. He waved for the others to follow and leaning towards Huw he whispered, 'courtyard is well guarded, so we will need to go through building.'

'To where?' Huw asked.

'Later,' came the reply.

They made quick progress through the corridors. Märt glided effortlessly along as if he had known the place all his life. He stopped outside the main hall and again beckoned Huw. 'There are not many Reds here, hardly anyone. I counted three around courtyard, one now dead in cells and two officers in hall. I want this officer as insurance.'

'You're mad,' Huw said, but could not help a vicious grin.

'Probably,' came the glib response. 'But then our world is mad these days. Use weapons only as last resort, we don't wish to wake this fort.'

Märt crept to the hall door, which stood slightly ajar, and signalled Huw to man the other side of the corridor. Märt then held up his gun and looked furtively through the gap. He stood motionless, waiting for the moment, then without warning, sprang through the doorway.

Oleg and Yuri looked up in surprise from the map they were studying. The sudden movement had wrong-footed them, especially as they viewed the faces of the new arrivals. Märt used his gun to indicate them to move sideways to the wall.

'No noise, no sudden movements. Maarja, watch the door.'

'Who the hell are you?' Oleg shouted, jumping to his feet. He slowed and brought his hands up as Märt's gun barrel raised perceptibly to the threat.

'We are Estonian scum that you left to dogs in Märjamaa,' Märt replied in Russian, then falling back into his own language. 'Huw, is passageway clear?'

Huw went across to the doorway opposite Maarja and looked through. It led to a small corridor. At the end of this was a door, which he vaguely remembered led to the courtyard. From the windows, Huw could see the main gate and the sentry that manned it, who appeared to be asleep. He spotted a faint red glow nearby; another sentry sat near the gate taking a furtive cigarette break.

'There are two men near the gate, waiting to be relieved. How the hell did you get inside here anyway?'

'This lot are hardly elite,' Juhan replied. 'When they change their guard, he walks to be relieved. Not other way round. Gate is free for few minutes.'

'My God, that simple?' Huw gasped.

'Yes, but then if they were good, they wouldn't be guarding gate.'

'How did you get here?' Oleg asked in Russian. 'It's impossible that you escaped.'

Märt snorted and glanced quickly at Huw. 'What have we here?'

'He wants to kill Maarja and I for what happened in 1919. His brother was in the Red Navy and executed here. We came into contact with the situation.'

'So, you are to blame, no?' Märt asked.

'We are all he has left to take revenge on,' Maarja said from the door. 'He was going to kill us tomorrow.'

'Oh well,' Juhan chuckled. 'Life is full of disappointments.'

Oleg resumed his seat and his composure, although he left his hands clearly visible. He looked slowly at Huw and said in English, 'Perhaps they would be polite enough to explain how they have managed to follow us here? I congratulate the enterprise and am curious to know how they have done the impossible.'

Huw shrugged. 'Here is a problem. This man wants to know how you got here. I want to know also. He only speaks Russian and English. I speak English and Estonian. You speak Russian and Estonian.'

Märt shook his head. 'Here is another problem. I will not fall for stalling tactics. We stay here talking, there is greater chance of being detected. He knows this, he banks on it.'

Oleg looked enquiringly, expecting a translation, but Huw shrugged. 'Tough shit, Ivanovic. We're busy. – Look out!'

Out of the corner of his vision, he saw a movement from Yuri. From his waist, the Russian produced a pistol and brought it up towards Märt, even as Huw yelled the warning.

In a split second, Juhan drew his hunting knife and threw it blade first. It hit Yuri full in the chest. A combination of pain and shock made him drop the pistol. Juhan ran to grab the weapon and stop the man from any further aggression.

Märt stormed up to Oleg, his finger tense on the gun trigger. 'I tell you how we got here,' he snarled in Russian. 'Because I am one of Finnish Boys. Because I was of Erna and we don't know when to give up.'

He slammed his gun into Oleg's temple, knocking him unconscious.

'Now is the time to go,' Märt said. 'Through to gate. Come on Juhan. Juhan!'

Juhan was on his knees, cradling the head of Yuri's dead body. His face was filled with misery, his lower lip trembling with anguish. Maarja moved quickly to his side and as he looked up to her, tears streamed down his face.

'I killed him, Mama, I killed him,' he whispered.

She gently brushed his tears. 'To save my life, kallis. To save us all. Come on, be strong. We need your courage now.'

Märt came over and pulled Juhan up. For a brief moment, the haunted look was back on Maarja's face. Juhan would not look at him.

'You did well, Juhan. Now we have to go. You know this.'

Juhan closed his eyes and nodded slowly, wiping his tears as he made for the doorway. Maarja glared at Märt, but there was no acknowledgement as he turned to follow.

'Ivanovic won't be out for long,' Huw said, as they reached him.

'It's fine. We have head start and that is all we need.' Märt said, as he scanned the courtyard for activity. He glanced at his watch, and began to time the nonchalant pacing of the guard at the gate. The man was clearly fed up with his lot and called out to his friend with the cigarette. There was no response. The guard called again and cursed. He shouldered his rifle and strode over to where his colleague sat.

'Quick. Follow me and keep in shadows.' Märt hissed. 'Maarja follow, then Juhan. Huw guard our back and come last. Quickly but safely, while they argue over cigarettes.'

He ran quickly to the fort wall, his footsteps only lightly scuffing the sandy surface. Then, having checked the area, he signalled for them to follow, keeping low. The sentry had prodded his colleague enough now to make him give up a precious cigarette, but not without a torrent of abuse and complaining. Märt reached the gate as the sentry threw a parting comment to his friend. Märt beckoned Maarja and pushed her through the slightly open gate. He looked to Juhan and Huw, but by then the sentry had turned and was walking back slowly, enjoying his drags from the cigarette.

As he reached the gate area, he bumped into Juhan, who had made a break for the entrance. Juhan had recovered now and Huw saw the sudden gleam of the hunting knife, as Juhan grabbed the sentry, harshly whispering something in Russian.

Huw watched the gleaming tip of the cigarette still being nonchalantly smoked by the other soldier to the side. He appeared oblivious to anything that was going on. Then when he called to his friend, Juhan grabbed the sentry's rifle and dragged the man into the shadows. After a few seconds of silence, the sentry hurled another curse and started to walk to the gate.

Huw waited patiently for the distance to narrow, counting the steps to when he could pounce on the man. He reached for his knife, but remembered it was taken when he was captured. He brought his gun up and took aim.

The sentry called his colleague's name louder and more urgently, a tiny bit of fear in his voice. Huw guessed Märt would be exposed as soon as the man came close enough. Waiting until the last possible moment, he jumped out into the courtyard to divert the attention of the second guard.

In a flurry of panic the man dropped his cigarette and tried to raise his rifle. He stopped abruptly when he felt the end of Märt's rifle in his back. Quickly disarmed, the two soldiers were told to face the wall with their hands pressed on the cold stone, as high as possible.

The three men slipped through the gate into the forest beyond. The extra rifles taken from the sentries were thrown into the bushes as they ran. Behind them, the two Russian soldiers had gathered their wits and overcome their fear of being assaulted again. A general alarm was now sounding in the fort. Maarja stepped out of the shadows further down the road and Märt stopped them all briefly.

'Juhan, you are faster. Go on ahead and get boat ready. We will follow as fast as we can. No time for delay, they have vehicles on this island.'

'Where? To the harbour?' Huw asked, but Märt shook his head.

'And advertise our arrival to them? No, we landed on beach further north. We need to leave quickly, before they get patrol boat out.'

Huw started to ask a question, but was met with a firm "later" as they ran through the forest. In the dim light, the slender silver birch trees stood out like ghostly sentries.

Sand entered his boots from scuffing them on the uneven ground, but Huw was just happy that he was free. It made him feel alive. Märt led them quickly down a narrow path. It proved impossible to see hazards like exposed tree roots and soft sand, so they stumbled on as best they could. Occasionally one of the three fell, but the fear of the chase got them up again quickly enough. They soon reached the edge of the forest and stepped straight out onto the beach itself.

The sand was now softer, making Huw imagine he was running through porridge. From the faint light cast by the moon and stars amid the clouds, he saw a long, flat strand with a small spit-like end onto which the forest had encroached until it almost reached the sea. Some boulders rose out of the sea like rounded posts.

Huw ran further down the beach and spotted a dart-shaped vessel amongst the boulders. He hoped it had a decent motor and tried to quicken his pace. Märt came out of the shadows ahead and made for Maarja, moving her down to the waterline. Huw followed, relieved at the firmer footing, despite getting wetter in the splash of the shallows.

Ahead of him, Juhan had already started wading out towards the boat. Märt and Maarja did not look too far behind. Huw glanced back, but saw no sign of pursuit. He prayed for this fortune to continue. The boat seemed close to shore, but the sea was above Märt's thighs as he helped Maarja on board, before quickly following up.

Huw waded to the boat. Juhan leant out and held onto the rocks to stop it drifting. Even with the adrenalin pumping, the shock of the cold water made him gasp. Firm hands helped him to a rope that allowed him to scale the sheer, sleek hull of the boat until he reached the cockpit, landing on something hard and metallic. With a rasping cough, the engine sprang to life. At last the craft was making decent headway and rode the gentle waves into the night. All four of the fugitives were sprawled around the feet of the boat owner, too breathless to speak. Maarja smiled at Huw in relief. He basked in the warm glow and clutched her hand.

As the boat gained pace, its prow rose with the pressure of the engine power. Huw looked back. Figures had started appearing on the beach. He recognised Oleg, who had begun to wade into the sea. The Russian raised his pistol and fired off the whole clip of rounds. It

177

was a token gesture of frustration and hate, for the boat was well out of range. Huw could not resist an ironic wave.

'He will have a lot to explain to NKVD,' he shouted to Märt.

Juhan and Maarja now sat arm in arm. Juhan was sheltering his mother from the cold spray as best he could, but looked totally beyond help in his woe. Maarja talked to him in low tones and for a moment, Huw felt a pang of envy that he was getting this, albeit necessary, attention.

'It will take Ivanovic a long while to get over what he tried, and failed, to do,' Huw shouted to Märt, over the noise of the boat.

'Perhaps never,' Märt shouted back. 'He had his revenge on us in his hand and he let us slip away.'

The man at the wheel turned at the sound of their voices. He was dressed in dark oilskin. His face, what was visible beyond the flat sea cap pulled down as much as possible, was lined from years of facing the salt air, and Huw could not catch his eye.

'Who is he?' he asked Märt.

'This is my good friend, Bjorn Lennartson,' was the reply.

'Swedish?' Huw was surprised at the name.

'No, good Estonian boy,' the man suddenly shouted, with a grin.

'He is Estonian Swede. Fisher folk driven out by Stalin in 1940,' Märt added. 'He escaped to Finland, like me, and joined army.'

Huw looked across to the few lights that signified where Tallinn lay in the distance. Then he took in the white wash from the boat engine behind them.

'This is all fantastic. Are you sure I am not dreaming?'

Märt grinned. 'For sure, when you wake we will go off to your pub and have jolly ale.'

'Okay, okay, but now you have your breath back, I deserve a story.'

Juhan turned briefly to look at them, before turning away again and staring back to shore. Märt nodded and moved to sit closer, keeping watch as he spoke.

'In Märjamaa we had fallen into carefully prepared trap. They were watching roads for us. They caught and killed our decoy. I heard them talk of this in jail. They felt they were heroes. Fools were too interested in you. Ivanovic was talking too much about taking you to Tallinn. We were thrown into cell that had one window. Mortar crumbled around bars and although they took our weapons, I had small sheathed knife still. It was hidden in front of my trousers, where most man do not want to touch.'

'It took all night, but we worked iron bars clear. This window was small, but we got through. They were too busy anyway, excited from roughing you up and putting you into van. They had probably not had so much fun since they had followed army in. Some were local Reds, who had crawled out of wood and were eager to show they were true. While they were busy, we found our jeep. It was still loaded, for those fools had not even bothered to secure it. I hot wired ignition and we drove off after you.'

'You hot wired it?' Huw still sometimes had visions of his meek friend, the baker, of years gone by, but they were slowly disappearing.

'Sure, don't they teach you anything in spy school? We set off after you and I gambled you would be on main Tallinn road. NKVD did not disappoint. We had one bit of bad luck when we met roadblock, but Juhan got us through. He shouted *Quick! We are escort for the special lorry. Which way?* Believe it or not, they not only told us, but told us where you were heading – Pirita. Obedient these Reds, if you talk to them right.'

The engine note cut to a throb and Bjorn called over the sound of the sea: 'Easy now, I thought I saw light ahead. We may have to ditch radio for more stealth.'

His Estonian was delivered with a heavy accent that Huw had not heard before, but his words were a shock.

'Radio?' What the hell?' Huw gasped in surprise.

'We got to harbour before you, for I know Tallinn and these Reds do not. We parked our jeep and walked to jetty. We were close by enough to hear their words, very careless. Soldiers were complaining about going to this God-forsaken island. "What the hell does he want with Naissaar?", they said.'

'What? Did you go and ask?'

Märt shrugged. 'For sure. I have been Russian soldier for long enough now to know how they act. Is this boat for Paldiski? No, it's going to Naissaar. There are still many Estonians around there and they talk as if their lives depend on it, for chance to survive and stay in their land.'

'And so it was that easy?'

'The Germans have retreated far away. The Reds are confident they won't be back and it makes them careless. We drove up coast and used radio. As I said, in Märjamaa, they left jeep loaded.'

Huw rolled his eyes in disbelief and shook his head, Märt ignored it.

'I still can talk to Finland. We Finnish Boys did good work. I still have friends, those I know can help.' He shrugged off the absurdity of it all.

'And this boat? It is not Finnish?'

'It is one of your English boats, you left it behind in Biorko when you fought Russian navy in 1920,' Bjorn shouted. 'I found it and we repaired it. She's good for speed, but not for passengers. There is not much space here, so hang on or go below – if you can stand engine fumes.'

Huw had to look away to stop laughing at the way things had turned out for his friend.

'Märt, I don't know how or why the gods smiled on us, but they have, for now. I am glad you came back.' For a second he succumbed to laughter. 'Where would I have been if it wasn't for you all along this journey?'

Märt did not return the smile, as he scanned the waters for signs of company in the dark night. There was nothing to be seen and all that could be heard was the lapping of the sea on the sides of the boat. 'I think we are alright here, Bjorn,' he said after a while. 'Let's get past headland and then signal. Are you sure you won't take us to Sweden?'

Bjorn shook his head and tapped the engine. 'I have just enough juice to get to Hiiumaa and then back to Finland as it is.'

'Then come to Sweden,' Juhan said.

Bjorn shook his head again. 'No, I won't be impounded and have boys say I deserted them.'

'You have woman, I think,' Juhan replied.

Bjorn pulled his cap down and muttered an oath. 'Make your message so that we can move, Märt. Longer we stop, more chance we have of Reds waking up.' He kicked the tarpaulin, producing a dull metal thud from beneath it. 'Then once you have worked out where you are getting picked up, I can work out where to drop you.'

Märt looked back to Maarja, who glanced at Huw. They appeared to want a decision, but Huw could only shrug apologetically.

'I'm sorry but my mind was back at sunny day on Kasari river.'

'Kassari!' Maarja exclaimed.

'No Kasari,' Huw protested.

'No, she is right Kassari Saare,' Märt said. 'That spit is long enough to be far away from land patrols. Good idea.'

Bjorn shrugged. 'That's fine, but there will be many places where patrol boats may berth on this east coast. I'm not sailing past Vormsi Island. I would prefer to chance minefields on north coast than that. If you go that way, you have to get by Sõru and God knows what else is happening on Saaremaa.'

'For sure, but then we hope to evade patrols and to do that we need speedboat like yours,' Märt said, straight-faced.

'I said no, my friend,' Bjorn replied. 'Besides, Swedish people do not really understand our *Rannarootslased* accent so well. I take my chances with Finns.'

'Aren't you missed at base?' Juhan asked, as he went to lift the tarpaulin.

'My commander approved of this mission, he is good Estonian. Come on, make this transmission and I will take you south on Hiiumaa. I don't want to go close to north coast, so I'll drop you on east coast. I know it's a long way from Kassari, but you can find your own way from there.'

Huw started helping Juhan. He felt the radio and decided that though battered it was still intact.

'I don't know this island. Why aren't we dropping off and making our connection on north coast?'

'Too many minefields,' Bjorn said. 'And Tahkma has great defences. Germans were busy there.'

'Haven't the Germans gone?' Huw asked.

'We have to assume this is so,' said Märt. 'If Reds are not already there, it is only short time before they come. Juhan, how is radio now?'

'The battery is low, so we must be quick.'

Huw stepped up and started tapping away. The response was almost immediate. Huw gave his call-sign and came straight to the point. 'Request evacuation, immediate.'

'Will confirm.'
'No time, compromised. Hiiumaa, Kassari point, how soon?'
'Stand by.'
'Battery low.'

Huw received no acknowledgment. It was silent for nearly 30 minutes and then came a crackling reply, as the battery started fading: 'Pick-up 48 hours from now. Confirm.'

Huw glanced at his watch. 'Confirm.' He tapped again, then looked up. 'The radio is dead. I don't know if they got my last send.'

'Let's get out of here then,' Bjorn said. 'They'll have probably heard you in Moscow.'

He gunned the engine and as they started making headway, they saw lights off the coast, gliding slowly towards them.

'Patrol,' Märt hissed.

'Can't be Reds,' Bjorn replied. 'Their navy couldn't fart around Kronstadt bay, let alone get to Estonia.'

'Maybe they captured a German E-boat?' tried Huw, 'or maybe it's the Germans?'

Bjorn gave out a bleak laugh 'Possibly, I doubt if there are any Germans this side of Konigsberg. I will try and lose them around Osmusaare island. Hold on.' They watched the lights slowly move across the horizon, then apparently become static.

'They've locked on our trail,' Huw shouted. 'And I think are gaining slowly.'

'Throw radio away,' Maarja suddenly shouted. 'It will make us go faster.'

Märt needed no second invitation, grabbing the box and dumping it overboard. He looked across to Huw, who waved dismissively.

'Either they are coming to pick us up or they are not.'

Bjorn rounded the island, seeking shelter from the patrol's searchlight, which had started to sweep the sea behind them. The island became a dark shadow in a darker night.

'Haven't they got better things to do?' Juhan grumbled.

'I want to go cautiously around this island,' Bjorn said. 'The Reds put a base on here in 1940 and may have reopened it. I don't want to wake them.'

The patrol was still out of sight. Maarja began to shiver in the slight wind, as it picked out the cooling sea spray on her clothes. As

Bjorn increased the throttle, a blinding light swam across to them from the island.

'Patrol!' Märt shouted. 'He's coming round other side of Osmusaare.'

Bjorn took the engine up to full throttle.

'Can't you shoot light?' Maarja asked.

Huw brought up his rifle to take aim and cursed. 'It would help if we could keep damned boat still. It's too far away.'

Bjorn swung the boat hard to port and out of the searchlight beam. At top speed, the boat pulled away from the patrol. As they left the island waters, the searchlight was not so bright on them. The patrol began firing.

'They have moved to cut off our route south,' Bjorn shouted. 'Shooting to push us further outwards. They are pushing me to north coast. I will need to drop you off at Kärdla bay and then lie low before Finland.'

'It's a bit risky. Kärdla is main town. If there are troops they will surely be garrisoned there,' Märt said.

Bjorn looked up and gave a grim smile. 'We are all so close to Hiiumaa now, even a deaf cripple would know about this little piece of fun. If the Reds think they can mess around this close to the island, I would take it that Hiiumaa is now no longer German.'

The patrol now started to tail off, firing a final shot as a symbolic gesture, even though the speedboat was now well out of range.

'Consider ourselves chased away,' muttered Huw.

Bjorn took the boat past the glimmering lights of Kärdla and pulled into the lee of the peninsula. If it had been a German stronghold, they had now all left or fallen asleep, Huw thought. As the group departed, Märt clasped Bjorn's hand.

'I will never forget, friend.'

'We are even now, friend,' came the reply. 'Be lucky now.'

Then with a roar of the engine, the small boat was off into the darkness.

Oleg stormed into the imposing building in the centre of the city. His temper was fuelled by the throbbing pain near his left temple. He scowled at the front desk and demanded assistance, but was met only with disdain. In the end, a few soldiers moved to intercept him, with a view to getting rid of the loud stranger. They were waved away by a man in a brown suit, one who looked more at home at a desk than he ever would in an army. 'Comrade Ivanovic,' he said crisply, with the hint of an oily smirk.

They had met before, Oleg realised, arguing at the harbour over the custody of the prisoners. It only added to his sour temper.

'I need this lazy rabble to start finding things out for me.' Oleg snapped.

'Why is this?'

'The English spy has escaped. He had help to flee the island, but I still think he is in this wretched land. I need records of any radio intercepts, coded messages, reports of any sightings, anything out of character on the north coast last night.'

'I take it this spy was the one you so grandly took to a small island with a tiny force of second-rate soldiers? And now you want us to clean up your mess?'

Oleg went crimson with rage. He would have shot the man, but for the fact he knew the guards around him would have shot him in response.

'I have no time for your petty accusations, comrade,' he spat. 'This spy is trying to return to the English with a former aide to the Estonian National Council and a leading so-called Forest Brother.' His voice lowered into a growl. 'I would not have it said that you hindered the capture of so important a group of people.'

They locked gazes for a long time and then the man nodded slowly. 'There was word of a patrol encountering a speedboat last night. Also we intercepted a message from that vicinity. We are decoding it now.'

'I have the knowledge to decode this,' Oleg said simply.

The man gave a cold smile, making his moustachioed mouth appear almost demonic. 'Then you should come to my office while I have the information prepared. I will get someone to patch your head wound. You appear to have had a mishap. Such a wound could seriously impact one's judgement if not treated.'

'Thank you for you concern, comrade. Your assistance is welcome.'

'Anything to assist, comrade,' the man said, with equal insincerity. 'It would be in everybody's interest for you to succeed. I know how dedicated you are to this goal and you will follow it to the end. Even,' he staged a false cough. 'To come back with your hands full or to perish trying. There is mention of Hiiumaa in the communication. That much we know.'

'Do the Germans still hold the island?'

'We think not, but perhaps you should help our glorious soldiers find out, and be part of the assault to liberate it.'

Chapter Twenty

The hill of crosses

It felt as though they had hiked forever during the night. After landing on the island, Märt had taken them around the edge of the town of Kärdla then, as soon as he found a way, steered them into the welcoming shadows of the forest running parallel to the road. The place he had chosen to rest in was eerily quiet. It was as if those who were left had hidden before the returning Red storm.

October was not a hot month in Estonia. Not as cold as the vicious winter months yet to arrive, but there was still a coolness to the morning air and a mist in the trees. Huw was glad the outcome of their journey would be decided before the snows returned and the sea froze. However, snow and ice would have enabled him to walk across to this island from the mainland.

He had woken in a forest glade. His first thought was that the trees in the distance were strangely shaped. Fallen branches seemed to have lodged between trunks, forming crosses. Then he looked again, noticing how the crossed branches had been tied with twine. Twisting round, he looked at his hand, now numb and tingling from leaning on a pile of stones – stones that were also placed in a cross. Nearby, somebody had left a cross woven from thin reeds on the ground. Everywhere he looked, there were crosses shaped out of natural forms. Huw shivered, thinking he had stumbled on an ancient graveyard.

Even the breeze had stopped, making the sombre glade strangely silent. Huw got up and went to check the others. Märt awoke on his approach and with a curt nod, got up and walked to a bush. Juhan gave a sleepy sign of greeting, but it was tinged with the sadness he had carried since Naissaar. Huw moved to where Maarja sat gazing around in silent contemplation.

'What is it?' he asked. 'Have I disturbed somebody's final resting place?' He was embarrassed at the sound of his own voice.

She shook her head. 'No, this must be Ristimägi,' she murmured. 'It is beautiful and so sad.'

'The hill of crosses? What happened here?' Huw asked.

Maarja looked around and gently picked up a cross of straw standing proud in the sandy soil.

'I read of this. A long time ago, Catherine was Empress of Russia. Estonia was part of empire. This island had always been heavy with Swedish settlers from older times. Gotland is not far to northwest from here. She decided Swedish had no place here and wanted them moved to Ukraine. These people were given little time to pack. Legend is that here is where they gathered with their belongings before they were sent away. People leave crosses here in memory and perhaps to feel sorrow, for this is sad place indeed.'

'It is beautiful, Huw murmured. 'It shows my mood, for I am heartbroken to leave Estonia.'

She gave him a quick peck on the cheek. 'Perhaps we should leave crosses also.'

Märt called them over. 'Come, we must go. There is road to south. It is straight and will lead us close to Kassari, but we must stay close to forest as we walk.'

'I have found some mushrooms.' Juhan appeared clutching them to his chest. 'It is not much, but at least we have something.'

The golden fungi were hardly enough to fill the stomach, but Huw felt his energy returning. He glanced around, wishing he could wash the snack down with a handful of blueberries and a scoop of river water, but there was no sign of either. The clouds were grey above and the wind ominous.

'It may rain,' Juhan said.

Märt shrugged. 'There is enough forest to keep us dry.'

They set off slowly and quite soon Märt was cursing to himself and moving towards the road.

'Ground is too uneven. I think we can take our chances on road now we are outside town. It is so straight we will see anything coming for miles and hear them also.'

Märt was soon proved correct. The road was straight and slightly undulating, but empty, and all around appeared still. The many storms that had beset the island had come and gone. The calm before the storm thought Huw, imagining the great Red wave to come.

The party trudged on, nursing their empty stomachs. Huw dreamt of finding a family of wild boar nearby. He ached for the taste of meat, and a clean stream of water. Mentally, he rummaged through their remaining possessions. The adrenaline-fuelled adventure in

Naissaar had taken all their provisions and accessories. A pistol and two rifles with limited ammunition remained to them, and two hunting knives.

Somehow Märt had lifted two hand grenades from the fort – not much use in a pitched battle at close range, which is what Huw expected they would have to face.

Märt decided they had to avoid rests where possible. Kassari, the gateway to safety, still lay far ahead.

Huw had had enough of espionage. He knew the past was not to be relived, but this mission had driven him to revisit it. He had found Maarja and knew she still shared his feelings, but he remained confused by what Märt meant to her, and lost as to why Märt, the estranged husband, father and rebel leader, seemed to use every opportunity to push Maarja back into his arms.

Had there really never been time for an explanation? Huw knew all too well that the perils of this land left no leisure for personal issues – but he cursed himself for ineptitude none the less. Märt had faith in him. He expected him to deliver the message that would bring support to this blighted land, but it no longer felt possible. The only thing Huw had proved to be good at on this mission was killing people. The fact that it had been so easy did not sit well with him at all. He looked at Juhan. The young man had always managed to lift the group's spirits with his ready smile and a particular knack for doing the impossible. Now, Juhan was struggling to come to terms with killing a man. Something he had vowed never to do in this turbulent land.

'Juhan, my friend,' said Huw, 'I am glad you have been with me on this journey. I could not have done it without you and Märt.'

Juhan smiled weakly. 'In time I may wish to remember fondly our journey also.'

'Time is a healer, Juhan,' Huw replied.

By midday, Märt reckoned they were in the middle of the island, half the distance to Kassari.

'I don't think I can keep this pace up,' Huw finally admitted.

'I would prefer to be at Kassari by nightfall, in case there are soldiers to avoid,' Märt replied.

'But perhaps we can stop,' Huw persisted.

'There are men ahead,' Juhan warned. 'Armed too, they have seen us.'

'They do not wear uniform, do you think they are Destroyers?' asked Maarja nervously.

'They may be Metsavennad,' Märt replied. 'Let's shoulder our arms. Don't do anything aggressive.'

Märt called a welcome as the men approached. In contrast, the newcomers kept their rifles to hand and looked over the group suspiciously. Although dressed in working clothes, one wore a light grey jacket with blue lapels and two stars: a Finnish army officer. Huw hoped it was a good sign. The conversation was clipped, with the leader's tone accusatory from the start. 'What do you want here?' he demanded.

'We are passing through to south coast, while we still can. We would be grateful for any food you may have spare.'

The men laughed unkindly. Their leader continued: 'Where are you from?'

'Mainland, we escaped before Reds took us.'

'How do I know you are not Reds,' the leader's mouth took on a sneer of contempt.

'How do I know you are not Germans or Destroyers yourself?' Märt replied evenly. Huw kept himself on his toes, ready to spring if the situation went wrong.

One of the men cursed. 'Destroyers would have shot you without thought and those damn Germans left us with no weapons, so they can go to hell.'

'Urmas, shut up,' the leader warned.

'Why?' The man scratched his forehead under his old army cap. 'They are not Destroyers. They look half-starved and they have woman with them.'

'Nevertheless, I trust no-one carrying guns,' the leader replied.

'You are Estonians though,' said Märt. 'Nationalists? Swedes? You must understand this; we are taking this man and woman to be rescued away from Reds.'

'Why is this?' Huw was asked.

'He does not answer,' Märt replied quickly.

'No it is alright,' Huw replied with a hand on Märt's arm. 'They need to know. I am a British officer.'

Urmas spat and loaded his rifle. 'Pah! English are friends of Stalin.'

'Not if I get back they won't be,' Huw growled. 'I have seen enough here to change that.'

The men looked at each other for a moment, and then the leader gave a curt nod. Urmas lowered his rifle. 'You say you pass through.'

'Yes,' Huw said. 'We will not stay.'

'Then you will trade, food for your weapons and ammunition. You give them now and I will send food.'

Märt laughed mirthlessly. 'What guarantees do you give us?'

The leader shouldered his rifle. 'None, but what choice do you have? My men are in forest, watching you as we speak.'

Märt locked gazes with the man for a long time, until they both began to grin.

'Trust in this world is given sparingly and should be treated with respect,' Märt said. He slowly unslung his rifle and handed it over, with a handful of bullets. The others followed suit, but very reluctantly.

The man nodded in approval. 'Wait in smoke lodge in that farm, I will send your food.'

The men returned to the forest, leaving one posted close to the perimeter. Huw felt Märt was right, trust was given sparingly.

'Either my stomach will be happy or we've been fooled with ease,' Juhan muttered, sitting down on the road.

'We had little choice,' Märt said. 'But if they lie, I'll go and leave them my grenade without pin. We'll keep watch from barn. It will give us slightly more warning of trap. We'll give them two hours and then I will be happy to be called fool.'

'We have limited defence, Märt,' Huw said.

'We needed to travel light anyway,' Märt replied and set off for the farm.

They waited two hours and the land seemed even more deserted than before. Huw needed to stretch his legs and made to move out of the barn, but Märt gave a warning whistle and shake of head.

'You may have been wrong, Märt,' Huw warned. 'I want to look around.'

'For sure,' came the reply. 'It was good try and we had little choice. We cannot solve every problem with gun. Besides, we have no need of weapons on Kassari. We either succeed or we fail, weapons won't make difference.'

'What if we don't get picked up?' Maarja asked.

'We join Metsavennad,' Märt replied simply.

'They look as if they need new leader,' Juhan chipped in from his vantage point, looking across the fields from a gap in the rotten wooden walls. 'He is losing control of his men.'

A realisation gripped Huw like a hammer blow. 'You must come with us, Märt. We would not have got this far without you. We would not be here, had it not been for you. I cannot just leave you here.'

'I see someone,' Juhan called. 'Looks like small girl.'

They all strained to look, just making out her head as she walked through the long grass. As she approached, they saw she was carrying a basket.

'I will go,' Maarja said. 'You will all scare her.'

She walked out to the girl and met her on the path, crouching down to her height. Maarja smiled a lot as she talked and the girl shyly gave her the small basket. Huw looked on, feeling a pang of regret for the days when it was a common sight to see that beautiful smile. He looked across at Märt and saw pain in his expression. Maarja opened one of the flaps of the small basket. The girl ran away, then turned and gave a shy wave before skipping away again. Maarja came back to the barn.

'Smoked sausage, two small cucumbers, roll of bread, three apples and bottle of water. I think you made good trade, Märt. At least my stomach tells me so.'

'We need energy. Chew slowly so it stops your stomach complaining. Then we leave.'

They ate and set out again for Kassari. It was hard to get started – aching limbs complained mercilessly and chafed feet screamed for recuperation. Soon they were back in their stride, though the pain remained on the fringes of their thoughts.

'I think we should have had smoke sauna,' Juhan muttered. 'It has been such long time.'

The road south remained straight and undulating. The forest was a curtain on each side, interspersed with glimpses of small farmsteads through the trees. All still appeared deserted, as if life had stood still in the land. By the afternoon they had reached the main road. In the distance, they could make out the coast and the faint outline of the long spit that was Kassari point.

'Why would the Germans leave the land undefended?' Huw asked.

'We were not willing sub-nation they expected us to be,' Maarja replied bitterly. 'It is of no matter who has come in, they have all tried to change us, to weed out those they do not like. It would be good for us if world left us to get on with being Estonian.'

'I wish I could have said something that would make them feel there was hope,' Huw muttered to himself.

'Think of what you will say when you return,' Märt snapped. 'That will be worth more than empty words here.'

'August said that Metsavennad in Märjamaa attacked German army as it left,' Juhan remarked. 'Trying to liberate weapons to help defend themselves, as Germans had left nothing. They said they lost many men and gained few arms. Germans had no interest in saving us, when we could have protected their backs as they ran away.'

'I hate this war,' Huw replied, looking to Maarja for some reassurance. There was none. She had closed up since they had left the farm. Huw could not read what she felt.

The road to the small peninsula of Kassari was dotted with small homesteads. Once or twice, they caught sight of life. On one occasion they knew they were being watched furtively by someone from the safety of a barn.

'Don't do anything aggressive or strange,' Märt warned. 'Some may sell us to save their own skins from Reds, if they haven't already. It is as well we have no rifles to show. We need to get nearer to Saare tip and find some cover. It wouldn't look good, sitting there all day like we are waiting for bus. We may as well fire flare and wave to approaching Reds.'

They reached the coastline after a hard walk. The forest gave way to open ground at the start of the spit. Juhan found a place to rest on the edge of a clearing of dusty ground and pale rock, interspersed with clumps of grass and reeds.

'I think we can move out some way here, grass is tall enough to hide us from prying eyes,' Märt said. Nobody argued.

The afternoon wore on as if it would never end. When at last they stopped, Juhan quickly fell asleep in the reeds, the rest found it difficult to break the tension of the day. Huw missed the simple tasks to keep him occupied, such as cleaning a rifle. Something he had done on countless occasions since he had landed in Estonia. He felt vulnerable now, being unarmed on an exposed point of land that could easily become a trap. He smiled to himself; perhaps there would be a nice desk job at the end of this?

'Märt, I will need to start teaching you English – or will it be Swedish?'

There was no reply, bar the haunted look in his friend's eyes.

'Märt, You cannot still say you will return to the forest after all this? You cannot possibly be thinking of staying, not with Ivanovic out there probably hunting you. There is nothing left to stay for, is there?'

Märt swallowed hard and looked at his boots.

'I will take my chances with local Metsavennad. I have good experience and they would not lose out by having me with them.'

'Märt,' Huw ran his fingers through his hair in frustration. 'I can't do this without you. I realise that now, I've been a terrible agent, totally unsuited for this work. I fear they may not listen to me, but with you there by my side they would have to. Why will you not come?' There was no reply. Märt continued to look at his feet and Huw was struggling for words. '...You are my friend. I cannot leave you here. You never abandoned me.'

Märt's eyes closed hard and his brows furrowed in pain as he whispered. 'You have not told him.'

The sound of the sea lapping on the nearby shore seemed to swallow them all up in the silence that followed. The smell of rotting seaweed made Huw think of better times back home – times when people said what they meant.

'I did not feel it was appropriate,' Maarja replied softly. 'And perhaps you should think also. The past is gone.'

Märt shook his head and stood to walk away, Maarja took a deep breath.

'There is much guilt in taking the woman of your best friend,' she said. 'It is not something that perhaps we both feel proud of, but time was hard and such things happen. Huw, you had been taken away and Juhan was due and...'

'What?' Huw exclaimed, then in a very unsteady voice he continued. 'What are you saying?'

'Juhan is your son,' Maarja replied gently.

Huw looked at Juhan, who appeared to still be in a deep sleep, possibly even out of earshot.

Maarja continued: 'I discovered this soon after your arrest. We never had got married and I was afraid that scandal of bastard son of foreigner would be hard on us. Märt agreed to marry me, to make Juhan his legal child. I am full of guilt for not waiting for you and I see Märt feels it also, but for Juhan's sake we had no choice.'

Huw groped for words. He wanted to walk away but his legs refused to work. 'You never said,' he finally gasped. 'I assumed Märt was the father. But this is still no excuse, Märt. I understand this and have no reason to be angry.'

Märt turned to face him and Huw was shocked to see his friend's eyes red with weeping. Tears rolled down his cheeks, he still could not meet Huw's gaze.

'Maarja is kind but you are right, it is not enough. You are right also, that you would not be here in this position were it not for me.'

Märt took a deep breath and found a stick. He took a knife that Huw had not known about from his boot and started whittling the stick as he spoke.

'How did they know where to find you? You were so far from sea, how did they know where to come? I did this, I reported you as deserter to local police. They fed it back to government and when English navy came to port, they delivered you up to English ships. I brought them to your farm and set up trap. You were my friend, when others were not. You were my brother. Yet Maarja was so beautiful and I could not help myself. I sinned, for when opportunity presented itself to send you away, temptation was too great. I took it and then I took your woman to wife.'

Huw stared straight ahead, watching the world fall around his ears.

Märt tried a smile, but his lips quivered too much. 'When Maarja found out, she wanted nothing to do with me any more. I was monster to her. I left and joined Estonians who went to fight in Finland. I hoped war would allow me honourable death away from those I had hurt. It did not happen, so I looked to learn what I could and make my actions absolve my crime. Erna was my saviour. I could look in mirrors once more without distaste.'

Märt wiped his eyes and then cast the stick away. 'Then you came back. Fate had given me one chance to redeem myself. Luck grew stronger and allowed me to bring you both back together and get you both away from this hell. If you stay here, both of you will die and soon. If I get you out of here, I have at least redeemed part of my actions. But that is also why I will not come, friend Huw. I can hardly look into your eyes for shame.'

Huw passed a hand over his eyes. 'All those years,' he whispered. 'All those years.'

He looked at Märt and saw a man broken in grief.

'It is not enough. Not enough to stay. We can talk of these things tomorrow, but now we need to get out of here and away.'

'We will see,' Märt replied softly.

Chapter Twenty-One

Our time is done

The remaining daylight hours were spent in silence, as everybody became swept up in their own thoughts. Gulls wheeled in the sky, searching for food on the shoreline. A butterfly wafted across the long grass, playing tag with shadows. A stoat appeared on the path, making his cautious stuttering run into the sanctuary of the long grasses.

'It will be dark soon.' Huw's words broke the silence.

'Yes,' Juhan agreed. 'Do you think we will find some decent food in Sweden?'

'I hope so,' Huw smiled.

As the sunlight fell into cloud and the daylight became patchy, an engine note could be heard in the distance. It was coming from inland. Huw looked in horror at Märt.

'We must move further up the shingle.'

Märt grabbed Juhan's arm to help him up. Huw did the same for Maarja. Energised by the tingling sensation as their hands touched, he gazed into her eyes for a moment and then murmured, 'there are things to say.'

'Yes,' she agreed, but said no more.

A lorry was approaching, the headlights carving faint beams in the forest. Huw saw the outlines of soldiers in the back. The lorry came to a stop and an officer jumped out.

'Ivanovic!' Huw swore. 'How the hell did he get wind of this?'

'They must have intercepted our radio message.' Märt said.

'But it was in code,' Huw growled.

'Was Kassari in code?'

'No – no time to translate it.' Huw swore again. 'Not this now, not when we are so close.'

'Shall we move to Saare point?' Maarja asked.

'In this light we will be easily spotted. We have to hold out a bit longer and move up when it's darker.'

There was a faint rustle of grass and they were joined by Juhan. 'They don't think we've arrived yet. They are getting ready to surprise us.'

'Don't you know the meaning of the word fear?' exclaimed Huw, then shook his head. It was a bit late in the day to get paternal with someone he had only just found out was his son.

Juhan grinned. 'I don't think they've got enough time to search grass. They may post guard on shingle spit, though not until dark.'

'We can try to work our way around them then,' Märt said. 'If I pick right spot I can use grenades to make diversion if we need it.'

Huw felt his breath catching in his throat as the truck disappeared into the forest and the men took up positions. The fugitives were not exposed yet, but they had passed the point of no return. The only clear escape was down the shingle spit that extended far into the sea towards the neighbouring island of Saaremaa. It was the moment Huw had feared the most, one chance was all they had, and it depended on the arrival of a single boat, making a hazardous journey to rescue them.

The soldiers' movements had ceased and the birds returned to their foraging. Swallows swooped low in their quest for flies and always, in the background, was the lapping of the sea. Then Huw heard the soft crunch of boots on gravel. He ducked his head to hide as the boots passed by, then dared a look. Oleg had passed by with two soldiers. They moved to where the grass began to thin out and Oleg could be seen giving his orders to the men. The men ran back past the hiding place to fetch a drum of cable they had left further down the path. They began to set an elaborate trip wire across the path and worked hard securing the ends, before taking cover nearby.

'They'll have rigged some explosive with one-second detonators, I guess,' Huw whispered to Märt.

'Where's Ivanovic?'

'He's lying down at edge of shingle, Märt replied. 'Last line of defence. Our one hurdle to freedom.' He looked around for a long time and then lay close to the others so his voice did not carry. 'This is it. When boat gets close, Juhan, you run like hell for end. You make sure boat stops and waits for us. We will distract Ivanovic. Maarja, you go next, then Huw. I will be last.' He paused. 'Make sure there is room for me on boat.'

Maarja smiled and stroked his cheek.

The darkness swept in and soon all that was left was the memory of where things were. Huw wondered how he used to pray as a child.

Tonight was the night for conversion back to religion for sure. Hymns played in his mind but they were the sad, Welsh ones he remembered from family funerals. It did not bode well.

The time stretched forever. Although Huw could hear their breath and feel their presence, he could no longer see his friends. There was nothing for it but to listen and wait, hope for a short break in the clouds to allow them to check the land and then for it to go dark when they ran. It felt like an age, but the faint note of a high-geared motor began to drift over them, coming from the sea. Huw heard Oleg mutter something, but it was lost to the night. The boat was drawing closer across the bay, with excruciating slowness. Then he heard Märt breathe one word. 'Ready,' then the world went mad.

The scramble of footsteps. The rush of air as a grenade was thrown. The grenade bouncing on gravel. An explosion, and a brief array of light between the two groups of soldiers stationed on opposite sides of the path. The soldiers instinctively returned fire. Soon they were embroiled in a shooting match and Huw heard Oleg race forward bellowing what was certainly a ceasefire order.

A rustle nearby, and the outline of Juhan, sprinting into the night. Huw heard the rasping of pebbles rolling under his feet and Oleg's curse. Then a pistol shot rang out. A flare exploded in the air, leaving three purple stars creating an unwelcome light in the sky.

Juhan was a fair way down the spit, moving fast. A speedboat approached the head. Huw heard a deeper throated engine and to his horror, spied a boat crossing the sound from Saaremaa. It had to be the patrol boat from last night. Another trap had been sprung.

Then he saw Oleg tracking Juhan's sprint with his rifle. Without a second's thought, Huw charged him from behind. Oleg fired and the shot went wide. Both men fell to the floor. Oleg recovered first, dropped his rifle and drew a pistol.

Huw looked towards the spit and saw two figures running. His mind flooded with relief. He had done his best. He knew nobody could have tried harder to get his family free. He felt a sharp pain and blood flowed inside his shirt.

A warning scream was followed by an explosion that knocked both men off their feet. A few soldiers had run to Oleg's aid but fell foul of the tripwire laid by their comrades. The lethal hail of shrapnel floored them and put the rest off following.

'Huw! Run!' Märt was on his feet racing to Oleg. Huw took a second to measure the situation. He had no weapon and his shoulder was useless. But Huw was the one Märt was placing all his trust in to deliver a message. He was the goods to be delivered. Huw snapped 'Follow!' and ran.

Out to sea, the patrol bore down on the small speedboat, which appeared to be taking a wide circle and making a break for it. Huw sprinted as fast as he could. The pebbles skidded underfoot and his shoulder screamed pain. The sea crashed on either side, making him feel like an unworthy Moses. He wished his body could do more than a loping gait. He'd seen a few miracles already, so perhaps one more would not be too much to ask?

Märt was quick enough to kick the pistol out of a rising Oleg's hand. He tried a lunge with his knife, but Oleg blocked the cut and threw him off. Märt recoiled from the defence and Oleg kicked him in the stomach. Märt recovered, but not quickly enough. Oleg picked up his pistol, turned and fired. Märt fell to his knees, screaming white agony and clutching his stomach. Oleg staggered to stand, feeling for the first time the deep cut Märt had inflicted on his face. He cursed and steadied his pistol with both hands, ready for the coup-de-grace.

'It ends here, bandit,' he snarled.

'You're right,' Märt's voice was a wheeze between gritted teeth. 'Our time is done. We should leave life to those who deserve it.'

Oleg heard a metallic clink and saw a dark shape drop between them. He looked back at his adversary, seeing the grenade pin still held in Märt's outstretched hand. Then all he saw was white that faded into nothing.

Chapter Twenty-Two

In the light of a star-shell

Huw had turned to look back when the explosion rang out. He saw Oleg's body fly backwards in the rapidly fading light of the star shot. He scanned for any other movements and saw a second body slumped on the path by the fallen Russian. It was Märt, Huw was certain of it, and certain that his friend had perished. In the fading light of the flare, he focussed on the path that would take him to his family. He had to make his way to Juhan and Maarja quickly. He had to turn his back on his fallen comrade and move.

Another star shell was fired, this time from the sea patrol. The speedboat had moved on west, the Soviet boat in pursuit. In the light of the flare, the spit was a dark crescent in a shimmering sea. Even though there was a long way to go, Huw glanced behind. The soldiers were advancing, stopping briefly to check the bodies. Huw continued his loping scramble up the shingle, clutching his bleeding left arm and desperately seeking a way they could defend themselves. The shingle path was now less than six foot wide. The loose stones moved under his feet, making it hard to go fast without stumbling. He feared injuring himself further. If he fell, could he stand back up with one shoulder out of commission?

He focused on the end of the spit and saw Maarja moving towards it. Juhan stood there waiting. By the time Huw reached them they were at the water's edge. The sea lapped on three sides of them in cool invitation. Saaremaa loomed in the background, a faint and tantalisingly distant shadow. Maarja reached to cushion his descent, as he fell to her side.

'Huw, what is wrong?'

'Shot in shoulder,' Huw panted. 'A glancing blow only, but I think it still bleeds.'

Without a word, Maarja produced a linen hair band and began to fashion a bandage.

'I wish it were cleaner, but it will have to do,' she muttered.

'Where's Märt gone?'

'He didn't make it,' Huw muttered. 'He sacrificed himself to stop Ivanovic.'

201

Maarja gave a low moan and he gasped as her grip tightened involuntarily on his arm. Then she composed herself and sighed.

'What now?'

'What choice do we have? We wait and see if the soldiers dare to come up here. Perhaps with Ivanovic dead, they may lose heart and just go back to base.'

Juhan began to sing softly. It was a simple folk song about a lost hero. His voice cracked with the strain. His parents listened calmly, waiting for their fate.

Then Huw realised the sound of the waves had changed; there was a quickening of the rhythmic lapping of the sea on the pebbles. Behind the continuous draw back and forth of the stones he heard a separate splashing or paddling.

'Is there anybody there?' he called out.

'There you are,' came a voice from the gloom. 'I thought I had lost you in this dark night. It was as well you have that singer amongst you. Keep talking and I'll get close by.'

'Bjorn?'

'Hello English, I would recognise your accent anywhere, even stranger than an Estonian Swede. There.'

A sudden burst of small arms fire began – too far away to be of any danger yet, but the soldiers would soon get into range.

'I think it would be wise for you to come on board now,' said Bjorn. 'Your rescue craft very kindly drew patrol away. He's been looking for me for a while. I've had to hide in nearby cove since I dropped you. Then I thought about my friend Märt and I knew he would need help, so I thought I would come and check. As well I did. Where is he anyway?'

Huw was last on board and made sure he had settled down before he replied. 'He's dead, Bjorn. He fought the bastard that was following us.'

'Did he kill him?' Huw nodded, and then realising the light was still poor, said 'yes'.

Bjorn grunted, then sighed. 'Then he died for purpose. Shame, he saved me when we were Finnish Boys. I wanted to re-pay him. Well, his last mission was to get you out safe, so I guess I will complete it for him. I knew he needed old Bjorn to come and help him one more time. Besides, I need to go and visit some relatives in Sweden. Hold tight, this will be bumpy ride. I think I know where German minefields are. If not, we'll have to talk about it in next world. Try to shelter, under the canopy. It won't protect you from waves that break high, but it will keep you from worst ones.'

Huw thought Bjorn finished with a bleak laugh, but it was the engine coughing to life. The boat swung around east and away from the sea patrol, the soldiers, and Märt's final resting place.

At first, each jolt of a wave sent a thrill of pain through Huw's shoulder but he soon grew numb to it. Maarja moved close to help him keep his balance. Relief flooded through him, both spiritually and physically, fed by her proximity. After a while, he realised she was sobbing. He drew her closer and kissed her cheek. She hugged him fiercely in return. Her words carried only faintly over the crash and roar of the waves: 'I never got to tell him that I forgave him.'

Tears ran down Huw's face. He could no longer stop the pain. 'Neither did I, but I think he knew. I hope he did.'

'I can never repay what he did at Naissaar,' she said.

'We can – by staying alive and free.'

There was a long pause and then he felt the warmth of her hand in his, and her voice in his ear. 'Promise me you will never leave me again.'

'I promise.'

Juhan was again singing over the sound of the sea. Huw tried to focus on the song, and the comfort of Maarja by his side. It dulled the pain, but the tears still fell.

'I never knew what friendship was, before now.'

It was a great relief to see the first rays of light on the eastern horizon. Huw was bruised and battered from the buffeting of the speedboat as they raced north. His shoulder ached but it seemed that the blood had finally clotted. Hopefully they would get medical help when they reached civilisation once more.

Maarja shivered, snuggling closer. 'I feel I cannot move for cold,' she murmured.

'Let's try and solve that,' Huw replied with a gentle kiss on the lips.

He would always be a lousy spy. His loved ones meant everything to him. He looked at Juhan, who had fallen asleep. Only Juhan could do this, he thought with a chuckle.

Huw realised his main fear, of traversing the mine strewn Baltic, had passed, and the disturbing flashbacks of the stricken *Cassandra* had faded with it. In fact all his memories were mere murmurs in his dreams. Now he had found Maarja, he wanted to live in today.

'Are we close to Sweden, Bjorn?' he asked.

Bjorn stirred from his own reverie. 'Closer, friend, but I'll not slow until I know for sure. There are enemy boats active on the surface and below, and they have little to do but cause trouble.'

And aircraft too, Huw thought, looking to the skies. He elected to keep his own personal gloom to himself.

'I hope this doesn't get you into trouble,' he said to Bjorn, who laughed.

'I'll be interred for rest of war, so at least until then I'll be safe. My orders were to come to aid of Finnish army officer in occupied territory. I'm rescuing his unit, so I'm following orders.'

Bjorn spent a long time quietly staring out to sea, before he added: 'Did he go quickly?'

'I think so, Bjorn. I hope so.'

'Best friend you could have had,' the boatman replied. 'This bloody war... Ok, it is light now and you may as well help me keep watch for anything. Objects, boats, debris, whatever. It could tell us if there are mines around or if there are predators about or if they are coming towards us. If it's that, pray they fly a blue flag with a yellow cross.'

They saw the first patrol boat an hour into daylight. It had spotted them and began heading in their direction. Huw watched the white spray at the front of it as it carved a path through the sea.

'Whose is it?' He asked.

'Not sure,' came the reply. Bjorn slowed the boat to a virtual stop and took a small telescope out of his pocket. 'We are close enough, but I don't know any more. I can see Swedish boats in every wave crest at present.'

'Perhaps they may have some water?' Juhan grumbled.

Yes, I am sure they are frying eggs for you as we speak,' Huw replied with a grin.

The boat drew closer and Huw tensed. He was sure he had seen this kind of craft before, associated with this current adventure. He racked his brains to remember. Was it Murmansk, when he flew in? Or the port where the submarine left? He was sure, so sure...

'Oh my God, they are Reds,' he cried, and he felt Maarja tense and moan in dismay.

'No, no,' Juhan shouted. 'They are Rootsi Vikings, look!'

The boat turned to come past and Huw finally noticed the Swedish flag fluttering at the stern, high and proud.

'I think I love those colours,' he smiled.

The boat pulled alongside and Bjorn worked his way close so that they bobbed against the hull. A ladder was thrown out and three men dropped down to board, an officer and two armed sailors. Huw looked up to the deck and noted the sailors there, who were covering their colleagues.

Bjorn spoke at great length with the officer then turned to Huw. 'They accept that you are refugees and will take you into their care. They have doctor on board and will send down harness to lift you.'

'I will climb,' Huw replied, and Bjorn shook his head. 'No time to be stubborn. You put on harness, and then you try to climb.'

'And you?'

'We are on border of territorial waters, not quite in. They will let me go, I may even trade some oil and supplies for my hidden bottles of vodka,' he said with a sly wink.

Huw shook his head in disbelief, but the humour and relief washed over him and he had to smile, despite the pain.

'My friend, if I ever see you again. I will buy you a crate of vodka. Märt would be proud.'

'Yes, yes,' Bjorn waved away his embarrassment. 'I will collect one day. Some of these speak English, you will be okay here, I think. Be lucky and look after your woman there.'

Huw woke in a bed, trying to figure out what had changed. After a few minutes of random memory flashes, he realised that although his body seemed to move in the rhythm of the waves, the floor did not follow. He was on dry land for the first time in days.

He was lying on a bed with sheets. He couldn't remember the last time this had happened; it was probably back in a camp before he had left the air base at Aberdeen months ago, in another life. He couldn't get over the way a mattress and pillow let his body sink in so far. He wanted to get up, but his limbs felt tired to the bones. The wound in his shoulder was still stiff with swelling. It now sported a large covering of bandage that reeked of antiseptic. Drowsiness reclaimed him. If this is Sweden, he thought, I can rest. If not, perhaps sleep would be the better option.

He was awoken again by the swishing noise of a skirt as somebody walked nearby. He tried to focus on the white uniform until the woman's face was visible to him and he could clearly make out her blonde hair and blue eyes.

'This is not a dream,' he said.

She laughed. 'No, you are in hospital. I have to dress your wound and check the infection.'

'There were people with me.' Huw muttered.

'Yes, one waits for you now. Perhaps when you are better, I think.'

Huw reached to gently touch her arm. 'No, please can I see.'

She moved away and he drifted to sleep again. When he regained consciousness, he slowly became aware of a figure approaching his side. The shadow lifted across his eyes and he recognised the broad smile on the man's face.

'Juhan?'

The smile broadened. 'Welcome and good morning.'

'Thank God!' Huw breathed. 'Where is your mother?'

'She is at refugee camp. We take it in turns to visit.'

'What camp?'

'For Baltic refugees. It is an old leisure camp, now full of Estonians and the bay has hundreds of boats used to get here.'

'You are not a prisoner?'

'No, the Swedes are good hosts. They gave us food, clothing and a small allowance of krona. We have beds. I do not remember when I last had a bed.'

Huw smiled weakly. 'I know, I know.'

He stared at Juhan for a moment, before he finally put into words what had been disturbing him for a long time. 'Märt spoke to me before the end, about your birth.'

Juhan nodded. 'Yes, I know.'

'You were asleep,' Huw whispered accusingly.

Juhan smiled again in apology. 'No, I pretended to be. What could I have said?'

'Were you surprised?'

Juhan shook his head. 'No, I already knew.'

Huw fell back into his pillows, but even though dazed, he still managed to match the smile of his son. 'No, nothing surprises me any more. I don't know what to say. It is a bit late to be more than friends.' He reached out his hand. 'If it is not patronising, I am proud of all your work in this little adventure of ours.'

Juhan took the proffered hand and squeezed it in affection. 'I am happy also, but perhaps I will say that if I ever have son, he will be named Märt.'

'Good choice,' Huw whispered, his eyes stinging with tears.

The door opened and Maarja stepped into the room. She looked a changed woman – washed, with fresh clothes and a touch of make-up. To Huw it was a vision from heaven, but his injured body still made him groan as she hugged him tenderly.

'Marry me now,' he whispered. 'Before somebody catches you looking like that.'

She laughed and cried. Juhan smiled and gave a cheery wave as he got up to leave the room. 'I need to rest. Later we will talk.'

'You slept for two days,' Maarja said, stroking Huw's lank hair. 'Doctor said shoulder was infected with dirt. Only salt water stopped it from getting worse.'

'What have I missed?' Huw asked.

Maarja spread her arms wide. 'Bath, warm house, everything really. We are processed as refugees from Estonia and I have been to British consul also.'

'Perhaps you should have told them I was Estonian.'

She shook her head. 'They already knew about you. Patrol crew reported on their return and Swedish government then talked to the British.'

'I don't remember talking.'

'That is not a problem. You were in great pain and doctor gave you morphine.'

'There is something else here.'

'What do you mean, Huw?'

'You are holding back, my love. I know you too well.'

'Would it be better for English to tell you?'

'I would prefer you to tell me, Maarja.'

She sighed. 'They have asked me if I think you would go back to Britain and plead for Estonia.'

Huw shook his head. 'I will never leave you again.'

Maarja patted his hand. 'They want me to go also. Estonians want me to be their representative.'

'Haven't they had enough of using us yet?' Huw asked bitterly.

'Message is not enough. Estonians have been trying to say this to west for ages. Our consul thought it may be better if we could get you over there to give your first hand account.' She paused and pursed her lips. 'I said I would go also.'

Huw dropped her hand in shock. He suddenly felt very tired. 'Why?'

She grabbed his hand back and kissed it.

'You must understand this. You have been in my land. You have seen how people are destroyed, forced to live in forest like wild animals. You see how people roam around killing, hurting and destroying, all in the name of an invader. There is talk, Huw that Reds will be on another bloody crusade now. Just like Red terror of 1941. People think war is turning. Germany will survive twelve months, no more. Russian bear is stronger and more aggressive. They think Reds will try to take back us refugees at the end and Sweden may not feel strong enough to resist. We must get England and America to stop them, give us back our freedom and persuade them not to abandon us.'

Huw felt tired as the news sank in. 'How long will they keep me here?'

'Five days they say, but there is much to do. Papers, connections. They have contacts here and will get us out. The Swedish will not know – or will ignore.'

'So we run from safety and shelter.'

'I don't think it will last, Huw. The Swedes are good people, but that won't be enough in this new world.'

'What do you want to do, Maarja? Do you want us to go to war with Russia? Do you want the next generation to suffer with us?'

Her eyes burned fiercely. 'If that is what it takes.'

Huw expected nothing else, though the words dismayed him.

'How do we get over?'

'Through Norway and across.'

He nodded slowly, deciding that he was going to get one thing out of this prolonged insecurity: 'One condition, Maarja.'

'What is this, Huw?'

'You marry me now. I'm serious. I lost you once and I am not going to do it again.'

She blushed and he continued: 'Märt lived for two things once I had arrived back in Estonia. To make the West pay attention to what is happening in Estonia and to bring us together. He gave his life to both. Do you think I would let him down now?'

Chapter Twenty-Three

Cymru am byth

After what felt like months but was only a week, Huw was finally pronounced fit to leave the hospital. He celebrated with a warm bath and clean clothes, whilst he prepared for a briefing at the British Embassy regarding the journey. He elected to take Juhan with him, as he still did not feel strong enough to do the journey alone.

It was so refreshing to walk through the streets without fear of any military conflict. His arm was now in a sling, but this would not be needed by the time they left. He walked easily, looking about him. The atmosphere in Stockholm was positive and relaxed. The place oozed calm and its people looked content. It was so long since he'd seen such a phenomenon in a city. He admired the people who sat leisurely in the parks, whiling away the benign day. He had to feel a tinge of jealousy at their lot, thinking of Tallinn in 1919, with everyone hungry and wondering if they would survive the assaults from the Russian and German armies. It seemed unfair that the Estonian capital had seen so little of this peace in its free life.

The odd thing for him was that here was a chance of some peace in his own life and he was rejecting it, choosing to pass it by again for a journey of great danger. At least this time he wouldn't be alone he thought, and felt a warm glow inside.

He tapped Juhan's shoulder. 'Do you have money?'

Juhan nodded and Huw indicated a small café. 'Let's take a coffee first.'

Huw took a seat about half way in, facing the door, and indicated for Juhan to sit opposite. 'Next time the waitress walks past, turn and look as if you are checking her out. The man to the left of the door in the brown trilby has been following us since the camp.'

Juhan frowned. 'Why do you think this is so?'

Huw grabbed a menu. 'I think NKVD. I am sure there are listeners in the camp and that word has got round about our arrival, what with Maarja being ex-ministry. I don't want this man following us, so I will need to do something about it here.'

'So what do you want me to do?'

Huw looked hard at the menu. 'Be ready for my lead. I want you to come with me to the consul. There is something for you to do for me. After all that has happened, it seems you are the best man for the job, literally.'

'What do you mean?' Juhan frowned.

Huw knew he was blushing and it made him smile sheepishly. 'Just that, be my best man. I am marrying your mother in two hours in the Lutheran church.'

Juhan's eyes widened in surprise and then his broad smile seemed to light the room. 'Huw, my friend, this is sudden, but very Estonian. Tonight, we find some vodka.'

'And this time not for insect bites.' Huw's smile suddenly dropped and he stood up. 'Come, we have to move.'

He walked quickly for the door, just timing it as the waitress reached the stranger's table. She was placing a cup of coffee on it when Huw pretended to stumble. His momentum took him into the waitress who squealed with dismay as she fell into the man, tipping his coffee over him. Huw and Juhan moved quickly, turning their backs on the angry shouts and curses that ensued. They spotted a tram and jumped on, to lose themselves in Stockholm's busy streets.

At the consulate, Huw could not help remarking, 'Did your mother ever tell you I first met her in a waiting room like this?'

Juhan nodded. 'She said you were surprised to see an Estonian.'

'It wasn't quite like that,' Huw flushed as the door opened for them to be ushered into the consul's office.

The man seemed to have everything prepared for their journey ahead and he went through the papers in a very officious tone. 'These are for Sweden. Here you are a police auxiliary, so you have to speak Estonian at all times. Your train tickets are valid for just before the border, a contact will meet you there. He will get you to the mountains, where the Norwegians will take over. Be careful, Germany may be losing, but Norway is still an occupied territory.' He reached for another set of papers. 'As soon as you cross over, burn your Swedish papers. In Norway, you are migrant workers from the Weimar republic of Ostland. These are your permits. This will get you towards Trondheim, where your new contact will be waiting. Speak Estonian to him also, though keep it simple.'

'What happens then?' Huw asked.

The consul slowly removed his half-rimmed glasses and blinked at him. His accent was educated and the words came out in a tone that showed little understanding, or interest. 'I am told you will be catching the Shetland Bus.'

When they left, Huw had managed to get some krona from the consul, successfully arguing he was due a rather large amount of back-pay. His next port of call was a florist, where he insisted on buying white roses.

'Juhan, my boy,' he said, as he organised the buttonholes. 'We may not be in the best suits, but we sure as hell are going to look the part.'

'What do I do with other flowers?' Juhan asked.

'Oh, give them to girls that you like while we walk there. It's time you started charming the ladies.'

'Ok.' The grin was back on Juhan's face and to Huw, the world felt complete.

The street where the church was sited was busy with people. Huw suddenly realised from the way many smiled at them, that they were there for the wedding.

'Has the whole refugee camp turned up?'

Juhan shrugged. 'Probably, but then it gives them all chance to be Estonians and celebrate.'

Huw sighed. 'I would not begrudge them that.'

There were more surprises in store. Many hands had assisted in making Maarja's dress. She appeared as an Estonian maiden of old, floral patterns on her skirts, flowers braided in her hair and headband. The camp had lent what they could, and made what they did not have. Her big day would be a memorable one for the whole community.

The music was provided by the voices of the congregation, singing traditional songs. By necessity the ceremony was in Swedish, though two Estonian Swedes stood by to help translate the words of the minister. Finally, when the vows had been made, the minister stood back and there was a pause. The church echoed with the remnants of his last words. The translator muttered something to Juhan who leant forward to whisper in Huw's ear: 'They are waiting for you to kiss my mother.'

'Oh, okay!' Huw was completely thrown. His words echoed in the church. As word passed down the aisles, friendly laughter rippled through the gathering. Huw looked sheepishly at Maarja, but her smile robbed him of his embarrassment.

'Not how I expected the first wedded kiss to be, but today, I really don't care.' Huw said.

'So, get on with it,' Maarja replied sweetly.

The journey from Stockholm was not simple. Huw had been asked time and again at the wedding feast where they would honeymoon. 'Örebro,' he had replied. The people always laughed, making him wonder if he had told them the location of the local coalmine.

They caught a tram out of town. Huw felt the easiest way to remain anonymous would be to meet their train at a smaller station. He was on alert for strangers who dallied too long, just on the edge of their vision.

Juhan stood apart from them and got on the carriage at one end with Huw and Maarja at the other. Huw had impressed on them how much easier it would be to spot potential stalkers if they sat at either end. There would be no communication between them until they were out of town.

The train to Örebro was fairly full, the internal warmth of the carriage a blessing after the sharp autumnal wind outside. It was now the last week of October and the weather was most definitely on the turn. They had this one chance to make it across Scandinavia before winter's white carpet made movement difficult at best and impossible in the higher passes.

Their goal was west of Stockholm and not on the route to Norway at all. Huw was still certain that they were being watched. Was it the Swedish authorities – or the NKVD? Whoever it was, he wanted them confused as to the journey they were planning. The trek across Sweden into occupied Norway and then across the sea would be epic enough. To have interference from third parties would render it impossible. Their flight from Estonia was enough excitement for one lifetime, Huw mused. There was no need to go looking for more.

Örebro lay on a lake, on the bank of which sat a prominent castle that split the town in two.

'Why have we left station?' asked Maarja.

'We have been followed,' Huw replied. 'No, this is for real. I'm certain of it. I think he's a Russian agent. I don't think the Reds have ever considered dressing their men in any other way but a suit and trilby.'

'What do you want to do?' Juhan asked.

'We have an hour and a half before the train to Östersund, let's try and lose him. We'll scout the town and then nearer the time, we'll all split up and lead him a dance.'

The trio made their way through Örebro and Huw began to relax. It was still a novelty to walk around a place and take in its beauty. The matchboard houses and the imposing round towers of the castle reminded him so much of towns in Estonia.

'This is no surprise,' Maarja replied to him. 'We were once part of Sweden. It is known as good years.'

Her eyes misted as she took in the town bustling gently about its business. Huw wondered where she was going back to in her mind.

'You are showing me Toompea again, I think,' he muttered.

She smiled sending warm sensations down his back. 'Yes and perhaps I was dreaming of showing you around Haapsalu also.'

'You never did that.'

Her tongue-tip perched on her lips in a coy smile. 'No, but I am doing it now. There are many occasions that I see that you have yet to experience.'

Huw coughed uncomfortably and her grin became mischievous.

'Juhan, are you ready for a bit of exercise?' Huw asked. He got a ready smile in reply.

'Yes, where do you want me to take him?'

'I have a feeling the man will follow me if we split up,' Huw replied. 'Go right for a few hundred metres and then double back. Maarja, you go left and around the castle. I will do my best to get rid of this pest. See you back in the station.'

Huw moved off down the road and picked up his pace. There were two parallel roads and he meant to make use of them. The snoop was fifty yards behind, Huw could see him in the reflections of shop windows and parked car mirrors. He would make this man's life hell.

He reached a road junction and bolted across it in front of the traffic. The cars honked their extreme displeasure, but his timing had been perfect, for the road became a river of moving vehicles. Racing down the street and keeping as close to the buildings as he dared, he darted across a side road and down an alley between two shops. He put his back to the nearside wall and waited in hope that his shadow was small enough to evade a cursory glance. Finding some refuse bins he crouched down in time to see the spy rush past the entrance in an aggravated trot. Huw waited a few seconds before nipping out to the edge of the alleyway, hoping that the smell in his nostrils did not run to his clothing. He took one quick look and then retreated back to the main road he had come from.

He was back on the station platform in time to see his train pull in. Maarja beamed, reminding Huw where Juhan had inherited his broad smile from. They boarded the train as if it was the most natural thing to do.

As they sped northwards Huw began to doze. He remembered a summer's day trip across the lowlands of mid Wales, through the green plains of the Dyfi estuary. A beautiful place where the wild birds hunted for food and sheep and cattle grazed in the marshes. It was a memory that had not surfaced for a long time and, in his dreamy state, he was there, floating along the train track and taking in the salt air.

He woke with a jolt. The train had come to a stop and there was a movement of people to and from the carriage. A blonde man walked past their compartment, his dark trench coat covering a brown suit. Huw eyed him with suspicion then moved to sit by the compartment door, leaving Juhan and Maarja at the window. He hoped he could somehow get an edge on any attack, for certainly if the NKVD were still following, then it was to ascertain their plans or stop them. If they found out what the plan actually was, they may try and expose them to the Swedes or worse, try and eliminate them.

There was movement outside the compartment and a shadow appeared. Huw tensed like a spring as the door swept open and the man sat down between Huw and his family. Nobody spoke in the compartment for a long time, making the tension unbearable. The new arrival slowly removed his hat and twirled it in his hands, staring intently at the ground. Then he muttered a few words.

'Cymru am byth.'

'What?' Huw replied without thinking.

The man sighed and continued in English. 'You really must guard your reactions, for I may not be who I seem.'

'And who is that?' Maarja asked.

Huw closed his eyes at the mess he had created.

'I'm a postman,' the man replied. 'I have two deliveries to make.'

'Three,' Maarja replied firmly.

The man frowned and his hat managed a few more rotations, until he finally said, 'that is... awkward.'

'That is your delivery,' Maarja snapped.

The man gave a hint of a smile and then nodded.

Maarja returned the nod in satisfaction. 'I am called M...' she began, but the man held up his hand.

'I do not want to know.'

'Can we trust you?' Huw asked suddenly.

The man shrugged. 'That's your problem.'

Huw winced at the memory of Märt on a windy Estonian beach months back.

'What is wrong?'

The man's voice broke through Huw's thoughts. Huw stared at the deep blue eyes and the haunted feeling returned. 'Someone once said that to me.'

'Who?'

They locked gazes.

'A friend,' Huw replied eventually.

With a flicker of understanding, the man nodded approval. 'There will be a long journey to Storlien, so you can rest. I will keep guard. Tell your man to relax.'

Huw looked across to Juhan and noticed the way he sat, tensed up and ready to spring, his hand closed on the hunting knife he had demanded to carry and eyes gleaming with a new desire for action. Huw had a sudden concern for his son. Their flight could easily turn Juhan into a killing machine, eager to find revenge wherever he deemed it was needed.

Huw smiled gently. 'Juhan, everything is alright. I trust this man.'

A fragment of the old smile returned, as Juhan settled back down in the corner. 'That's good, I need to sleep.'

'Me also son, I want to go home.' Huw turned back to the man. 'What is Storlien?'

'A town close to the border.'

'We only have tickets to Östersund.'

The man shrugged again. 'This will be no problem, there are many who help, even if our country stands apart from this war. Best sleep now, I will wake you in time enough.'

Huw settled down. There was nothing to do but rest and see where the fates took him. Either this man was real or not. He would check out Östersund station for signs of problems, but something led him to believe that this time, things were alright. He drifted off to sleep.

He was woken by the sound of sharp voices. A policeman was standing in the compartment talking to Maarja. The blonde postman was nowhere to be seen.

'You have not left at your stop, why are you going to the border? Do you think to leave? You cannot travel with refugee visas.'

Maarja was stumbling for a reply, though her face was full of innocence and charm. 'I am so sorry. We must have slept through our stop. We are all so tired, but we can go back on the next train.'

The compartment door opened and their contact appeared. The policeman stopped his interrogation and paused, then nodded and handed back the papers. 'See that you do.'

He moved past the contact without a word. Huw was impressed and slightly amused as the man sat down and took out a cigarette, as if nothing had occurred.

'We are near to Storlien. There the locomotives change and you will need to hide.'

He did not expand on this statement and Huw looked across to give Maarja a smile of support. Juhan appeared bored by the whole affair.

'Can we get something to eat and drink?' Maarja asked.

The man smiled and produced a small bar of chocolate.

'This and a hip flask is all I have. When you arrive, stay on the train to Trondheim, where you will be met.' He took a long drag and stubbed out the cigarette on the floor with his toe. 'We are near, please be ready.'

'This man seems to know his business,' Juhan suddenly said in Estonian. 'If he was Red, he wouldn't be so smooth.'

On arrival at Storlien, they got out onto the station. Their contact walked the platform with them to the top of the train. He kept them at a steady gait, despite Huw's strong desire to run. The steam engine gently hissed at the platform end as they approached. The crew was busy on the footplate and as Huw passed the cab, the driver leant out and called to the station staff. Huw looked back to see the station master walk towards the engine.

'Keep close to the engine and go around to the cab on the other side,' the blonde man muttered, then peeled off and started talking to the driver. Huw looked back to see the stationmaster had joined the conversation. The two men stood quite broadly on, so the view from the carriages was blocked. Huw held back to ensure they walked in single file and then moved to the end of the engine. He indicated quickly to his family and stepped off the platform to rush around the front of the engine. He hoped they were hidden from view from the platform. If they were seen, it would be obvious what they were up to, as they made their way along the darker side of the engine. Huw peered up the steps to the cab. There was no sound of life, so he grabbed the handrails and levered himself slowly up to the cab floor. The driver was still leaning out of the cab, talking to the men on the platform. The fireman, standing on the coal, looked up from the tender and flashed a dusty grin.

'Hej!' He mouthed and beckoned furtively. Huw needed no second offer and scrambled up to sit, at the fireman's indication, on the cab floor against the front of the coal bunker. He was out of sight of any prying eyes on the station. Maarja followed, then the fireman made to stop Juhan, but Huw tapped the man's leg and shook his head. 'My son,' he whispered and pointed at himself and Maarja. 'My wife.'

'You have been busy,' the man said, glancing around to see if there was anyone watching. Then he rushed to the tender and dug away a small hollow at the front of the coal pile. He motioned for Juhan to sit and received a grin of thanks.

The train moved out slowly. Huw took a quick look out and caught sight of the self-styled postman. He gave a parting nod and a smile. The fireman's shadow danced in front of Huw with flowing movements as he fed the hungry furnace, fuelling the engine's lurch into the cold night. The locomotive roared in response to the crew's ministrations. After a kilometre or so, the fireman climbed onto the coal pile in the tender and began to attack it with a greater gusto than before. Finally, he beckoned Huw to follow.

219

From the glow of the firebox, Huw could faintly make out a gap at the back of the coal pile. A piece of corrugated iron could be seen under the coal, leading to a small pocket of shelter. He squeezed into it, finding it cosy and already warm. When Maarja followed a few minutes later, she snuggled up with a giggle and a kiss. Juhan followed after and then they were like sardines in a can. The shadow of the fireman loomed over them.

'Tight for three, but you will live. Only fifteen kilometres to go.'

He pulled the cover over them and soon their tiny world was full of the percussion of coal rattling on corrugated iron. Huw tried to relax and regulate his breath. He felt Maarja's hand and his mind started dreaming of better times.

They were cooling off in the river by the farm, before Märt appeared on the scene and... The loss washed over Huw like a raw wound. He knew he would always feel this pain, but it gave him a new determination to succeed. He owed it to his friend at the very least. His attention drifted back to the dream of the river.

The air was poor and getting worse for the three of them. The close confinement meant the heat soon built up. Huw felt they were in a moving coffin. Only fifteen kilometres, the fireman had said, but it may as well have been fifteen hundred to Huw. The train lurched to a stop and there was a faint sound of shouting. He imagined he could hear someone moving about on the coal. He prayed for release and fresh air in his lungs.

The engine roared again and the train lurched forward, much to his bitter disappointment. He was growing woozy and light-headed. He wondered how long they could last, before they were overcome by carbon monoxide. Soon, he would have to chance breaking out to save them from suffocation. If he still had the energy – how many hundredweight of coal had been shovelled on them? He thought of stricken submariners. He shook his head to clear away the morbid image. Panic wouldn't help. He squeezed Maarja's hand and to his relief received a similar response.

The train lurched to a stop again. Huw realised he had been dozing. A surge of fear hit his throat, exacerbated as the motion started again, albeit slowly. Then there was a sudden relief, as he heard the sound of shovelling from above. Finally, the corrugated roof was pulled clear. Huw rejoiced as his lungs filled with cool, clear air. His body tingled as a movement sent his blood flowing around his legs. The sweat that slicked his body began to cool and he shivered.

'Come quick.' The fireman's voice was a harsh whisper as his hand appeared in view. 'Can you get up? Before the German guard comes back. I've got him sharing a smoke and a chat with the driver on the station. If we keep low, he won't see us.'

Huw grasped the man's hand and pulled himself up onto his unsteady feet. His workmen's clothes were not going to look as new as he had feared they did at the start. He moved haltingly to the top of the pile and looked back for Maarja.

It took a few seconds to see the shawl she had wisely tied to her hair and then he found her outstretched hands and pulled her to safety. The fireman waved her towards a ladder at the back of the tender and she was soon out of sight. Juhan was very wobbly as he descended the back of the tender in his turn. Huw heard him retching. It made him want to swill his own mouth in water. The fireman took his Swedish papers to burn on the fire and pointed to the dimly lit station a few yards away.

'Go to the platform. There are some people there who will help you clean up a little. Good Norwegians.' The fireman's white teeth suddenly broke through the blackness of his coal dust smeared face. 'Welcome to Norway.'

They shuffled up to the station, where a sign proudly stated the name "Koppera". Huw was surprised at the lack of attention being shown by the German soldiers around. Perhaps in resignation that the glorious future promised by their leader appeared to be crumbling, they were biding time – and bored with it.

There was little time to wash hands and faces at the station. Huw argued that to do so would arouse suspicion – they'd look cleaner than their clothes. But Maarja was insistent: 'Even the poorest people have some pride. I do not need to look as if I have been down a coal mine,' she said with a tired smile.

Clambering into the train was almost too much. The oxygen deprivation caused by their stint in the tender had exhausted them all, but they found seats in an open carriage of the train to rest in. Juhan elected to sit farther down the carriage, facing his parents, as he had done in Sweden. He gave Huw a faint wink and the ghost of a smile, to say he was still enjoying the journey.

Huw fell back to talking in Estonian and squeezed Maarja's arm.

'Would that I could hug you now, kallis,' he whispered.

She smiled demurely and lowered her eyes. 'There will be time, now I've got you back. You are not going anywhere from me now.'

'I look forward to that time,' he said, in a tone that made her narrow her eyes in mock disapproval.

Huw quietened abruptly as he realised the carriage was silent and no longer deserted. Among their fellow passengers, a German officer sat, eyes closed, oblivious to the world. His grey hair and lined face told of a long and busy life. Given the turnaround in fortunes of Germany, Huw wondered how far that would continue. How long would any of them survive? He began to think again of the circumstances of his posting and how it had all turned out. Was it fate or just foolishness that had Huw chosen in the first place? He'd certainly not shown many qualities for the role – except perhaps that of a loner – from the time the navy imprisoned him in Portsmouth.

The train's motion was calming. Maarja drifted off to sleep. Huw felt comfortable with her head resting on his shoulder. It proved too cumbersome and she moved to rest against the window. Huw had a sudden desire to relieve himself and began to rise, slowly letting Maarja's arm drop to stop her waking.

'Back in a minute,' he whispered.

He made off to the next carriage in search of a toilet. There were compartments and Huw had a thought about it being better for them to be hiding in one. Easier to rest and stay unnoticed as they raced across Norway. Perhaps on his return, he would wake Maarja. Juhan would follow in time.

Leaving the toilet, he found himself walking towards the German officer, who asked to see his papers. The man sounded curious rather than authoritarian, as he gave a stiff nod.

'Hier bitte,' he said, indicating an empty compartment. Huw stepped inside and turned to find himself staring down the barrel of a Luger pistol.

Chapter Twenty-Four

The smell of fish

'I think we need to talk,' the man said in English. Huw feigned ignorance, but his adversary shook his head.

'Nein, that is not good enough. I have studied your actions, watched your movements and heard your words. Your woman is of Ostland sure enough, you are not.'

He sat down slowly, keeping the pistol trained on Huw and motioning for him to sit. The man showed Huw his ID card again.

'Yet your papers say you were born in Dorpat, this is wrong surely?'

'I was born in Finland,' Huw said quietly.

'So, I have to ask myself questions.' The man continued in Estonian, 'I was born and brought up in Ostland – in Dago, where our manor was. I learned to speak with locals, I know their voices and way they say things. I know Finnish people also. I say your accent is west of there. English perhaps?'

Huw could not believe how his luck had changed, switching between triumph and disaster since that plane had touched down in Murmansk. Here, disaster loomed again. He looked around for a weapon or an escape route, but nothing presented itself.

'So, I ask myself,' the officer resumed in English. 'What is an Ostlander speaking Englishman doing with an Ostland woman in Norway? Nothing good, I think – or maybe there is another story. For why would the British send a man into Norway from Sweden, when the Norwegian resistance is perfectly capable of landing you anywhere on this damned impossible coastline, hein?'

The door opened and in one swift movement, the German grabbed Maarja's arm and dragged her inside. She was spun towards Huw in a way that stopped any chance of escape.

'Madam, you may as well be present, so I can keep an eye on you,' the man said calmly in English. 'Your husband has a story to tell me.'

Huw sat in silence. The situation appeared hopeless. Could Juhan possibly arrive unannounced and cause confusion? As if Huw's mind was being read, the German pulled the blinds down.

'Now we have the privacy. I need to know the truth. I do not wish to play games. My next move depends on what you say. Come, come. You are too quiet.'

'This is my wife,' Huw finally replied. 'We were married in Sweden a few days ago. We are refugees from Estonia.'

'And your papers?'

'Burnt to allow us to travel through Norway unhindered.'

'Why do you run?'

'The Reds are not liberators, they are murderers,' Maarja spat. The officer nodded in understanding.

'You were fugitives, why was this please?'

Huw looked into the man's eyes for clues. Some instinct told him there was a spark of humanity still within, he hoped to God he was right.

'Maarja was working in the government. I was an officer of the Royal Navy. In 1919, we both had exposure to the capture and execution of some sailors in the Russian navy at this time. It seems Mother Russia has a long memory.'

The man appraised Huw's every facial expression, his whole body language. It was worse than his day in court, when he'd been in the dock for desertion. The German pursed his lips.

'How were you involved?'

'I was an officer on board a ship that captured a Russian vessel.'

'I heard that two were captured.'

Huw nodded, unsurprised now at the man's knowledge.

'Indeed, I was assigned to the consul by the time the second one was got.'

'I worked for the ministry,' Maarja said.

The German nodded slowly. 'So? And then?'

'I jumped ship and we went to live on a farm near Märjamaa.'

'For twenty-four years?'

'Yes,' Maarja said quickly.

'No,' Huw said. There was something in the eyes of the German that was compelling him to tell the truth. He was watching like a hawk and Huw felt sure he would pick out the lies far too easily. There was something else there also, hidden deeply. Huw wanted to trust the man, even if it was wartime and he was the enemy.

'Thank you,' the man replied. 'Madam, it is very important that you are honest with me, very important.'

He indicated for Huw to continue.

'I was captured and returned to England, where I was sent to prison for my crime. When released, I struggled to find any work.'

'But you did not return to Ostland, why?'

Huw stared at a dark grease spot on the floor. 'I had no money, my parents had died and there was no family left. I had been in prison and I felt... wretched, useless – and I hated myself for it. I could have tried, I damned well should have tried, but I did not have the courage. I felt I could not survive travelling in foreign countries with no money. And I was scared of what I would find when I got there.'

Maarja flushed but said nothing. There was a long silence before Huw continued in a subdued voice. 'Prison broke me. I felt ashamed that I had let everyone down. I couldn't look anyone in the eye again.'

Maarja sighed. 'You are so filled with your sense of honour. Think how many years you wasted.'

Huw nodded and closed his eyes. 'I do, constantly.'

'You were sent back by the English to Ostland to the resistance against the Reich.'

'That's what we told the Reds we were doing.'

'Why?'

'So they would take me there.'

A flicker of a smile played on the German's lips. 'And they pulled back your leash when they were ready.'

Huw shook his head. 'They did not know where I was.'

'So how did they know where to look?'

Huw shrugged. 'They intercepted my signals perhaps?'

'In code, ja? So they broke this easily?'

Huw was silent, for there was no answer he could give.

'But I am surprised,' the German continued. 'That you did not receive the Reds with open arms. The resistance attacked our men as we fell back.'

'Germany left us to die,' Maarja snapped angrily. 'When the Wehrmacht left, they left us with nothing. They disarmed our men who had driven the Reds back and left us defenceless. Why else do you expect they were attacked? We needed weapons.'

The German frowned and began to speak, but Maarja was at boiling point and was now in full flow. 'You left us, you bloody landlords, with your big houses and airs and graces. You took what you wanted with you and then just ran away.'

Huw felt they were dead. He hoped Juhan could escape, at least. He even prayed now that his son would not intercept them. A mixture of anger, surprise and embarrassment seemed to choke the air in the compartment. The officer smiled thinly and slowly began to put his pistol away. He reached inside his tunic.

The door flew open and Juhan stood in the entrance, his hunting knife in hand and a look of murder on his face.

'Juhan, leave him!' Huw snapped.

Juhan reacted slowly, the white anger confounded by doubt.

'Juhan, it is alright,' Maarja said softly. 'We are just talking. Come inside.'

Juhan sat down, but the knife was still gripped firmly in hand – waiting for the first sign of betrayal. The German quickly shut the door and then brought out a small wallet.

'This man is your son, no? This is my son.'

He produced a photograph and handed it to Maarja. A young man stared back at her proudly, his formal uniform belying the carefree smile as he sat on a riverbank. A young woman sat laughing by his side. Maarja's face softened as she took in the scene.

'He was killed in an air raid in Berlin. It was as well perhaps, for he was being posted to the eastern front. To die there would be harsh. To be captured would be a living hell. It is a harsh fate for a German now to be told he will be posted east, not west. In either front you can die, but in the West if you are captured, you are still a man, not an animal.'

He smiled again, but there was no warmth, only deep sadness.

'You place your future, all your dreams, in your children. You hope they succeed where you have failed. When they are taken from you, you are left with no hope. I am returning to Trondheim for orders. I think they will send me east. I think this is my death sentence. I am an old man now. Perhaps I have lived too long. At this time, the world is not kind to us all.'

He looked out of the window for a long time

'Do you not have a wife? Other children?' Maarja asked gently.

His eyes closed for a moment.

'She died in childbirth. My daughter has little to do with me. She is perhaps not proud that her father chose the path he did, in days when the new ideas seemed glorious. It is a fitting punishment for me.' He sighed away his burden. 'But now I am facing an English spy. One who has journeyed far to find his family and lead them to safety. Is this man a threat to me? Only if I hurt his family, I think. I am old and I am tired. One escaping family, looking to find a way out of this mess, will not change the world. Or perhaps it will, but for the better, hein? I want to believe there is still good in this world.'

He gathered his hat and reached out to touch Maarja's arm.

'I would like to have seen your wedding day, my dear.'

Maarja leaned forward to kiss his cheek.

'Write to her, tell her everything you feel. It will help both of you.'

The ghost of a smile played on his lips. 'Perhaps.'

He stood to attention and gave a slight bow, clicking his heels, before he stepped through the door and was gone. Maarja gave out a soft sob.

'What is wrong, mother?' Juhan asked.

'That is a poor man who needs to forgive himself,' she replied.

'Perhaps he just did,' Juhan replied.

Maarja reached out to hug her son. There was nothing that could be better than the right words at the right time, Huw thought, as he settled down to sleep off the remaining journey.

They were picked up by their contact ahead of the main station of Trondheim. The contact just seemed to glide into their lives, as if he had been there all the time.

'Come with me,' the man said, his sharp eyes scrutinising Huw from under his trilby hat. Huw knew better than to ask questions; it was better to observe what was going on around. The man sat with them, but when they left the train, he could have been walking alone. At the ticket barrier, they were stopped by an officious German officer demanding papers. Their contact had already melted into the shadows.

'Ostlanders? What are you doing here?'

'We are working. I have papers,' Maarja replied.

'Ja, ja, but you are of Ostland, why here in Norway?'

'My country is gone, buried under the Reds. We escaped by boat.'

227

The officer studied the papers carefully again and then his eyes narrowed.

'This allows work for two men. What about the woman?'

Maarja quickly translated to Huw in Estonian.

'I will not leave my woman behind to Red Army,' Huw growled, putting as much indignation into his Estonian accent as he could. 'Would you do such thing?'

The German gave a curt nod.

'Genau.'

He handed back the documents and spoke again to Maarja. She walked through the barrier without a word, Huw and Juhan quickly in tow.

'What did he say?' Huw asked.

'Behave and work hard. These *men* are so superior after all.'

'Superior enough to have a job collecting tickets at an anonymous station,' Huw replied. 'Let's go.'

They began to walk down the road and Huw noticed his contact walking towards them. He passed by as if he did not know them at all, but as he passed, he muttered, 'a truck lies round the next corner. Get in the back.'

The truck looked deserted as Huw got them on board. The back was full of boxes and Huw began to move them to make room.

'Empty,' he said.

'And it stinks of fish,' Maarja muttered.

Juhan started to make a space by stacking the boxes closer to the end. 'If we sit over here, smell will be less.'

The truck started up and began to move and soon their noses alerted them to the mounting smell of diesel fumes.

'It seems to me we are damned if we move and damned if we don't,' Huw said. He cleared a space toward the back and loosened the canvas cover, to let the air flow. 'There.'

'I feel sick,' Maarja said through gritted teeth.

'Please stick your head out of back then,' Juhan said with a grin. 'I don't think I would be able to take that smell also.'

The truck wended its way along a bumpy, twisting road and they all began to doze. After a while, Huw became aware of a bobbing arc of light playing on the canvas flap. He peeked out and cursed at the sight of a German jeep following them.

'Don't these people ever stop?' He muttered.

The vehicle, a Kubelwagen, was driving close for quite a while, before it sped past with an angry parp of the horn. The darkness reclaimed them and their world resumed around the monotonous rise and fall of the lorry engine, as it lumbered through the countryside. A few miles on, the truck came to a stop, amid a lot of shouting. The flap was thrown open and Huw looked straight into the hard face of a German soldier. His shouted commands, even though Huw could not understand the words, were obviously a demand for their disembarkation. The soldier shouted for papers. Huw looked for the Kubelwagen, but it was nowhere to be seen. They had stumbled on an established roadblock. Huw tried to imagine what to say, even though he knew he did not have the language to say it.

Maarja stepped in to stem the doubt created by Huw's confusion. Talking calmly, she took the papers from Huw and Juhan and presented them to the soldier. The man looked at them and then barked a question at the driver, who just shrugged and said something in his own language. Maarja spoke at length again and a flat look of boredom came across the soldier's face. He virtually threw the papers back at Maarja and snapped commands at her. This was punctuated by a dismissive wave and a shove in Juhan's back.

'We get back in now,' Maarja said, pointing out the cab to the Norwegian, who shrugged and sloped off.

'What happened?' Huw asked.

Maarja smiled stiffly. 'He was frustrated that neither you nor Juhan could speak German. He became angrier at driver for not speaking also, because he thought this man could. He was then again angry that I could not speak Norwegian, so could not translate for him. He told me a lot about how useless we all were and how pathetic this country was. Then he said that I smelt of fish and told me to go and wash. I think he was trying to imply that fish had nothing to do with it.'

'There is a man who will remain as bachelor,' Juhan replied.

The lorry engine droned as they made their way through the Norwegian countryside. Huw and Juhan managed to prop open the canvas flap to give them more ventilation. Maarja found some sacking, miraculously not soaked in fish oil, and used it as a mat. She sat gazing at intently on something cupped in her hand. After a while she looked up with a shy smile and showed Huw the pencil sketch of the rose that he had drawn years ago for her. She stroked the frayed ends gently.

'I may have lost you, but I never forgot you,' she said, her eyes welling with tears.

'I'll draw you another, when the world slows down for us,' Huw promised. 'On nice fresh card that will last forever.'

She turned to look back at her picture.

'And then I will have two,' she said. 'But they will be different, as we have all changed.'

'I will build you a garden of roses,' Huw offered.

'But then it may be that land is cold where we end up, ' she said with a mischievous look.

'Then I will make a greenhouse,' he said.

'We are near sea,' Juhan called. 'Do you think we should hide in case there are more roadblocks?'

'Probably,' Huw said. 'There will be plenty of military installations by the coast. No, perhaps not. We know what will happen. If the Germans stop us, they will search the back. We will be safer if we look as though we are supposed to be there.'

To illustrate that, he moved to lift the flap, letting the light of day flood in.

Soon after this, the lorry stopped in an area that appeared uninhabited. Huw looked out, seeking a reason for this latest delay. The driver leant out of his cab and pointed to a narrow path leading down towards the seashore. No words were spoken. Huw waved his thanks and got a "V for victory" sign in return. This was followed by a crash of gears that heralded the swift departure of the lorry. They were left standing in a rocky wilderness facing the wind blowing from the sea.

The path led them down to a small shingle beach, sheltered from the road. It was flanked by sheer cliffs leaving a narrow inlet. A rowing boat was beached there, in a small rocky indent, out of sight from the sea. As they picked their way over the rocks, a man appeared beside them.

'Here you wait,' he said. 'Two hours, German patrol will come and then we go. Here,' he offered something wrapped in paper.

The smoky, tangy smell of cured fish came out, leaving Huw to think of their recent journey. His stomach heaved, but he had not eaten in a day and a half, so he forced himself to chew some of the fish. The other two joined in, although with such looks of disdain, it was clear it would be a long time before they would enjoy the taste of fish again. The man supplied a canteen of water, which was nectar to their dry throats. Huw settled down to doze, out of sight of prying eyes as he waited for the next stage of this relentless journey.

He awoke to the drone of an engine, which pulled him into an immediate state of alertness. He crouched to peer over the rocks sheltering him from the sea, heard a low whistle and spied the Norwegian guide on a ledge above, indicating to the water.

'It is ok,' he said. 'This is German patrol; they come every day this time like clockwork. They should be Swiss,'

'Why are they so obvious with their patrols?' Huw whispered.

The man shrugged. 'They know they are losing. They know the time is short. They have stopped caring.'

He looked over the top with a quick grin. 'Do not worry about talking; there are only good Norwegians in this area. We know when strangers come.'

'Why bother hiding then?'

'Losing makes them lazy, but not completely. If you present them with a fight, they will still take it.'

Huw lay back again and sighed. After so many weeks of living on the edge, keeping one step ahead of pursuit, it felt bizarre now to be lying on a beach with nothing but the sound of the sea and the lazy breeze wafting over him. Maarja crawled over to him and lay by his side. Huw's mind drifted.

They had gathered hay from the fields for the winter. It was a beautiful clear sunny day and the sweat was running off his shirtless body. The hay was bundled onto the cart and they broke for lunch late, when the land was at its hottest. Huw wished he was by the coast and looked forward to the day's end, when he would wash in the river or by the water pump. He lay down and Maarja joined him. Overcome by heat and fatigue, he dozed until he felt something tickling his nose. He brushed it away and settled into the black openness of sleep. The tickling returned, he swatted at it and caught a grass stalk. He opened his eyes and saw Maarja's impish grin.

'I have more flowers to tickle you with, if you try and sleep again,' she warned.

He groaned and grabbed her waist, tickling her ribs. She squealed and laughed as she turned to break away. He gazed deep into her deep blue eyes. They were as beautiful as the rest of her. He moved to kiss her...

Now, he really looked into her eyes as he had not done for a long time. They were still beautiful and still gave him the rush of feeling that he remembered. It had never gone away, nor would it, he knew. For the umpteenth time, he thanked Märt silently for his sacrifice.

'I never stopped loving you,' he muttered.

She smiled sweetly. 'I am old and fat.'

He shook his head. 'There is still what lies within.'

'So, I *am* old and fat,' her brows arched in mock surprise. He reached out and tickled her ribs. She gave out a low shriek, which she quickly stifled and they both laughed softly. The Norwegian crept over from his perch.

'As dusk falls we will leave. There are no active guns here, but there are a few down the coast who might take an interest in us. Be patient.'

'I have waited twenty-five years,' Maarja replied. 'How patient do you wish me to be?'

The light was fading when the Norwegian roused them and they gathered around to launch the rowing boat into the oncoming waves of the beach. Juhan held the boat through the gentle waves and then was last to hop in. 'Should I swim alongside?' He grumbled as he struggled to jump.

'You could do with a wash,' Huw quipped.

Juhan grinned. 'Yes, it is tempting.'

They rowed clear of the headland and slowly pulled out towards one of the hundreds of islands dotting the horizon. There was no sign of shipping in the area at all. Huw was certain that would not have been the case before the war.

Faintly, above the gentle lap of water and the dipping of the oars, he could make out the hum of an engine far off. He scanned the air, looking for signs of an aeroplane. The last thing they needed at this moment, whilst they were this exposed. Nothing happened for a long time and then he became aware of a shadow of a craft looming from around a nearby island. It seemed to be a fast patrol; it altered course and bore down on them. Huw's heart sank.

Chapter Twenty-Five

Everyone but the Germans

'It has Norway's flag,' shouted Juhan.

'This is the Shetland bus,' The Norwegian man remarked calmly.

The ship pulled up sharply alongside, the wash making their rowing boat bob like a cork. A rope ladder was hung down and Huw steered the rowing boat toward it with difficulty. The loud thrum of the ship's engine suggested a beast demanding to be given rein.

Huw marvelled at the ship. It was like the speedboats being tested when he was at sea, but much bigger. Huw guessed it was of torpedo-boat or search-and-rescue origin: fast, manoeuvrable and with a light wooden hull, it would be difficult to intercept if used for fast, covert operations.

On climbing the ladder, they were helped on deck by some of the crew, who then shared a joke with the Norwegian guide in the rowing boat, before the man pulled away with his oars. He did not acknowledge the fugitives.

Their new hosts looked a strange bunch for a navy crew. Many were working on deck and appeared to be dressed in a mixture of navy uniform, stout fishing Guernseys and bobble hats. In effect, whatever appeared to be comfortable. They would pass as seamen, but possibly not navy. The captain stood on the small bridge wearing a military hat and tunic, but even this was unbuttoned at the top. A true motley crew – Huw warmed to them immediately.

'Are you navy?' Maarja asked.

'Sure,' the man replied. 'This is a Norwegian navy boat. Sorry we are late, but we have been busy.'

He grinned and pointed to the horizon, where a dirty black cloud was rising from the south.

'Resistance?'

The man shrugged. 'They call us that but we fight for our country and our king in exile. We are his navy.'

'Where are we bound?' Huw asked and the man grinned.

'Home. Scallowa. Shetland. We are the Shetlandsjegen – the Shetland boys. You will like it there.'

'And – "the Shetland Bus"?'

233

'It is so named because we come over so many times on business,' the man laughed, patting the superstructure of the boat affectionately. 'I am called Lars,' he added. 'Come with me, I will show you your bunks.'

Huw turned to Maarja and Juhan and gave them a strange smile.

'You are home,' said Maarja. 'I see it in your eyes.'

'If home has a bath and a bed, I will love it,' Huw replied. His smile broadened. 'But I'm home with my family, also.'

They were taken below deck to a cabin which had bunks set out ready. Lars pointed to a doorway across the corridor.

'Our shower is here, there is soap and towels. I will leave fresh clothes for you. You need to wash.'

Huw knew what he meant. Not a criticism of their odour but an acknowledgement of the journey they had undertaken. Even so, it was still unbelievable.

'These are American boats,' Lars said to the unasked question. 'And you know Americans do not go anywhere without comfort.

'Next thing you tell me they have hot water.'

Lars made a face.

'Possibly, depends on how much has been used. We will be too busy working, so nobody will use them also. I need you to stay in your cabins after, for we will be travelling back fast in the dark. We find the Germans leave us alone in this way, because they cannot catch us, hey?'

'I will ask the cook to find you some hot food and coffee. Please do not come up, I do not wish to lose any of you overboard. Nor do I wish you to be in the way if we have to fight off an attack.'

He nodded and left.

'I love Norwegians, they are so practical,' Huw said, in the silent void that Lars had left behind. Maarja shook her head in wonder. 'What is this world? I do not know it.'

'I suggest you find out,' Huw said. 'Juhan and I can smell a bit longer.'

When Maarja came out of the shower, Huw and Juhan were sat drinking coffee. Used plates were stacked on the floor and a warm plate of fried bacon and eggs sat on the bed.

'Come and eat, mother,' Juhan said with a grin.

'I don't think I can,' she replied, looking a bit pale. 'I feel terrible.'

'Lie down then,' Huw said, clearing the plate out of sight. 'If the smell of the food is bad for you, I will open a porthole. We cannot have the light on though. It may be seen by patrol aircraft.

'How do you make this stop?' She moaned, and Huw smiled.

'Lie down and imagine a small ship on the sea. Imagine you are watching it bob around in time with the ship you are in. Soon you understand what the ship is doing. It helps. You lie down too, Juhan.'

Juhan had walked back in from a shower and now looked paler. He was quiet and swallowing heavily. Huw made for the welcoming waters of the shower, hoping he would not return to a sea of regurgitation. Once finished, he noted the remaining plate of food was untouched. Although it was cold, he wolfed it down. He was still hungry and had long ago adopted the dog-mentality of eating anything when it was available, as you never knew how long you might go without.

His now full stomach made him feel drowsy and he settled into his bunk to sleep. His family appeared to be ahead of him in that field, but Huw wondered if they were just trying to make the swirling, swaying journey somehow go away. They both breathed as if they were still awake. Huw closed his eyes, losing himself in the hum of an electricity generator and the pitch and yaw of the boat as it sped across the boisterous North Sea.

He was woken by a crashing sound in the sea – a staccato thudding on the hull. It was certainly not a storm that caused it. He was out of his bunk and though the door to the base of the stairs in seconds. The ship started rocking violently from a nearby explosion and the hiss of returning spray washed down the hatch. Too damned close, Huw thought. The sound of sporadic automatic weapons fire was now in the air.

He heard footsteps behind him and turned to see an ashen faced Juhan standing in the doorway, wiping his mouth.

'I made it to toilet,' he said. 'What's happening?'

'We're under attack, a coastal patrol aircraft, must be a clear night out there.'

'Do we stay down here?'

Huw had visions of *Caradoc* chasing Russian ships in another age.

He stood with his group in the depths of the ship, timber and tools ready to plug any damage at a moment's notice.

'Steady boys, steady,' he growled as the ship vibrated with the percussion of a gun salvo from its turrets. *'Get ready for work.'*

Huw shook his head.

'Not this time, Juhan. This girl is lightly armed to make her fast and what is missing makes us easy to send down without a whimper if we are caught. This time, I'm going up on deck. I won't leave this world without a fight.'

'Ok,' Juhan said, staggering to Huw's side, a sheepish grin on his face. 'So don't lecture me when I follow you.'

Maarja appeared at the doorway, looking ill.

'I managed to reach toilet in time,' she said.

Huw managed to stop himself commenting about the importance of this knowledge. Speak in haste, repent at your leisure, the chapel parson always said.

A cacophony of shouting and groaning came from the stairwell and a man came down fast, half dragging a wounded comrade. The man was bleeding heavily. Maarja changed gear in an instant.

'Take him to your sick bay, I will help.'

She looked at Huw and the world missed a beat. He could see the fear in her eyes, mixed with the love, as she answered his unspoken words.

'Just do whatever you need to get us out of this mess,' she said.

Huw and Juhan needed no second telling and raced up to the deck above. One rake of fire had hit amidships and caught the machine gun turret, which was now gleaming with someone's blood. The bridge was peppered with holes and shattered glass. All this was illuminated by a small fire that two men were desperately trying to douse.

'I'll get this gun working,' Juhan shouted.

'I'll go to the bridge,' Huw replied.

He raced up through the door and saw two men. One by the wheel was clearly dead. The captain remained, clutching his shoulder whilst trying to steer.

'I've got the wheel,' Huw shouted, grabbing hold of it. 'You give me directions, I will steer.'

The captain's face was lined with stress and pain. He muttered something in Norwegian.

'Captain, I am ex Royal Navy. I can steer this boat. You can't do that and think of a way out of here.'

The captain cursed, but he nodded and let Huw take over, moving to the side to grip the bridge walls.

'Hold on!' Huw yelled. The silhouette of the aircraft lined up for its run on the starboard of the boat. He prayed his timing was up to this. Below, a heavy machine gun started up. Juhan had begun to work his passage.

'Port!' The captain yelled, and Huw instinctively spun the wheel. The boat lurched sharply. Huw braced his legs. The bomb blast made the ship leap and plunge. Huw moaned as the jolt pummelled his shoulder wound. He spun the wheel starboard. Now he had a clear view of it, and he yelled, 'It's a Blenheim! The damned arsehole is one of ours.'

His shoulder was raw with pain and wet with blood, sweat or both. The next bomb blast threw him against the side of the cabin. The captain caught him and pushed him back. Huw screamed with rage at the situation. To be so close to freedom and to be caught in friendly fire? His family put in peril by his own people after all they had escaped from? His anger was white hot and he looked to the open window and the machine gun post.

'Juhan. Take that bastard down!'

The captain gave him a quizzical look and Huw sighed and nodded back.

'I'm alright. This is just the last straw. It seems only the Germans haven't shot at me recently.'

'Well, we could go back and ask them to if you like,' the captain replied.

Huw grinned and shouted an obscene reply, drowned in the captain's sudden call for hard to port. Huw pulled the wheel with all his might and lost his balance, so that the captain had to throw him back. The ship spun on a sixpence and another bomb missed them by inches. This time Huw felt the shudder of the ship's guns returning fire. The aircraft circled again and began to start a low run.

'He's going for cannon fire,' the captain shouted. 'Turn to full and meet him head on. Narrow the silhouette.'

The Blenheim came closer and closer. They were looking down the barrels of a gun.

'We move to port on my order,' barked the captain. 'Now!'

237

The salvo went down the side of the boat, but it avoided major damage. Huw was now hugging the wheel more for support than action.

'I don't know how many more of these I will be able to do,' he groaned.

The captain, gripping the side of the bridge, gave a wry smile. 'Me neither.'

'Well, there is a few more in me at least,' Huw said.

There was a faint sound of cheering and the captain steadied himself and looked out.

'They have broken off the attack. Thank God.'

'Why?' Huw gasped. 'He all but had us.'

'I don't know, maybe low on fuel or ammunition. I thought I saw an engine smoking. It could even have been Lars standing at the stern waving a flare close to the Norwegian flag.'

'What?'

Huw clambered to stand as best he could and looked out. The deck was now a smoking mess, a mass of debris and crawling with men clearing up and repairing. Standing on the rail, clutching the flagpole in one hand while waving a flare in the other, was Lars. He caught them looking and gave a weary wave with the flare.

'Christ, that was close,' the captain murmured.

'I can keep to the wheel while your men recover,' Huw said.

'You are tired and hurt,' the captain replied.

Huw grinned. 'So make sure they don't take too long resting. At least I can get you time to get the ship back to some order and you can plot our course.'

The captain nodded slowly and then held out his hand. 'Jan Ronaldsson.'

'Huw Williams. Glad to be on board.'

Juhan and Lars came onto the bridge much later. Lars took over the wheel, whilst Juhan helped Huw to get below deck. They found Maarja busy tending to the wounded, her eyes burning with fatigue. She sported a heavy bruise close to the temple.

'Come, let us look at your shoulder,' she said to Huw.

'I'm alright,' Huw muttered tetchily.

Maarja glared at him.

'I am too tired to argue, get your shirt off.'

She added some ointment, which Huw felt sure was mustard. It certainly stung as if it was, even through his exhaustion.

'You've got this infected again. I will bandage it up, but we need it seen to when we land.'

'I'm alright,' Huw grumbled. 'There are worse injured here.'

'Fine,' she snapped. 'You want gangrene? Don't come near me.'

'When did you become a nurse?'

'They taught us enough when Tallinn was under siege in 1919. There, now.'

'Why the bruise?' Huw asked

'Because there is an idiot here who does not know how to steer a boat,' came the angry reply.

'I need to get back up top,' Huw muttered, and kissed her cheek.

The ghost of a smile played on her lips, as she whispered, 'be careful.'

Huw scrambled back up to the deck. The crew was busier now; most of the sailors looked in better shape and showed a newfound energy after beating off the aircraft attack.

'Captain Ronaldsson, it is your turn now,' Huw said as he climbed onto the bridge.

Jan's expression suggested he was in pain. He looked to Huw and back at the chart. As he did so, a drop of blood hit the table. He picked it up with his finger and stared at it for a while and then slowly nodded.

'You are navy man? Then keep an eye on this heading. Compass is here, this is the bearing. Keep to it, I will be back soon.'

'Just don't tell her I was anywhere near the wheel, Captain,' Huw said.

The grin of understanding made Huw feel part of the crew. He looked out of the bridge and noticed that the wind had picked up. The waves now rolled so tall that their peaks were above the height of the cab when the boat was in a trough. Huw didn't care, he felt so right about it all. He had to check himself when he realised he had started to whistle a shanty.

The craft was checked for its seaworthiness and a few urgent repairs were made. The Norwegians made little weather of patching up the ship or patching up themselves.

Huw's eyelids became leaden after a few hours and he was fighting sleep, although the boat was taking water and the injured needed treating. They had to make port soon. His shoulder burned, but even that could not stop him falling into a dangerously dozy state.

He woke sharply. They needed a direct course and they needed an accurate one. The possibility otherwise was to miss Shetland altogether and sail right past into the Atlantic Ocean, between the tip of the islands and the Faroes to the north. He had to stay awake.

He was woken by a hand gently shaking his shoulder and his heart leapt in panic.

'Easy,' said Jan, his calm voice filling Huw's mind. 'I bring coffee, it will help.'

The coffee was black and so strong that Huw felt the boost like a kick up the backside.

'I will not blink for the rest of the journey after this drink,' he remarked.

'I relieve you, friend Huw. Go below and rest. We are half a day perhaps from Scallowa and I will need your help later. We have some men who will not be of help any more.'

Huw nodded slowly and tried a weary salute. Jan waved it away nonchalantly.

'This is a Norwegian boat and we are fishermen at heart. Here we are more interested in the sailing.'

Huw found their bunks empty and moved down to find his family. Juhan looked up when his father entered the galley. He had started cooking and looked quite at home among the pots and pans. Maarja sat in the room that held the wounded. She was sleeping, her head rested on her hands. Those that had been treated looked comfortable, so he staggered over and gently roused her. She rubbed her neck and groaned.

'Come, Maarja. Our bunks are next door. You can hear if there are any problems. You have done all you can.'

Chapter Twenty-Six

Scalloway

Huw woke in his bunk, the morning sunlight beaming at him through the porthole. Maarja slept in his arms. He managed to roll off without waking her or causing his wound to grumble too much. Finally, he could take in the sight through the porthole.

'Oh, thank Christ,' he whispered. 'Thank Christ indeed.'

'What is wrong,' Maarja murmured from the bunk.

Huw went to kneel by her side, and put his arm around her shoulders.

'If you can, come with me to the deck, there is something I want you to see.'

'If it's a proper bed, I say it is worth seeing, or sleeping in perhaps. Where is Juhan?'

'Cooking probably, he seems to be enjoying himself and it takes his mind off the journey.'

'Come on then, surprise me.' She rolled off the bed and slowly stood up and stretched.

On deck they were greeted by a bright, glorious dawn. The sky was clear blue and a breeze was in the air. Maarja shivered, but she could not take her eyes off the red-brown cliffs that loomed close to starboard. A squat lighthouse stood proud at its peak, looking out to sea. The sun's fledgling rays began to glint off the glass panes of the light in pulses, as the ship bobbed up and down on the waves. Breakers foamed at the base of the cliff, washing it clean time and again.

'We are in the Roost,' Huw said, keeping his arm around her shoulders. 'The channel between the southern tip of Shetland and Fair Isle. This is Sumburgh Head; the shadow over there is Fair Isle. *Caradoc* ran aground there in 1919, after we'd taken the German fleet to anchor in Orkney. That was fun, I can tell you.'

'I'm home,' Maarja breathed.

Huw, too excited to listen, continued: 'Straight ahead is Newfoundland, Canada. About three thousand miles away. Not for today, perhaps.'

Maarja took a deep breath and looked at Huw with dewy eyes. 'I need to see my wounded, but thank you for this sight. It is most beautiful I have ever seen.'

She moved back below and Huw went back to work on deck.

The land behind Sumburgh Head was shrouded in mist, making the lighthouse more prominent, as the only clue that there was civilisation around in front of the infinite oblivion.

'We take a wide berth, until the mist clears,' Captain Petersson said, one arm now in a bandage splint. 'I will be cautious though, Shetland waters are shallow, not like Norway. I want to get to Scallowa.'

Huw was posted as a lookout to ensure the limping craft steered clear of the small reefs. The journey began to feel routine, as if the whole world relaxed in front of him. A few dolphins elected to race the boat, their sleek grey bodies rising and falling from the sea, a permanent smile etched onto their faces. Huw's mind raced with them.

Seabirds began to trawl the boat. Some fished in the waters around them and Huw wished he had a line to join in. The puffins especially were curious to watch, with their clumsy flight, like bricks with wings.

'Reef to starboard ten,' he shouted.

Jan nodded an acknowledgement and gave an order to change course. The first signs of life began to take shape on the shore, as small crofter's cottages began to show through the slowly lifting mist. Finally, they made their way towards an inlet, where a small fishing village nestled between barren hills. It looked to Huw like a typical Scottish village, but with a ruined square castle tower by the harbour, dominating its centre.

'Scallowa,' Jan nodded. 'Time to wake them. Our fuel is spent and I need a tow.'

He sounded the ship's horn. The notes echoed all around the bay before the place settled back to its silence, the wash of the sea and the throb of the engines dominating their ears. Then suddenly a cacophony of noise – a rousing chorus of ships' horns rang out in reply.

Jan chuckled to himself. 'I hope they did not stay up for us.'

A small launch had put out to intercept them. On arrival, it was as if the whole crew were eager to shout greetings and banter. As soon as they were close enough, a man wearing the khaki of the British army was transferred by rope ladder. In spite of his ungainly appearance, he managed to achieve this in quick order.

His manner was familiar and easy going. He greeted the men by name. Huw felt a pang of jealousy for what must be the liaison officer. To be able to interact with partisans of an occupied nation from a well-organised base on home territory was a luxury he wished he had been given in Estonia.

'Trouble, Jan?' The liaison asked the captain. 'You are a bit late home.'

Jan nodded. 'Two dead and shot up by a stupid English coastal plane.'

'Funnily enough, the RAF have been on the phone complaining about having their planes shot up by you.'

Jan's jaw stiffened. 'Tell them to come here and we can argue the toss.'

'Steady now, what was the damage?'

'Sven and Fredrick.'

'Packages safe?'

Jan grunted. 'Yes and they earned their passage also.'

The officer turned to Huw and thrust out a hand in greeting. 'My name is Craig, Captain Craig, I suppose. I've got a man from the ministry being an arse on the dock, trying to throw his weight around. I assume you are one of the cloak and dagger brigade and he thinks you boys are a law unto yourselves. Even so, welcome to Scalloway, what the bloody hell is going on?'

Huw was amused by the way Craig pronounced the port name differently to the Norwegians. He was sure the sailors had blended in with the locals, while poor Craig probably was stuck trying to speak English correctly. He remembered something similar with his own training, when someone had referred to the Estonian island Dago as if it was a derogatory term for a swarthy foreigner. That's the one thing we Brits do badly, he thought. Adapt.

His mind suddenly sprang into processing events and he realised, after all this, what was going on. More importantly what had gone on. Taking matters to hand, he quickly focused on the latest threat.

'Huw Williams, British intelligence, I suppose,' he said. 'It's a long story, but these events make me see the light a bit. If you have a few minutes to delay this man, I will explain.'

'Twenty minutes are all I will have, before we get to shore. Assuming my happy Vikings don't swing him from the yardarm first. You'd best talk fast. You've had a hellish journey from what I can see and this crew have lost some of their own, which will make them even more stubborn than normal – especially when some pompous Whitehall ass tries to walk through them.'

'Well, let's start talking now, and then you can meet my wife. Is there a chance I can get a message to someone in the war office? An officer by the name of Taylor.'

They berthed at the quayside that played host to a few more of the torpedo boats. Other ships sat dormant in the bay. Some questions in Norwegian were thrown from the shore to the crew as they were secured to their berth. The answers were tinged with sorrow for the fallen.

There was shouting from the deck and Huw looked over to see a commotion on the quayside. A group of men had made their way to the gangplank. Huw noted a man in a suit accompanied by two squaddies. The soldiers had bayonets on their rifles and the Norwegians' reaction was not pleasant. As the man climbed the gangplank, Lars raced down to block his way. Many on the boat grabbed machine guns. A mechanical whirring made Huw turn to find even the gun turret trained on the gangplank. Lars chose not to speak English but his tone left no doubt that the group were unwelcome.

'You are not coming on my boat,' Jan shouted.

'I have the authority to board this vessel,' came the curt reply from the man. Huw knew this man was from intelligence, although his actions contradicted the word totally. Why was he in such a hurry? Did he look vaguely familiar?

'Not on my boat,' Jan replied. 'Tell your toy soldiers to put their little guns away and get off my gangplank.'

'I am here on the business of His Majesty's Government and I expect to be let on board,' the suit demanded.

'Don't let this get out of hand, Jan,' Huw heard Craig say in the background.

'Okay, the soldiers can piss off,' Jan shouted. 'You come up alone.'

The man's reaction was to go almost purple with rage. He began to protest his outrage, but the situation was resolved by a sharp order from the liaison officer.

'Sergeant Watson!' He shouted.

'Sir!' Came the response from shore.

'Get these bloody squaddies off my quayside now.'

'Sir!' A burly man in a khaki uniform leapt onto the gangplank and started to scream orders at the poor hapless men. The suit stared in disbelief as the soldiers meekly retreated from their perch and he was left alone. Huw looked across at Craig, who smiled back.

'A grunt always responds to stripes before a civvy.'

Chapter Twenty-Seven

The spy unmasked

Thirty minutes later Huw, Maarja and Juhan were shown into the wardroom of the boat. The suit was pacing around angrily, and glared at them as they came in.

'I'm not used to being kept waiting, Williams,' he snapped, 'and I certainly did not expect you to bring your menagerie.'

'What's going on?' Juhan asked his mother.

'Don't worry, let Huw talk,' said Maarja.

'I will be waiting, this man is threat,' he replied.

Maarja nodded, safe in the expectation that the new arrival knew no Estonian.

'Have they finished?' The man growled. 'Can you not tell them to be quiet? I have no need to be interrupted by gibberish.'

'Listen, Godfrey,' Huw retorted, 'if you keep talking like that about my family, I'll rip your head off your shoulders. Stop griping and start talking.'

'You remember me?'

'Last time I saw you I broke your nose. Your manners have not changed and neither have my opinions of you. Don't make me break your jaw.'

Godfrey looked even colder than before. 'I have no time for this charade, sit down.'

Huw remained standing and Godfrey cursed. 'You are a fool, Williams. A waster, a loser, ideal cannon fodder. I have been charged to bring you in and I will not hesitate to take you back dead if I need to. You deserted your post, you ran. You did not carry out your orders to liaise with the Reds. If anything, you appear to have fought them, from what they tell me. So, a traitor to boot.'

'It was not much of a choice,' Huw replied. 'And a stupid mission, bound to fail, as you damn well know.'

Godfrey sat back on a table and began to master his temper. Slowly, the confident arrogance crept back, as he tried a new tack. 'I give you a simple choice, you can come with me now and follow orders for once or I will take you by force. If you come now, your family will be treated as refugees. If not, I will ensure they are

247

repatriated back east as Soviet citizens and our allies will look after them as only they know how.'

'Refugees?' Maarja spat the words in distaste. 'Is this man a fool? I am here representing Estonian government in exile. I am no refugee.'

'There is no Estonian government in exile.' In spite of his surprise at Maarja's English, Godfrey's tone reached Arctic proportions.

Maarja's eyes flared in anger. 'Is this arrogant arsehole what we came back to see?'

The door opened and Jan moved in slowly. Although injured, he had smartened up his coat and looked more the naval officer than before.

'This is not your concern, Captain, please leave,' said Godfrey.

'This is my bloody boat,' the Norwegian replied, sitting down on the nearest chair. 'I'll go where I bloody well like.'

'Captain Craig!' Godfrey shouted, and the liaison officer soon followed.

'Control your charges, Craig. Remind them they are guests in this land.'

Craig leant against a wall and folded his arms, but made no attempt to assist. Godfrey mouthed another curse and turned his attention back to Huw.

'I have come a long way to this godforsaken backwater to get you, and I'm not leaving without you. I arrest you for desertion, dereliction of duty and failing to obey orders.' He turned to Maarja and Juhan. 'As citizens of our allies, the Soviet Union, you will be repatriated as soon as is feasible.'

'What is he saying?' Juhan asked Maarja.

'He wants to send Huw to prison for running away and us to Russia,' said Maarja.

'This man is born fool,' said Juhan, and Huw had no need to look, he knew Juhan would be readying his knife.

'Transportation is available to take you to Lerwick. Craig, you can arrange this straight away.'

He stood up to leave, tucking his gun in his back, but Jan put his leg across the door to block his exit. 'Nobody is going anywhere.'

'Do not try my patience,' warned Godfrey. 'I will not have British justice obstructed by a foreign force in our waters.'

'This is a Norwegian matter,' Jan replied coldly. 'We settle this in Norwegian territory.'

Godfrey swiftly pulled out a revolver from his belt and waved it at the group. 'This has nothing to do with Norway.'

Jan stood up slowly facing Godfrey. 'I've faced British guns before. You don't scare me. I've had worse problems with Germans. These people are members of my crew and as such are subject to Norwegian law and justice.'

Godfrey was outraged. 'Craig, control your charges. This is obstruction of justice.'

Craig continued to stand calmly with his arms folded, although a small smile now played on his face.

'The problem here for you at any rate Godfrey, is that he is right – this is a Norwegian base. That makes it Norwegian sovereign territory. These people are of the Norwegian navy and as such fall under the jurisdiction of the Norwegian crown. Basically, you haven't a leg to stand on, so put that bloody gun down and stop being an arse.'

'What's happening?' Juhan whispered, his knife now clear of the scabbard.

'We have joined Norwegian Navy,' Maarja replied.

'Great!' Juhan replied, with a large grin, made the more vicious by the tension in the room.

'Whitehall will hear of this,' Godfrey blustered.

'Ja and so will the King of Norway, he will also be informed, Mr Godfrey,' Jan replied.

'It's over, Godfrey,' said Huw, stepping forward, 'it's finished. I realise now what's been going on and you haven't a chance. You are not going to kill us all, so you had better just put the gun down.'

Godfrey brandished his gun, aiming directly at Huw, who stared back at it calmly. There seemed no fear left in him.

'You see,' Huw continued, 'I had some thinking time recently, when I wasn't being shot at that is, and I just started wondering why.' He moved slowly towards a seat. 'Why train an operative of my age? Why take me through Russia? Why did the Reds know my every move? The answer was simple in the end. Someone told them our codes. They read my messages. Why do all that, unless you wanted me captured? The Reds would perhaps work on me on the journey and make me their puppet, by torture, I suppose.'

Huw stretched, it felt so relaxing now to have all the answers. It was even satisfying to finally have his true enemy in plain sight.

'The Russians were keen to play their part. They wanted to use me for intelligence behind German lines, then after they broke through, to turn me. Except that too was foiled. Incredibly, the man who took over that mission wanted my blood for another reason – one from a long time ago. It all got me thinking, did Britain want me turned or was there a cuckoo in the nest? One who worked for our eastern friends against the interests of Britain? I think we can safely say we know the answer to that now, Godfrey. Don't you think?'

Godfrey shook his head. 'You are a dreamer, Williams. Trying to cover up your trail of incompetence.'

'But that is precisely what *you* are doing,' Huw replied. 'I couldn't put it together, until now. Now I see the act of a desperate man, trying to dispose of the evidence. You must have been that fearful of being shown up for the traitor you are, that you shot up to Shetland to greet me. But you lost your chance when you failed to get on board. You thought you could gain control of the situation simply by being a spook. A pretty poor strategy, wasn't it? What you've never done before though is come up against Norwegians. They don't jump through your hoops and they are bloody good at telling people what they think.'

'What you say is…?' Maarja began.

'Godfrey is a double agent; he works for Stalin. He and people like him are why Estonia fell – or he helped. I wouldn't give him so much credit.'

'Then he is a dead man,' Maarja said, in English.

Godfrey smiled coldly. 'Perhaps you should remind your woman that I am the one holding a gun.'

'But you are not going to use it,' Huw replied. 'You shoot all four of us, then what? How do you get off the boat? How do you get off the quayside? How do you leave Shetland? What were you thinking? That after all I'd been through, I would just come quietly like a lamb to the slaughter?'

'You have no proof of this,' Godfrey said. 'You are the rogue, not I. A failed spy, one who shot his bolt and ran. Nobody's going to put faith in your word. Same as no one will believe a foreigner.'

'They'll listen to me,' said Craig.

Godfrey's eyes were gleaming now with fear. He licked his lips nervously. 'You're first, then the captain. Then I shoot Williams because he is trying to escape. The rest I'll throw to the New World Order. You can't get away from this. No one escapes destiny.'

'Very true, very true,' Huw murmured. 'But you do admit you are working for the Soviets against your own country. Why?'

Godfrey laughed. 'I'm looking forward. Germany is finished and this hulk of a country is done for. The Soviet Union offers the only true answer. I was a green shirt long enough to know the answer is sharing the wealth.'

'What is green shirt?' Maarja asked, as she moved slowly to sit away from Juhan.

'A minority who dreamed of the country being run as a business and the profit being divided up equally as a dividend,' Huw replied. 'Not my cup of tea. I've got my feet on the ground.'

Godfrey's eyes narrowed to the taunts, which was exactly what Huw wanted. The angrier Godfrey got, the quicker he might make mistakes. Craig had not been disarmed.

'I can see you wouldn't have been much of an intellectual to have been so gullible. What did the Soviets offer you? Riches? Hardly in keeping with the communist ideal, unless you are a hypocrite, of course. Was it women then? Or was it boys perhaps? Nice clean little mummy's lamb like you?'

'Why do you keep doing this? Godfrey said tightly, his gun was shaking now, his fingers white with gripping it.

'Because you are a traitorous whoreson who's killed thousands of innocents for his own greed. Tell me this, if Stalin's such a good master, why are so many people running away from Mother Russia's embrace?'

Godfrey raised the pistol and put his other arm under it to steady it. Huw tensed, his mind flashed back to *Caradoc*. He thought of Maarja, back on that first day that she walked into the embassy office and sat opposite him. Her blue eyes, her beautiful hair, he looked over to her standing in the wardroom of the Norwegian boat, and smiled. 'Having you back, I am complete,' he said. He turned back to Godfrey. 'Because of *you* my best friend died. He sacrificed himself for me. How can I see you any other way but with contempt?'

The tension broke as Jan made a sharp movement and Godfrey spun to meet the threat. Juhan's knife sailed through the air to bury

251

itself in Godfrey's shoulder, making his arm jolt upwards as he fired. The bullet hit the ceiling. Godfrey collapsed to his knees in pain as Craig moved in, holding his own pistol to Godfrey's head. He gripped Godfrey's gun arm to keep it pointing upwards.

'Game's over, old son. Time to face the music.'

Jan opened the wardroom door and called for support. There was an answering pounding of feet down stairs and three sailors burst in. They secured Godfrey and made ready to bundle him away. Maarja stepped forward and planted a heavy kick straight between Godfrey's legs. He went ashen. The rest of the men gasped in sympathy.

'I think you got off lightly, Godfrey,' Craig said dryly, as he was bundled out of the room.

'Thank you for believing me,' Huw said to Craig, who nodded acknowledgment.

Jan trusts you,' he said. 'That's enough for me – and besides you have an honest face.'

Juhan had his arm around his mother's shoulders. Tears streamed as she looked up to Huw. 'I wanted to kill him, Huw. He does not deserve to live while so many perish.'

'His day has come and gone.' Huw replied.

Juhan whispered something to his mother and she smiled.

'Captain. My son wants to know if you are good to your word and we are now of Norwegian navy.'

'Why yes,' Jan replied. 'For without you three, we would not be here.'

'Time to go ashore,' Craig said. 'Shetland offers little in comfort, but a lot in hospitality. If you are staying, we must find you quarters.'

They made their way up to the deck and Huw and Maarja stood hand in hand close to the gangplank. Maarja was still crying softly as she looked around the small town and the hills behind.

'I want to stay. This place, I cannot explain, but it feels like home.'

Huw smiled and kissed her gently. 'That's good. I won't need to worry about trying to find you again. You and me, we have a lot of living to do. Over here, so far away from the ghosts of our past is a good place to start.'

Chapter Twenty-Eight

The gentlemen of Whitehall

A week later Huw and Maarja were in London, at the end of a long overnight journey by train. Huw was growing used to sleeping rough in carriages. His neck felt stiff and he was grumpy, but they'd managed to get a cup of tea from a mobile WVS unit outside Euston and it cheered him up a bit. London was bustling; people were getting on with things, in spite of the ruins and other signs of damage from the blitz. Huw's new navy uniform itched around the neck, but he kept looking at the Norwegian navy insignia on his cap. It still raised a smile.

Whitehall looked strangely intact, cocooned as it was by sand bags and windows decorated with white tape criss-crossing the windows.

'Still dogged with stuffiness and formality,' Huw muttered.

Maarja gave his hand a squeeze and then stopped to straighten his tie. 'Come on, let's tell them.'

The man was courteous in the extreme but his face gave away no emotion. Maarja told of the experiences of the two invasions of her homeland, Huw added his own observations and the pain of it all came back. The remains on the road at Kadrina, Toomas lying dead in the forest, and finally the crumpled figure of Märt on a shingle spit in the fading light of the star shell. He closed his eyes, unwilling to show any sign of weakness in front of those who may provide the succour that his former world needed. Then, like the surf on the shingle, reality broke through. The shock numbed his skull.

'You're not the minister, are you? I've been really dense, been away for so long and forgotten who is in government. You're not the man we need to talk to.'

The man leaned back and gazed at his fountain pen for a while, exuding disapproval. 'You must understand, the minister is very busy and obviously cannot be in a position to see as many people as he would like. I am to provide information and feedback to the minister and this has been very succinctly put, sir, madam. I will relay your message to the minister and a reply will follow to the Estonians in due course.'

The silence was as if the world had shifted and needed a second to regain its spin. Huw felt a cavern open in front of him. 'What about the Atlantic Accord?' he asked. 'Churchill and Eisenhower pledged that countries would be restored at the end of hostilities.'

The man gave a bland smile in reply. 'But hostilities have yet to cease and a lot of rebuilding work will need to be done, in our own cities for example.'

Maarja's words were tinged with frost. 'I am here as a representative of a sovereign nation to deliver plea for assistance. We need British government to use its influence to stop bloodshed that is taking place on Estonia's soil. I would expect that at least a junior minister would have met me, not a civil servant.'

The man put his pen down gently and bridged his chin with his clasped hands. 'I am sorry that you feel this way. As I say, I have heard your message and will relay it to the ministry, from whence a reply will be forthcoming in due course. The minister will decide whether a message needs to be sent to the Soviet ambassador.'

'Needs? Needs?' Maarja almost spat. 'Do you believe I am lying?'

'Madam, I believe that you have given an honest rendition of your government's message. I will pass this on, but please bear in mind that we will need to consider what to say to our ally in the east very carefully. The Estonian people have recently given a lot of support to the German cause, after all.'

'There was little choice,' Maarja said bitterly.

'Indeed, but regrettably, I must now close this meeting. As soon as the ministry has the information a message will be sent to the Estonian government via our embassy in Sweden. Good day to you, madam.'

There was a ruthless polite efficiency in the way that Huw and Maarja were courteously shown out of the building. Huw steered up towards Trafalgar Square, to find some space from the crowds of people going about their business. It was very much a normal scene in the city, although most people were in uniform and everyone shouldered a gas mask.

'Let's head towards Buckingham Palace,' he said. 'There is at least some greenery there.'

A rush of footsteps made him turn around to see an older, bearded man jogging towards them, apparently heading for the Admiralty. Then Huw realised that the man wanted to catch up with them.

'Hello Williams, it's been too damn long.'

The beard was greyer perhaps, but the face was friendly, and familiar.

'Taylor? Is that you? Have I been gone so long that you've become a greybeard?'

'Yes, hello my friend,' Taylor panted as he stopped. 'I was told you were in and I nearly missed you. I just had to see you, what on earth are you wearing?'

'Norwegian Navy,' Huw replied with a grin.

'That's where you ended up? I thought I heard you went looking for that girl in Estonia, after we'd left and forgot to come back. What happened to her?'

'That as well, my friend and,' Huw nodded towards Maarja and Taylor beamed with delight.

'Oh my word, so it is. I remember you my dear, you are as lovely as when you turned up to our banquet. No, I do. Someone so lovely who had my friend swept off his feet, I don't forget that smile.'

'I wish I could smile now like I did then,' Maarja replied.

'Yes, I know certain events have taken place,' Taylor stopped smiling. 'You petitioned for assistance?'

Maarja nodded and Huw narrowed his eyes. 'You already know, don't play games.'

Taylor nodded. 'You're right, I was aware and because of the time you have taken to get here, I knew a lot already. I wanted to see you, personally.'

'Were you sent?'

Taylor pursed his lip. 'Let's say, a blind eye is being turned. I would dearly love a catch-up drink with you, away from here. There's a good place I know down by the Law Courts, which is just the business. Come on, I'll grab a taxi and you can fill me in on the details – and tell me about that beautiful city of yours.'

They settled into a pub. Beyond the long entrance was a cavernous bar. The lofty feel was accentuated by three large vats towering above the few people there. Opposite the bar was a line of alcoves, each containing a table and four chairs. Taylor got drinks and steered them to one of the tables. He sat down and smiled at them.

'I like this place; the old lawyers used these snob corners to come and talk to their clients where they couldn't be overheard easily. It makes you feel more relaxed.'

Maarja did not touch her drink – the fury still boiled within her and Huw was about to apologise when she cut over him.

'I think this man already knows story, Huw.'

'Madam?' Taylor smiled.

'It seems strange to me that Huw's old friend, who sent him to Estonia, appears after our meeting. It is too simple. You are more than messenger. You are too comfortable with story.'

Taylor leaned back and sipped his drink in silence for a while, his eyes focussed on Maarja's face.

'I was once of Civil Service,' she said, 'and I have learnt much in this time since.'

Taylor closed his eyes and nodded. 'You are a lucky man, Huw. Your lady misses nothing. It is very true. I was instrumental in getting you into SOE[2] operations. I was the one who confirmed you were fit for service.'

'Why did you do this?' Huw asked, his beer left hovering in front of his lips.

'Huw, word of your elopement and recapture reached the ears of those who had been on *Caradoc*. I knew you had been back in the country a long time and when I needed a man in Estonia, one who could blend in with the people, I sought you out.'

Huw's brows furrowed. 'Out of sentiment?'

'No, old son. I needed someone for my work.' Taylor paused. 'But I would also say that when I found out your plight, I believed you deserved another chance.'

'You looked to turn me over to the Russians?'

A boisterous group of squaddies had come into the pub. Worse for wear, they began to break out in song. One leant back too far and staggered onto the table. He turned around quickly and glared at the group in the alcove, then noticed the gold braid on Taylor's tunic.

---

[2] A British government organisation in WWII, that ran covert operations in occupied lands.

'Beg pardon, Admiral,' the man muttered, then staggered away to clap his mates on the back.

Taylor sighed and looked back to Huw and Maarja. 'No, I wanted you to spy on them. I wanted to get information about what they are up to. I even wanted you to find your woman. That much at least was a success.'

'But they are not interested, in Whitehall,' Maarja said.

'No, they are always interested. There are some problems that make it awkward, one of which is that the Soviets are good at catching our people.'

'But now you have the man to blame.' Huw said.

'Yes, but I wonder if he acted alone. You are right, Godfrey managed to steer the mission towards the waiting trap that the Soviets had set.'

'So we were lucky to have come up against a man with a grudge,' said Huw, 'or I might be roasting in hell as we speak.'

Maarja placed her hand on Huw's arm for reassurance. 'But it did not happen and we got here, to deliver the message.'

Taylor smiled and took a sip of his drink. 'I assure you that your testimony was treated as of great importance.'

'So why aren't the navy ready to go back there, like 1919?' Huw snapped.

Taylor rubbed his beard. 'Simple problem, I'm afraid. Last time, Russia was only menacing and here it is triumphant. And there is still the war to be won. Germany is a bit in the way.'

'What about the Atlantic Accord?' Huw asked.

'Huw, I have to tell you something that we don't bandy around to people – bad for morale and all that. This country is near bankrupt. We spent a fortune in the Great War and now we're mortgaged to the hilt. We have taken up loans with the Americans and bought their ordinance to replace ours, where our factories are either unable to build fast enough or have been flattened. We are in debt, we can't afford things to go on after Germany. The war will not continue.'

'So you will leave us to die?' Maarja asked, her face was like stone.

'We will do what we can to change the situation, but there will be no military solution.'

Huw sighed and banged his fist against the wall. 'So all this was in vain? Good men died to get us here – and it was for nothing?'

257

'Many good men have died Huw, some because of Godfrey – and he will be punished, outside of the public eye, naturally. Others have died on the battlefields of Europe, Africa and the Far East. I wish I could have provided you better news, but I thought you deserved an explanation.'

'What now then?' Huw asked.

'I am quite happy for you to remain where you are. Those Viking chappies are a good lot and I also think you deserve a quieter time.'

'Quieter?'

'Yes, you won't be allowed on ops, but there's plenty to do ashore.'

He stood to leave and picked up his hat. 'I have to go, I will be missed. I am so glad I got to see you again, Huw and I am delighted that you found your lady once more. Look after her, she's worth a million.'

Maarja looked up to Taylor, her eyes full of tears. 'So there is nothing we can do? We have lost?'

'No talk of losing, there is always hope,' he said. He took her hand, bent and kissed it. 'Keep talking of your land and make sure that this country never forgets you. One day it will count for something.'

Huw and Maarja were left alone in the alcove. The place was bustling, the blue smoke from cigarettes formed a cloud floating around the vats. Huw had been so long away from this environment that his eyes began to sting. He felt like a caged animal among so many people and the noise was echoing in his ears.

'What do you wish to do now?' He asked Maarja.

'Go back to Scallowa,' she said. 'Go back home. This land is not welcoming.'

Epilogue

They gazed in wonder at the television screen. The news report had pictures of thousands gathered in an arena. Many were in national costume and all were singing. Some danced, all appeared to be smiling. Then the pictures changed to a helicopter shot of a long line of people standing hand in hand.

'It appears to stretch over the horizon,' the old man whispered. 'Do you think they reached Latvia?'

'Weren't they going to Lithuania?' Came the reply.

'Well, you'd have to go through Latvia first,' he answered.

The picture changed, ground camera crews now showed a close-up of the line. They had found a particularly beautiful woman to focus on. She beamed as she sang, her face glowing with passion. The man remembered times past and looked fondly at his lady.

'She looks as you did, Maarja, when you took me dancing.'

'She is full of spirit that one,' Maarja agreed.

'As you were, my dear. As you were. Juhan visits us today after church, we must make sure he sees this – and his children, they must understand.'

Maarja said nothing, but tears ran down her cheeks. She grabbed the hand of her husband of forty-seven years and squeezed it.

'What are you thinking, my love?' Huw asked.

'Happiness. Like a weight is taken from my shoulders. I have lived through a long winter, a harsh cruel winter. Now it is spring and I am content.'

Her beautiful blue eyes stared at his, making his mind warm with pleasure, as they always had.

'It has been a long time coming and now Estonia feels free.' Maarja said. 'As do I.'

About the Author

Geraint Roberts left school with ideas of becoming a mining geologist, only to end up working for a renewable energy company via a bank and a brief stint as a manager in a drug rehab clinic. He lives close to his home town in mid-Wales, with his Estonian wife and two children.

Having visited Estonia many times, he is now quite happy with the cuisine, beer and long quiet sandy beaches. He sees Welsh experience mirrored in Estonia's psyche, which is a comfortable feeling.

He developed an interest in writing to defend his sanity after being outsourced to a dusty corner in an office in Milton Keynes. He quickly realised that he only liked geology if it involved scrambling around in old mines and so a latent interest in history emerged to dominate his writing. Geraint is currently working on a new novel, *Promise*, based in late Victorian Aberystwyth and a play, *Senghenydd*, based on a mining disaster in South Wales.

www.geraintroberts.com

About Circaidy Gregory

A small press based in Hastings, Sussex, Circaidy Gregory publishes novels, short stories, plays and poetry. Most of our titles are by authors we have met through the Earlyworks Press Writers' and Reviewers' club projects and competitions. They include both new and established authors and, we think, offer the independent reader well-crafted work in well-produced editions that take them off the beaten track of the mainstream best seller lists to offer new ideas and intelligent, satisfying reads.

A genre-smashing novella by Mark Rickman

Unable to pull his life together after the death of his wife, Michael Brent neglects himself, his family and his work, resorting instead to the whisky bottle and recreating a formidable new version of his childhood hero, Crazy Bear.

But he cannot conquer his nightmares, or his feelings of guilt and responsibility for her death. Only when he calls the police to report finding the body of a murder victim – and gets treated as the prime suspect – does he find the will to fight back.

A page-turning thriller, a satisfying dark comedy, a breath-taking murder trial and a message of hope for anyone who has suffered the lingering death of a loved one – how can one book do all these things? Read 'Crazy Bear' and find out.

Crazy Bear – a novella by Mark Rickman

paperback ISBN 978 1 906541-19-6
ebook ISBN 978-1-906451-33-2

Left of the Moon by Monica Tracey

from the author of 'Unweaving the Thread', a runner up for the Irish Prize

Family secrets and dramatic encounters reach from Ireland to Italy and across the generations

Monica Tracey writes with sympathy, warmth and wisdom. Her gentle, assured storytelling will please a wide readership, and her composed and confident prose is a joy. She writes about the big and universal themes, love and loss, war and a kind of conditional peace, bringing to these topics two qualities that rarely go together: a depth of experience, and a keen appreciation of life's pleasures and possibilities.

— Hilary Mantel

Against her family's wishes, the recently widowed Isabel agrees to leave Ireland and accompany her cousin Grace on a holiday to Italy. Their journey takes them to a British Military Cemetery near the Adriatic, to the grave of a young soldier who died in 1943. With the help of a veteran of the Italian campaign, Grace and Isabel unearth family secrets that have lain hidden for more than half a century.

The novel shifts between the contemporary perspectives of Isabel and her manipulative mother, Rita, and the 1943 diary of a young Venetian woman. Isabel and Grace realise that the past is not dead and can still change their families' lives forever. Out of the sorrows of war, both women see a chance of happiness.

Can these new discoveries heal the rifts between the women, and explain Rita's apparent rejection of her daughter?

Left of the Moon paperback ISBN 978-1-906451-35-6
ebook ISBN 978-1-906541-40-0

www.circaidygregory.co.uk